LUCIFER'S STORY : BOOK 1

EDDREN AND BEYOND

ISBN: 9780994110725 (paperback)
ISBN: 9780994110749 (kindle)

Published by Little Red Hen Community Press,
Tauranga, New Zealand.
Printing: Createspace.com
Retail: Amazon.com
Cover art: Microsoft Images; adapted from Guido Reni's painting of *St Michael banishing Satan from heaven.*

ABOUT THE AUTHOR

Jocelynne Jones is the pen-name of a writer living in New Zealand. Retired, with two grownup offspring and a granddaughter, she is a quiet-living family person whose writing has, up until the age of ebooks, been little more than a hobby. With the establishment of 'indie publishers' Jocelynne has found an outlet for a passion that was hitherto stifled by previous publishing systems.

Other titles by the same author are:-

'*Lucifer's Story: Book 2*' – The second part of this fantasy tale of good-over-evil, which envisions the end of evil forever. It is set in a parallel universe called Eternity.
'*Whiskey Rose*' – The story of a family faced with the constraints of caring for an elderly relative.
'*Guarding My Angel*' – A drama based on the author's autobiography.
'*Freedom: Ours for the asking*' – A work of non-fiction under the genre of 'mind, body, spirit,' which explains how people have become separated from their intrinsic identity, and what to do about it.

To Jenny.

With grateful thanks, as always!

LUCIFER'S STORY : BOOK 1

EDDREN AND BEYOND

Jocelynne Jones

CONTENTS

PART ONE: OUT OF ETERNITY

CHAPTER 1

The track leading up to the lodge was narrow and winding. On its left, a high bank where the road had been created out of the hillside; to the right, a gentle slope fell away to meadowlands below.

"I don't know why they couldn't have sent a levitated carriage for us instead of this rickety old bus," the angel Lucifer complained to his companion, Angelina.

He was tired of being bumped around on the hard seat, and had already banged his head against the window. As a member of an elite group of angels in Eternity he felt he deserved more consideration. Certainly, he was used to the best of everything.

Angelina sighed, but said nothing. Lucifer was always complaining about something. It comes from being spoilt, she thought, and looked patiently out at the view.

Lucifer, Angelina and all the other angels in Eternity had been summoned to attend a seminar. Entitled, 'Facsimile', none of the angels knew what the seminar was for; just that their master Yavros had arranged it.

At last the lodge came into view. Well-known for its panoramic location, the multi-storied venue, aesthetically perfect for the spot on which it was situated, had always been a favourite with angel communities from all over the realm. But it was best known for its excellent convention facilities.

The bus came to a halt before an impressive portico; signifying to the angels on board that their journey had ended. An ornate front door opened automatically as the inquisitive guests approached the building.

Once inside, the angels paused to get their bearings and, along with many others, to seek further directions.

Lucifer took control.

"It looks like we have to go over there," he said to his companions, and gesticulated to towards a large, brightly coloured noticeboard, on which were displayed the words, 'FACSIMILE SEMINAR,' with an arrow pointing to the right.

"Well, that was easy enough," he thought when all the angels had located their seats in the hall specified, and sat down. "I hope this thing doesn't take too long. I've got an ethereal massage booked for later on, and I'll need it after that bumpy ride!"

While she waited for the seminar to begin, Angelina took stock of their surroundings.

The hall was oblong with a stage at one end. A rostrum stood in front of full-length drapes the width of the stage.

Angelina turned around to watch as groups from other parts of Eternity came in. Then she spotted an old friend, and waved. Once the room had filled with the chattering angels, a gong sounded for silence.

The hush of expectation was broken when a sole Being; an impressive figure, splendidly dressed in dazzling white, drifted in from one side of the stage and took his place at the rostrum. The angels rose to their feet respectfully, and applauded their appreciation of his greatness.

"Thank you, my angels. Please be seated."

The booming voice of Yavros, the Grand Master of all Eternity, commanded instant obedience, and immediately everyone settled back into their seats.

"It is good to see you again," he continued. "We don't have many opportunities to get together these days. You are all so busy with your appointed tasks; having a break from them now and then is most beneficial. A function like this gives us a chance to catch up with each other."

'Cut the small-talk and get on with it,' thought Lucifer. He was curious to know what this 'Facsimile' business was all about.

Just then, three Golden Angels entered the stage. They stood quietly to one side of Yavros, as if awaiting further instructions.

Angelina pointed to the Golden Angel standing in the middle of the three, and whispered to Lucifer, "There's Miekaale. He's Yavros' personal protector, and the Captain of the Guard."

Lucifer opened his mouth to comment that he did have a brain and knew who they all were, but then changed his mind when Yavros began to speak again.

"Well, friends, I won't delay you further. I'm sure you're wondering what this seminar is about, so I'll get straight to it. The reason I called you all here today, is to inform you of an innovative idea that I have had in mind. Accordingly, I've now come to a decision."

He paused briefly as murmuring from the angels halted his train of thought. Then, unaffected by the interruption, he continued.

"Although the decision has only recently been made, the seed of my idea was originally sown in a previous epoch, when Eternity was still in its infancy. But now the time has come for me to act.

"As you are aware, Eternity was a creation of mine; the result of a dream. That's how all of you angels came to be: I created you. If you recall from legends of old, I dipped my ethereal fingers into the ocean of my Being, and flung the

3

droplets of my spirit out to the four corners of Eternity. Each one of them became a loyal and valued angel. Ever since, as a reward for your loyalty to me, I have given you my all. But now...I feel there should be more to your lives than privilege alone, and that I should once again exercise my boundless creativity."

The attentive angels looked at one another quizzically.

"Have you any idea what he's talking about?" mouthed Angelina to Lucifer.

"No, and I don't like the sound of it," he replied rigidly.

Yavros then turned to one of the Golden Angels, and said, "Would you be kind enough to unveil the map while I explain to these good souls what I intend to do."

Without touching them, the Golden Angel drew back the immense drapes, revealing a map that filled the entire screen. Then, as if rehearsed, the other two Golden Angels stationed themselves each side of the map, ready to assist in the demonstration when needed.

"My children, this is my idea..."

With a sweeping gesture, Yavros introduced the map to his riveted audience "Whatever is that?" he heard an angel remark, and laughed at the reaction.

"What indeed," he said for all to hear. "Well, I will now tell you."

Yavros was beginning to enjoy himself. Hitherto he had been concerned about telling them of his decision, but now he could not wait to share it with them.

"I called this seminar 'Facsimile'. If you think about it you will realise what I mean by that. When I formed you angels I did so to resemble myself. But now I'm restless and am ready to broaden my horizons, so I've decided to create a whole new realm; a different kind of world."

He turned again to the map.

4

"I want to create a world of great beauty. I intend it to be three dimensional; to be tangible, visible and audible, and I want to create..."

Yavros stopped mid-sentence, realising he was getting carried away. '...Better not explain it to them all at once,' he thought.

"I'm sorry. I can see you are mystified. I'll slow down. In fact, I think we'll take a short break. I've given you enough to absorb for the moment."

With that, Yavros left the stage; followed closely by the Golden Angels.

Angelina looked at Lucifer. He had a strange expression on his face: one she had never seen before. A feeling of foreboding went through her, although she had no idea what foreboding was. None of the angels had experienced something of that nature; for in the paradise of Eternity, there had never been cause for a sense of foreboding; not until now.

"What's wrong, Lucifer?" she asked.

"Nothing!" he retorted, avoiding her enquiring look.

Angelina was right, all the same: Lucifer was worried. And looking at it from his perspective, he was right to be worried. Lucifer's world was about to be turned upside-down, as the birth of a new baby turns the world of its older sibling upside-down. But as yet he had no inkling to what extent.

Angelina and Lucifer had been friends for what seemed like forever. They evolved from droplets of spirit together, progressed to maturity together, and worked in the same quadrant of Eternity together. They were inseparable, as though their souls were in some way bonded.

And yet, as separate personalities they were completely different. Angelina, like most of the angels, was gentle and easy-going; ever the peacemaker. Lucifer was headstrong and liked everything to be just so. Many accused him of being selfish and very negative – too much of a free spirit to be an angel of Yavros. Yet, Angelina knew differently. She knew that he couldn't help it. During the course of his inception into angelhood Lucifer's spirit somehow drew the short straw. His negative demeanour was not due to an unpleasant nature, but because he had missed out on some of the blessings bestowed upon the other angels.

For some reason, when Yavros dispensed the droplets of his spirit into the four corners of Eternity, Lucifer did not develop in quite the same way as the others angels. Not only did he behave differently from the rest, but he also looked different. Whereas most of his peers displayed a serene youthfulness, Lucifer seemed restless, and looked old right from the start.

To some he was even considered ugly, and had been hurt many times over by derogatory comments made by other angels. It was the negative effect they had on Lucifer that endeared him to Angelina.

In effect, she felt sorry for him. She felt he was much maligned. She wanted to protect him, and to do what she could to establish in him the same essence of spirituality that she saw in her other colleagues.

But she had been fighting a losing battle to uplift his soul, because she was never able to influence him. Lucifer could no more change his character than he could change his looks. ...Not because he didn't want to change – he and Angelina had had numerous conversations about it – but because he did not know how to. Nobody before him was ever faced with such a problem. Thus, none had preceded him to offer counsel on how to change one's ingrained personality from negative to positive.

Of this, Angelina was keenly aware. On the outside Lucifer was always brash, but underneath the veneer she knew there was still something of the spirit that created him; the same spirit of Yavros which was within herself and all the other angels. And it was this fact that kept her at his side.

While the angel gathering completed its short recess, she wondered what effect Yavros' news would have on Lucifer. Would it serve to encourage his spiritual growth, or hinder it? She felt sure her angel colleagues would be amenable to new ideas and welcome whatever changes they brought. But Lucifer would need some coaxing.

The gong for silence sounded again, and once more Yavros and the Golden Angels took their place in front of the map.

The voice boomed out again. "Now, where were we?"

Yavros turned to face the huge map. It was in the form of a large circle, with light areas at the top and bottom, and patches of colour on a blue background in between.

"This is my idea," he said, pointing toward it. "This is my objective: to create another world; a realm which, as I said earlier, is very different from the realm we inhabit here. Whereas you angels are ethereal in substance, this will be physical. Whereas Eternity is ever-present, the new realm will be one of time and space. I intend to have this world known as 'Eddren'. I will fill it with colour, and with joyous sounds such as have never been experienced before. I will breathe life into all manner of terrestrial forms, and then, when everything is in place, will come my masterpiece, my greatest triumph. For just as you were originally fashioned as an expression of me, so will I now take the concept one step further. I will manifest my spirit in physical form."

7

Yavros paused briefly while the angels took in his grand pronouncement and responded accordingly.

Continuing, he said, "To create Eternity and everything that's in it, I flung droplets of myself into the ethers. Now I intend to do it again. Even though my progeny will be very much like you angels in spirit, there will be some variations that will set them apart from you.

"The main difference is this: I will bestow upon them the gift of individuality. An angel is an individual; yet at the same time is under obedience to me. This new being will also be connected with me, but will have much greater autonomy. I will give him intellect and intelligence as well as intuition. I will enable him to reason independently of me, so that he can learn about me and realise for himself the greatness of Yavros and all his creations. I will call it 'freedom of will'. This will be a challenge both for him and for me. And this..." he said, pointing with pride at the map, "...is where he will live: Eddren! Well, everybody; what do you think of that!"

Yavros' exclamation of delight was short-lived when he remembered there was also an audience to consider; an audience of angels who by now were both excited and dumbfounded by the revelation. It was time to include them.

"Alright, that's all I have to say for now. Are there any questions?"

At first the angels remained silent, each absorbed in their private thoughts; not yet knowing how to process the information. To some, as Yavros had suggested, it would be a challenge, to many others it was an honour that he was sharing this monumental decision with them; but to just one, the news came as a threat.

It was Lucifer.

Somehow he suspected this was going to affect him, and affect him adversely.

Lucifer responded first, and stood in order to catch Yavros' attention. At the same time, he looked at the faces of his peers, hoping to see others who showed signs of concern. But he saw none.

Yavros reacted immediately.

"Yes, Lucifer. What do you want to ask me?"

Suddenly Lucifer felt horribly out of place, sensing that if he asked his question he would be shouted down.

He wanted to ask how the new world would affect each of them. Yet, in an instant he realised that no matter what he said, his fellow angels would interpret his comment as criticism; such was his reputation.

"Nothing, Sire... I just needed to stretch my legs," he lied, and sat down again.

"What are you doing?" chided Angelina, confused by his actions; for she sensed his concerns. "Why would you not speak out?"

Angelina's intuitive connection with Lucifer had picked up his feelings, and she would have also liked to hear the answer to his unasked question. Yet, she could see how disconcerted he was, and backed off from quizzing him any further.

"Don't worry," she whispered kindly. "Everything will be alright."

An angel sitting near the back was the next to stand.

Yavros acknowledged him.

"Master, where will this new world be?"

"An interesting question," Yavros replied. "It's one that's not easy to answer. I doubt if you have grasped the concept of time and space yet, and perhaps you won't be able to until Eddren has been formed. But I will attempt to explain it in familiar terms.

"Eternity, the realm in which all of us dwell, isn't just a place; it is a state of being. You are accustomed to living this way and cannot conceive of any other. But if you try to imagine another state to be a different dimension, then close your eyes and meditate upon it and you will be able to perceive it; for that is where Eddren will be. I suppose you might call it − a parallel dimension to this one. I'm afraid I can't explain it better than that at the moment, because it is also new to me. Does it answer your question, though?"

The angel politely nodded in affirmation, expressing his thanks in the process, although he didn't really understand the explanation.

Yavros continued.

"Do you have any more questions before we move on?"

Another angel stood up.

"Sire, you told us you want to be more creative, but you also said there should be more to our own lives than just privilege. Could you please tell us what you mean?"

"Yes; I was just coming to that," Yavros replied. "Please be seated again, and I will elaborate on my remark.

"When Eddren has been established, which in our own time-scale will happen quickly but in terrestrial terms will not eventuate for a very long time; when the physical life forms have evolved to the point where I can develop my new strain of beings...then I will call upon you angels for a special purpose. I'm telling you this now, because you will need to prepare yourselves for the tasks I have in mind for you all.

"In essence, I will be giving you all the responsibility of looking after my blossoming progeny; to which incidentally I've decided to allocate the term 'terran spirits' to indicate their physical form. Serving terran spirits as well as me will be different for you, but also rewarding. A change is as good as a rest, and you've all had plenty of rest so far; so you should be ready for a change – and a challenge!"

This last exclamation was made with a flourish; his arms flung open as though offering the challenge and seeking acceptance. In response first one, then several, and finally almost all the angels rose to their feet; again applauding their leader. Only Lucifer, Angelina and one or two others remained seated; not yet joining in the enthusiasm of their colleagues.

Angelina actually accepted Yavros' latest missive. She always did. But her primary concern just now was for her friend's state of mind. He had slumped back in his seat; his expression lifeless, his eyes black and empty. Is this the final straw for him, she thought forlornly; that will prevent his recovery from all he has suffered in his time? She knew what he was thinking: how he might be relegated further to the lowly status of servant to some upstart adonis. The thought distressed her terribly.

His directive delivered, Yavros expressed his gratitude to their hosts at the convention centre, wished everybody well, assuring them he would keep them informed of all the terrestrial progress, and with a gesture made his exit.

The ensuing chatter became deafening. Gradually the various groups made their way out of the building to the waiting transport, and embarked on their journey home. Angelina and Lucifer were among the last to leave.

They sat in silence during the bumpy ride down the hill: Lucifer adhered to his seat with despondency; Angelina deeply concerned for his state of mind.

Neither had anything to say.

CHAPTER 2

From that day on, Lucifer behaved as though he had lost touch with his soul. So low were his spirits, he functioned only instinctively; performing his daily routines and rituals with an automation never before seen among the angels. In the main he kept to himself; interacting with his peers only when obliged to.

But of most concern to Angelina was the fact that he became quietly courteous and uncomplaining; so out of character for the normally outspoken angel.

Lucifer's domain within the realm was one small room in an apartment complex housing over a hundred angels. The complex was self-contained. Except for their routine work requirements, the angels had little reason to stray too far; for their lives were connected to Yavros and his will.

Although the angels were individuals, there was little freedom of choice. This was one aspect of being an angel with which Lucifer always had a problem. Frequently he had an overwhelming desire to break free, but was forced to accept that he couldn't. So, when the directive arrived from Yavros, sent to each of the angels who had attended the Facsimile seminar, he systematically read it, yet with neither interest nor response.

The directive consisted of a list of contemplations each angel should regularly undertake while Eddren was being formed; this, in order to prepare themselves for the task of looking after the terran spirits. The directives ranged from contemplating the greatness of Yavros, to focusing on the secrets of translocating to the new realm when the time came. Each contemplation was to be repeated daily until the formation of Eddren was complete. After that, Yavros would issue new directives.

The dutiful angel communities organised themselves into groups: to pray and contemplate as instructed, but not to discuss. Discussion was something angels generally would never engage in; so spontaneously did they accept Yavros' will for them. When Lucifer was approached to join a group, he politely declined; stating that he would prefer to work on the directives alone.

It was not long before Angelina, away on a scheduled mission, heard of Lucifer's decision.

Shortly after her return, she called in on him; concerned about his strange behaviour.

"It worries me that you're not handling this very well," she told Lucifer; knowing of old that he would welcome her expression of understanding.

She waited, anticipating his appreciative response.

When Lucifer lowered his head, seemingly in remorse, Angelina assumed he was quietly embracing her concerns. But then he shot her a fiery glance.

"I wish you'd all mind your own business!" he snapped, causing Angelina to recoil in alarm. "What I do with Yavros' directive is nothing to do with anybody else!" Then, before Angelina could respond, he added, "Now, if you're through patronising me, I'll thank you to leave!"

Angelina was stunned. The shock from Lucifer's treatment of her was overwhelming.

13

Never before in their long history had she been spoken to in such harsh tones – by him, or by anyone. His unkind remarks cut the normally placid angel to the quick.

So severe was her reaction to his brutal rejection that she quickly came to a realisation. If she was to perform her regular duties in a normal manner ever again, she should first seek counselling. Lucifer had knocked her composure out of kilter. It became obvious, much to her dismay, that she could not regain it by herself.

But who could she confide in? Certainly not Yavros; for under present circumstances that would only alert him to Lucifer's frame of mind; an attitude which might change. There was still time. Eddren was not yet ready to house the terran spirits. Evolution in the physical realm still had countless millennia to go before the planet was ready for its terran inhabitants. Lucifer could still be persuaded to change his mind in the meantime. But it would require a miracle. Yavros was definitely not the one from whom she should seek counsel.

There was only one other angel whose reputation as a confidante and sage she could trust. He was a mentor from an ancient order; an original angel, whose wisdom was respected throughout all Eternity. His name was Masian. But would he be willing to listen? Would he even grant her an audience in the first place? There was only one way to find out.

Timidly, Angelina approached his quarters, and knocked.

Masian lived in a complex only a few blocks from her, and yet it could well have been in another part of Eternity altogether. Angels were grouped according to rank and responsibility, although this did not affect the manner in which Yavros regarded them. The Grand Master of Eternity loved all angels equally – even Lucifer. The fact that, over

14

the ages since their creation, some angels had moved through the ranks more quickly than others did not mean he loved them any better, and neither did they seek it. An angel's disposition was a constant state of love: each for Yavros and all for one another. At least, it had always been that way. Lucifer seemed to have altered the status quo of just lately.

The door to Masian's home opened abruptly, indicating that when Angelina arrived the occupant had briefly been elsewhere in mind or body, and scrambled to respond to her gentle knock.

Masian's normally calm demeanour returned instantly on seeing his visitor's sweet countenance.

"I'm sorry, my dear. I didn't mean to keep you waiting," he said, his tone profoundly apologetic. "Won't you please come in?"

Angelina was dumbfounded. Masian seemed not at all how she expected him to be.

She had never before come within the presence of this highly respected sage, and had assumed he would exude the magnificence of the Golden Angels, or even of Yavros. But Masian was different. The impression that formed in her mind, as she passed inside and waited while he closed the door, was one of quiet insignificance.

The same could also be said of his surroundings. There was nothing of the glittering palace she had imagined for angels more eminent than herself, but more like the pure simplicity of her own humble dwelling.

All at once Angelina sensed the atmosphere in Masian's room. It enveloped her in soothing serenity, which made her want to stay in there forever. She was allowing herself to drift into its ambience when Masian spoke again.

"Now, what can I do for you – Angelina isn't it?"

Angelina's eyes sparkled with delight. 'He knows who I am!' she thought in amazement.

Masian caught her surprise.

"There are a great many angels in Eternity, yet few that I know by name; and you, my dear, are one of them. Your gentle compassion is much talked about!"

"Really!" exclaimed Angelina, but then checked herself. She was not there for praise, but to talk about Lucifer. So, before she became lost in Masian's admiration she applied herself to the purpose of her visit.

"I would like to discuss Lucifer with you, if I may."

"Lucifer! Now I understand. Am I right in stating Lucifer is your friend?"

"Yes. How did you know?"

"I know much of what transpires in Eternity. And I have also observed Lucifer's guarded response to our master's directives. He's not very amenable towards them, and that worries me. I wondered if you might seek advice on how to deal with him."

"You did?"

"Does that surprise you?"

"A little. …Well, actually, I'm very surprised. I'd begun to assume I was alone in my concerns. Nobody else is in the least bit perturbed.'

"I'm sorry, but you are right to be concerned."

Angelina groaned. "Oh, no! Why do you say that?"

"Because Yavros won't be very happy if Lucifer does not change his attitude."

"But Lucifer can't help the way he is. For some reason he developed differently from the rest of us and has had a difficult time of things. Surely Yavros would take that into account!"

"Not necessarily. Yavros requires complete obedience from all the angels, including Lucifer. If your friend cannot

16

accept that, then he must work all the harder to achieve it. Remember, obedience is his sole purpose for living."

Angelina inwardly howled with frustration; for it was becoming apparent she might fail in her quest.

Masian didn't know Lucifer the way she did. He could no longer change his underlying nature than could Masian. He had a free spirit; not unlike the free will Yavros was planning to bestow on the terran spirits. She knew, from Lucifer's unusual behaviour that he was actually struggling with it. His rejection of her was exasperation and nothing more. After all, who else could he lash out at but her; his closest friend?

"...And if he can't change his attitude?" asked Angelina in despair.

"Then I doubt he will get any sympathy from Yavros."

"You can't mean that! Yavros is renowned for his loving and fair treatment of us all. He wouldn't single Lucifer out. He wouldn't be so spiteful as to make him a scapegoat. Surely he would be forgiving and understanding! Instead, he would try to help Lucifer. He would..."

"...Again, I'm sorry to say this, but if you want to protect Lucifer from serious trouble before Yavros' terran spirits are introduced, you don't have very much time left in which to achieve it. I would, however, advise you to remember just who and what you are."

"What's that?"

"Why, you are an angel, of course. In other words, your consciousness is spirit. A wealth of spiritual resources is at your disposal. You should utilise them to help Lucifer. Get back into that state of consciousness now. You seem to have slipped lately because of your concerns about him."

Angelina pondered Masian's words as she made her way back home.

Her mind was in a spin. A sense of panic threatened to consume her as the serenity of Masian's presence slowly faded and was replaced by the reality of the situation: her closest friend was in serious trouble. His future, it seemed, depended on her intervention.

All of a sudden Angelina felt helpless; as if everything she had gained in her existence had deserted her, and she was little more than a fragmented soul with no substance and no inspiration.

While still lost in her musings, she rounded the corner near her home and was abruptly brought to her senses; for pounding on the door stood the object of her concerns: Lucifer.

He spotted her immediately.

"Where've you been?" he snapped.

"I've... I visited a friend," Angelina stuttered, caught off guard by the sudden confrontation. "Why all the fuss?" she asked tersely.

"Don't you know?"

"Know what?"

"We've all been summoned before Yavros. The notice for it arrived a short time ago. ...But then, if you'd been here you would have known. Now get a move on or we'll both be late!"

"Alright, but let me get my breath. ...Why are you being so pushy, anyway?"

"It's a directive! You know we can't ignore a directive! You might not care if you get into trouble for ignoring him, but I do."

"Why the switch?" asked Angelina, striving to keep up with him as they hurried to the meeting place. "Not long ago you were against these new instructions from Yavros, and now you're rushing to obey him. What has changed your mind?"

Angelina's heart was in her mouth, hoping to hear that Lucifer had adjusted his attitude towards the terran spirits.

"Oh, I haven't changed my mind!"

"What do you mean? Lucifer, you're not making sense."

But there was no time for Lucifer to answer, for they had reached the bustling crowd of angels already gathered outside Yavros' dwelling.

Soon Yavros appeared on the balcony; his latest missive at the ready. This time he was alone.

Angelina looked around for the Golden Angels; Yavros never appeared before his subjects without at least one of them present.

And then she saw them; each purposefully stationed at intervals throughout the multitude.

Though somewhat disturbed by the spectacle, Angelina was relieved that Lucifer had finally shown some interest in Yavros' directives. Yet at the same time his statement worried her. Had he really not changed his mind?

Out of earshot, she quietly wailed, "Oh, Lucifer, what's going on with you?"

Just then, Yavros raised his arms – his characteristic way of hushing an audience.

Silence quickly ensued; each angel as intrigued as the others to know what this meeting was all about.

"My friends," began Yavros. "I am pleased to advise you that the time is now right to introduce the first terran spirits to the face of Eddren. Everything is at last in place to cater for their wants. Unlike you, they need to have a special environment in order to survive. They need air to breathe, water to drink, dry land on which to live, and a source of heat, which I have decreed shall come from a nearby star. They will need vegetation to provide shelter, and a variety of foodstuffs to sustain their bodies. These resources, and many more, I have already prepared for them to utilise.

"But most importantly; they should be protected from any harm that may befall them. You angels will provide that protection. This is the challenge I have prepared for you all."

A buzz of excitement went round the gathering.

"What does he mean by 'harm'?" asked one angel of his companion.

Yavros sensed concern among the angels, and called for silence.

"My progeny have always been very special to me, as you know from your own experience. My latest creation, the terran spirits, are extra special to me. They're not just my subjects as are you angels, they are my offspring. It would distress me if any harm should come to them. By 'harm', I mean that they may dash a foot against a stone, or sustain an injury to their physical bodies in a fall. With their minds fixed on me they might inadvertently forget to look out for their own safety. Your task will be to stand beside them, and forewarn them of any imminent dangers."

Yavros turned and retrieved from inside the vestibule of his abode several bundles of scrolls, which he delivered to each of the three Golden Angels.

Angelina wondered what was on the scrolls, and voiced her enquiry to Lucifer.

"More instructions, I suppose," he responded with little enthusiasm; then reached out as a scroll was handed to him. Immediately, he scrutinised the document.

Indeed it was a set of instructions – but not in a general sense like the previous ones. This was specifically for him. As he glanced over its contents, Lucifer saw that his name was mentioned in several places, together with the name of the terran spirit he would be assisting and the location in Eddren where they would be domiciled.

A look of trepidation crossed his face; a look that went unnoticed by Angelina while she concentrated on her own instructions.

"This is weird," she said, unaware of Lucifer's reaction. "All mine says is, 'Angelina, angel of Yavros, is required to minister to the terran spirits.' But it doesn't say which one, or how. What does yours say?"

Lucifer hastily rolled up his own instructions so that the contents could not be seen.

"My instructions are none of your business," he barked.

"Lucifer! Don't start that again! You know you have to obey Yavros. You've got no choice!"

Angelina's retort erupted a little more forcefully than she intended, attracting the attention of other angels.

This was no place to get into an argument, she decided. So before Yavros summed up and dismissed the gathering, she tugged at Lucifer's robe, urging him to follow her.

"Come on, let's get out of here," she said.

"Take your hand off me!" Lucifer growled, but followed her anyway. He had already decided there was no further reason to stay.

"Lucifer, I hope you're not going to be foolish over this," Angelina remarked as they threaded their way through the crowd. "It might not fare very well with you if you are."

"Rubbish. There's nothing Yavros could do to me, even if I did disobey him."

"I wouldn't be so sure about that! He's never been put to the test before."

"What would he do...give me menial duties? Yeah; that would be really difficult!"

Had the two of them stayed a little longer, they would have heard Yavros advise the angels that they needed to register their acceptance before beginning their tasks, and as soon as possible.

"The time is at hand," he told the crowd. "Conditions on the planet are perfect. Your services will be required as soon as my progeny have completed their own evolution. So please get your acceptances back to me quickly."

But Angelina and Lucifer did not stay. Lucifer would not have heeded Yavros' instructions, anyway. His mind was already made up.

CHAPTER 3

Some time later, with the deadline for acceptance expired, it came to light that three angels had not yet responded. Puzzled that even one of them might fail in his obligations, Yavros ordered them to come before him for questioning.

Lucifer was also puzzled, and interrogated his minder as to why he'd been singled out to appear before Yavros. He wondered if it concerned his irrational behaviour of late, and was amused to learn that it was merely because he had failed to return the acceptance on time.

What's more, Lucifer found he was not the only one.

"Don't tell me there's even more angels who refuse to serve those stupid terran spirits?" he chuckled under his breath in delight and relief.

The first to be questioned by Yavros had actually brought his acceptance along with him. Apologising sincerely for his tardiness, he explained that he had been absent on a mission till only recently. Yavros forgave him straightaway, and dismissed him with an affectionate handshake.

The second offered no apology for his lack of response. The angel, it turned out, had also recently returned from duty; to be greeted by the news that one of their number had set his mind against Yavros' instructions. This caused him to wonder why any angel of the realm would want to resist such a definitive order. It worried him. Was there something in Eddren to fear? There must be a reason for it, he had assumed, but was too bashful to investigate further. The look of concern on his face as he stood before his master was touching.

Yavros took pity on him. He well understood how the prospect of working in a completely new dimension might be intimidating; in conditions with which nobody was yet familiar and with entities that were still evolving. This, he conveyed to the anxious angel, setting him more at ease. Then, when Yavros assured him everything would be fine and that he really had nothing to worry about, the angel handed in his acceptance with profound apologies for his reservations about it.

"That's alright, my friend; you're forgiven. Go now, and I wish you well in your endeavours."

Then it was Lucifer's turn. While he was waiting to be seen, he had again speculated on the fact that the other two angels shared his lack of enthusiasm for working with terran spirits. To see first one dissenter and then the other leave their interviews in good spirits offered him some hope that all would be well for him, too. Encouraged, he leapt up to see Yavros.

...And his demeanour did not waver when his master greeted him cordially.

"Well, Lucifer, and what's the reason for the lateness of your acceptance?" he asked casually; expecting a similar explanation to the first two angels.

"Oh!" remarked Lucifer with a cheeky laugh. "Did you think I was just late handing it in?"

"Of course...what else?" responded Yavros in a slightly less cordial tone. "Is there another reason why you have not accepted your assignment?"

Suddenly Lucifer felt uneasy; his disquiet noticed by Yavros who now scrutinised the angel standing before him.

"Please give me your reason, Lucifer. I would really like to hear it."

Yavros had already learnt about Lucifer's reluctance to join in with counselling sessions and preparatory exercises. Yet, he refused to believe there could be undertones in the rumours. He had convinced himself that no angel of his could possibly refuse an instruction, for they weren't made that way. But then he recalled something he had almost forgotten about: that when the angels were created, one of them evolved differently from the others. Was Lucifer that angel? And if so, what has made him anti-social now?

With caution, Yavros addressed Lucifer again.

"I'm waiting..." he said guardedly.

"It's quite simple," Lucifer told him, expecting the same friendly reception as the other two angels. "I have decided to decline your invitation to serve the terran spirits."

"What?" Yavros said with the hesitant tone of disbelief.

Unaware of Yavros' reaction, Lucifer continued.

"It seems to me that an angel of my standing should not subjugate himself to a lesser being, and especially not to a mere mortal, even if he is a creation of yours. It would be beneath my dignity to do so."

If Lucifer was assuming Yavros might accept the rationale behind his statement, he was mistaken.

Instead Yavros, his eyes wide with increasing rage, rose to his full stature; a phenomenon never before witnessed. With fury in his heart, he bellowed at the top of his voice, "Miekaale! Get in here this minute!"

"Why all the fuss?" asked Lucifer more plaintively, now he realised his explanation was not well received. "What does it matter if one of the angels refuses to carry out your instructions?"

Miekaale the Golden Angel appeared instantaneously.

An ordinary angel is a diminutive spectre, even when in its most splendid state of consciousness; but a Golden Angel is so much more. And Miekaale had only been seen by the angel community in a subordinate role to Yavros. Yet the abrupt arrival of a Golden Angel summoned to his side, especially the Captain of the Guard over all Eternity, took Lucifer's breath away.

Miekaale exuded the energy of a thousand stars as he responded to Yavros' summons; and when Lucifer realised that the same energy was about to be unleashed upon him, he suddenly felt afraid. For reassurance, he tried to recall what he had said to Angelina... Oh yes, that was it: 'What is the worst that could happen to me?' He pondered this while Yavros spoke privately to the bristling Golden Angel. And then he had a brainwave: he would appeal to Yavros' sense of justice.

"Sire," Lucifer butted in, causing the two conspirators to halt their conversation and look his way.

Yavros, still seething from Lucifer's offensive remarks, regarded him with indifference; as though a mere wisp of breeze had briefly distracted him. Then he turned back to his deliberations.

Undaunted by the rebuff, Lucifer tried again.

"Yavros! Please! Won't you allow me to speak with you about this?"

"I've heard as much as I wish to hear from you," Yavros replied, irritated by the additional interruption.

"But I need to explain something to you!"

Suddenly Yavros lost his patience.

"Miekaale," he said. "Would you be so kind as to escort this reprobate to the ante-room, and secure him there? We will deal with him later."

Before he realised just what was happening, Lucifer found himself in the grip of Miekaale's energy field, trapped with no hope of escape. He could have been bound hands and feet, for all the movement he was permitted.

In an instant he was transported to the adjoining room, while Miekaale returned to Yavros. There was no need of further bondage. Lucifer could not move an inch.

But he could still talk, and once he realised this fact, he began to roar at the top of his voice. There was something he still needed to say to Yavros, and he was going to say it; come what may.

"You can't treat me this way!" he bellowed. "It's not my fault I can't obey your instructions! You made me different from all of the other angels. They are subservient because they've got no choice. But I do have a choice. I already possess the free will you're giving the terran spirits. And now you're calling me a reprobate! Damn it, Yavros. I have a right to choose my own destiny!"

This time, Yavros had no alternative but to listen. Once again he reluctantly paid attention through the open door; not out of regard for Lucifer's sensitivity, but in an attempt to shut him up.

"I am sorry, Miekaale; I can't think with him bellowing like that," Yavros confessed to his Captain of the Guard. "Bear with me; this won't take a minute."

He strode to the doorway; filling it with his presence. Without attempting to make eye contact with Lucifer, he said, "Well, what else do you want to say to me?"

"About time, too!" panted Lucifer, more to himself than to Yavros. "Can we talk properly without these wretched bonds?" he asked, looking down at his confined form. "I really am entitled to do what I want, you know."

With a fiery glance, Yavros turned on him.

"How dare you fabricate excuses for disobeying me!" he screamed into the face of the now apprehensive angel. "May I remind you that despite the free will you claim to have, you are angel; not terran. Whether you like it or not, you are and always will be under obedience to me. And whether you like it or not you will obey me or..."

"...Or what!" retorted Lucifer, mockingly. "What could you possibly do to me that's more of a punishment than serving your terran spirits?"

"You're trying my patience, Lucifer! Be very careful! You have never seen the kind of justice the Grand Master of Eternity can exact upon someone who crosses him!"

Lucifer roared with frustration. How was he going to get through to the One who created him – who supposedly loved him – that he had an intrinsic right to make his own decisions?

Receiving no response to his vociferous appeal, Lucifer slumped back to draw breath and review his situation. He appeared to be in trouble. If he did not want to incur a heavy penalty for his contrary attitude, his only course of action was to relent and agree to subjugate himself to the terrans. ...He couldn't do it! The thought of it nauseated him! He would not become a servant of anyone, let alone one of those creatures!

While Yavros returned to Miekaale, Lucifer hung his head dejectedly. To him, it seemed to take forever for them to reach some kind of conclusion.

At length, as the pair of mighty beings approached him, a pang of fear shot through his traumatised soul.

"Right, Lucifer," began Yavros. "I have given you a few moments to reflect on your faults, and assume that you've had the wisdom to change your mind. Are you now willing to follow my instructions? I strongly advise it."

"I can't do it!" came the sorry response. "I will not obey you on this. It's not that I'm disobedient; I just can't make myself do it. I'm sorry, but you'll just have to banish me to the furthest reaches of Eternity, or something..."

"...Oh, I have something far more appropriate in mind for you," responded Yavros scathingly. "...Something more in keeping with the seriousness of your transgression."

Lucifer lifted his eyes to behold the angry glare of his accuser, and the silent affirmation of compliance from the Captain of the Guard. Somehow, Lucifer knew he was not going to like what Yavros had arranged.

"Miekaale," instructed Yavros. "Would you please take this scoundrel, and remove him from Eternity altogether."

With a flap of his mighty wings, the great Golden Angel scooped up the protesting rebel, and banished him.

In less than the blink of an ethereal eye Lucifer, the only angel to have ever fallen out of favour with Yavros, found himself alone.

He quickly looked around, hoping to glimpse a familiar landmark: any object that might help him to identify his surroundings; but there were none.

It appeared, to his shocked and puzzled mind, that he was somewhere else. But where could it possibly be? After all, there was nowhere else – except perhaps for the new physical realm of Eddren, and he surely would not have been sent there.

Had Yavros put one over him? Was he playing a trick: to intimidate him and encourage a change of heart?

Angrily, Lucifer stamped his foot; at least he could move now. As he did so, the surface or substance on which he stood shook with the stomping, causing him to almost lose his balance.

He swore violently.

The ground shook again; accompanied this time by a rumbling coming from deep within.

But within what!

"Where am I..?" Lucifer yelled out into the ethers.

"...Where you deserve to be," a voice boomed back.

"Yavros... Is that you?"

Lucifer's demeanour was mellowing slightly, now that the reality of his situation had begun to sink in.

"Of course it is. You are now sampling the consequence for disobeying me. I recommend you keep perfectly still."

"Why?" Lucifer sneered, sarcastically. "I may be in some strange place, but I'm now free! Your servant Miekaale has no hold over me anymore – look!" Lucifer jumped around in glee. "You may think you've disciplined me, Yavros, but look again. This place is all mine, whatever it might be. By the way...just what is it?"

"You are in your own world now. I've called it 'Hellion;' which means, 'a naughty child'. ...Quite appropriate, don't you think? This will be a realm of your own making. If you harbour negative thoughts against me, your surroundings will deteriorate. If you begin to repent of your ways and turn back to me, then the atmosphere will slowly dissipate and you will be restored to your place in Eternity. ...But not until! It's entirely up to you, what you do...and where you go from here."

"You can't do this to me!" yelled Lucifer in response.

"Oh yes I can. I created you, don't forget. I gave you life as an angel; a servant of Eternity. You are not nor ever will be independent. Because of a flaw in your original makeup you have acquired a sense of autonomy, but that doesn't mean you can behave as an individual. You are; or rather you were an angel. From now on you are stripped of your status. From now until the day of your repentance, you are nothing more than raw spirit: without form or standing."

Lucifer could say nothing. He was defeated. Yavros had left him without a leg to stand on; though come to think of it, looking down at himself he saw that it was also literally true. He had no visible legs – or anything. Even though he felt the same as before, in actual fact he could see nothing of his former self.

The fallen angel, so it seemed, was now no more than a spirit: part of the ethers. As Yavros had so precisely put it, he was 'without form.'

Yavros left him alone to ponder the future.

His hope was that Lucifer might contemplate both his wrongdoings and the change in consciousness he needed in order to find favour again.

For a while, Lucifer did just that. A strange calm came over him as resignation slowly replaced resentment. Soon the atmosphere around him seemed lighter. For a moment he could see the outline of his old self.

But then something dawned on him; something that he knew would seal his fate forever. He realised, with a groan of anguish, that if he relented and went back to Eternity he would still have to obey Yavros and serve the terrans.

"No!" he bellowed out into the ethers as they began to swirl around him again. "I won't do it! I would rather be a nothing in freedom, than an angel in chains!"

As he fixed the determination in his soul, the world of Hellion opened up before his eyes; revealing a fiery void where the anger he was generating had taken shape.

Lucifer regarded it with despair.

31

"If this is where I have to live from now on, then so be it," he stated with feigned dignity. "At least it's mine...all mine. And I shall make of it what I like!"

Back in Eternity, Angelina had heard of Lucifer's downfall, along with many others of her community. She rushed over to Yavros' quarters, in the vain hope that she might be able to persuade him to back down and forgive Lucifer.

She needed to tell him that Lucifer couldn't help the way he was, and that Yavros should help him to reform rather than punish him. But if she was hoping to speak with Yavros in private, she was to be disappointed.

When Angelina arrived at the assembly area in front of Yavros' home, she saw that a large crowd of angels had gathered. And they appeared to be holding an animated discussion with Yavros about his unfair treatment of one of their own.

The angels, she learnt, were not happy about it; not if it meant any one of them might be next in line for the same punishment.

"Of course I will not be punishing any of you," Yavros assured them. "Lucifer brought this upon himself because he would not serve the terran spirits. But he was the only angel to refuse. So why would I want to punish you?"

Yavros also assured his attentive and anxious subjects that he had not, as had been put about, made a scapegoat of Lucifer to demonstrate that their kindly creator also had a sterner side. Lucifer, he told them, was exiled because he had sinned against his master and against his fellow angels by acting in a disgraceful manner.

Not only had he refused to serve the terran spirits as instructed but also committed a crime hitherto unheard of in Eternity: he had actually argued with Yavros. Could such behaviour be overlooked?

"...I think not," Yavros insisted before dismissing the crowd. "I have done the only thing I could do under such circumstances. I have banished Lucifer to the new realm of Hellion until he decides to repent. Then, and only then will he be forgiven and his status as an angel restored."

Angelina turned away from the gathering; dismayed that she had failed to speak on Lucifer's behalf. But her feelings were eased by the knowledge that Yavros was still hoping for repentance from Lucifer.

"...If he ever has a mind to repent," Angelina reflected; not assuming that Lucifer was likely to repent of his own volition any time soon. "Maybe, when he's languished long enough in his new realm, he'll feel more like repenting. ...Poor Lucifer, I wonder what he's thinking right now."

Angelina moaned sympathetically.

"His life will be different from now on; that's for sure."

Lucifer, by now, was thinking very little at all. There was nothing to think about. He had quickly discovered that his thoughts and feelings acutely affected his environment. Yavros had assured him they would. Furthermore, his surroundings remained intolerable because, right from the start, his thoughts were only of anger, of frustration and of plots for revenge; although he had no idea just how he could exact any revenge.

In fact, his initial scepticism was slowly being replaced by an annoying realisation that Yavros wasn't joking.

Yet, he declared with conviction, in refusing his master he had merely followed his own instincts. Was it not his right to do so? The fact that he was the only angel who thought that way didn't come into it. His instincts were ingrained in him – he certainly didn't fabricate them!

With the passage of time, when it became evident that the burning ethers would not abate as long as he was angry, Lucifer's resentment, out of necessity, began to dissipate.

Slowly his anger turned into a feeling of abandonment: that he had been dumped in the scrap heap of Eternity, to fragment and ultimately rot in his own self-pity. But even that sentiment, he discovered, got him nowhere.

Then, when there was no more emotion left in him and the last whispers of thought had faded from his mind, he sat motionless: in silence and solitude; blankly suspended in a ocean of emptiness, with nothing to do and nowhere to go. He desperately wanted to scream, but suspected that all it would achieve was more of the same.

And so Lucifer, in spirit, separated himself from existence altogether.

Yet, as he did so something remarkable happened. He found himself with a feeling of peace. Nothing mattered any more: not even his own misery. In Eternity they called it 'the peace which passes all understanding.'

That was how he felt now.

"Watch it, Lucifer," he warned himself. "Be careful you don't get too sloppy. You'll start thinking good thoughts and find yourself back there– back at square one with the same decision to make!"

And yet, he couldn't help it. In the stifling confines of Hellion there was nothing else to do than sit in a state of apathy – and dream of being somewhere else.

It was during one such reverie that Lucifer's life changed forever; not intentionally, but purely by chance. It was a real eye opener for the prisoner who was becoming more bored with each passing moment.

Lucifer's state of inert peacefulness was becoming so transcendent that he could not stop himself from drifting into it. Then one day, when he drifted off again, he sensed something unusual:

He was on the move.

At first Lucifer was too comatose to notice that something different was taking place. But then, as reality broke into his trance, he felt like he was falling; that he was somehow being pulled through a slowly revolving tunnel. The whole incident was so strange he barely realised it was taking place...until he shot from the end of his phantom tunnel.

The realisation of the incident startled him so much that he snapped back to full consciousness, and found himself once more in the swirling masses of Hellion.

But what Lucifer beheld was unforgettable.

When he fell out of the tunnel, Lucifer briefly witnessed a vista, the like of which he had never seen before. It was a completely different kind of world from anything he came across in Hellion or Eternity. There was light and colour; sound and texture in everything. The ground beneath him was green, and seemed to be solid. Above him the sky was hazy, but blue. Furthermore, there were objects around him; far too numerous to mention, and now that he had awoken from his dream, they were too indistinct to recall with clarity.

"What was that all about?" he said in wonderment.

He tried desperately to retain the startling image. But the picture faded quickly, and all he had left of it was the knowledge that something strange had occurred.

Lucifer shook his head to clear away the blurring effect of lethargy which now threatened to invade him. He knew his daydream had been a real experience, but what was it? ...And how could he get it back again?

After further contemplation on the matter, he figured out that the only way he could retrieve the experience was to duplicate the state of mind he was in at the time. Yet, relentlessly though he tried, he could not reproduce the calmness which had allowed his escape to take place.

That was how he now regarded the experience – a way to escape.

He had no idea what the place was; only that it must be somewhere far away from the awful realm that had been created for him alone.

Then one day, when it seemed the illusive dream had slipped from his grasp forever, he once more switched off to reality...and the tunnel opened up again.

It was the sensation of movement that alerted him to it. Straight away, he switched to full awareness; determined not to lose the experience a second time. But in doing so, he once again broke the reverie and jerked back into his own dimension.

"Damn it!" he cried out in frustration. "Am I ever going to get out of this accursed place?"

While Lucifer swore, the ground beneath him rumbled, and churning ethers caused him unbearable torment.

"...And damn you, Yavros!" he wailed, trying to fight off the onslaught. "It's all your fault! You should have listened to me instead of sending me here!"

In despair, and for the first time ever, Lucifer wept; he'd had enough. All the hate and hurt had left him scarred and defeated. He had no more fight left in him...couldn't take any more of it.

He just wanted to let go and die.

If only he could really die, he thought miserably. If only he could just become absorbed into the ethers and cease to exist completely. If only...

As Lucifer's mind drifted off into oblivion again, the tunnel appeared. But this time, Lucifer was so lost in his distant musings that he failed to notice it.

...Not until he arrived at the other end and was hurled out into the same scene as before.

"Good grief!" he exclaimed in disbelief.

The pitiful sprite, though startled and shaken, could not help being amazed by his sudden good fortune...and this time he had not been pulled back into Hellion!

"I made it!" he chuckled in surprise; but then retracted his careless claim when he realised he didn't actually know where he was.

He wondered if he had slipped through to an unknown part of Eternity. After all, he'd let go of the anger before hurtling through the tunnel again. Was this Yavros' pledge of redemption taking effect? Could he go home and never have to return to Hellion?

What a wonderful thought!

But then the rapture ceased abruptly when he recalled what would happen if he was redeemed to Yavros.

"Oh no! I would have to go through the whole business all over again. What am I to do?"

Lucifer looked around to see if anyone was there. Perhaps he could remain incognito; invisible even, and not have to front up to Yavros.

He expected to see a member of the angel community at work, or at least something he recognised that would give him his bearings. But nothing was familiar to him; not even the landscape.

There appeared to be things coming out of the ground such as he had seen nowhere in Eternity, and organisms up in the sky which could not have been angels. He looked down at himself as a reminder of what an angel actually looked like, and was shocked to discover that he was not yet visible. It appeared, for some reason, that his angel status had not been restored, even if his spirit had.

"Where in all of Hellion am I?" wailed Lucifer; not really expecting a response. "Could I be wrong about this place?" he cried. It certainly didn't look like anything he'd seen in Eternity or Hellion.

And then it dawned.

This wasn't Eternity, and it certainly couldn't be Hellion: it was much too pretty to be part of a scrapheap like that. ...Which meant there was only one other possibility.

Had he in fact landed in Eddren?

A thrill of excitement and expectation filled his soul.

"Well, what a windfall!" he cried, taking an enthusiastic interest. "This place is fascinating! Yavros, you've really out-shone yourself. Eddren is incredible!"

Everywhere he looked, Lucifer saw new and intriguing expressions of his master's inventiveness. What other kind of power could possibly produce such a diverse display of creativity? he mused.

All at once, Lucifer felt a new sense of awe at Yavros, who had designed both the splendour of Eternity and now this new realm of Eddren.

"...And living things, too, by the look of it," he marvelled as he recognised life in a creature soaring above him.

The bird was dark and had a wing-span not unlike the span of an angel's wings. It dropped onto a wide expanse of mirror-like substance not far away, and as it did so the water rippled away from it in increasing circles.

Lucifer was fascinated.

He shot to the edge of the lake, and looked inquisitively into crystal clear water. Despite the disturbance from the ripples, he marvelled how the lake reflected the trees and distant hills.

He wondered whether he could see his own reflection if he leant over the edge, and then realised he wouldn't be able to: he was still only spirit.

Yet, as he peered into the depths of the lake, it took him by surprise to discover that he could in fact see a reflection staring back at him.

Intrigued, Lucifer looked more closely into the mirror-image. He blinked, trying to make it out.

Looking back at him out of the now still water, was the reflection of a mighty angel, its splendid wings unfurled.

He gasped with surprise and awe.

"My goodness, it's me!" Lucifer exclaimed with puffed up pride. "This is how I look now!"

And then he realised something: It was not his own reflection he saw, but the mirror-image of someone else.

Quickly, Lucifer looked up.

What he observed filled him with alarm; for hovering above, a piercing look in its eye, was the one entity Lucifer presently feared the most: Miekaale, the Golden Angel.

"Oh, rats!" cursed Lucifer, sensing what might follow.

Unceremoniously, Miekaale gathered up the protesting spirit in his great wings.

In an instant, Lucifer found himself transported through the veil of consciousness and back into Hellion.

Yet, once the shock of his extradition had subsided, far from being dispirited he felt a welcome glow of success.

He may have been thrown out of Eternity and also out of Eddren, but he now had a clever little trick up his sleeve: something nobody could take away from him.

He now knew, albeit by accident, how to translocate into Eddren.

What fun he was going to have there in the future!

CHAPTER 4

Yavros was furious. His feelings of vexation towards Lucifer intensified when he heard of his audaciousness in escaping from Hellion; even more so that he had found Eddren.

"Miekaale," he instructed his concerned Captain of the Guard. "Please don't let this happen again!"

"I'm sorry, Master," came the reply. "It did not occur to me that Lucifer would be able to escape from his prison. ...But I'm sure he has learnt his lesson now."

"Let us hope so!"

If Lucifer had indeed learnt a lesson, it was not the one Miekaale and Yavros supposed.

He had certainly realised something; except it was not how to repent of his sins, but that he could now come and go as he pleased between Hellion and Eddren – and there was nobody to stop him.

Lucifer laughed as he embraced this; for it meant that even though he may be sent home from Eddren time and again, it would not prevent him from returning. At least, this was what he presumed. As yet, he could not reliably claim the ability to outwit his master. That assertion remained to be seen, but the idea tickled his fancy.

It was not long before he tried again. If practice leads to perfection, then in double-quick time Lucifer perfected his technique for translocating.

His first few visits to Eddren were furtive and brief in duration in case Miekaale, more sensitive now to his antics, got wind of it and whisked him into Hellion again.

"But what does it matter?" he chuckled; "I'll just come back another time!"

Lucifer had fun on his visits to Eddren. With great interest, he investigated each of the planet's regions, and learnt as much as he could about Yavros' terrestrial creation.

He saw how mountainous regions had evolved, where desert scapes had been formed, and areas where the land was pure white. He gazed in admiration on the forests and green meadows; especially the colourful flowering plants. But the life forms that fascinated him the most were the ones that moved.

His master, during the long formation of his physical realm, had evolved living creatures of various shapes and sizes. Some of them had four legs, others only two – many of which could fly like the angels – and there were even creatures with no legs at all.

But he was never able to spend much time observing them because of his perpetual need to keep his visits brief.

Meanwhile, in Eternity, Yavros had finalised the plans for his angel guardians.

The angels now had their guardianship duties firmly embedded in their minds, and were ready to spring into action when the time came. The first to go was a young angel called Mercer; chosen only as a trial run, for as yet the role of angel guardian was untested.

Yavros had selected an angel of the most recent epoch because the younger mind, he had guessed, would be less immersed in angel dogma than the more mature members of Eternity. He would therefore be flexible in his thinking, and better able to learn from the brand new experience of looking after terran spirits. Then later, according to Yavros' theory, he could report back to the others, and pass on his newly acquired knowledge before they began their own missions in Eddren.

And so it was incumbent upon Mercer, as the first angel assigned the position of angel guardian, to be responsible for terran spirits in Eddren.

Although inexperienced in the role, Mercer approached his preparatory tasks with enthusiasm.

He successfully completed all of the spiritual exercises required to translocate out of Eternity, and having been warned that the transition from an ethereal plane into a physical one might prove to be traumatic, he wisely gave himself a period of time to adjust to the conditions in the new realm.

The world of time and space, he discovered, was vastly different from the ever-present state he had just left.

Following well-rehearsed directions, he homed in on his two charges.

The first terran spirits, already gifted with the names of Hominus and Womah, had no inkling they were different from other life forms. Neither did they recognise that the sole purpose of their lives was to worship Yavros. They just got on with living.

They did, however, appreciate the wonders of the place they knew to be called 'Eddren', and marvelled at both its creation and its creator.

When Mercer caught up with them, they were standing alongside a waterfall, admiring the fine gossamer mist as it reflected the colours of the spectrum. He was immediately spellbound, and gazed upon them with affection.

By the end of his third day in Eddren, Mercer began to realise that he had little to do by way of guarding Hominus and Womah. Everything in their lives was so ordered and so perfect that his presence became nothing more than a token gesture. In fact, he wondered why he was there at all, but merely an unnecessary minder of two beings who did not even need minding.

He was about to report this observation back to Yavros, when something happened to change everything.

Lucifer, on one of his fleeting visits, had arrived in Eddren at a place of great beauty and serenity. As such, he could not help noticing how peaceful it was.

All around were colourful flowers, and hillsides dotted with trees in luxuriant foliage; it was a wonderful sight to behold. ...And the abundant bird-life took his breath away. The place was beautiful. Not even Eternity filled him with such awe.

"Yavros, I never thought I would say this, but I've come to really admire your omnipotence," Lucifer said out loud as if the whole of creation was listening. "You sure know how to throw a party!"

But then he remembered that good thoughts might put him back in Yavros' favour. Hastily, he tried to think how he could reverse his good intentions in case he suddenly landed back in Eternity.

Then, as if by magic, an opportunity presented itself.

One of the birds he admired so much had landed only a short distance away from him; looking for fallen berries. Lucifer wondered if it perceived his presence, and when it took no notice of him he assumed that it did not.

He wasn't especially thinking about how he could repay the spiritual credits he may have just earned; he'd merely noticed the bird's presence. But then something inside of him seemed to take over. Before he realised what he was doing, he cheekily whispered, "boo" to it.

The bird, though not actually hearing him, instantly felt the disturbance in the atmosphere and flew off, squawking indignantly.

"Aha! Did I do that?" cried Lucifer with pleasure. "Did I actually upset one of Yavros' creatures? What a bonus!"

He decided to give it another try, and looked around for something else to play with.

Soon he spotted a tiny creature with a long skinny tail scurrying through the grass. A much larger bird was flying overhead, so he urged it to swoop on the little mouse. With a squawk it obeyed, flying off with the helpless life form in its talons.

"I don't believe it!" he shrieked. "This is just incredible! Lucifer, old chap, I never knew you had it in you!"

...And then he saw the terran spirits.

To begin with, Lucifer didn't realise what they were, but looked on them as just another life form; except there was one noticeable difference, which caught his eye.

Whereas everything else was covered with fur, hide or feathers, these appeared to be clothed in nothing but skin.

Lucifer was transfixed. In Eternity he was used to seeing others of his kind displaying the raiment of angelhood; garments which differed from each other according to rank only. But these two had nothing to cover their skin at all. And what's more, he hissed while unable to draw his eyes away from them, "They look foolish! Don't they know that? Whatever were you thinking of, Yavros? I'm afraid you missed the mark with this life form!"

It was only when he noticed the phantom form of their angel guardian that he realised just what they were.

"Can these creatures actually be Yavros' terran spirits?"

At that precise moment, Mercer was a short distance away from his charges. Lulled into a false sense of security by their innocence he had taken leave to investigate a nest of baby creatures.

Still feeling playful after his manipulation of the birds, Lucifer decided to play a trick on Mercer; yet his instincts advised caution.

"Best not reveal your presence until you know exactly what's going on," he thought, and concentrated again on the terran spirits.

As Hominus and Womah danced for joy, Lucifer had an idea. It suddenly occurred to him, while he observed their strange behaviour, that the terran spirits were not aware their unclothed state made them look foolish.

He wondered if they even knew what 'foolish' meant, and decided to put it to the test.

Telepathically, he disturbed their composure.

All at once, Hominus awoke to both his own and his partner's nakedness, and hid in the trees.

Alarmed by his actions, Womah chased after him. Then, seeing Hominus through different eyes, she let out a shriek of revulsion and ran away.

"Yes!" cried Lucifer. "I've done it! I can control Yavros' progeny! This is too good to be true!"

But in his excitement, Lucifer forgot about Mercer, who had now been alerted to the goings on.

The anxious angel guardian, who was fully responsible for Yavros' first terran spirits, rushed back to the waterfall to find that both of his charges had disappeared. There, he sensed the presence of the alien spirit.

Mercer panicked.

"What have I done?" he wailed.

From above Yavros, who was contentedly meditating upon his success in Eddren, heard the shocking commotion and took notice.

The scene below filled him with horror: Mercer, the angel guardian supposedly looking after his creations, was running around frantically; his terran charges nowhere to be seen. And laughing out loud at the panic-stricken young angel was Lucifer, as large as life; evidently involved in all that had just taken place.

"NO!" Yavros wailed despondently.

The booming voice of Yavros resonated throughout the whole of Eternity, Eddren and, had anyone been there, even in Hellion.

On the ground, where Lucifer was watching the drama unfold, the earth shifted with the shockwaves.

He knew in an instant that Yavros had seen him.

"Whoops," he said coyly. "I've been spotted. ...Best go before Miekaale gets hold of me."

But he was too late.

Miekaale, who had instantly reacted to Yavros' distress call, shackled Lucifer before he could even contemplate a return to Hellion.

Ruthlessly, he dispatched the brigand to his own realm again; this time, Miekaale informing him, "You will remain bound until such time as Yavros recovers from the shock of what you've done."

Yavros was inconsolable. "Lucifer, why are you tormenting me?" he cried into the ethers.

To think that the angel he exiled to Hellion had already negatively influenced his beloved terran spirits, was more than Yavros could bear.

He swiftly sent for the trembling Mercer for an account of the incident.

"I'm sorry, Sire," sobbed the distraught angel. "I didn't know he was there...I couldn't see him!"

"That's alright," replied Yavros with hollow compassion. "Just tell me what happened."

"That's just it – I don't really know what happened! One minute the terrans were enjoying their surroundings, the next there was mayhem; and I'm to blame for not keeping watch. The two of them were playing, so I slipped away to examine one of your creations. Then, when I turned back, Womah was running into the forest, and Hominus crept out from behind a shrub; only to disappear into the forest as well. After that, everything seemed to go mad. So all I can say is...I don't really know what happened – but it did. Is there anything I can do to make amends, Sire?"

"No, Mercer, just go off home. It's not your fault Lucifer out-smarted everyone. I forgive you."

"Thank you, Sire," gushed Mercer, and carefully backed away from Yavros' presence.

Word spreads quickly in an ethereal realm, and the news that something dreadful had happened in Eddren was no exception; such was the telepathy between the angels of Eternity. Yet, none really understood what all the fuss was about. From all accounts, the terran spirits merely had a disagreement and went their separate ways. What was so terrible about that?

But Angelina was suspicious.

"Lucifer has turned their heads, that's what he's done," Yavros explained none too calmly, when she plucked up the courage to question him about it.

"Sire, what do you mean by 'turned their heads'?" she asked cautiously.

48

"I don't know how, but Lucifer has influenced their way of thinking," Yavros replied. "He has somehow tainted my terran spirits with an improper knowledge of physical life. It's more like the way he behaves than the spiritual path I planned for them. At no time did I foresee something like this happening! ...What can I do?"

Yavros was shaking by the time he'd finished his heart-felt account; so much so that Angelina became fearful he might fragment with rage. She tried to reassure him.

"Sire, please don't trouble yourself so. I'm sure Lucifer was only playing a trick on them and meant no real harm."

"That may well be the case, but Lucifer's not the one I'm concerned about; it's the terran spirits. They have free will. Lucifer has sown his seed in them. They might choose to germinate his seed, rather than honour me as I initially intended; and there is nothing I can do about it."

Angelina felt deeply sorry for Yavros. He had invested so much love and effort into the creation of Eddren and his terran spirits. To see him lose the devotion of the race so soon after their inception must be devastating...

"There must be something you can do, Sire," she said with encouragement. "You could visit Eddren yourself and remind them of their birthright. ...Let them actually see their loving creator. That might help!"

"I haven't considered going to Eddren," said Yavros. "I wouldn't even want to go there now; not when Lucifer has spoilt everything. I might scrap the whole idea of a utopia, and start again."

"That's a bit drastic isn't it? Surely you wouldn't want to kill off everything you've given life to, just because of one set-back; something that might be of little significance."

"I suppose you're right. I'll give it some thought. Thank you for your insightful comments, Angelina."

Yavros did indeed give it some thought – a great deal of thought. Yet, what he failed to take into account was the fact that while he was considering the problem, on the physical plane a thousand or more years had flown by. And a lot can happen on the face of a planet in the space of a thousand years; especially one like Eddren.

While Yavros took stock of the situation, reports started to come in from angel guardians stationed in Eddren.

They complained that many alarming traits had been noted throughout the terran community. Some were at a loss to know how to handle their charges now, and needed instruction on how to proceed.

After a while, Yavros was forced to break off from his musings and attend to their problems.

The terrans, he was told, were behaving oddly; not at all the kind of behaviour the angels had anticipated – and indeed had been led to expect when they trained for the role of angel guardian.

"In what manner are they different?" Yavros enquired, when the incoming reports became too numerous to deal with individually.

The angels informed him that after the first terrans had been infected by Lucifer, their newly acquired behaviour traits, and those of successive generations, became self-perpetuating. This, to the extent that after a millennium of terran habitation, Lucifer's self-serving nature had become ingrained in them.

In effect, his nature was now the terrans' nature.

The beings Yavros created as a facsimile of himself, the angels told him, could no longer be termed in that fashion; for they now recognised no authority but their own.

Several angel guardians advised him that they were unable to shepherd the terran spirits on the right path anymore; for they took no notice of the gentle wisdom which the guardians tried to impart. Rather, they insisted on going their own way with no acknowledgement of the One who created them.

"...But this is terrible," declared Yavros. "We must do something about it! Miekaale! Summon a gathering of the angels. I wish to address them – all of them!"

The angels listened, speechless, to what Yavros had to say.

It was already common knowledge that conditions had deteriorated, now that terrans were spreading throughout Eddren. However, nobody was prepared for the worrying news that degeneration had taken place.

And none was more distressed about the developing situation than Angelina.

She, more than anyone else, felt a weight of concern for the legacy her interfering friend had left for the master's treasured progeny.

Angelina waited solemnly for Yavros' judgement on the matter.

Would he really put an end to the physical realm; or maybe just visit Eddren himself, as she had suggested.

In fact, his decision turned out to be neither, much to her relief. It would have been tragic, she considered, if the new realm was destroyed merely on account of one disgraced angel's resentment. Instead, his ruling was that someone from Eternity who was considered trustworthy should go to Eddren, and teach the terran spirits who they really were, and where they came from.

"...But not me," he insisted; sighing wearily. "I couldn't stand to see how spiritually bereft my latest progeny have become. No; it would be inappropriate for me to venture away from Eternity just now. That being the case, I have selected from among you a knowledgeable angel whose reputation is faultless."

Yavros must mean Masian, thought Angelina excitedly, remembering how she valued the wise advice he gave her on a previous occasion. Surely nobody in Eternity could be held in higher esteem than Masian?

But it was not the name of Masian that passed Yavros' lips. The angel he selected as his ambassador to Eddren was a respected member of a lesser angelic order – one of more recent lineage than Masian; a name Angelina had barely heard mentioned before.

His name was Salutat.

.

PART TWO: AN ANGEL CALLED SALUTAT

CHAPTER 1

The chosen angel, Salutat, had for a while been counselling angel guardians on their return.

It transpired that as time went by in Eddren, the work had become an arduous and draining experience for the more sensitive angels; many of whom needed counselling on the completion of their mission. Salutat, out of concern for their wellbeing, had volunteered to help them.

This was a task well suited to his temperament. As a result, he became an expert in helping the angels re-adjust to life in Eternity, once the psychological wounds inflicted by their callous terran charges had healed.

However, it was not because of these skills that Yavros chose him, but for one other: Salutat learnt a great deal from returning angel guardians about life in Eddren. He would therefore be forewarned as to what he could expect in the current epoch; and more important still, he now had a better idea than most about the terrans themselves.

The decision made, Salutat was brought before Yavros to receive his instructions.

It was clear-cut what he would be doing: His mission on Eddren was to re-educate the terrans as to their spiritual connection with Yavros, and to guide them back along the true path.

"It should be quite straightforward," Yavros told him. "Once the terran spirits realise how they've lost track of their spirituality and resumed their devotion to me, you may come back home."

The dutiful angel accepted the brief without question. But there was one matter which troubled him.

"How am I to function on the physical plane?" he asked. "I am an angel. The terran spirits won't be able to see me, and presumably wouldn't be able to hear me, either."

Yavros had not thought of that.

Angel guardians were originally empowered to convey suggestions into the minds of their charges by telepathic means, but terran nature now had such a stronghold on them that telepathy alone no longer worked. If the terran consciousness stood a chance of being restored to Yavros, then an alternative method of communication would need to be found.

"Now I come to think of it," announced Salutat after some consideration. "What I need is a physical body such as the ones the terrans utilise. I believe it's the only way."

"I'm sure it is!" added Yavros laughingly. "But have you any suggestions as to how we may procure one for you?"

Salutat thought back to the many accounts he received from angel guardians. One particular aspect of terran life came strongly to mind. He thought it best to mention it to Yavros.

"They seem to go through a lengthy process in order to become fully grown," he informed his master. "From what I have heard, they begin life as tiny infants and slowly grow into adults. In physical terms it takes a great many years to accomplish full growth. It would be a simple matter if I was born into a baby and waited until I am mature enough to perform my task. ...But I don't think I can wait that long. Even as we speak time is passing on the physical plane. If it takes twenty Eddren years before I can begin my mission, a further generation of bad habits may have taken hold in the terran consciousness, and the task will be harder still. Better, I think, if I use a mature body that already exists."

"You can't do that!" exclaimed Yavros indignantly.

"Why not?"

"Because each terran spirit has its own soul! You must not possess the body of another spirit! It just isn't done!"

"With respect, Sire, that doesn't mean it can't be done. And we won't know whether or not it's possible until we try. Anyway, what choice do I have? The angels have been unable to communicate with the terrans telepathically for some time now. While I am with them, working in terran form is our only choice."

Yavros sighed. Salutat was right. He did need a body, and quickly. In haste he sent a party of angels into Eddren to seek a suitable candidate. It didn't take long to find one.

Salutat's host body was to be a young man who went by the name of Tagaar. The youth was a simpleton; a trait inherited from his father. As his brain was actually intact, Yavros saw nothing unethical about introducing another spirit into his body.

"It might even improve his life," he added when giving Salutat the news.

Straightaway, Salutat began to focus on the techniques for translocating into Eddren. He had no problem finding an instructor, for thousands of angel guardians had already followed the procedure; and many of them offered to help him in gratitude for their successful rehabilitation.

"It's very kind of you all," he told the willing angels; "but I only need one of you to show me how to do it."

Alone again, with the procedure for reaching the physical realm now embedded in his mind, Salutat set to work.

The technique involved a series of meditative exercises; each taking him more deeply into his own consciousness. And then, when a particular state had been achieved, he would slip through what was described to him as 'a long revolving tunnel', before his entry into the physical realm of Eddren.

That should be simple enough, he thought, and settled himself into the meditative state.

Very soon, there before him lay the strange vision of a revolving tunnel. True to expectation, he felt the pulling effect that drew him into it. But as soon as he sensed the movement, Salutat accidentally lost his meditative state, and snapped back into full consciousness again.

"Whatever happened there – did I make a mistake?" he asked of himself, and tried a second time with the same outcome.

Dismayed by his apparent failure, Salutat sought advice from his angel tutor. To confess to Yavros that he couldn't even enter Eddren, let alone begin his mission, would be unthinkable.

"You're trying too hard," he was told. "Just relax and let it happen without thinking about it."

"That's easy for you to say; you've done it before," was Salutat's response.

"Yes, and I had the same trouble to begin with...we all did. You just need more practice at relaxing; that's all."

'Alright then,' thought Salutat. 'If relaxing is what I must do in order to translocate, so be it!'

From then on, as often as possible, Salutat practiced putting himself into a state of relaxation. He had to admit, though, that relaxing was something he was not very good at, having spent the major part of his existence on the go in one way or another.

In fact, relaxing was something angels indulged in but rarely, as nobody ever became sufficiently weary to need it. So trying to make himself relax did not come easily to the energetic angel.

Yet, once he had acquired the knack, he practiced it all the more.

Then one day he became so relaxed that he drifted off into the meditative state he had endeavoured to attain.

In an instant, Salutat was through the tunnel and out into Eddren.

He landed with an undignified yelp.

"My goodness!" he cried, stunned by the experience. "Have I translocated to Eddren without even trying?"

In the welcome knowledge that he had arrived, Salutat sprang into action. There would be no time to lose if he was to redeem the terran spirits before many more years had passed.

But then he remembered: he was now in a realm with opposing forces. This was a physical dimension: a world of time and space; not the 'eternal now' of his own realm.

From here on, he realised, everything will be happening for me at a very different pace.

"So take it easy," he advised himself. "There's really no need to rush into things. Now, where's my host body!"

Tagaar, the young man selected to house Salutat, lived with his parents on the outskirts of a township in a desert region. His family were poor, as were most people in those parts, and they relied on each other for companionship and support.

Though simple in mind, Tagaar was an affable soul who knew just about everyone in the region; and most people in his settlement were on friendly terms with him.

Quiet by nature, he was used to following his mother around; hardly uttering a word. His mother saw no harm in this, and expected it. So she was somewhat taken aback, on rousing him from sleep one morning, when he came to with a start as though awoken from an intense dream and curtly said, "What is it…where am I?" And, on looking up at his mother: "Who are you?"

Salutat timed his arrival to enter the boy during sleep in order to minimise disturbance for them both.

The angel Salutat knew exactly what to expect during his mission in Eddren – he'd been well informed by the many angel guardians he counselled on their return. Yet as a novice terran spirit, he had no idea about the conditions he would actually have to face; nor the feelings he might experience as a result of those conditions. So when Salutat awoke in a strange body at an unknown person's behest, the rush of emotions took him by storm.

Entirely without thought, he had demanded to know the identity of the woman looking down at him: a reaction to the shock of being awoken so abruptly in a strange and bizarre environment. If he had but given himself a second to think about it, Salutat would have recognised the need for diplomacy in his dealings with the terrans. This was something which in time he would become very good at, but just at the moment the experience of arrival took him quite by surprise.

And Salutat wasn't the only one to be taken by surprise. His host's mother was also astonished by her son's atypical response to their usual routine; for she regularly had to wake him up, otherwise he would sleep the day away and be of no use to her at all. On this particular morning, she attributed his startled reaction to a vivid dream.

Thus excusing his odd behaviour, she said, "I'm sorry, son. Did I frighten you? Here, take some water; you look parched. It's freshly drawn from the well."

As Salutat struggled to sit himself up, experiencing for the first time the unaccustomed weight and restrictions of a bulky physical frame, he realised that he was in fact very thirsty. ...And not just thirsty, but also ravenously hungry.

Salutat had a lot to learn while he adjusted to living in a terran body. He soon discovered that a physical form was extremely confining and often uncomfortable.

"You have to force every part of it to move in order to accomplish anything," he later told an angel colleague.

But he resigned himself to the fact that he had a job to do as a terran spirit, and so must make the most of what had been supplied for him.

One of the tasks Tagaar's mother regularly assigned to him was a weekly trip to market for their provisions. The soil in their surroundings was too sandy to grow much; necessitating the need for the purchase of fresh produce.

This was an outing Tagaar always looked forward to. It gave him an opportunity to get away by himself, even if it meant that he had to balance a heavy basket of food on his head all the way home; something usually undertaken by the women of the household. But he didn't mind; for it proved to him that his mother believed in his abilities.

Salutat, on the other hand, had no interest in trudging the distance to market. He was quickly discovering that in order to travel from one place to another, he needed to walk. Furthermore, not only did he have to walk there, but he also had to walk all the way back again. This irritated him immensely. He argued silently with Yavros that doing the household tasks was not a part of his mission; that walking made his feet hurt, and it was much too hot to be out during the daytime, anyway.

Yavros assured him that it was all part of his training, and that as he would be doing a lot more walking from now on, he had better get used to it.

Reluctantly, Salutat complied.

It was on one such visit to the market that his struggles intensified.

Salutat was waiting in line to be served by a stallholder, when somebody called from behind, "Tagaar, is that you?"

At first Salutat took no notice; for the fact that he now bore another name had slipped his recollection. This, on account of the fact that he was so thirsty from walking that he had briefly drifted back to Eternity.

However, when the man poked him and said, "Tagaar it's me, Moesa! I'm right behind you," Salutat snapped out of his reverie and turned round to respond.

With a little bow, something he had seen other terrans do when greeting their friends, he apologised for being so negligent.

"My mind was in another world," he said with a degree of accuracy, and then went on, "How are you?"

"I'm well, thank you," replied Moesa. "We haven't seen much of you lately. You weren't ill, were you?"

"No," Salutat responded blindly, not knowing what the term 'ill' meant.

"I guess your mother has kept you busy."

"Yes, that's it. I've been busy," he said, hedging around the real issue of not knowing who this person was.

But then, just as Salutat began to feel overwhelmed by the situation, Yavros rescued him from his dilemma.

A young woman seemed to appear out of nowhere, and joined them. Excusing herself for interrupting their private conversation, she said, "Moesa, how is your sister? I hear she broke her leg in a fall."

While Moesa and the woman talked, Salutat uttered a silent prayer of thanks to Yavros for helping him out. Then, once his consciousness had returned from its angelic state, he listened to the account from Moesa on how his sibling was injured.

So far in his mission, Salutat had not had occasion to consider that a terran might become injured or ill. He had assumed that, as they were supposed to be a reflection of Yavros, they must be perfect in every way; except, so it seemed these days, in consciousness. To discover that a terran had been incapacitated distressed Salutat.

Was this more of Lucifer's vengefulness?

He decided to remedy the situation, and restore the girl to health.

With the mind of an angel, he raised his consciousness and projected it towards the injured person. Then, when he felt spiritual energy go out of him he relaxed; somehow knowing that it had been effective.

Later that day, after Salutat had made the arduous journey back home, the household was disturbed by animated knocking on the door of their stone house.

It was Moesa.

"You'll never guess what's happened!" he breathlessly said to Tagaar's mother, who had rushed to see what the fuss was about. "It's my sister. Her leg is better!"

"Surely not," was the response. "She hasn't been able to walk on it for ages. It can't have healed so quickly!"

"But it has, I tell you. It's miraculous!"

Salutat listened in; sharing in their surprise. Were his prayers earlier on so effective that they completely healed her; or was it just coincidence?

Soon afterwards, Salutat's query was answered when Tagaar's mother began complaining of an aching back.

"I must have strained it hauling the bucket up from our well," she grumbled, rubbing her lower spine.

Feeling her pain, and concerned that the woman may also become incapacitated, Salutat placed his hand on the painful area.

"Is this where it hurts?" he asked.

"Yes son, it is," was her reply. But then she changed her mind. "...At least, it did hurt until you put your hand over the spot. I can feel only tingling there now. The warmth from your hand is going right through me! Whatever are you doing, Tagaar?"

"Nothing," he replied truthfully. In fact, Salutat had put his hand on the woman's back only out of compassion; yet in doing so he had inadvertently released a further flow of spiritual energy, instantly correcting the imbalance in her aura and healing her sore back.

"That's amazing!" she cried when she realised she could move freely and without pain. "I don't know how you did it son, but thank you!"

She kissed Tagaar lightly on the cheek, and then rushed off to tell her friends what had happened.

It was not long before Salutat began to receive calls for help from other terrans.

Word quickly spread that Tagaar possessed the power of healing. Moesa wondered whether his sister's recovery from the broken leg could also be attributed to his friend's newfound abilities. After all, he reminded himself, Tagaar was present when his sister's condition was discussed.

"I really don't know," was Salutat's reply when Moesa questioned him. "I remember raising my consciousness to send spiritual thoughts in her direction, but I can't claim any credit for her healing."

"This is fascinating," said Moesa. "Will you tell me some more about this special consciousness or yours? It sounds very interesting."

Salutat could not believe his ears. Here was someone actually asking about the very topic on which he'd based his mission. Did that mean it had it now begun?

Over the next few weeks, Salutat had many conversations with Moesa.

He explained how Eddren came into being, and about the Grand Master of Eternity; referring to him as 'the Spirit Father'. To refer to Yavros by his proper name seemed somewhat premature.

He did, however, explain that the Spirit Father, though unseen by mortals, gave life to all living things in Eddren, including terrans. And then he sadly told Moesa how, over the centuries, they had lost track of their spiritual identity, preferring to follow worldly pursuits of their own.

Yet, he refrained from mentioning Lucifer's s influence. It seemed irrelevant just now; for his whereabouts had not even been an issue of late...

Tagaar's message of hope to a people weary of struggle became a popular topic of conversation, and he was often invited to talk to family and community groups about it.

This was something Salutat relished. He felt that at last he was making progress with his mission.

Yet, one aspect of the work caused him a great deal of hardship: the walking – and the heat. As an angel he would have soared from one location to another, but as a terran spirit he had little alternative but to walk everywhere; sometimes for several days, and often through hot, dusty or mountainous terrain to reach people who were anxious to both hear his message, and be healed of their ailments.

Exhausted, Salutat lifted his hands to the heavens.

"Yavros! This is your work. Please help me to do it!"

Relief and Yavros' response came by way of an old man's kind gesture.

The man had been a neighbour of Tagaar's family for decades. As his health had deteriorated, he was brought to Tagaar for healing. Salutat soon set to work; giving the old man many more years of life. Then, to express gratitude, he offered Tagaar something he could not refuse: the use of his horse.

"I'm unable to ride it now," he told Tagaar. "I'm too old to even climb up on it, and won't be getting out and about like I used to, anyway. So, please take it with my blessing."

After that, Salutat's mission became much easier – once he learnt how to ride it.

The idea of sitting astride another of Yavros' creations in order to get around seemed rather strange to his angel way of thinking. However, with perseverance he finally got the hang of controlling the unpredictable beast without falling off, which enabled him to accept invitations from further afield.

Terran spirits, he was finding, were hungry for a message such as his. They knew nothing of their spiritual origins. All they had experienced on a physical level was hardship.

When they learnt from Salutat that an invisible energy sustained their lives and could help them to recover their spirituality, they joyously grasped the message and made it their own.

As an angel on a mission, Salutat was delighted – as was Yavros. Unfortunately, so was Lucifer.

Yavros had been receiving some encouraging reports from Salutat. As a result, his focus gradually shifted from anger over what Lucifer had done, to a renewed interest in his physical creations.

In addition, his feelings of appreciation for the manner in which Salutat was helping the terrans also lifted his own spirits. Unfortunately, this also caused the shackles which had bound Lucifer ever since his manipulation of the early terrans, to be unintentionally relaxed.

Hardly believing his luck, Lucifer found himself liberated once again.

Not even Miekaale realised he was free. Having allowed himself a moment to share in Yavros' happiness, Miekaale briefly diverted his attention away from his captive; this fact duly noted by the captive himself.

So, as opportunity had presented itself to him, Lucifer couldn't help but capitalise on it and slipped unobtrusively back into Eddren.

On his arrival there, it soon became apparent to Lucifer that something must have occurred to bring about Yavros' change of heart, and Miekaale's timely distraction.

Intrigued, he set himself the task of finding out what it could be.

As he travelled the realm, he could barely believe how different everything was...and just how many people were on the planet! Lucifer knew a lot of terrestrial time must have passed since the days of Hominus and Womah, but it did not occur to him that they would procreate so much in that time. To his reckoning, a million or more terrans now inhabited Eddren.

However, the difference that interested him most lay in their demeanour.

The innocence of early terrans seemed to be a thing of the past. Whereas Hominus and Womah showed their love for the creator and delighted in the world he created for them, in the main these people exhibited neither quality.

Lucifer observed their lack of spirituality straight away. They seemed more like a reflection of himself than Yavros.

Was this the 'terran nature' he was accused of instilling in them? Had he in fact turned Yavros' progeny away from their creator completely?

The thought of that appealed enormously.

Yet, it wasn't intentional, he insisted privately. Not back then, at any rate. He'd just played a trick on Hominus and Womah: a ruse to get back at Yavros. But apparently that was enough. His little prank succeeded in sowing in them the seed of terran nature – his nature! ...And it had grown all by itself in the millennium since then; how wonderful! ...Poor Yavros must be beside himself with frenzy!

So what, he wondered, has happened recently to cause Miekaale to relax his vigil on me?

Lucifer soon found out.

The revitalisation of terran spirits rippled out from Salutat in increasing circles. Lucifer's keen senses quickly picked up on the subtle changes.

Whereas the atmosphere around the terrans generally was that of a depressed people, in pockets here and there a brightening in their mood became evident, which gave Lucifer cause for concern. It annoyed him that he had not been in Eddren when this turnaround occurred. The last thing he wanted to see was a planet filled with dancing nymphs; for the recollection of Hominus and Womah still sickened him. But what could he do to thwart the upsurge, and who was responsible for it?

"There must be a root cause behind this unacceptable rise in spirituality!" he declared.

One disadvantage Salutat encountered as a physical being was the irritating restrictions to his mobility. As Tagaar, he could not move about as readily as his angel alter ego.

Furthermore, his field of vision was restricted to what he could see from his elevation when standing or riding his horse – a little more if he climbed to the top of a hill.

On the other hand Lucifer, still in the invisible form of raw spirit, had no restriction of movement or vision, and was able to flit from one place to another with ease. Thus, as he converged on the nucleus of the rippling motion, he took himself up to an elevation from which he could see everything for miles around. Very soon he noticed in the distance a small band of travellers leaving a trail in the soft sand. The source of spiritual energy seemed to be coming from there.

"This is interesting," he thought, and decided to take a closer look.

On the ground, a whirlwind suddenly funnelled past the travellers, stirring up sand in the faces of both the terran spirits and their horses.

Salutat drew his cloak over his face for protection.

Moesa, now his mission assistant, exclaimed, "Where did that come from?" He looked around to see where the whirlwind had gone, but it had vanished altogether.

At the same time, Salutat felt a chill run down his spine, as though something sinister was at hand; yet he couldn't determine what it might be.

That Lucifer might be present did not occur to him.

By now, Lucifer had seen enough to answer his queries. He now knew what was causing the spiritual energy: an angel, cleverly disguised as a terran male.

Out of earshot of the teacher and his followers, Lucifer cried into the ethers, "Angel of Yavros, you may be able to hide yourself from the terran spirits, but you can't hide from me. I know who you are – you're Salutat; I remember you of old. But what in all of creation are you doing here?"

And then it dawned. Salutat had been commissioned to return the terran spirits to Yavros!

"How quaint," Lucifer chuckled. "Yavros must be really worried about this place to send one of his minions!"

After their day's teaching, Lucifer covertly followed the evangelising group back home. It so happened that Tagaar had been invited by Moesa to stay overnight at his family's dwelling, so Lucifer wasted no time in inviting himself, too.

There, Salutat met his friend's family: his hard-working mother, his young sister who's leg Salutat had healed, and Moesa' father who, it transpired, disagreed with his son's new concept of an invisible creator.

Out of respect for his host, Salutat chose to refrain from arguing this particular point. He recognised in him a man whose opinion was regarded as law in his own house, and so kept away from the subject of their mission. Instead, as Tagaar, he spoke only of their respective families.

Lucifer regarded all of this with interest. It offered him an objective on which to work.

After Salutat and Moesa had departed again the next morning, he remained behind at the parents' home, and attached himself to Moesa's father. Then, when the man indulged in an afternoon nap, he made his move.

While the father slept, Lucifer entered his subconscious mind and, finding in it the chamber which contained his beliefs, added another concept. He encouraged the man to accept that Tagaar was right in part: that there was indeed a creator of Eddren, but rather than some invisible Spirit Father, this creator was very much visible.

It comes into the world every day, Lucifer taught him. It sends to the face of Eddren warmth, light and colour, he declared subliminally.

The creator of Eddren, he convinced his naïve student, is none other than the sun.

When Moesa's father awoke later on, it was as though he'd been given a revelation in a dream.

He hurried off to tell his wife and then his neighbours that he had received a message from the true creator of Eddren. He told them he was wrong in judging his son's opinions so harshly. Tagaar and Moesa were on the right track after all – they'd merely been looking in the wrong direction.

The creator of their universe was actually the sun!

After that, there was no stopping him. Lucifer saw to it that the revelation burned in his soul with a passion. As far as Lucifer and Moesa's father were concerned, the earlier teaching needed to be corrected forthwith.

Hot on the heels of the mission party the father, goaded from within by Lucifer, followed along their route; voicing his own thoughts to inhabitants of the camps, settlements or dwellings where the evangelisers had already preached.

Yet, rather than reinforcing their teachings, he replaced them with Lucifer's contrived version of the truth.

He advised the people that Moesa and his friends were only partly right in their beliefs, for it was the sun they should really be worshipping. And, he added for emphasis, the others had paved the way for the coming of the real truth: that the sun is the creator and centre of all.

71

As each listener embraced the adjunct to the message they had already received, they turned their faces skyward to feel the warmth of their new creator – and away from Yavros once again.

The first Salutat heard about the travesty was when he found himself back in Eternity, leaving the hapless Tagaar in control of an undertaking he really knew nothing about.

It was with abject horror that Salutat discovered what had taken place. In near panic he sought to defend himself against Yavros' accusations of spiritual carelessness where Lucifer was concerned.

"...But, what makes you assume Lucifer is behind it?" he asked as a last resort.

"Because Lucifer has escaped from Hellion again. You should have been more vigilant, Salutat. Have you any idea of the impairment that has befallen the terran spirits yet again. Not only are they not returning to me, but they've firmly embraced a false teaching initiated by Lucifer. ...And he will make sure they adhere to it!

Is there no end to his machinations?"

Salutat's soul froze with shock and disbelief. How could everything have changed so dramatically when it was all going so well? And what, he thought forlornly, will become of his Moesa, now that Tagaar is his bumbling self again? With Lucifer's influence prompting the headstrong father, how can their mission possibly proceed?

Moesa must be devastated...

Unsure what to do about the situation in Eddren, Salutat went into decline. He felt completely helpless.

Not since Lucifer's banishment to Hellion had an angel of Yavros disappointed his master so.

Yet Yavros did not censure Salutat, as with Lucifer. Despite his dejection over what happened, Yavros could not rebuke the angel who was only doing his best. Instead, he allowed Salutat to slip away into self-imposed exile – at least until the furore had quietened, and he could resume his normal duties without fear of recrimination; for the angel community was deeply distressed by his departure from attentiveness. Salutat's part in it would take a lot of living down; of this Yavros was certain.

Salutat, on the other hand, just wanted to get away to lick his wounds and ponder his transgression.

While he was isolated from the rest of Eternity, Salutat had plenty of time to think. At first he condemned himself for his stupidity, but as time went by he began to reflect a little more clearly on what had happened.

In actual fact, Salutat began to realise, he hadn't done anything wrong at all. The mutation of their teaching was not his or Moesa's doing, but Lucifer's. He couldn't help it if Lucifer found out about his mission and followed him.

"It's funny," he reflected. "I knew something sinister was going on when the whirlwind came close by and then disappeared. That must have been Lucifer. I should have known to heed the warning signs...but I suppose it's easy to be wise in retrospect."

And later on, when sorrow was replaced by a growing sense of indignation, he began to think further.

"It's not my fault that I didn't sense Lucifer's presence!" he bellowed into the furthest reaches of Eternity. "I was working in the form of a terran spirit. And when you're terran, you're stuck with physical limitations. I couldn't see him following me with his false teaching! It's unfair that I've been ostracised for not thinking like an angel when I was living the life of a terran!"

Salutat grimaced in despair. He was stuck in a position that seemed hopeless. How could he possibly resolve it?

And then the solution presented itself...a solution that would send him off in a completely new direction.

He received a visit from Angelina.

The gentle angel had heard how hurtfully her peers spoke of Salutat's blunder.

Angelina felt sure they must have been exaggerating, so she set out to locate him and hopefully learn the truth. He was not hard to find.

Suspecting that none of the angels would go near him while he was exiled, she looked for an area of Eternity that was devoid of activity.

"Who are you, and what do you want?" Salutat asked gruffly when he saw her approaching.

He expected only further criticism; after all, why else would anyone want to visit him just now?

"Please forgive this intrusion," she said meekly, wishing to cause no discomfiture for the unhappy recluse, but also undeterred in her resolve to speak with him. "My name is Angelina. I would like to talk to you, if I may."

Salutat lowered his tone when he realised she wasn't there to condemn him.

"You shouldn't bother with me, Angelina? Can't you see I'm in exile?"

"Yes I know. That's why I wanted to speak with you. It's a while now since you were recalled from Eddren. Don't you think it's time you came out of exile?"

"On whose authority do you ask me that?"

"Well, nobody's, really...except I'm concerned for your wellbeing. It's unlike an angel to become so downhearted about something over which he had no control."

74

Suddenly Salutat realised that Angelina was serious. Here was an angel who apparently saw no reason to condemn or criticise him. In fact, she was giving him the impression she supported his stance.

"Why do you think that?" he asked. "Everybody else in Eternity is out to condemn me."

"...Because you couldn't help what happened. It was all Lucifer's doing. I know him only too well. The first terran spirits fell under his influence, as did the one who initiated sun worship. And indirectly, so have you for not realising what was going on."

"I must admit, I didn't believe it was entirely my fault either. It seemed to me that Yavros treated me a little too harshly. He doesn't understand what life as a terran spirit is like these days."

"What do you mean by that?" asked Angelina, pleased to see Salutat opening up.

"It's a different experience, living in a physical body. I couldn't do nearly as much as in spirit form. They think in a different way from angels, too. All in all, I reckon terran spirits have a difficult life. Did you know a physical body is heavy compared with ours? They can't even fly! They've got no sense of telepathy, and they have to put up with all manner of conditions – which, in my case, was hot and dusty. ...How I hated that part!"

Angelina listened compassionately. "Have you told all of this to Yavros?" she asked at length.

"No, what's the point?"

"...Because these are justifiable reasons why you failed to notice Lucifer's presence. And also, Salutat: don't forget you had no idea Lucifer had even escaped from Hellion, so how could you have known to look out for him? I suggest you speak with Yavros if you're ever to come out of this ridiculous exile."

"Well, maybe I don't want come out of exile!"

Salutat's indignation at the idea surprised even him.

"Of course you do! Please remember you're an angel! I think something of the terran person you occupied must still be present for you to react this way!"

"I'll say again. What's the point? Yavros has it fixed in his mind that I'm not to be trusted. I can't change that."

"Yes you can! If you explain to him what you just told me, he'll have no choice but to accept it. You can ask him for another chance."

"Another chance for what? ...My mission?"

"No! ...Another mission! Ask him for a different mission! Ask him for a chance to prove that you can be trusted to work in Eddren again."

"Now just hold on; I'll take this thing one step at a time, if you don't mind. I'm not sure I even want to speak to Yavros about it. I'm a bit disenchanted with him, too. And as for another mission – do you honestly suppose he'd go along with that!"

"I don't know! But you won't find out unless you speak to him. What's the worst he can do? ...Refuse you; that's all. Yavros is not likely to banish you to Hellion, like he did Lucifer. He'll probably just give you back your old tasks in Eternity, and you can carry on from where you left off. But if he doesn't refuse you, then..."

"...Alright, I'll go and see Yavros for you – if only to get you off my back!

With mixed feelings, Angelina left Salutat to ponder her suggestions. Had she asked too much of him? At very least she had got him to open up somewhat.

Who knows, she thought; this might turn out alright for both Salutat and Yavros.

CHAPTER 2

Sometime later, Angelina answered a knock on her door. To her amazement, the visitor was Salutat.

Since the day she sought him out she had heard nothing of him or from him, and had become so immersed in her own work that she barely gave him a thought. As far as she was concerned, her message to Salutat had been delivered and that was all she could do. Whether or not he took any notice of it was entirely up to him.

Therefore, when he turned up, beaming so broadly she hardly recognised him, Angelina realised her efforts were not in vain after all.

"Come in," she said enthusiastically. "This is a surprise!"

I hope you don't mind me calling on you without prior arrangement," he said, brushing past her. "I know it's not generally acceptable."

"No, of course I don't mind. I'm glad to see you...and can tell from your cheerful mood that you're happy to be back in circulation."

"Yes; and I have you to thank for it."

"Dare I ask why?"

"Oh, I think you can guess the answer to that."

"Forgive me for saying so, but it's not in the nature of an angel to play guessing games!"

"I'm sorry. It's just that after so long in exile, being here again is like a new lease on life for me; what with my new mission and everything..."

"...New mission? Salutat, what are you saying? Are you telling me you took my advice and discussed your feelings with Yavros?"

"I certainly did! My friend, you have a way with words. Discussing it with Yavros straightened everything out for me. Yours was the best advice I could have had. Thank you so much."

Angelina was dumbfounded.

After a moment to compose herself, she said, "Please tell me about your conversation with Yavros."

"It was all just as you predicted. I explained to Yavros about the conditions. Then I pointed out that he has never been to Eddren, let alone lived as a terran, and so cannot possibly know what it's like. I told him I thought it unkind of him to adopt such an attitude towards me when he has no idea what I had to go through on his behalf – especially the unbearable heat! And lastly, I reminded him that I had no idea Lucifer had escaped, because nobody told me; so how could I sense he was undermining my operation. And then, when I thought Yavros may have relented somewhat in his attitude, I asked him about a new mission as a terran spirit! ...You do remember suggesting it, don't you?"

"I do indeed. So he's giving you another chance?"

"Yes. But that's not all..."

"...Salutat, that's wonderful news! When do you start?"

"Wait – I haven't finished yet..."

Salutat had something to say to Angelina: something he proposed to Yavros and for which he received permission. Yet it was also something for which he needed Angelina's full attention in order to explain what he meant.

"...Angelina, before I tell you what the mission is, I need to ask you a question."

"What's that?"

"I want to ask you..."

Salutat suddenly tailed off, unsure how to broach the subject with her.

"Go on," said Angelina, fascinated with the mystery.

"I've already received Yavros' consent to do this..."

"To do what!"

"...Take you with me!"

"You're joking! Do you realise what you're asking?"

"Yes, of course. I've given it a lot of thought."

"I can see that! But why do you want to take somebody with you...and why me?"

"Because working among terran spirits is lonely for an angel. I had nobody of my own to share my thoughts and concerns with. And, as they say, two heads are better than one; especially when it comes to being on the lookout for Lucifer. What do you say, Angelina? Will you come with me this time, and work in Eddren?"

Angelina could not believe she was hearing this. Here was an angel, a stranger to her until only recently, asking her to take part in his mission to another realm. How could she? Somewhere she still had the directive from Yavros about her own mission to Eddren. As such, she must keep herself free for further instructions.

"I don't think I can," she said. "I appreciate your asking, though. It's an honour to be considered for a mission in Eddren. But I'm still waiting to hear from Yavros regarding my own work with the terran spirits. I should not neglect that just to accommodate somebody else's whim; I hope you understand."

Salutat was disappointed. He felt sure Angelina would jump at the chance. Yavros had seemed keen about two of his angels working together.

"As you already support my mission in Eddren," Salutat said; "perhaps you could also confirm with Yavros that this suggestion has received his approval."

Yet, Angelina remained undecided. She wasn't even sure if she wanted to go with Salutat. Her duty, as always, was to Yavros. Salutat really had no right to manipulate his way into another angel's obligations.

Later on, she decided to take a second look at her own set of instructions. Maybe the wording would help throw some light on what she should do.

Carefully opening the ageing scroll, she once again read, 'Angelina, angel of Yavros, is required to minister to the terran spirits'.

"This doesn't really tell me anything!" she complained, and read it again.

In fact, to Angelina the wording just seemed ill-defined, and was of no help to her whatsoever.

"I wonder if anybody else was given such ambiguous instructions," she thought.

Mystified, Angelina set out to question her colleagues about it, but without success. Not even one matched the vague wording of Angelina's orders. Each reported similar instructions to the ones Lucifer received; theirs differing only in the names, locations and time-frames involved.

"Am I the only angel who wasn't given specific orders?" she queried.

At length she could bear her perplexity no longer, and went to see Yavros.

"You are right," he told her when she poured out her grievances to him." I did not specify what your assignment was to be."

"But why?" she asked him.

"I deliberately left your instructions 'ill-defined', as you put it. I knew that something important would come up; although in the beginning I certainly didn't anticipate what that might be. ...And I knew you would be the right one to tackle it. Then when Salutat asked if he could have you accompany him on his second mission to Eddren, your assignment in my scheme became clear. My dear, this will be a very special mission– both for you two, and for me!"

"What do you mean – are you coming, too?"

"Oh no! Goodness me! I have no intention of ever going to Eddren! No; I mean there is a special challenge ahead for the two of you, and I will be interested to see how you are both getting on. There is nothing more important to me than following the progress of my dear terran spirits as they prepare for their rebirth. To have them return to me has been my dream. Do you now accept the challenge?"

"Certainly, Sire. If it's your wish that I go, then I consider it to be a privilege. ...And I like the way you described the mission: a return. In fact, henceforth I shall refer to it as, 'The Return'."

"Then bless you both in your venture, Angelina. You will always be in my thoughts."

Angelina suddenly felt a glow of pride. Was this really the mission planned for her all along, even though there was no mention of it beforehand? She would actually be going to Eddren – not as an invisible angel guardian, like so many of her peers – but living as a mortal terran spirit.

"I am truly honoured," she reflected modestly. "Not too many angels can claim they have lived a dual life!"

81

Excitedly, she hurried to Salutat with the good news.

He smiled appreciatively; not revealing the delight in his heart to have this special angel as his companion. Angelina was right in an observation she made: that a trace of his terran life had remained in him. Ever since her advice to him, he had found himself becoming fond of her. He knew instinctively that not only would she be a reliable worker on the mission, but also a like-minded companion.

With their preparatory exercises completed, Salutat gave Angelina a time-slot for the translocation itself.

She said farewell to her closest associates, and taking a deep ethereal breath to calm her, joined Salutat to begin their exciting mission.

As with all who had translocated before her, Angelina experienced the same jerk back to full consciousness when she felt the strange sensation of falling; and then again on the realisation that she had slipped out at the other end.

Discouraged, she confessed, "Salutat, I don't think I can manage this!"

"Don't worry," he said kindly as he turned back with her for the second time. "You'll get the hang of it with a bit of practice. Translocation itself is not difficult. You just need confidence – and you need to relax. That's what I was told, and it's true."

But Angelina's confidence had deserted her. In fact, she felt quite jittery: an unwelcome sense of anxiety that as an angel she had rarely experienced before. She began to question whether Salutat really knew what he was doing. Maybe other angels had succeeded in getting through to Eddren and remaining there, but it didn't necessarily mean that she could do it! Nevertheless, she had accepted the mission, and was duty bound to at least try.

On her next attempt, Angelina attempted the journey with enforced assistance; for as she began to feel the slipping sensation, she grabbed hold of Salutat; almost ruining the translocation.

At any other time, Salutat would have objected to such a lack of propriety on the part of an angel, but in this case he understood perfectly why Angelina had lunged at him. In fact, he reflected once the pair were safely through to the new realm, he rather enjoyed being held by her.

But familiarities aside, Salutat needed to focus on more pressing issues: such as the fact that they had actually arrived, and that his passenger, who was doubtless in a state of shock, needed his undivided attention in order to adjust to the physical plane.

Angelina noticed the difference in their surroundings right away. As they slid from the end of the tunnel, she gasped in wonderment; for far from being in a state of shock, she was transfixed.

"This is amazing!" she exclaimed; still holding on tightly. "Is everything really the work of Yavros' hand?"

And then she remembered where she was — no longer in the known environs of Eternity, but in a strange realm; one which she knew would take some getting used to.

"Are you feeling okay, Angelina?" asked Salutat, having now disentangled himself from her.

"Yes, I'm fine, thank you," she replied.

She turned to face him and discover that, although she heard what he said, she could not see him.

Fearing he had somehow disappeared, she called out, "Salutat — I can't see you! Where are you?"

"It's alright, I'm still here!" he reassured her. "You can't see me because we are no longer angels but spirits, and on the physical plane spirits are invisible."

"I thought we were supposed to be terran spirits."

"We will be eventually. We'll need to find a couple of suitable hosts in order to begin our work. But right now I want to concentrate on getting you adjusted to being in Eddren."

Salutat, too, found that he needed a moment to adjust. And this time he liked what he saw.

Whereas his previous mission, hundreds of years ago in physical terms, had been in a hot and dusty country, this was different. It was warm — that, he could tell from the humid air — but it certainly wasn't hot, and not the least bit sandy. In fact, nothing of the countryside could be seen in their immediate surroundings.

For, on translocating this time, he realised; he and his companion had arrived in the environs of a city.

The realisation of this had barely sunk in when Salutat's observations were disrupted by an unfamiliar sound.

Responding to a rumbling noise behind them, he swung round to see that they were in the path of a fast moving, colourfully decorated horse and chariot.

Directly, he enveloped Angelina and swept her out of harm's way, while the vehicle rushed by; momentarily fragmenting the terrified pair as they were dragged along in its wake.

"Whatever was that?" gasped Angelina while trying, in a manner unfamiliar to an angel of Eternity, to pull herself together; a task even more difficult than translocating.

"I think we were run through by a racing cart of some kind," suggested Salutat, regaining his own composure. "What sort of world has this become, where terrans need to travel at such speed? How can the realm of Eddren have changed so dramatically in only a short space of time – or has it been a short space of time just in Eternity?"

The incident with the chariot brought home to Salutat the fact that nothing in Eddren was likely to be familiar to him on this mission.

As they moved cautiously along the side of the roadway which had served as their point of entry, it occurred to him that for a city very few terran spirits were out and about. Looking around, he realised why: it was still early morning. Elongated shadows suggested to his sluggish memory that, although he couldn't see it, the sun was low in the sky.

But throughout the morning that all changed. As they drifted along the road the sun climbed higher, brightening up their surroundings; a feature which dazzled awestruck Angelina by its intensity. Gradually more people appeared. Mostly they were men dressed in loose white garments with coloured swathes of cloth slung across one shoulder. It soon became apparent that the terrans were all heading in the same direction down a narrow street.

His curiosity aroused, Salutat decided to follow the now steady stream of people. Shortly, the cobble-stoned street opened out into a splendid, paved plaza: the city's meeting and business area.

It reminded Angelina of the meeting place in front of Yavros' dwelling back home in Eternity. For a moment she felt nostalgia creeping over her, but then chided herself and shook off the feelings. She could not afford to become home-sick. Instead, she followed Salutat's lead.

The pair halted briefly in order to gain perspective on what appeared to be the focal point for life in the centre of this major city.

The plaza was surrounded by tall, impressive buildings; gleaming white in the bright sunlight.

One in particular stood out from the rest, and seemed to be the place to which all the people were heading. At the top of a flight of steps stood an imposing entrance, with pillars of immense height featured on either side.

Again, Angelina's mind returned to another place, and she briefly travelled back to the day all the angels were summoned to the convention centre in Eternity: to attend Yavros' 'Facsimile' seminar, where he informed them of his innovative decision to create Eddren; that awful day which became the catalyst for Lucifer's undoing.

'Ah, Lucifer,' she mused; sadly. 'I wonder how he is; and where he is...'

However, Angelina's reflections were short-lived, partly because her sense of duty brought her back to reality, but mainly because things were starting to happen; things that would take both Angelina and Salutat by surprise.

They had by now ascended the steps leading into the huge building.

As they entered between the giant pillars they could hear chanting coming from within; a sound that grew ever louder when they moved deeper into the building. Then, as they reached its interior chamber, the reverberating sound became deafening.

"What is that awful noise?" asked Angelina of Salutat.

But Salutat could not hear her for the din – and for the distraction that occupied his mind. He had now realised what the purpose of the building must be.

Sculpted into the far wall of the assembly chamber he could see a massive replica of the sun.

"Well I never," he muttered. "A temple has been built for the worship of the sun! This must be a religion based on the lies Lucifer spread last time I was in Eddren!"

He turned to Angelina and ushered her outside.

"What did you do that for?" she asked indignantly.

"We can't stay here," he said with a sense of urgency.

"Why not? It's a fascinating place."

"This is a temple for sun worship: a place of idolatry!"

When they could hear themselves think again, Angelina said, "Sun worship: that's what Lucifer introduced. Did the people really take his twisted message to heart?"

"It sure looks like it. Yavros will be horrified! We must inform him."

However, before they had time to discuss it further, a man's raised voice caught their attention.

The two angels strained to see what was going on.

At the top of the steps, a portly man in fine vestments had arrived at the temple; his way ahead blocked by a shabby woman standing in prayer. The angels' attention had been drawn to him when he shouted at the old woman to move.

Yet, at that moment the woman was in an elevated state of consciousness; closer even to Yavros than to the sun she assumed she was worshipping. In effect, she could not hear the rude shouting.

To the angels' dismay, the man roughly shoved her to one side. Losing her balance, she fell headlong down the steps. The heartless man watched her fall, then haughtily turned away and continued on into the building.

Angelina gaped in disbelief.

"Is this what Lucifer's sun worship does to our master's creations?" she protested, her eyes boring into him.

Angelina rued the day that her one-time friend planted his seed of deceit within the terran consciousness.

For a moment, she shared Yavros' disappointment that her mission partner, in ancient times, had failed to notice Lucifer. With a feeling of dread, she wondered if there was now any point to the mission on which they were about to embark. By the look of it, returning terran spirits to Yavros was already a lost cause.

Salutat, too, had trouble believing what had just taken place. But, aware of how much a physical body can suffer, his primary concern was for the woman.

Softly groaning, she lay motionless; face down on the temple steps.

Unable to help her while in spirit form, Salutat could do nothing except elevate his consciousness. Then, when his efforts appeared to have no effect, he telepathically yelled into the minds of worshippers as they stepped over her to get to the temple; also to no avail

...Except for one gentleman who gave the impression he had heard something. Also clad in the simplest of clothing, he looked to be of little social standing. Yet he stopped, knelt at her side, and quickly assessed her situation.

The woman was now bleeding badly from a gash in her forehead. The kindly man called to two youths who were approaching the steps, and told them to fetch the wagon which had been their transport. While they obeyed their father, he rested the woman's head in his lap. From the perspective of the angels, he appeared to know her.

Salutat and Angelina looked on with concern. As they did so, the man started to wail; agonising over the wounds inflicted on her. Then he went quiet and gazed deeply into her inert face.

Just as the two youths arrived with the wagon, he said sorrowfully, "It's too late, your mother has passed on."

Suddenly Angelina felt a pang of anguish, as though it was Yavros himself looking on: seeing the life of a beloved terran snuffed out by an arrogant sun worshipper who had placed himself above her.

But then something remarkable happened.

By now a small crowd had gathered; attracted by the unfolding drama.

While the angels watched the sons lift their mother's body into the wagon, Angelina caught sight of something unusual. It was a form of some description: a gossamer replica of the woman herself; rising up from the body and clear of the crowd. Quickly she nudged Salutat.

"Look!" she said urgently. "Can you see that?"

"What?" asked Salutat, following her line of vision.

"Over there – hovering above the woman's body. Can't you see? I think it's her spirit! It seems to be looking down on her body. I wonder if Yavros will call it home."

Then, just as the spirit was about to dissipate into thin air, Salutat noticed it, too.

"Yes, I do see it! And you're right. It is her spirit. Well, fancy that! I never before considered what happens to a terran spirit at the moment of death. Now we know!"

With mixed feelings, the mission angels continued on their way. The brief sojourn at the temple had taught them much about the terran spirit of the modern era.

On the one hand, the arrogant worshipper of the sun epitomised all that Lucifer had injected into the terrans; both in the beginning and more recently.

Yet, there was also the poor, humble terran female and her caring family. Angelina prayed, as they moved away from the scene, that Yavros would welcome her soul back home, and maybe reward the unselfishness of her family when others ignored her sorry plight.

"It seems to me, that not all terran spirits here have turned away from Yavros," she told Salutat. "Their current beliefs inhibit them because they seek him in the wrong place. I suppose that's where we should concentrate our mission: on re-introducing them to their real creator."

"I tried to do that last time; only Lucifer somehow got wind of it and wrecked the whole thing. I can't believe he once was a friend of yours."

"He wasn't always a scoundrel," remarked Angelina. "We actually got on very well until the whole business of Eddren began. He felt he just couldn't be subservient to the terran spirits. I often wonder if he realised, the day he tainted those first ones, just how much it would alter the whole race, and how different they are now from Yavros' original ideas for them. Yavros called it 'terran nature' and condemned it. But it's not all bad. There's still a lot of good in them, if what we witnessed is anything to go by."

Slowly the angels made their way beyond the outskirts of the city and into the country; observing their environment as they went along.

At last Salutat was able to see the landscape created by Yavros in the region: wide belts of grassland, rolling hills and not far away, a fast-flowing river.

"This is more like it," he stated contentedly. "I am very grateful to Yavros for allocating this particular area for us to work in. It's so much more pleasant than my previous region. Did I tell you about that?"

"Yes you did. Don't you remember? It was when you were still in exile."

"...That's right; I'd almost forgotten. My exile seems like another lifetime, too."

As they continued, the ground began to rise up ahead of them. Soon they found themselves elevated above the valley through which the river flowed.

Looking back, the silhouette of the city and its buildings away in the distance seemed far less important now. Even the great temple seemed insignificant against the expanse of land and sky surrounding the city.

But as they went higher still, they discovered they could no longer see into the valley. A peculiar mist seemed to descend over them. Soon it developed into a clinging fog that both obscured their view and felt uncomfortable in its clamminess; even to a spirit. And when it started to rain, the two angels felt a need to seek shelter.

Not even Salutat knew what was happening; for at no time did he encounter rain in the desert. This was a new and unpleasant sensation for him. He was discovering that, although an angel does not feel in a physical sense as does a terran, the effect of rain trickling through an ethereal form is strange to say the least.

Up ahead, set back on a wide expanse of tussock, they spied a structure which had no walls but only four corner posts and a roof.

Compared with the city buildings it looked dilapidated, but Salutat realised it might provide some shelter until the rain eased. He guessed the barn may have been used for stock feed, as it was filled with a rough stack of hay that almost reached the roof.

The pair settled in; expecting a long wait, for the rain was becoming heavier.

They had not long been in the barn, when a commotion nearby startled them.

Angelina sensed movement within the hay, and gasped; unnerved by the unexpected occurrence.

"Let's get out of here," she said to Salutat.

"No, don't be silly!" he chided. "It's probably rodents come in to shelter, too."

But then, one of the 'rodents' spoke.

"Dymas, I'm getting wet!" cried a female voice; its owner emerging from the haystack.

"There must be a hole in the roof," came the reply.

Then a scantily clad young male appeared and leapt up; soon to be followed by an almost naked young woman.

The girl stood for a moment looking out at the rain. "It's not going to stop any time soon. I should make a run for it; my father will have my hide if I'm late home."

"Yes, I suppose we should go," said Dymas, replacing his scattered attire, which appeared to have been hastily shed some time earlier.

He handed the girl her own garments.

Quickly she threw them on and ran out into the rain.

Dymas watched her leave; then as an afterthought he cupped his hands and called to her, "Cefire! Will I see you again tomorrow?"

The girl stopped briefly, turned back to him and replied, "Of course," before running on.

Angelina was fascinated. What strange antics the terran spirits engage in, she thought, while she watched Dymas as he waited for a break in the weather before making his own getaway.

After both terrans had left, she asked Salutat if he ever encountered such behaviour in the terran spirits when he was last in Eddren.

"No, I actually had little to do with them, except when I preached; and then their conduct was, I would say, quite normal."

"I'm curious about this couple," said Angelina. "Can we hang around till tomorrow, and see if they do come back?"

"If you wish. But what makes you so curious?"

"There seems to be something endearing about them; something spiritual, even – I'm not really sure. I just feel a need to stay here for the time being."

"Alright then. We can take a look around when the rain stops. It's such a lovely region."

Late the following afternoon, the girl Cefire came back to the barn.

She called out to Dymas in case he had preceded her there, but she was the first to arrive. Sitting quietly in the hay, she rested her chin on her hands and stared out at the view now bathed in bright daylight.

Angelina felt an empathy with her. The compassionate angel regarded her with interest, as though they were in some way connected. The girl seemed sad, she perceived; certainly, reflective.

"I wonder what she's thinking," Angelina whispered to Salutat; forgetting that a terran spirit cannot actually hear an angel.

A short time later, Dymas turned up. He was dressed more formally than on the previous day, as if he had come from a place of business. Cefire took a moment to admire his appearance; he looked so handsome. How she loved him.

They kissed passionately; then silently moved round to the back of the haystack.

The angels looked on as the terran lovers removed their clothing. For the first time Angelina saw terrans in their raw skin.

She felt compelled to comment.

"The male looks so different from the female," she said innocently; not realising that public nakedness in Eddren was considered an impropriety.

Salutat chuckled.

It did not occur to either that they were spying on the private lives of others. From their perspective, it was all part of their ongoing education about terran behaviour in the modern era. After all, Salutat had long ascertained; if ever they were to become terran themselves, they would need to be well acquainted with all aspects of terran life.

Nevertheless they could not tell what the couple were doing; not even when they disappeared beneath the pile of hay, their bodies moving rhythmically and groaning noises coming from the girl.

Is she in pain? Angelina wondered; concerned for her well-being.

They emerged, panting and dishevelled a few minutes afterwards.

Angelina was relieved to see they were alright. But still she was none the wiser about what had caused the girl's apparent anguish.

"I'll never understand Yavros' progeny," she confessed to Salutat.

"Well, you'd better try," he responded. "Hopefully, we will be terran in the not too distant future!"

Cefire and Dymas returned to the barn regularly after that. The angels began to recognise that they were engaged in a covert relationship. It was a supposition that turned out to be painfully accurate.

In fact, the young terran couple were very much in love but could not openly display their love, for they came from different backgrounds.

The family of Dymas had always been enterprising in the field of business, whereas Cefire's father had close affinities with the sun temple and frowned on the pursuit of money. Had he known about the relationship between his daughter and a broker's son, he would have forbidden the association outright and punished his errant daughter accordingly.

Thus, Cefire and Dymas, out of necessity, resorted to furtive meetings in the hay barn.

It was the only way they could be together.

Several weeks later, Cefire arrived at the barn in a state of great agitation. She paced up and down while she waited for Dymas to turn up; alarming Angelina who instinctively knew something was amiss.

When her lover arrived, Cefire tried to cover up the fact that she was upset. Yet, intuitively, Dymas saw through the masquerade and questioned her.

At first Cefire would not respond to him. Lost for words, she instead gazed mindlessly out towards the distant city.

Dymas sensed trouble.

"Cefire, you're really worrying me. Please tell me what is wrong."

The girl fidgeted awkwardly, reluctant to confess that there was indeed something wrong.

Dymas persisted.

...And he was not alone in waiting for an explanation. Angelina, too, strained to hear what Cefire had to say.

"I don't know how to tell you this," she said eventually, "but I think I'm with child."

For a moment Dymas fell silent; deep in thought. His first reaction was one of joy – what could be sweeter than to have a child with your beloved.

He wanted to share his joy with her, knowing as he did that his enthusiasm would gladden both their hearts. But before his feelings could be indulged, certain practicalities arose in his mind.

Although Dymas was the son of a business man, he had little means of his own. His parents were against a liaison with Cefire, and had already insisted that they could not support him if they were to marry. Furthermore, Cefire's father was likely to retaliate if he knew about the tryst. Certainly he would be displeased that the boy he berated had been intimate to the point of pregnancy with his precious and only daughter; for he had secretly pledged her to the sun temple: to become a priestess when she reached the age of maturity; although of this she was mercifully unaware.

Then Dymas had a thought: maybe; hopefully, Cefire was mistaken. At length he found the courage to ask her.

"Cefire, are you certain you're with child?"

"Yes," she said mournfully. "I have not had the menses for a couple of months now. Unfortunately, that can mean only one thing."

"What are they talking about?" Angelina asked Salutat. She had no idea about physical conception and pregnancy, babies or motherhood, and especially about the need to be monetarily responsible for both. So, rather than feel any concern for their plight, she was puzzled as to cause of the dilemma.

"I don't know," Salutat said in all honesty as he tried to remember back to his previous life. The only females he encountered when living as a terran spirit were members of Moesa and Tagaar's families; and nothing like this ever transpired with them that he could recall.

The unhappy couple remained in a state of isolation for some time, each absorbed in their own thoughts; neither able to come up with a solution to their problem.

At long last Cefire said, "I'd better go. My father will be wondering where I am, and it will be getting dark soon."

With only a peck on the forehead, she said goodbye to Dymas and told him she would be back again tomorrow.

As the love of his life hurried away, Dymas looked on forlornly; wondering what would happen to her. Of one thing was certain, though: he could not leave Cefire in her father's control.

Angelina waited anxiously for the following afternoon, in the hope that they would both turn up.

She was now very concerned for the mental well-being of these two terran spirits: people she had become fond of lately, but to whom she could not offer practical help.

The next day, Dymas arrived as usual, but there was no sign of Cefire.

He waited as long as he could, hoping against hope that she was just running late. He would not allow himself to think she had forsaken their relationship, or even that she considered it prudent not to see him for a while. Yet, still Cefire did not come.

Every day for a week he came, in the hope that she may be waiting for him at their usual meeting place. And after that, he roamed the city streets in an attempt to connect with her. But all was to no avail. Cefire seemed to have disappeared altogether – until one day, some weeks later, she managed to get a message to him.

It was but a brief missive, delivered verbally by a mutual acquaintance, instructing him to go back to the barn the following day at their usual time.

Anxiously, Dymas complied.

Cefire was already at the barn when he arrived; Salutat and Angelina nervously in attendance.

She seemed different, Dymas observed. Her face was gaunt and expressionless, and despite her condition Cefire appeared to have lost weight.

He approached her cautiously, unsure whether to be friendly towards her or guarded. He decided on the latter in case her spirits were so low, as was the impression she gave, that she might not be able to return the friendliness. But when the time came, he could not contain himself.

"I am so glad to see you!" he said breathlessly, hurrying the last few steps to where she sat.

He dropped beside her and awaited her response.

Cefire glanced at him; then looked away again. Her expressionless features belied her true feelings. Beneath the numbness she felt in her soul, a spark of recognition was painfully re-igniting within her: a remembrance of the love she shared with this young man. She tried to force it back; the pain of recollection too much to endure. But it would not go away.

She began to weep softly.

Dymas slipped his arm around Cefire's shoulder and pulled her to him, resting his head against hers. Then he took hold of her hand and lightly kissed the fingers. They were icy cold, and she appeared to be trembling.

Cefire was obviously very troubled.

"Tell me what's wrong," he said quietly; trying to hide the worry. "Has something happened?"

Again she remained silent, unable to put words to the grief she was feeling: grief for the terror she had been through since she last saw him; for the hopelessness of a future they might once have had together. ...But most of all, grief for her empty future without him.

As a result of rumours initiated by her father's gossiping friends, Cefire was forced to confess to him that she was with child. He then turned on her, beat her soundly and banished her to her room while he pondered the scandal she had brought upon his household. Later he admonished her, labelling her as the biggest disappointment in his life. He said to her, "Do you not realise that I had lofty plans for you? And now you have brought shame upon me, and on my name within the temple. I cannot describe the disgust and hostility I feel towards the daughter in whom I had such high hopes!"

At first he had insisted Cefire get rid of the baby. He procured potions, the like of which Cefire did not know existed, in order to end her pregnancy. But she would not take them. At the risk of another beating she refused to kill the unborn baby of the man she loved, and although she would never express her reasoning to her father, she could not allow him near her with the deadly brew.

For her stubbornness, she received another beating.

"What's to be done with you?" he exclaimed in the end. According to his own point of view, there was only way to deal with the appalling situation. He would keep her shut in at home during the remainder of her confinement, and then surreptitiously dispose of the brat.

It was only when Cefire could no longer bear the agony of everything her father was putting her through that she succeeded in getting a message to Dymas.

Cefire explained all of this to her lover. She found it more difficult than she could cope with to describe it coherently, without causing him to rush off and seek revenge.

The angels listened intently. They could not believe how someone, with deep religious convictions, could behave so atrociously to his own flesh and blood at a time when she most needed his support. This must be Lucifer's influence, Angelina decided, and for the first time intense feelings of animosity towards him began to surface within her.

"Lucifer, you have become a nasty piece of work!" she hissed, as though Lucifer was within earshot. "Look what you've done to our master's creations. Is your resentment of Yavros such that you must take it out on innocent souls like these? How can he ever forgive you for it? ...And why would he want to?"

Dymas' horror at Cefire's tidings knew no bounds. It had been obvious, from the look on her face when they first met up again, that something was terribly wrong. But this was inexcusable! Who did the man think he was, to treat his daughter in such a way?

Without hesitation he jumped to his feet and held out his hand to her.

"Come on; we need to leave," he insisted, helping her up. "We can't stay here any longer. If we and our baby are to have any kind of life, then we must go far away from your father – and from my parents; for they won't be very happy when they learn what he's doing."

"But how can we?" Cefire wailed. "We've nowhere to go. ...And how would we survive?"

She sat down again: a dispirited heap upon the straw. Dymas gently stroked her hair as he pondered what to do. And then an idea came to mind; an idea so preposterous as to be not worth considering.

He dismissed it immediately.

A minute later Cefire looked up at him and hesitantly said, "I think...you should get away by yourself. ...It's my problem, not yours. I don't want you to suffer on account of my father and me – I love you far too much..."

Cefire tailed off, her throat constricted; the heaviness in her heart dulling any further inspiration in her mind.

Dymas squatted in front of her and touched both of her chilled hands to his lips.

"Do you honestly think I could leave you here?" he said passionately, gazing into her frightened eyes. "We're in it together – and we'll see it through together." Then, as the thought that glanced across his mind reappeared, he went on, "Besides, I have an idea."

"What's that?" she meekly asked, only half interested; her state of exhaustion finally getting the better of her.

Dymas sat down next to her again, the seed of his idea now germinating. The more he thought about it, the more logical a solution it seemed. But how to broach the subject with Cefire?

Be careful, he told himself. Think this through properly before you say anything.

After a moment he took a deep breath, and began.

"I don't know how you will react to this. You'll probably think I'm mad – and maybe I am! But I've just had an idea about how we can free ourselves from this predicament, and be together forever. ...Only you might not like it."

"I might not like what?" said Cefire, now looking at him curiously. Her instincts told her it was something alarming, worrying or at very least: arduous. But anything would be better than going back home to face her father.

Dymas shook his head, reluctant to mention it.

Why did I have to get such a stupid idea in my head? he thought. I just can't do it. ...I can't even say it!

But now Cefire's curiosity had piqued. She urged him, "Please...tell me what you're thinking!"

I have no choice, he continued to reflect.

He held his hands together as if in prayer; not knowing where to start.

"Dymas, you're frightening me. I want to know exactly what you're thinking, and I want to know now!"

"Alright! I'll tell you!" Dymas felt like a cornered animal with nowhere to hide. He gasped with dismay that he needed to actually voice his intentions, and wished again that he had never thought of it. "...But I really don't know how to put it into words," he added ruefully.

"It can't be that bad, surely? After all, you're not going to kill anyone, are you?"

Dymas suddenly went quiet again, as though Cefire had touched a nerve. Then he said, "No, of course not! Well, not exactly..."

"..Now you're not making any sense."

"Well, I'm not thinking of actually killing anyone."

"Then why did you shut off when I mentioned it?"

"Because..."

"...Because what!"

"Because I realised a good way we could get out of this and stay together, would be to end our lives!"

"What – kill ourselves? You must be joking!"

"Kill themselves?" mouthed Angelina to Salutat. "What does she mean by that?"

"I knew you would think I'm mad," said Dymas timidly, regretting the whole notion.

While Cefire tried to absorb what Dymas was thinking, Salutat also attempted to grasp his meaning.

How can anyone end their own life? he asked himself. It's not possible! We are all eternal: immortal.

But then it came to him. Perhaps Dymas meant he wanted to kill off their bodies so that they could go on together as spirits. Yes, that must be right – it can't really be anything else.

He explained his theory to Angelina.

"Oh no!" she exclaimed; so vocally that for a moment she thought the terran spirits may have actually heard her. A little more quietly she added. "...But we can't allow that to happen! We must help them!"

"And how d'you suppose we do that? We're still spirit."

"I don't know! We can help them to escape! Show them a way out, or something!"

"That's not a bad idea," replied Salutat, thinking fast. "Stay here. I'm going to have a look around."

In a flash he was gone, leaving Angelina to watch over the two young people by herself.

What am I to do? she pleaded silently into the ethers; terrified that the couple might take off and do something over which she had no control.

"Lucifer," she growled. "It's all your fault!"

Cefire had no intention of going anywhere; partly because she was too exhausted, but mainly because the shock of Dymas' revelation had frozen her to the spot.

Sitting on the hay, her head bowed; her senses numb, she closed her eyes, as if in doing so all the horrors of her world would go away. But when Dymas gently prodded her, urgently seeking a response to his bleak suggestion, she glanced up at him, only to find herself in exactly the same predicament. Then she began to wail mournfully.

"Alright, we won't kill ourselves," Dymas cried; in fear for her well-being. "Everything will work out...you'll see."

Meanwhile, in another realm a spirit was stirring. Lucifer had heard his name mentioned.

The voice sounded familiar. Could it be Angelina; trying to reach him at long last? But then, he realised, the voice did not sound particularly friendly; which made him feel very unhappy.

"I must look into this," he stated, and slipped unnoticed into Eddren.

Lucifer stumbled upon a scene of terran turmoil when he homed in on Angelina. There before him were a male and a female who seemed far from content. Furthermore, they weren't alone. He also sensed the presence of an angel; and not just one angel, but two.

If one of the angels was Angelina, then who could the other one be?

"Oh no!" he groaned when he saw Salutat's spirit not far away. "It's him again! ...And with my Angelina! This is just too much!"

Lucifer quickly grasped the reason for the terran spirits' distress, and why the angels were interested in them.

It's the girl's father, he asserted with uncanny accuracy. ...And he worships at the sun temple!

"What a good fellow he is," he proclaimed sarcastically. "I'm so flattered he's devoted to a religion I invented. That really fooled you all, didn't it? Maybe I can have a bit more fun with this. My loyal subject would love to know where his daughter is – and I'll show those meddlesome angels what I'm capable of, too!"

It was with horror, some time later, that Cefire observed in the distance her father approaching on horseback.

"Oh no!" she howled in terror; already traumatised by her current plight.

Dymas glanced around for somewhere they could hide; but the man had them in his sights.

At Lucifer's instigation, Cefire's father had been tipped off by a local stockman that his errant daughter and her lover were together on the hillside; the intention being to make life difficult for both the angels and their pet project.

"That way," Lucifer chuckled; "I'll be able to disrupt two sets of plans at the same time."

While Dymas hastily sought a way out for himself and Cefire, Angelina began to panic. For once in her life, all her spiritual resources seemed to evaporate, leaving her with no recourse except to cry out, "Salutat! Where are you?"

Responding to the urgency in her call, Salutat reappeared and instantly weighed up the situation. As luck would have it, he had already chosen the path for their flight.

"Come this way, you two," he called out, but the terran spirits were unable to hear him.

In their distress it did not occur to them that help might be at hand. So when Dymas grabbed hold of Cefire's arm and hauled her off in the opposite direction, Salutat shot over to him and yelled into his mind, "Go the other way, you fool!"

"Salutat!" exclaimed Angelina, shocked at the way in which he had spoken to one of Yavros' beloved offspring.

But Salutat's rudeness in the face of danger had paid off; for Dymas suddenly halted, turned to Cefire and said, "Wait – this is no good. Let's go up the hill!"

With relief, Salutat drove the fleeing couple over a low stone wall obscured by shrubs, and up the steep incline. The two angels followed close behind.

They had barely made progress, when the horse and rider reached the hay barn that had been their haven.

Restricted now by difficult terrain and an obstacle the horse refused to negotiate, its rider hurled abuse at his daughter from the saddle, before jumping down to pursue them on foot.

By now, Salutat had guided his two charges up through the trees and out into a clearing.

Soon Cefire began to tire, and lagged behind. Although she had always kept herself fit, her delicate condition now left her breathless.

"I need to rest," she insisted, flopping down onto the soft grass while Dymas forged ahead.

Reluctantly, he stopped to urge her on.

"Cefire, we can't rest now! Goodness knows what your father will do if he catches up with us!"

Dymas pulled her up and together they ran off; only to stop again further up the hill.

"I can't do it!" she declared emphatically, the strength in her legs failing. She had been exhausted even before the need of flight, and now had no more stamina.

She implored him, "You go on, Dymas. Get away from him while you can. I will always love you, but we obviously weren't meant to be together!"

CHAPTER 3

Time stood still for the desperate couple. Dymas, at a loss to know what to do next, paused to think. However, he need not have worried; for the decision had already been made. Salutat knew exactly what they should do.

Quickly he seized the moment.

While he kept the two terran spirits suspended briefly in time and space, he checked out something he noticed while looking for a means of escape. Over to their left, on the far side of a rocky out-crop, he had seen a ledge which might provide them with a safe place in which to hide for the time being. He felt sure Cefire's father would not be able to find them there.

Again he entered Dymas' subconscious mind with the idea; and again the perceptive terran responded.

Dymas would never understand how he instinctively knew where to go, or that they would find such a perfect hiding place. He just blindly acted on his hunch.

In an instant, they were through the rocks and shuffling along the ledge; fully obscured from the sight of anyone else on the hillside.

The ledge on which the pair now stood had been worn down over many centuries by fleet-footed animals that inhabited the slopes. It was narrow and high up; not really suitable for terran use and far too dangerous for anyone to safely remain upon for long.

The fugitives realised this as soon as they stood on it. Yet, what they did not know was just how short their stay would need to be; for, hovering close by was a third spirit; one whose unwelcome presence even the worried angels were yet to detect.

Lucifer gleefully watched the pair's futile attempt to evade Cefire's father.

The man's senses, sharpened by Lucifer's intervention, told him exactly where the fugitives had gone. And he was more than ready to ambush them just when they thought they were safe.

As he approached their hiding place, crashing through the bushes like a stampeding bull, Cefire screamed, "It's too late!"

Dymas looked on in horror, aware that their fate was about to be placed in the hands of a maniac.

"Let's do it!" he shrieked. "Let's end the agony and be together forever!"

"Dymas! No!" Cefire cried pitifully, and held onto him for all she was worth.

"What choice do we have?"

"There must be something!"

"No there isn't...look!"

Dymas shrieked as the father stepped confidently onto the narrow ledge.

"I can't!" Cefire pleaded.

"Alright, I'll go alone."

"No, Dymas! Don't leave me – I couldn't bear it! My father will kill me!"

"Then let's die together!"

"There has to be another way!"

And then he was upon them, his black eyes flashing with rage; an anger fuelled by Lucifer's lust for revenge on the terran spirits – and on the One who created them.

"Wait for me," shrieked Cefire.

Without faltering she grabbed the hand of her beloved, and together they flung themselves off.

"No!!" Salutat shrieked as the young lovers leapt from the ledge to certain death.

"Quickly!" Angelina screamed in despair. "We must save them! Their love is too pure to end this way!"

Without being sure of what she was doing Angelina, followed closely by Salutat, lunged after the pair.

In only a split second, they caught up with the falling bodies, cradling them as best they could; hoping somehow to break the fall.

Yet, still the two figures continued to plunge towards the ground...

It was strange, Angelina later recounted to Salutat, just how peaceful they each looked as they fell, when a second in time seemed more like a minute, and in retrospect she was able to recall every detail of that frightening event.

She told him afterwards that when the couple began to plummet, she saw two gossamer apparitions detach from their bodies and disappear into thin air. At that moment she wondered if they were, in fact, the spirits of Cefire and Dymas as they left the physical plane to be forever united in love.

But relating the observations to him was as yet in the future. For just now, the more pressing need was to stop the terran spirits from being smashed on the unyielding ground below.

Once Salutat realised that enveloping Cefire and Dymas in spirit would not save them, he could see but one workable alternative: He and Angelina must enter the falling bodies, and support them at least until they had safely alighted onto the ground.

Instinctively, he slipped inside the body of Dymas, and urged Angelina to do likewise with Cefire. Thus, together the angels were able to control their descent.

As they did so, the rate of fall slowed, so that by the time they had descended to ground level they were able to step onto it unhurt. It was only when they were safely down that Salutat noticed the absence of the former inhabitants.

Angelina rejoiced that she was right in her observation: that the souls of Cefire and Dymas had indeed departed for another realm. It appeared the angels were now the sole occupants of two physical bodies.

Yet, for this development, neither felt like celebrating.

At the same time Lucifer, having assumed the death of the terran spirits, chortled with delight at the success of his spur-of-the-moment initiative, and scurried back to Hellion before his presence, and therefore his involvement in all that had taken place, could be detected.

On the other hand, Cefire's father – now released from Lucifer's influence – looked on in horror when he realised they had thrown themselves off the ledge.

At first he had averted his eyes; too cowardly to watch the outcome. Yet he had no alternative but to check what had happened to his daughter.

The scene, as he plucked up the courage to look down, was not the gut-wrenching carnage he expected to see, but something else altogether. Cefire and Dymas appeared to be alright. He could not believe his eyes. All at once the residue of Lucifer's poison fired his emotions once more.

"You needn't think either of you will get away from me!" he shouted through tears of humiliation.

His angry voice, echoing across the valley, was clearly audible to the angels and their precious vessels on the ground below. It then occurred to them that the father, on seeing the two terrans alive and well, presumed that they were still Cefire and Dymas.

A problem now arose for Angelina and Salutat: Although they had successfully entered the terran bodies, it was not in such a way as to take control of them. For, despite their need to flee Cefire's angry father, they found they could not move.

In alarm, Angelina said, "What shall we do? That man is after us now – and he's already left the ledge!"

She looked up: to the place from where the lovers had taken their final leap.

Did they – did we – really jump from way up there? she marvelled.

But then she snapped her attention back to the present situation: What could be done about the two living, yet cumbersome bodies?

"If I recall," replied Salutat, while struggling with the unruly frame he now occupied. "When I took possession of my last body, I had complete control."

"Then what's wrong here?"

"I'm not sure. Maybe entering their auras has upset the polarisation, or something."

"Perhaps we should get out, and leave the bodies here. After all, their previous occupants don't need them, and we must make our move soon. That awful terran will be on his way back down the hill by now. It won't be very long before he catches up with them – with us! Oh dear, this is terrible! What shall we do?"

And then it dawned on Salutat. Was this incident in fact Yavros' strange way of providing the bodies they needed for their mission? If so, why did he have to go about it in such an unfortunate manner? And how were they to take control of them?

"It was never like this before," he lamented.

Let's get out of them," repeated Angelina plaintively. "I don't want to be stuck in such a strange organism when he gets here."

"I think the problem is, we've occupied only the bodies. We should enter their minds, too, in order to take control of the bodies. That's what happened when I was Tagaar."

"When you were what?" asked Angelina, starting to feel trapped in a shell.

"...In my last terran life. The name of the boy I occupied was Tagaar."

"Oh! So how did you manage to take control when you entered his body?"

"I don't know. One minute I was leaving Eternity, the next I found myself waking up in Tagaar's body. Although it took a while for me to get my bearings, I gained control of the body quite quickly. But then, Tagaar's personality was still present, even if it wasn't in control. The spirits of these two seem to have gone."

"Then maybe we should 'take control' – and quickly!"

"That seems logical under the circumstances."

"Okay. Shall we give it a try?"

"Alright. On the count of three..." said Salutat, readying himself; "One, two, three..."

The action of taking charge using mind control had the desired effect. The terran forms, now fully-fledged people

112

again albeit with new identities, could move and function as well as their predecessors.

Salutat needed only a moment to adjust to being terran again, but for Angelina it was a different experience.

She panicked. Restricted for the very first time within the confines of a physical form, she felt imprisoned as if in some kind of armature. More frightening still, she could no longer communicate with Salutat telepathically.

Immediately, her spirit began to fragment.

Salutat grabbed her hand before she lost her balance and keeled over.

Reacting, Angelina grunted: the first sound she heard herself emit from Cefire's body. It sounded odd – nothing like her own melodic voice.

Salutat laughed.

Telepathically, Angelina tried to say, "It's not funny!"

Unable to understand her comment, Salutat enunciated the words, "You need to speak by moving your mouth;" and pointed at her lips.

This time, her voice had a more familiar sound – that of her predecessor, Cefire.

Angelina was fascinated.

"We'd better get out of here before the man catches up with us," Salutat remarked while adjusting to the weight and drag of his own body.

Angelina tried a few steps unaided; a task easier than expected, now that she had taken control of her body. She looked around for a glimpse of their pursuer; yet he was still nowhere in sight.

It transpired that Cefire's father, on returning to the spot where he left his horse, discovered that the animal had vanished. He swore violently, and went off in search of the prized beast. All thought of chasing his wayward daughter dissolved in favour of retrieving something infinitely more valuable to him.

"Let her go off with that no-good youth," he grumbled as he searched for a creature that was already well on its way back home. "...And good riddance to the pair of you!"

However, of this fortuitous turn of events the terran angels knew nothing. As far as they were aware, Cefire's father was still in pursuit, and unless they made haste, it would be only a matter of time before he finally caught up with them.

"Come on," Salutat urged Angelina. "Let's get back up into the hills. He'll probably think we've headed towards the river, and track us there."

When Angelina tried to hurry, she found she could not; for she felt extremely heavy as though a weight was strapped to her belly. And then she remembered.

"My goodness! Cefire was with child, wasn't she? That must mean I'm with child, too! Oh Yavros; what have we got ourselves into!"

The ascent proved to be a long and arduous climb for the two lumbering angels, as the drop from the ledge had been considerable.

To get high enough up to escape detection demanded a great deal of stamina; especially from Angelina. Just like her predecessor, she stopped frequently; understanding fully why Cefire refused to go on when she did.

Her legs ached, and her mouth was so dry she thought her tongue might soon adhere to its roof.

"I saw a stream earlier on," said Salutat. "Maybe I can find it again. Stay here while I take a look."

A few minutes later, Angelina saw him cheerily coming back from the trees.

"Yes, I was right – and it's not far away. Up you get; we could both do with a drink."

Soon Angelina, unused to the concept of drinking, was gulping down handfuls of the sweet, refreshing water.

"This is wonderful," she said at length; having relished every drop. "Water must surely be a gift from Yavros!"

And then they were off again.

The day was drawing on now. Lengthening shadows had already plunged some hillsides into early nightfall. Salutat remembered of old that they would need to seek shelter for the night.

Angelina was exhausted. She had insisted on more than one occasion that she could go no further, and reasserted her stance on it now.

Salutat felt for her.

"Alright," he conceded. "We'll call it a day. I think we've given Cefire's father the slip, anyway."

Salutat stopped and surveyed their whereabouts. They were not far from the top of the hill. He scrambled up and looked over the ridge, expecting to see the land drop away again, but it did not. Instead, it stretched out in front of him: an ancient volcanic basin full of lake water. The lake was edged with shrubbery, and inviting grass that swept up to a rim pock-marked with caves.

Yes, this will do nicely, he thought, and called back to Angelina, "Come up here."

Angelina laboriously got to her feet. With difficulty she climbed up to join Salutat.

"Look at this," he said, gesturing out over the lake.

"My goodness," she responded weakly. "It's so pretty!"

The last golden rays of sunlight glanced off the high banks, reflecting flawlessly in the lake's glassy surface.

Angelina was entranced. Never before in Eternity or, more recently in Eddren, had she seen anything so lovely.

"Can we please rest here?" she asked.

"Yes, I think so. There are caves on the other side of the lake. We should be able to find one we can shelter in."

By the time they reached the roomy cave that would serve as their refuge for the night, Angelina's energy had all but run out.

Salutat raked up dried leaves, and placed them thickly on the cave's hard floor as a mattress. There would be little comfort for either of them that night.

As yet, Angelina knew nothing of discomfort, for just now she was too tired to do anything except gently lower herself onto the makeshift bed. The sense of relief at being able to lay Cefire's weary body down was soon overtaken by the need to sleep, and Angelina drifted off.

Salutat, through the eyes of Dymas before him, looked on the countenance of Angelina; asleep behind the face that shone with Cefire's radiance only a short time ago.

He was terran again now, with terran emotions. Some of the love expressed towards Cefire by her suitor began to resurface, catching Salutat offguard; for he experienced no such emotions as Tagaar; only a deep desire to spread the word about Yavros.

As he gazed at the sleeping face of Cefire, he saw also the pure graciousness of the angel, and his heart went out to both. Lying beside her, he cradled the now chilled body in his arms, and together they slept.

Yet, the night did not treat them kindly. Sometime after the full moon began its descent, Angelina sat up; groaning and clutching at her stomach.

Awakened by movement and her anguish, Salutat knelt to try and render assistance to her. As he did so, his hands came into contact with a sticky substance seeping through the leaves that served as their bed. In the dim moonlight he could not make out what it was, and as his first concern was for Angelina, now writhing in agony, he gave it no further thought.

All of a sudden, Angelina screamed and then fell silent. The echo of her scream in their homely cave seemed to linger endlessly.

An eerie silence followed, unsettling the neophyte terran and his ailing companion.

Salutat held his breath, not knowing what to make of it. He now realised the mysterious substance was somehow connected with her, and wondered what had happened. Had the body Angelina occupied died?

He attempted to communicate with her in case she had reverted to spirit, but to no avail. Then he heard a faint sound coming from the body. It was the gentle sound of breathing. With relief he realised that Angelina was alright, and settled back down to keep her warm; the stickiness still oozing all around them both.

When the dawn finally came, Salutat awoke to find he was completely alone.

He shaded his eyes from bright daylight entering the cave, and noticed that his hand was stained dark red.

In alarm, he leapt to his feet, but they slipped out from under him on the moist mat of leaves, and he went down with a bump.

Salutat was afraid now. Whatever was happening, and what had become of Angelina? Had she melted away and left only this offensive goo? Surely something sinister was at work here?

Terror-struck, he let out a blood-curdling cry.

"Yavros! Help me! I need you!"

Just then, from the back of the cave another light began to appear with growing intensity.

Confused, Salutat shielded his eyes again and glimpsed a form within the light, before in a flash it disappeared. Yet Salutat knew without doubt what it was.

The form had stayed long enough for him to recognise a swift response to his cry for help.

It was Miekaale.

All of a sudden, a voice behind him said, "Salutat, what's the matter?"

With a yelp of anxiety, Salutat swung round and saw a terran form silhouetted against the daylight.

Angelina quietly stood in the cave entrance as though nothing had happened to her during the night.

Salutat looked at her, then back into the cave; now dark again. Did she not see the bright light, or was he starting to imagine things?

"Angelina! Are you alright?" he said weakly, bewildered by all that had just taken place.

"Yes, I'm fine. ...A bit tired still, and I feel unclean, but otherwise I'm quite well. By the way," she said, almost as an afterthought. "I shed the baby in the night." And then added with regret, "It would have been Dymas and Cefire's baby. ...I wonder if they know."

Salutat was of two minds now – pleased that Angelina was alright, but also confused.

Angelina had given him the impression, by her casual demeanour, that she didn't see the apparition in the cave.

Wasn't she even aware that their magnificent Golden Angel had helped them in their hour of need? Yavros must have wasted no time in responding to his plea and sent Miekaale to dispel the negative atmosphere.

Surely she saw him!

...Or did Miekaale appear to him rather than to both of them? If so, was it because he alone made the invocation?

By now, Angelina was more concerned about Salutat than he about her.

As her eyes adjusted to the darkness within the cave, she saw he was agitated and apparently not coping with the situation.

Determined to set his mind at rest, she said, "Do you realise what it was that happened during the night? ...And why I – or should that be 'we', from the state of you – are both covered in blood?"

"You said you shed the baby. What does that mean?" responded Salutat, trying now to re-focus onto what she was trying to tell him.

"It came away from my body. I suppose all the stress Cefire was under – and the hardships the baby must have endured since we took over the bodies – was all too much for an unborn child. It's a great shame that one of Yavros' creations will not now have a chance at life."

Salutat listened sympathetically while Angelina explained how, at daybreak, she awoke feeling a lot better but very thirsty, and went down to the lake to take a drink.

"It's beautiful out there; the sun is lovely and warm," she told him. "While you slept I sat by the edge of the lake and dabbled my feet. They'd been covered in blood, but after a while they became clean again. ...Oh, and I also found us something to eat!"

"You did? That's wonderful."

"Yes – while you were resting. Come and look."

Salutat had recovered from his confusion now, and was curious to know what Angelina was referring to. He stiffly negotiated the rocky entrance of the cave and went out into the sunshine. Immediately his flagging spirits lifted in its warmth – and at the sight of the sparkling lake, which, he decided, must also have been gifted to them by Yavros.

"That's not all he's given us," said Angelina, reading his mind. "Yavros has supplied us with food, too." She pointed at the grassy embankment by the lake's edge, dotted with what looked like small white stones.

"They're pebbles! We can't eat pebbles."

"No they're not. They're food! Look!"

Angelina picked one up and turned it over. Whereas the surface had been firm and rounded, the underneath was soft and fluted. She bit into the mushroom and handed the rest to Salutat.

"They're delicious," she said. "Here, try it."

He took a bite and indicated that it was quite tasty.

Instantly, hunger pangs reminded him that the terran in him was starving; that neither he nor Dymas before him had eaten for a very long time.

Between them they ate their fill.

Never before had anything tasted so good although, Salutat recalled; he had not actually tasted anything for a long time, and Angelina not at all. Yet the mind of a terran spirit remembers much, and the new inhabitants of the bodies ate with enthusiasm.

As the warming sun rose higher, Salutat ambled down to the lake to cool his feet; still sore from all their walking the previous day.

He sat quietly, his feet dangling in the water. Nothing disturbed the silence except for a gentle lapping sound as he swished them beneath the surface. He noticed that his feet, once grubby and stained, had become clean again. It made him wonder if a good soak in the water would have the same effect on the rest of him, including his clothes; so he slid his whole body into the chilly water.

Salutat let out a shriek as the cold of the water hit him; waking Angelina who had been dozing on the grassy bank.

She looked up quickly.

Amused, she said, "What are you doing in there?"

By now, Salutat was used to being in the water. The feel of it caressing his body was both soothing and invigorating, and he realised he had been right that it would also clean his clothes.

He called out to Angelina.

"Why don't you come in, too? It's wonderful!"

She wandered down to the edge, and timidly pushed a foot into the water. It was cold to her thoroughly warmed up body, and she withdrew her foot smartly.

"I don't think so," she called out to him.

But then the unexpected happened. A piece of turf on which she had been standing gave way; causing her to lose her balance.

Before she realised what was going on she had fallen, splashing and shrieking, into the lake.

Salutat howled with laughter. He waded back to check if she was alright.

Shaken and embarrassed, Angelina insisted she was. Then she noticed something different about him.

"Hey, look at you!" she exclaimed. "You're clean again!"

Salutat looked down into the water. Sure enough, his clothes and skin were now free of stains.

Inspired by the cleansing effect of the water, Angelina splashed around, too.

"Watch out!" cried Salutat when he received a face full of spray.

He slapped the surface at her to return the favour.

Angelina squealed with laughter and splashed him back.

What fun this is, thought Salutat, as the pair engaged in a brief but fierce water fight.

He had never experienced fun before, certainly not on his previous mission. Was it a natural part of terran life, or were they just indulging in one of the many traits inflicted on the terran spirits by Lucifer? It was hard to tell. Yet one thing was certain: for the moment the terran angels were thoroughly enjoying themselves.

The laughter brought welcome respite from the rigours of the last couple of days.

Their recreation at an end, the angels cheerfully emerged from the water. Unobserved by Angelina, her wet clothing clung seductively to her curvaceous new body.

Salutat stared at her, unable to take his eyes off the shapely form; the image captivating.

All at once, the passion Dymas bore for Cefire fired up in the loins of Salutat, leaving him less than composed.

Angelina sensed a change in his demeanour and looked at him; then gasped ashamedly and quickly averted her eyes from the unexpected sight.

"What's wrong?" he asked.

"Nothing!" lied Angelina, her cheeks turning crimson; embarrassment leaving her confused as to why she should feel that way.

While they struggled up the bank, Salutat wondered what was going on.

He looked down at his body; at his own wet clothing which also clung to his form, concealing little of his fully aroused manhood. For the first time, he understood the raw element of terran nature which had become so potent a part of Dymas and Cefire's relationship.

Alarmed by the episode and by Angelina's reaction to it, Salutat covered himself as best he could. Then he moved away to silently recover from his embarrassment.

For some time the pair remained apart; not sure just what had changed between them, but certain that some of their casual innocence had been lost.

Angelina, too, fought her feelings. Cefire's love for Dymas had been intensely physical as well as from the heart. The purity of the angel's spirit had been severely compromised when she witnessed Salutat's arousal.

This was an unwelcome feeling about an intimate part of the lovers' relationship. She felt ashamed that she had inadvertently seen it, and that it had stirred up her own passions. Such raw terran emotions were unfamiliar to the angel, and unwelcome. They were not something an angel of Yavros should allow to tarnish her spirituality.

...Although, she had to admit to herself, the feelings were not altogether unpleasant.

A part of her wanted to address the issue rationally and discuss the new development with Salutat. Another part of her wanted to forget anything had ever happened, and get straight on with their mission. She decided on the latter, got up off the grass and calmly walked towards him.

Salutat had also recovered his composure; yet it startled him to see her take the initiative and head over to him.

He shifted awkwardly, and would have preferred to ignore her; but the angel in him took over and he lifted his head ready to receive his colleague's dialogue.

"Salutat," she said as if indeed nothing had just taken place. "I think we should get going. Who knows how far we will need to travel today, and by the look of the sun it must be close to the middle of the day already."

"You're right," said Salutat; relieved that the spell had been broken. "I've no idea what lies beyond the ridge here, but there's only one way we can find out!"

The way down was less steep than the hill's incline had been.

Just ahead they could make out a river snaking its way through a valley. Whether it was the same river as the one which guided them out of the city was unclear. What was clear, though, and which offered them a suggestion as to which way to go, was the sight of a roadway alongside the river, weaving into the distance.

The road had been laid down stone by stone in ancient times, to accommodate the migration of heavy vehicles. Up and down, a trickle of wagons could be seen; indicating the continuity of trade.

"This road must lead somewhere significant," Salutat remarked when they eventually reached it.

Angelina, tiring after her ordeal the previous night, was close to collapse. She sat down on a boulder to rest briefly, while Salutat waited for something to come along.

"I thought there'd be more wagons along at this hour of the day," he said ruefully when, after some considerable time, nothing of use had come in their direction, and their feet were once again painful from walking. He had hoped someone might offer them a ride to the next township; perhaps a traveller with a wagon, or a chariot like the one that almost ran them down when they first arrived in Eddren. ...What a long time ago that seemed now, Salutat reflected; the thought tinged with regret that they still had not begun their mission. He felt like apologising to Yavros. But then he remembered they had only just received their bodies, so how could they have started on it.

They walked on in silence, each absorbed with their own thoughts; their energy all but spent with none in reserve for conversation.

Salutat began to think about Eternity and Yavros. He was getting tired, and his mind spontaneously drifted off to the one place he felt secure and at home. He thought again about the apparition of Miekaale in the cave. Was it real – or just the need of a troubled angel to see and feel something of his home realm again? After all, Angelina had not seen it.

But then, as if in answer to his enquiry, a voice spoke clearly inside his head.

"Of course I sent Miekaale to you," it stated. "Do you really think I would abandon my mission angels when they were in need? You invoked me, and I responded. Such is my way. You know that!"

"Yavros!" said Salutat laughingly.

Angelina, also suspended somewhere between Eddren and Eternity, heard him.

"Why did you say that?" she asked.

"It's a long story," he replied, still chuckling to himself. "I'll tell you about it some time."

But as they continued to walk, Salutat chided himself. Angelina has a right to know about Miekaale, he thought. She's my partner on this mission, and I can't keep anything from her. I must discuss it with her as soon as..."

Salutat's musings came to an abrupt end when a horse and wagon pulled up alongside them.

A kindly looking man, mature in age, leant down to greet the ailing angels.

"May I offer you a ride to the port city?" he asked in a friendly manner.

The angels looked at each other; then Angelina quickly said, with as much enthusiasm as her state of exhaustion would allow, "Yes, please...you are very kind."

The ride to the next town, a bustling port on a major trade route, was a bumpy one. Angelina and Salutat shared the back of the wagon with a cargo of squash which the driver, who introduced himself as Halished, was delivering to the docks for a local grower.

"The delivery of goods is my occupation," he explained to the weary pair, who would have preferred to journey in silence in order to rest for a while. "I also like to offer my services to good people like you. Helping those in need is my way of saying thank you to the Spirit Father for all he has given me."

Halished twisted round to speak with his passengers further. On finding them asleep, propped up against each other for support, he grinned to himself, turned back and cracked the whip over his horse.

"These two souls will be my house guests tonight," he declared. "They look like a young couple in need of some looking after."

Halished pulled up in front of his home. The wagon coming to a halt awakened the pair from the doze its rhythmic movement had sustained. Then their host lightly jumped down and beckoned them inside.

There, he introduced them to his wife.

"Will you excuse me," he said. "I must deliver my load before it gets dark."

"Why before dark?" asked Angelina, politely.

"There have been many sinister occurrences during the hours of darkness recently. Others of my trade have been killed, so we must all be vigilant."

Salutat snapped to attention. Sinister occurrences: that sounds like the hand of Lucifer.

"What exactly has been happening?" he asked.

"Well," began Halished, "There was an incident only the other day. ...But let me complete my delivery; then after some refreshments we will talk."

While the guests availed themselves of Halished's bathing facilities and put on fresh clothing provided by his wife, their benevolent host completed his trading for the day.

He and his wife enjoyed these occasions. They had set up their home to accommodate travellers such as Angelina and Salutat. A spare room was always kept ready; together with fresh clothing and linen for the bed, as the angels had just discovered. Their guests were usually couples; many of whom headed to the port to embark on one of the ocean-going vessels for a new life across the sea. Halished, on this occasion, assumed that Angelina and Salutat were just such a couple. Recently wed, he guessed from their youthfulness and from the manner in which they clung to each other in the back of the wagon.

On Halished's return, it was a different pair of guests he encountered – at least, they looked different: refreshed and well-presented before their hosts.

"Please come with me into the dining area. There will be six of us tonight. Two of my colleagues will be joining us for a meeting afterwards. Of need, we must meet in secret because..."

Halished suddenly stopped mid-sentence, realising he had begun to say something he should not mention; not yet, anyway. Not until he had ascertained if the pair were of like mind with him and his associates. His house guests usually were. He had a knack of knowing just who might be as he passed them on the road.

During dinner, he addressed his visitors again.

"Tell me," he continued. "Are you two members of the sun temple faith?"

Salutat and Angelina traded uneasy glances.

Why did he ask that? Angelina wondered. They now suspected sun temple authorities would prosecute anyone caught practicing another faith, and she distrustfully felt nervous.

Trying to disguise her feelings, she watched Salutat for his response.

"No, actually we don't belong to that faith," announced Salutat without hesitation. The spontaneity of his response surprised even him; as though something had prompted him to make such a bold confession. Could it have been Yavros again?

"Good," continued Halished with relief; and pleased his hunch about them was correct. "What I started to mention just now is that my colleagues and I must meet in private. You see, we belong to a secret society, comprising people who believe the real creator of Eddren is not the sun. Have you ever thought along those lines?"

"Indeed, yes," replied Salutat with astonishment. What could he mean? Do these people know about Yavros?

Halished nodded in acknowledgement that they were now of one mind, and continued.

"It has long been held that we did not originate from the sun, as religion teaches us, but from an invisible source of energy which exploded into life eons ago, giving birth to the sun itself, to Eddren and more importantly, to every living thing, including us."

"Really!" exclaimed Angelina in awe of their wisdom; but then sensed from the stares of Halished's colleagues that, as a female, she should remain silent. She would let Salutat do the talking.

"Yes," Halished went on. "It is believed that the religion of sun worship was established to give people something tangible to worship as they couldn't grasp the concept of an invisible creator..."

"...It wasn't quite like that," interjected Salutat. Then, when he also received critical stares, he reluctantly backed away. After all, he was a guest in someone else's house.

As far as Halished and his colleagues were concerned, they were the ones with the knowledge on the subject; not Salutat. He was there to listen and learn; not to teach as in Tagaar's days. It didn't seem quite appropriate just now to inform them that it was he, the angel Salutat, who initiated the ancient teaching of the invisible creator. ...Or that it was Lucifer who manipulated the teaching of sun worship – not to give the people something tangible to look up to, but to throw them off the right track.

Ignoring Salutat's remark, Halished went on.

"As I told you earlier, there have been some disturbing occurrences at night. Local inhabitants often report seeing furtive sprites with evil black eyes that we believe to be responsible for many of the killings round here. It is most worrying. We're convinced that there's a sinister element at work, but we don't exactly know what it is or where it's coming from.

How can I remain silent about this? thought Salutat while sensing the uneasiness in Halished's voice. I know exactly what's causing it – and how to deal with it!

In silence he again reflected on the events in the cave the previous night.

He wanted to inform them that if his new friends were to pray to Yavros, Miekaale would clear their region of negativity in an instant. But how, he wondered, could he broach the subject with Halished? A good kind man he may be, yet he was giving the impression of being single-minded in his beliefs, and not open to suggestion.

Salutat desperately wanted to impart his knowledge; not just about Miekaale, but especially about Lucifer. After all, he thought contemptuously, any sinister goings-on in Eddren must have Lucifer at its source.

Afar off, Lucifer's phantom was again alerted to an affront on his good name.

Apart from the angst he recently caused for the mission angels and their departed terran friends, he had lain low over the last few centuries.

His creativity in Eddren needed no further input from him in order to express itself; for it wasn't needed. When combined with terran free will, he had discovered, his negativity was self-perpetuating.

It pleased him immensely to see just how well his sun worship had progressed; especially as it was considered the principal religion, to the exclusion of all else.

"That's one in the eye for you, O mighty Yavros," he had exclaimed with pride.

Yet that was before Halished spoke with the mission angels about a secret society; one that did not follow the rules of Lucifer's established religion but rather honoured the original truth. And when Salutat aired his impertinent remarks in the same instant, the dormant sprite realised that something was going on: something that might prove to be contrary to his own interests.

"We'll soon see about that!" he declared.

The household's refreshments completed, Halished's wife cleared away their plates, so that the business of the evening' could begin.

The main purpose of the secret society's meetings was to perpetuate their faith; to recruit new devotees and to worship the one true creator.

With arms raised in supplication, Halished began his incantations to draw the creator down into their midst.

Salutat looked on in dismay.

They've still got it wrong! he moaned silently while the others chanted. Yavros is within their own souls, not up in the sky somewhere. It's no wonder so few terrans have returned to Yavros. Either they're involved with Lucifer's sun worship or they still reach outwardly to their creator! Damn you, Lucifer! If it wasn't for your interference, all of this would have been avoided!

It was during this outburst of condemnation that Lucifer dropped in on Salutat, causing the ground to shake.

Initially, the transcendent gathering suspected nothing sinister with this occurrence; but assumed an earth tremor was taking place.

Commencing its course as no more than a faint rumble, the quaking seemed to come ever closer, strengthening as it approached, until finally the house rocked and crockery fell to the floor.

Rudely awoken, the house's occupants hurried out into the garden.

In the midst of the chaos, Lucifer spied Angelina holding on to a tree trunk for support; it upset him to see her in terran form.

With the earth still shaking, he zeroed in on her.

Yet, the frightened angel could not see him hovering within arm's reach. Nor was she aware of his presence as he took in the loveliness of his beloved Angelina.

"Here is one of Yavros' terran spirits I wouldn't want to annoy," he thought affectionately, while gazing beyond the blue eyes that were once Cefire's.

He hoped to see some recognition on Angelina's part. But there was none. The terran emotion of fear prevented her from noticing him.

On the other hand, Salutat did notice Lucifer. At least, he noticed his devastating influence.

Yet again he called to his mentor for support.

While the ground continued to sway beneath them, he shouted, "Yavros, we need you!" much louder than he had intended to. And yet again he saw the great Golden Angel appear before him.

Awestruck, Angelina saw Miekaale, too.

…And so did Lucifer; but, for the now panic-stricken phantom it was too late. He was shackled and tossed aside even before a squeal of protest could escape him.

At the hands of the Golden Angel, Lucifer's extradition this time was no less dramatic than in the past; and the instant he left, the earthquake ceased.

Halished ran in search of his wife and their guests. All were unhurt by their terrifying experience, but his two shaken colleagues, concerned for the well-being of their families, apologetically left straightaway.

It transpired that damage in the dwelling was less than feared: a few pots broken and dust everywhere, but very little else.

The angels helped their hosts to restore a semblance of normality, and then sat down with them to talk about their harrowing ordeal.

At Halished's insistence, they gave thanks to the creator for their deliverance.

While Halished and his wife continued to pray, Angelina tried to catch Salutat's eye. She wanted to know what he'd been up to, and why Miekaale had appeared.

As though thinking the same thing, Halished said to a surprised Salutat, "By the way, who is Yavros? ...And what was that bright light all about?"

Salutat went quiet, suddenly thrown off balance by the unexpected question. Why did Halished mention Yavros' name just now?

And then he remembered why: he had loudly invoked Yavros during the tremor, forgetting there were witnesses present at the time.

"Yavros?" he echoed, frantically searching his mind for an on the spot explanation. This was something he had not anticipated doing just yet.

Salutat looked up at Halished. How he wished the man could read his mind, and learn telepathically all there was to know about Yavros. How can I explain in just one simple answer, he wondered, something that is intrinsically the same as your beliefs, and yet also very different?

Halished began to take offence at Salutat's reluctance to respond. The strange events of the evening, culminating in his guest's entreaty and the light that disappeared almost as soon as it came, both mystified and worried him.

Had he been wrong in offering this pair his hospitality? Did they in fact practice some other pagan religion and were bringing it into his home; thereby tainting its purity.

He wanted an explanation.

"I'm waiting Salutat!" he said expectantly. "Who were you talking to back there? Who – or what – is Yavros?"

It was Angelina who answered.

She, too, understood that Miekaale had been sent to save them, although she had no idea Lucifer was present.

With great joy she saw how Yavros answered Salutat's cry for help; and knew they needed his help again now if they were to appease their host.

In response to a silent prayer, Yavros came to her; then, seconds later, Angelina found herself speaking his words.

"Yavros is the name of the creator," she began, in a tone stronger than Cefire's sweet voice. "Salutat and I...know of another realm where the creator reigns supreme. Your knowledge of spiritual matters, your devotion to the Spirit Father and desire to spread the word about an invisible creator, are acknowledged and much treasured. However, terran spirits are now at a stage where they cannot move ahead in a spiritual sense unless they set aside handed-down beliefs and traditions. You need to trace back to the basics of spirituality and the origin of terran nature; to learn that Lucifer superimposed his own values on your souls. Your goal should be to cast off your terran nature and work towards the Return; namely: to recognise your spiritual identity, and then return to me."

Halished and Salutat stared open-mouthed at Angelina: Halished astonished that a female house-guest claimed to be more knowledgeable than he was on the subject of the creator of Eddren.

134

Yet Salutat's impression was that she'd suddenly taken leave of her senses – until, at the end of her dissertation, she said 'return to me'. Then he knew they were not her own words, but those of Yavros.

By this time, Angelina had also realised where the pearls of wisdom came from.

Her heart leapt with the knowledge that Yavros himself had spoken through her; but she was also keenly aware that the enquiring eyes of two men and an unassuming woman were now bearing down on her.

"What did you just say?" asked Halished at length; not because he had failed to hear her every word but rather, he wanted her to repeat the blasphemy: to use it against her if ever he saw fit.

Angelina looked blankly back at him. Yavros had by now completed his missive and withdrawn; leaving Angelina bewildered and at a loss to know how to answer.

After a moment she responded.

"I'm sorry, but I don't think I can say it all again."

Without a word, Halished got up and left the room; a look of displeasure on his face.

Salutat suspected his host did not take kindly to Angelina's missive, as it must have seemed to Halished that a woman was preaching at him.

Yet Salutat knew such was not the case. He, too, had recognised the sound of Yavros in his partner's voice, and empathised with her subsequent disquiet; for Angelina on her own would not have had the audacity to speak bluntly in the presence of a host.

Halished's wife, who had been tending to their needs, sensed Angelina's discomfort as well. Quietly, she placed a reassuring hand on her shoulder.

"Don't worry, dear. He'll get over it," she said. "These secret society people are as bad as sun worshippers for assuming they alone hold the truth. Personally, and just between you and me, I think you are right. We should get back to basics. But I'm curious to know who 'Lucifer' is!"

Angelina sighed, not realising she had even mentioned the name. The story of Lucifer would involve a complicated explanation, and she was too tired to get into it just now.

Maybe tomorrow, she thought – if Halished has cooled off enough to let me explain...and if he allows us to remain in his house. For the time being, her main interest was in sleeping, for the day had been harrowing for the first-time terran spirit.

"I appreciate your support," she said to Halished's wife; "but do you mind if I take my rest now – I'm very tired. We can talk some more tomorrow, if you like."

Salutat led her to the room prepared for them. Alone at last, the pair of angels regarded each other wearily.

"You look washed out," commented Salutat.

"I am," she replied weakly.

Then she noticed where they were to sleep: a large bed supposedly designed for a married couple.

Though little more than a hay-filled mattress placed on a wooden frame with basic bedding for warmth, it looked far more inviting than the scratchy bed she had to lie on the night before.

"Is this where we sleep?" she asked mechanically, her eyelids growing heavier by the minute.

"I presume so," replied Salutat.

"...Together?" she added, suddenly apprehensive about such closeness with an angel of Yavros.

"Angelina, I'm sure it will be alright. They think we're married already – and we did sleep on the same bed last night, if you recall."

"That was different – and we're not married! Our hosts may be unaware of our status, but we certainly are! Yavros would disapprove!"

"Don't worry about it! I'm sure Yavros doesn't care. And even if he did, what other choice is there? I don't intend to sleep on the floor!"

Angelina fell asleep the moment her head touched the coarse pillow. Salutat lay beside her and pulled a blanket over them both.

It was cosy and warm stretched out under the blanket; on a bed infinitely more comfortable than the pile of dried leaves in the cave.

Lying alongside a companion he was increasingly fond of, Salutat watched her as she slept. He studied the peaceful features, which were different from the Angelina he knew of old, but nonetheless graceful and very pretty. Her soft eyelashes flickered, and he wondered what insights were forming in her lovely head. Was she still with him in spirit, or back in Eternity with Yavros?

Suddenly Angelina turned onto her side; facing Salutat. He gasped at the closeness of her.

As her sweet breath combined with his own, a tingle went through him. Once again he felt the raw passion of his predecessor rising. Ashamed, he turned over and faced the other way.

Angelina is my companion on this mission, he chided himself. But then he heard a familiar voice in his head.

"Marry her!" it said.

Salutat sat upright in surprise.

"Yavros? Is that what I must do?" he asked secretly, at the same time raising his eyes to the roof for inspiration as Halished might do. And then, he felt a glow of affirmation warming his heart.

With a smile on his face, Salutat lay back down beside his intended bride; exhilaration flowing right through him.

Tomorrow, he would ask Angelina to be his wife.

In Yavros' physical realm, no one thing was more crushing than experience, when it came to awareness of terran pain and suffering; thanks in kind to Lucifer.

The angel terrans, however, suffered none of the pain Cefire and Dymas experienced when forced to dismiss the idea of marriage. In contrast, they expected no restrictions when they made their own plans to marry.

Neither did it occur to them that they might need to support themselves: another problem faced by the young terran couple when contemplating their future. The angels were on a mission for Yavros, and only that was important. In fact, so focused were they that nothing practical crossed their minds at all.

Salutat spent most of the following morning investigating how he might go about getting married in that town.

He received some strange looks when he enquired in unlikely places; receiving from them but one suggestion:

"...In the temple, of course!"

But marriage in the temple was out of the question for Salutat. They would need an alternative venue.

Then further questioning led him to a judge, who stated he could marry them later in the day.

When Salutat returned home, Angelina was waiting for the result of his enquiries.

Halished, too, had awaited his return. Having calmed down after the shock revelation of the previous night, he was anxious to continue their discussion; for by the time he awoke feeling refreshed, he had accepted that there were other interpretations of the religion he held dear.

In fact, he was so keen to learn more, especially about the bright light seen during the quake, that he completed his work early in order to continue the conversation.

But before he could do so, Salutat begged a moment's leave to have a word with Angelina.

She accepted the news about the judge quite calmly, as though he had merely informed her of an appointment. In her opinion, marriage was just something Yavros required them to do.

What more could there be to it, anyway? she queried.

Salutat's message delivered, there was no time left to discuss the marriage ceremony, or even to think about it. His obligations at that moment lay in two directions. The one had been put on hold for a few hours; the other he was anxious to get on with as soon as possible.

But how can I explain Miekaale to Halished in just a few sentences? he wondered.

With Yavros feeding him information at exactly the right moment and in precisely the right fashion for his hosts to grasp its meaning, Salutat's task proved to be easier than he had imagined.

Soon Halished understood as much as his guests about the Golden Angel and his role in cleansing Eddren of evil.

"This is just what we need around here!" he exclaimed fervently. "I've agonised over how to deal with the sinister occurrences for a long time. Now I know. What did you say his name was?"

"...Is. His name is Miekaale," responded Salutat. "He lives now, not just in the past. He's as eternal as Yavros. All the angels are, including Ang......"

Suddenly Salutat winced with pain.

Angelina, in trying to restrain him, caught him with a sideways kick to the ankle. Instantly, he realised why she had done it. Neither Halished nor anyone else in Eddren knew of their identity, and their secret must remain intact.

He shot her a distressed look; suggesting both apology and reproach.

"...You were saying?" urged Halished, too intent on the topic of discussion to notice the diversion. "Please tell me more about Miekaale."

"That's all there is to it," Salutat replied thoughtfully. "...Except, that when you pray to Yavros he sends Miekaale to rid the place of evil – but only if you pray. He doesn't even help Angelina and me unless we pray to Yavros first. When we do, though, his arrival can be instantaneous..."

"...Just like a flash of lightening?" asked Halished's wife, remembering how the bright light had appeared and then instantly vanished.

"Yes," said Angelina. "The effect of his presence is quite awe inspiring. Everything just seems to settle down again. It's amazing."

"Salutat, may I ask you something?" said Halished after a moment's reflection.

"Yes, of course."

"May I inform our colleagues in the society of this new perspective on our beliefs?"

Salutat eyed Angelina for her approval. She returned his glance with a look which said, 'I suppose that would be alright.'

But before he could respond, Halished continued with, "Better still, would you and your good lady be willing to speak to them instead? Then you could personally answer any questions they may have."

Again, the two angels exchanged glances. Together they replied, "Yes."

Halished was delighted.

The marriage preliminaries over with, Angelina and Salutat nervously stood before the judge. Neither understood why they might feel nervous; only that they did. When the judge asked if they knew of any reason why they should not marry, they glanced at each other anxiously, and Angelina said, "I don't think so." Then, with a stroke of a pen and the placement of his hands over theirs, the judge pronounced them married.

In disbelief at the speed of the ceremony, they left the courthouse.

"Well, that was easy," Angelina remarked to her new husband as they made their way back home.

But Angelina did not yet realise it was only the angel talking: the angel of Yavros, whose duty as a missionary in Eddren was to marry. And as an angel, she had none of the feelings which Cefire would be experiencing: feelings of elation and passion; feelings that briefly touched her when she witnessed Salutat's masculinity at the lakeside. For now, only the knowledge that she and Salutat were ready to begin their mission as man and wife was of importance.

On their return, Halished told them he had arranged for a discourse with the society for the following day.

"Does this mean our mission has now begun?" Angelina asked Salutat later on.

"It certainly looks like it!" he laughed.

CHAPTER 4

Excited about the development, the newlyweds retired to their room for the night.

As they lay next to one another on the massive bed, each reflecting on the day's activities, Angelina turned to her new spouse and said, "I think I'm happy."

Salutat laughed and flipped over onto his side, looking directly into the beaming face only a few inches away.

The look of serenity in Angelina's eyes was beguiling to the youthful male whose mind may have been Salutat's but whose body and passions still belonged to Dymas.

They were now so close, their spirits merged.

A quiver of anticipation ran through Salutat; a quiver that inflamed both Angelina's heart and her passions.

Suddenly the angel in her receded, and involuntarily the woman emerged. As though she were no longer Angelina but passionate Cefire, experienced in love and desperate for her husband's embrace, Angelina lunged forward and planted a kiss on Salutat's lips; at the same time snuggling up even closer to him.

Salutat was overcome. The need to marry for the sake of the mission all of a sudden became obsolete in favour of marriage for love. In an instant, Salutat realised as never before that he dearly loved Angelina.

He took her eagerly; his predecessor's expertise in the art of love-making blending with pure angelic transcendence. As they simultaneously reached the moment of ecstasy, their two souls became one – united with Yavros, and with each other.

"So this is what marriage is really all about!" exclaimed Salutat when, part way through the night, they made love again. Nobody had warned him about terran passion!

Angelina thought back to their first days in Eddren, to the time they took refuge from a shower in the hay barn, and were witness to their predecessors' antics. Now she knew exactly what they had been doing – and why!

"Is this our love, or theirs?" she asked Salutat when she awoke the next morning.

"I don't really know," was his reply. "...Perhaps it's a bit of both!"

The meeting with the secret society was exhilarating for the angel missionaries.

Now that Halished had endorsed an addition to their theories on the creator, it was received with great interest by the society's members. And when Halished announced with pride that his house guests had a champion to fight evil in Eddren, they were thoroughly convinced. So much so, in fact, that straightaway they prayed for Miekaale to relieve their district of the sinister occurrences.

Anticipating that the prayers would be answered, the members thanked the guest speakers for an enlightening talk, and made to leave. But then Halished recalled a part of Angelina's revelation they had not yet discussed, and questioned her about it.

"The other day," he said, "you briefly spoke of someone called 'Lucifer'. Who is he?"

Angelina offered Salutat the chance to explain.

"I'm still too close to Lucifer to be objective about his involvement," she told him in a whisper.

Salutat seized the opportunity.

"It was due to his interference right at the beginning that terran nature exists; even nowadays," he told his audience. "Lucifer was an angel of Yavros who refused to serve the original terrans. He was banished by Miekaale to Hellion, but then escaped. Ever since, he has caused problems in Eddren; especially with the souls of terrans. This, to the extent that terran nature has now taken on a momentum all of its own. As you have experienced in your own lives, many challenges have resulted from Lucifer's interference, ranging from bad behaviour to sinister occurrences. It is Miekaale's role to deport Lucifer when he appears, and to alleviate his legacy of evil. All terrans need to do is invoke Yavros, and he will send Miekaale."

Later, when the company had dispersed, Angelina said to her husband, "It looks like our real mission is to teach the people about Miekaale!"

"I don't think so," he replied.

"Why not? We know how effective he is. This can't be the only part of Eddren in need of his help."

"I'm not disputing what you say, Angelina. It's just that in Halished's home we've been lucky to meet with people who now understand about Yavros. Most don't even know about their spiritual heritage, or are too immersed in sun worship to be open-minded about it. Telling them about Miekaale just now would be like..."

Salutat searched his mind for an analogy to illustrate the point he was trying to make.

"...Like feeding a handful of precious gems to a flock of sheep. They wouldn't be able to assimilate it, and so the wisdom will be lost. Do you know what I mean?"

Angelina gave him a hug. "Yes; thank you. I'd forgotten to what extent Lucifer has turned their heads. Miekaale is important, but terrans aren't ready to hear about him yet. I guess our mission is just to reawaken their souls."

The next few months reminded Salutat of olden times when he travelled the countryside to spread his message. The difference now was that he had the companionship of his wife, Angelina – and he did not have to travel on foot, or even on horseback. This time, kindly donated to them by a friend of Halished, he had the most up to date form of transport available – a horse and covered wagon: to serve as both transport and their accommodation.

It was during this time away that Angelina conceived. The love they now shared, consummated at the height of passion, came to fruition when a boy was born to Angelina at the beginning of summer. Salutat gave their son the name Batim to honour Halished's father. As he informed Angelina, he could offer no finer gesture to the man who provided the stimulus for their mission than to so name their first-born.

"But don't forget," Angelina added. "All things happen through Yavros. It was he who led us to the right place, with the right people and at the right time for all this to come about. They were of Yavros' making. So it's not just Halished who should be receiving our thanks."

"I know, and I am truly grateful to Yavros. But there is a terran act of gratitude to perform here as well. And it must not only be acknowledged on our part; it should also be recognised by Halished himself."

Some time later, the new parents joined with friends to consecrate their child.

It gave Angelina a sense of satisfaction, that the son of terran angels had now received the stamp of Yavros: an affirmation of Batim's spirituality.

But her contentment would not last very long; for she had overlooked one important factor.

Angelina had forgotten that wherever spirituality is to be found in the realm of Eddren, terran nature in the form of Lucifer's influence is never too far away, and waiting to wreak havoc.

...And that does not exclude the terran son of angels.

PART THREE: BATIM THE SON OF ANGELS

CHAPTER 1

The terran child of angel parents, happily accompanied his parents on their mission during all of his formative years. Angelina taught her son in the ways of Yavros, while at the same time supporting Salutat in his missionary work. But soon she found the dual role impossible to maintain.

At length, they hired a reputable tutor to accompany them, and to educate Batim in the general knowledge of all aspects of Eddren life.

The nomadic family travelled extensively; in the process awakening terranity's sleeping spirit and, where necessary, warning them of the dangers: the supernatural snares set by Lucifer.

Although their messages received acclaim from those who had suffered under religious doctrine, the terrans also knew that they risked punishment if new teachings were leaked to the authorities. Yet this did not deter them; for discovering the truth about Yavros and Eternity was like a breath of fresh air to the stifled populace.

...And the angels would allow nothing to diminish it.

With a sense of camaraderie the terrans forged ahead, preparing for the Return: for the time of their death, when they would translocate from the physical world and be reunited with Yavros.

But not so Salutat and Angelina. The evangelists did not share in the sense of concord. Theirs was only a transient objective; affiliated to neither community nor nation. They belonged only to Yavros, and Batim belonged to them. And here lay their vulnerability, but as yet they did not realise it; until one ill-fated afternoon when Lucifer unexpectedly turned up.

Batim had grown into a fine young man, and drew near to the age of maturity.

Although he devoted the years of his childhood to his parents and their mission, he was becoming increasingly restless. Unknowingly, he was in fact ready to break away from their itinerant lifestyle and follow a new direction all of his own.

However, Batim kept these feelings to himself. Ever the dutiful son, he seldom voiced his thoughts; but he failed to take into account the fact that his parents were not just terran spirits, they were also intuitive angels.

Before too long, Angelina and Salutat picked up on his discontent and the reason why.

It was time, they decided, for Batim to fly the coop.

By now, the mission angels had completed their tour of the country and, more than ready for a break, returned to the port city where it all began.

Angelina remembered a pretty picnic spot; high on a hillside overlooking the port. She suggested one day that she, Salutat and Batim spend some leisure time together, so that they might enjoy each other's company detached from the rigours of touring and the city's noise. However, there was one other reason why she wanted the family to be undisturbed: Angelina knew that this would be the last opportunity they would have to socialise as a family unit.

It was time, she decreed, to bring their decision out into the open: to inform their adolescent son that he should leave the security of home, and further his education in a place of advanced tutelage – by himself.

It so happened that on the very afternoon the angels were enjoying their picnic, Lucifer translocated to Eddren.

He often found, these days, that he would translocate spontaneously and even unintentionally; as though some force was pulling him through.

In effect, he couldn't help it.

What's more, Lucifer was usually unaware that he had done so until he slithered out into the physical world; coincidentally to areas of either heightened spirituality or unrelenting negativity.

Thus, on the day of the family gathering, by chance he converged on the former. In this case: it was the angels' picnic on the hillside.

Lucifer's arrival went unnoticed by the contented group of family members.

As it was accompanied this time by little more than a distant rumble of thunder, it barely broke into their jovial banter and enjoyment of each other's company.

Lucifer had learnt that the more explosively he entered Eddren, the more swiftly he was likely to be removed; thanks to Miekaale. So this time, when he perceived from afar that his lovely Angelina and her two companions were engaged in social and private interaction, he paid them a visit; yet quietly.

His disgust, when he observed the intimacy of the little group, was profound.

"Whatever does Salutat think he's doing, cosying up to Angelina like that?" he grumbled as he viewed them from only a short distance away. "And who is that young terran with them? He certainly is no angel. This warrants further inspection from me!"

Noiselessly to avoid detection, Lucifer moved up closer. Now within earshot of the contented picnickers, what he heard astounded him: Angelina was referring to the brat as her son!

"I'm not going to put up with that!" he hissed, sending a gust of chilled air over the group.

Unsuspecting, Angelina pulled her shawl closely around her shoulders.

The port city boasted a superb place of further education, known locally as the 'Academie', which was renowned for producing highly qualified young men.

It was because of this that Salutat brought his wife and Batim back there to settle, in the hope that his son might be persuaded to enrol at the Academie. But broaching the subject would prove tricky. He did not want the boy to assume his parents were anxious to be free of him, for nothing could have been further from the truth. Salutat relished the fact that they had all travelled together, as Batim brought them immeasurable joy over the years. But now, their own feelings must take second place to Batim's ongoing needs.

Yet, as feared, when asked if he would like to attend the Academie, Batim's reacted swiftly with "You want to be rid of me, don't you?"

"No, of course not!" they replied simultaneously.

It took the rest of the day for the parents to convince their son that they only had his best interests at heart.

Batim sat sullenly on the grass, while each presented a plausible and justifiable reason why he should separate from parental control and branch out into the world on his own. At length, he admitted he had been feeling restless of late, and maybe he was ready for a change, even if the idea of going it alone intimidated him.

"It's bound to be a bit scary, son," Salutat concurred, remembering only too well his first experiences as a terran spirit back in Tagaar's days. "...But you'll get used to it and," he added with a wry smile, "In time you'll wonder how you ever stood being around your folks for so long."

"Father, how can you say that?" exclaimed Batim. "It has been wonderful, growing up with parents who possess such spirit. Being with you and mother while you spread the word about Yavros has been my inspiration..."

"...I was actually only joking, son," Salutat assured him. "I know you'll miss us as much as we will miss you."

The following morning, the wary youth accompanied his father to the gates of the Academie. "...Just to show you what it looks like," Salutat told him.

Batim was not impressed.

"An imposing building it might be," he said, "but it's the standard of tuition that counts."

"Yes, and it is the highest in the land, so I've heard," Salutat replied.

The day after that, Batim went alone to the gates of the Academie; coincidentally at the time when the students had finished their lectures and were beginning to leave for home. On this occasion, Batim ventured within the gates to get a better impression of the place.

It felt good, he thought: the prospect of studying within such an advanced place of education.

He leant against a tree for a few minutes and watched the intellectual young men. Some walked in pairs; others alone as they made for the gate and home. He wondered what interesting topics they had been involved with, and were perhaps still discussing with their friends.

Batim had never been among so many young people before. The sight of a crowd of boys roughly his own age unnerved him – until he remembered he was actually no different from them.

"Don't be silly," he chided himself. "Go and say hello – they won't bite."

Batim stepped out from the tree and made his way over to a bush-lined driveway that led up to the Academie's main entrance.

Just then, a student ran past him at great speed. As he did so, he inadvertently bumped into Batim; the accident causing him to drop a scroll he carried under his arm. Immediately the runner halted and ran back to Batim to retrieve the scroll – and to apologise.

"I'm so sorry," he blurted out, short of breath. "...How careless of me. ...You're not hurt are you?"

Batim was speechless; in part because of the incident and the fact that somebody had actually spoken to him. But mainly, he was hesitant because the scroll had burst open, revealing on it a strangely shaped symbol: some kind of symmetrical picture, the like of which Batim had never seen before; and it fascinated him.

While the student continued to apologise profusely, Batim could not take his eyes off it.

"...I said, you're not hurt are you?" the student again asked as he bent to pick up his scroll.

Suddenly Batim came to his senses.

"No, not at all," was his astonished reply. "The fault was probably mine, anyway."

The student rose to his feet and carefully began to roll up his work.

Hurriedly, Batim tried to see as much of the unfamiliar depiction as he could before he lost sight of it; his attempt noticed by the student.

He stopped rolling it up and said, "Are you interested in my mantra?"

"Mantra?" mimicked Batim, unsure of what he meant.

"Yes," said the student, opening the scroll again. "This is a mantra. It helps you focus on higher things. I have been working with it in my Ancient Philosophies course. By the way, my name is Resuval. Are you a student here?"

"No. ...Not yet, that is. I'm called Batim. Our family has just moved back to this city after many years away. My parents want me to study... Um...I'm thinking of enrolling at the Academie."

"Well, Batim, I hope you do."

"Would you tell me some more about your interesting mantra before you go?"

Batim's interest had been stimulated by the glimpse of advanced scholastic work, but then remembered that his newfound friend was in a hurry.

"Yes, of course. What would you like to...?"

A shout caught Resuval's attention. He spun round to see two other students hailing him.

Turning back to Batim, he said, "I'm sorry but I must go now. My friends are waiting for me – that's why I was in such a hurry."

Then, when he saw a disappointed look on Batim's face, he added, "Maybe I'll get a chance to discuss it with you when you begin your course."

And then he was gone.

Batim's head was in a spin. Nothing he learnt from his own tutor was ever like this. Life at the Academie, he deduced after one brief encounter, looked like it could be exciting as well as educational.

By the time he got back home he had made up his mind to enrol there.

After that, time flew by for the soon-to-be scholar. A lot needed to be arranged in advance: practical matters such as accommodation, for his parents were anxious to return to their mission once he was settled; and the all-important enrolment.

His eyes strained to absorb just how many courses he could choose from.

"I'll do them all!" he exclaimed to Salutat on the day of his enrolment.

"I wouldn't recommend it," came the registrar's cynical reply. "Your first year will be difficult enough adjusting to the pace of academic life – and to being on your own. You don't want to overtire yourself with too much study. Just take it quietly. Three subjects would be considered a good choice to begin with."

"Only three!" grumbled Batim, and looked enquiringly at his father. "Whatever shall I choose?"

"Well," said Salutat, pouring over the schedule. "You'll be taking philosophical and religious studies..."

"...Philosophical studies," echoed Batim privately. "Isn't that what Resuval's taking?" Then he corrected himself. "Oh, no – he said it was 'ancient' philosophies. The mantra must be from some kind of ancient ritual."

"So, what do you think?" asked Salutat, breaking into Batim's deliberations. "Decide quickly son. There are other students waiting to enrol."

Batim settled on Ancient Philosophies, Mathematics and Athletic sports. The last one appealed to him because he and Salutat had often jogged together to maintain their fitness. The young athlete was now keen to involve himself in competitive sporting events.

Only now did he realise what a cloistered life he must have led with his parents; even though, at the time, he did not think of it that way.

"I can't wait to get started," he said after everything was arranged.

Then, settling into his room at the Academie's hostel which he shared with another student, Batim said farewell to his parents; to begin his adventurous new life as an independent adult.

Little did he realise how much the experience would change him.

Meanwhile, in another realm Lucifer was fuming.

Two things irritated him now. To think that Salutat had formed a close liaison with Angelina, to the extent they now had progeny, consumed him with jealousy. However, of greater significance recently was his growing awareness that Hellion no longer belonged to him alone. Other errant souls were now being sent there.

After all this time as ruler and sole occupant of Hellion, Lucifer's exclusive position was no longer secure.

Actually, he had been aware of it developing for a while now. It wasn't difficult to notice all the other miscreants: fragmented and therefore harmless souls who posed no threat to him. Until now he had been so firmly entrenched in his executive role that there could be no dispute with homeless non-beings. But on his return to Hellion after the angels' picnic, he noticed a difference: the inhabitants of Hellion were becoming indifferent to him.

Did the newcomers not know who he was? Were his recent sojourns in Eddren so frequent that they had not even heard of the mighty Lucifer?

...And not only did they ignore him; some even pushed him out of the way.

"These vermin are too much!" he complained bitterly. "Everyone thinks they're kingpin. Don't they know there's only one master of Hellion – me!"

But, as self-praise is no recommendation, none listened to Lucifer's thunderous declaration. Instead, they rudely snubbed him and got on with their own empty existence as residents of Hellion.

"This is your fault!" Lucifer shouted at Yavros, as though somehow he could project his stance through the dense cloud of pathos and discarded souls. "If you didn't keep throwing your castoffs down here, I would still have the place to myself! Now I have nothing to call my own!"

Then later, when his annoyance had cooled slightly, he wondered, "...Anyway, why are they actually here? Surely, Yavros' precious little have-beens should now be prancing around in Eternity?"

And then it dawned.

"Of course! These defunct terran spirits are in Hellion because of something evil they did while they were alive – some kind of anti-social or criminal behaviour. And what made them evil...? Whoops!" said Lucifer cheekily. "I guess it was me!

Energised by the thought, a spark of optimism ignited within him.

"But there must still be a few wretches left who aren't pushy and rude; rejects of the old order who know their place in the scheme of things – well, my scheme, anyway. Somewhere in this seething mass of terran leftovers, there must be one gelatinous gobbet who respects old Lucifer!"

In desperation, Lucifer began a frantic search for a possible victim to restore his self-esteem and help him convince the other phantoms of his superiority. It was beneath his dignity, he proclaimed, to subject himself to these cretins any more than he was willing to serve Yavros' terran spirits in Eddren.

But where would he find one? The phantoms in Hellion were once the scum of Eddren; not the stupid pushovers Hominus and Womah had been. ...Quite the reverse, in fact. His terran nature, playfully instilled in them eons ago, had developed into a negative force with a momentum all of its own.

How ironic that he – the originator of it all – now found himself on the receiving end of his own barbarity.

As Hellion's residents grew more insulting in their attitude towards him, the greater became Lucifer's need of finding one that he, himself, could push around.

"...Just one!" he wailed plaintively into the stagnating ethers. "Is that too much to ask?"

And then, as if by magic...there it was.

The fragmented fool sat blubbering in a squalid corner of Hellion; nursing wounds still raw from the self-pity in which it wallowed; although it had no right to wallow in self-pity at all. In being exiled to Hellion, it was receiving its just desserts. Not only was it exterminated while in Eddren and denied entry to Eternity, but also it received some scathing comments from its fellow Hellionites.

It transpired that the heinous crime which resulted in its condemnation was so awful that not even Hellion was a good enough place for it.

And the reason for it was this:

A soul which fragmented on translocation to Hellion was invariably, when alive, a terran spirit with such low morals as to have been completely devoid of spirituality.

159

This, to the astute Lucifer and others of his kind, was blatantly obvious.

On its arrival in Hellion, this individual foolishly boasted that it had been a high elder in the temple of the sun, and had gouged out the eyes of its only daughter because she would not become a priestess in the temple.

Unfortunately, its bragging received no support from any of Hellion's other disreputable residents. In the main, they had little regard for religious doctrine, especially not sun worship, and exiled the now fragmented soul to the outer reaches of their realm; hopefully, to be rid of such scum forever.

It was from this unlikely spot that Lucifer would extract his primary ally.

Lucifer had no knowledge of the wisp's identity, or of its transgressions. However, he reckoned it must have done something pretty terrible, even by his own vile standards, to end up there – and in such a fragmented state, too.

He wondered if he could capitalise on the situation and win the misfit's trust; even help it to become whole again. And then, when its gratitude to the benevolent Lucifer was consummate, he could toy with it, manipulate it – enslave it forever...

The fragmented soul was so overwhelmed that Hellion's founder member – the knowledge of which Lucifer went to great pains to impart – was not about to denigrate it for its sins, that it ceased trembling and raised a sceptical but grateful eyebrow in Lucifer's direction.

So far so good, chuckled Lucifer and speculated that a little phoney compassion might go down well, too.

His syrup was received like warm sunshine on an icy lake, melting the phantom's soul and gradually making it whole again.

Its gratitude was so sincere, so absolute; so pure that for a moment Lucifer feared it might become righteous enough to be accepted into Eternity, and Lucifer with it; something he could not allow, considering the effort he had put into moulding it. After all, his plan of action had nothing to do with a moment's compassion that oozed out of his dark heart. He did it for one reason only: because he craved control. Lucifer was sick of being treated like filth by the other inhabitants of Hellion. ...And he wanted a scapegoat to boost his image down there.

...That was all.

But the soul saw Lucifer's attentiveness in a different light. It assumed he cared; that Lucifer was actually a kind-hearted character who tried to help the poor unfortunates of Hellion. It promised from then on to repay Lucifer one-hundredfold; to pander to his every whim, as a slave obeys its master.

From now on, the soul declared, Lucifer's merest wish would be its unconditional command.

Lucifer only had to voice it.

At first, Lucifer hated having the servile creep constantly in attendance. Now that he had achieved his objective and had fun in the process, he wanted no more to do with it.

"Will you quit pestering me – I don't want you hanging around me!" he pleaded in exasperation.

"But Lucifer," the soul cried pitifully. "What will become of me without service to you? Tell me your wishes, and I will be your willing slave!"

"Yuk! Go away!" shrieked Lucifer, flicking at it like one of Eddren's insects.

But then he had an idea.

If the nitwit really wanted to become his devoted slave, Lucifer mused, he would turn it into one; a duplicate of himself: his doppelgänger.

He would even give it a name: Slave.

Lucifer and Slave – as alike in appearance as identical twins. What a delightful concept!

Enjoying his own ingenuity, Lucifer applauded himself. How he would relish using his alter ego, and how much more could be achieved because of it – starting with that hateful lovechild Batim!

Lucifer skilfully trained his protégé in the art of deception. By the time he had finished, none but the most observant could tell them apart.

"Not even Miekaale will know there are two of us," he gloated, with the thought of possibilities opening up.

There was no time to lose, now. The realm of Eddren could be his for the taking.

All he needed to do, he decided, was to leave Slave in Hellion as a decoy – to fool Miekaale into believing he was still there. Then he would hasten to the coastal city where he was sure the boy Batim could still be found.

However, at the very last moment before translocation, Lucifer changed his plans. As he was about exit Hellion, he grabbed the unsuspecting Slave and pulled it through with him.

"Why should I be the one to do all the work?" he said in excuse. "My slave can do it for me. Miekaale will think he's seeing double. He'll have his hands full trying to figure out what's going on, and in the meantime I'll have double the fun in the process!"

Peals of laughter accompanied Lucifer's train of thought as the pair arrived in Eddren; startling the already terrified, formless Slave.

"What have I let myself in for?" Slave wondered; confused by everything that was taking place.

And then it realised something. It was back in Eddren; but without a body or any form whatsoever! ...And Lucifer, too, by the look of it. Slave could not see him, but there was no doubting his awful presence.

The ribald laughter which accompanied their arrival in the realm was unmistakably that of Lucifer.

"Why have you brought me back here?" it asked, in as vexed a tone as a formless sprite can manage.

"You'll see," replied Lucifer, still in the grip of mirth. "All will be revealed. I have plans for you, my friend."

At the Academie, Batim was adjusting to his new life as a tertiary scholar.

The first few weeks had been harrowing for the novice student. What's more, he was now completely on his own, as his hostel room-mate resigned soon after admission and had not been replaced.

Alone for the first time in his life, he missed his parents terribly. All the new students did. Yet none would admit it, and because of this Batim assumed he was the only one. To overcome the homesickness, he threw himself into his academic classes.

Batim revelled in the courses he was taking, especially athletics. As expected, he was very good at it, and found in it a welcome release from the mental strain of study.

He loved to run. Even when he was not participating in competitive games at the Academie, he would take off into the hills, or run the length of a wide, sandy beach just north of the harbour. It reminded him of the treasured times spent in his youth, running alongside his father – 'for a bit of exercise,' as Salutat told Angelina to justify their regular disappearances.

As the months passed, Batim became used to living alone. He grew to like having his room to himself. He could study in peace, and reflect quietly on all that his parents taught him about Yavros, and on everything he had learnt during the months since he started at the Academie.

"How fortunate I am," he said as he looked out from his window onto the well-kept grounds of the campus. "I am truly blessed to have such wonderful opportunities in life."

However, an important factor that Batim had failed to take into account was about to tear his world apart, and as yet he was both innocent of its substance and ignorant of its dangers.

He had neglected his parents' warnings about Lucifer. For, as he would later recall, when a terran spirit is full of contentment, he overlooks the need for caution; a lesson Batim would soon learn to his cost.

All this while, Lucifer had been keeping his distance from Batim; observing the student's every move, but biding his time until a perfect moment presented itself for intrusion into his life.

For many months, nothing transpired to present him with an opening. The brat, Lucifer growled petulantly, was too damnably perfect to do anything wrong.

...That was, until the day of the carnival.

Every year, at the height of the season, when studies were winding down and spirits in the Academie were high, the scholars grouped together to present a colourful carnival for the townsfolk.

It was always a huge hit, providing both release from the rigours of everyday life for the city, and much needed revenue for the Academie; for the generosity of the public on this occasion surpassed even that for the sun temple. Entertainers included singers, jugglers, clowns, and floats of every shape and size portraying, in comic relief, all the activities within the Academie. Batim's participation was in the field of athletics. He and his colleagues were asked to run in pairs, holding aloft standards depicting their sport, alongside the lead float as it slowly made its way around the carnival's circuit.

Scholarly students envied the athletes for this honour. There carried with the role of standard-bearer a certain esteem for the Academie, and a glamorous reputation for the runners themselves.

Young ladies habitually flocked to cheer nimble youths while they jogged along the carnival's route; and this for one reason only – the athletes wore nothing but scanty loincloths, which left little to the imagination of nubile young maids.

It was often said that the innocent young daughters of prominent citizens would return home less than innocent after the carnival. So it was not with unanimous glee that carnival day was anticipated.

Of these rumours Batim knew nothing. All he did know, when the day arrived, was the tremendous honour he felt to represent the Academie in this way, and that he was very excited about it.

Of the rumours Lucifer knew nothing, either. He did not even know about the carnival itself until the event began.

And then the opportunity he had been eagerly awaiting hit him between the eyes.

...Her name was Urla.

At first Lucifer did not notice her, and neither did Batim. She was just one of the many fresh, giggling faces lining the street to catch a glimpse of muscular young flesh. Nor did Batim recognise that he, more than any other athlete, attracted the greatest attention from her, for the fairness of his hair and the litheness of his physique.

The runners worked to a plan. Each time the leading float completed a circuit, arriving back where it started, a fresh pair of participants replaced the exhausted runners who preceded them.

During the course of the day, each pair of runners had three turns at the circuit.

At the beginning of his second circuit, Batim noticed a young woman jogging alongside him. The stronger runner of the two, Batim quickly left her standing; for she soon ran out of breath and disappeared into the crowd.

It fascinated him that the girl had apparently taken an interest, although he could not understand why – they had not been introduced, nor exchanged so much as a word.

Yet still, it fascinated him; so, during his third circuit of the course, his curiosity well ignited, he looked out for her.

This time, rather than begin the circuit with him, the girl started her run from halfway round the course. And when Batim arrived at the finish line, breathless and exhausted, she ended her run at the same place.

For a moment both stood panting.

For a while Batim paid attention to his carnival partner who complained of a sore back rather than to the girl. ...After all, he did not yet know her, and felt embarrassed that he seemed to be the object of a female's attention.

But then, as if aiming to attract him, she moved closer; her beguiling ways professionally played out.

Bemused, Batim's team mates watched as the girl made advances on their innocent and, they realised, rather naïve colleague; for they knew what she was. Some of them had even known her. At very least, they were aware of her reputation.

The girl, who went only by the name of Urla, had known a lot of the students in her disreputable career because it was her trade: the only way in which the young woman, orphaned at an early age and uneducated, could make a living in the hostile climate of the times. There were few openings for unattached women; only restrictions – except for this one. Yet, as she still had to provide for herself, she reluctantly made it her career.

However, in this instance, as Batim's friends sniggered and exchanged lewd comments, Urla had eyes for only one man. And that man was beginning to respond.

Batim could not help himself. The allure of a female was an element of physical life from which he had been well cloistered, although he never looked at it that way at the time. And now, here was a member of the fairer sex – and very fair at that – all but throwing herself at him.

How could he resist?

Having regained his breath, Batim smiled at her; not quite knowing what to say.

She fluttered her dark lashes, confirming what his heart was hoping – that she was very much attracted to him.

Without introducing himself, as his parents would have preferred, he gushed awkwardly, "You've got lovely eyes;" a comment that caused her to flash them all the more.

"And you have got a lovely... Well...you're just lovely," she responded cheekily while looking him up and down. Then she added, "By the way, I'm known as Urla."

Batim lurched forward, his hand outstretched ready to take hers in greeting. "My name is Batim; this was my first time with the carnival."

"Really?" she responded with marked interest. "And did you enjoy it?"

"Oh, yes. It was a wonderful experience: a real honour to represent the Academie. ...Are you connected with the Academie at all?"

Urla smirked. "In a way," she said hesitantly. "I suppose you could say I have a few connections with the Academie. But I get the impression you don't know about that yet."

"...About what?" asked Batim in all innocence.

"Oh, nothing..."

Again, Batim was fascinated. All these wonderful new experiences; most of which he had chanced upon in just one day.

He really had no idea how to deal with them.

But somebody else, observing close by, knew exactly how to deal with them; and how to utilise them: somebody neither Batim nor Urla realised was watching.

Silently; invisibly, Lucifer was working out how he could capitalise on the attraction growing between these two terrans. And he knew just who was going to help him.

He roughly pulled Slave aside and asked, "Weren't you a male in terran life?"

"Yes. ...Why?"

"Hmm... That's inconvenient. I need you to be feminine for a while."

"...A woman? Wow, that would be a challenge. I always took great pleasure in putting them down during my life.

But I could give it a try, if it is your will. What would you have me do?"

Lucifer ignored Slave's chattering; for he had already decided what its function should be. He would share none of his thoughts with the critter whose sole purpose, in his opinion, was to respond to his every command; not to question it.

Instead, he moved in closer to the chatty pair of terran spirits to get a fix on the rapport between them. It seemed they were really hitting it off.

While they strolled back to the Academie's gates, Urla said to the euphoric Batim, "Will you meet me tomorrow after your classes?"

"Yes, that would be very nice," Batim replied straight away; and then politely bade her good day

For some time afterwards he watched Urla mingle with the crowds; not wanting to turn away; still keen to retain something of the spell that had overtaken him.

Back inside the hostel room, with silence and solitude his only companions again, Batim's bewildered mind tried to take stock of everything that had happened.

He felt different: stimulated even, as though dormant senses in him had been awakened.

A spark had enflamed his whole being. He knew nothing of what it might be.

But Lucifer knew. He recognised infatuation between male and female when he saw it.

Were not the boy's parents also guilty of it? Here was a way he could get back at Salutat for stealing Angelina's heart: to have his son seduced by this slip of a girl who was obviously of loose morals.

The thought of it tantalised him.

"Slave!" he barked to the inattentive sprite who, at that moment, was mesmerised by everything going on around them: the sights, the colours, the bright and bouncy music. It had never come across anything like this during its time at the sun temple.

"What do you want?" it snapped in response; annoyed by the intrusion into its musings, and conscious now that Lucifer considered it to be little more than a lackey.

"He's treating me more like an object to be exploited than a person with thoughts and feelings," Slave grumbled as it tried to focus on the latest command.

"Just come here!" barked Lucifer. "I have work for you."

His instructions were to be carried out to the letter; without objection. Slave's opinion held no sway in any of his decisions; and that was the rule.

"Your job," he announced, "is to stand a way off the girl and instruct her in the art of seducing the son of angels..."

"...Angels!"

Slave looked around in alarm; fearing the news of its exit from Hellion may have filtered through to Eternity.

"Don't interrupt!" scowled Lucifer; frustrated at losing his train of thought.

Still worried, Slave tried to absorb Lucifer's instructions.

"As I was saying," Lucifer continued. "I want the woman Urla to make Batim fall hopelessly in love with her."

"Well, that should be a cinch!" boasted Slave. "All men are pushovers for a pretty face."

Lucifer frowned with contempt. But for Slave's lack of a body he would have cuffed it around the ears. Instead, he maintained what little patience remained in him and said pointedly, "Let's not take anything for granted, shall we? You are not dealing with a character who, like you, is so morally corrupt that he would fall for the usual female wiles. This terran was born of and brought up by angels.

He has scruples. I assure you that Batim, son of the angel Salutat, will take some defrocking."

Yet Lucifer could not have been more wrong. Batim, the terran son of terran angels, was already besotted by the attractive young woman.

He was indeed, although he did not know it at the time, a pushover for a pretty face.

...At least, for one in particular.

CHAPTER 2

Batim could not sleep that night.

His mind, still stimulated from the day's events, seemed set on reliving every detail.

He jerked awake just moments after falling asleep so many times that his nerves started to feel quite ragged. When morning finally rescued him, he was relieved but exhausted. Then, during an afternoon class, he nodded off to sleep; only to be prodded in the ribs by a fellow student and chastised by his tutor.

But Batim did not really mind, for there was a light at the end of this tunnel; something he had to look forward to: his upcoming meeting with Urla. And although the afternoon still dragged on, it was worth the tedium as far as he was concerned.

The pair had arranged to meet by the Academie's rear entrance after Batim's final lecture.

It amazed him how she knew precisely when that would be; for there she was, waiting for him.

Excitedly, he bowled up to her; this time all sense of formality melting away at the sight of her beguiling face.

"I'm so glad you've come," he said exuberantly.

"I wouldn't have missed it for the world," she replied, and then added in a syrupy voice, "I think you're the most handsome fellow I've ever seen!"

"Watch it, Slave!" interrupted Lucifer, as the sprite began to take its new role to heart. "Don't overdo it or you'll scare him off!"

Batim and Urla grabbed a bite to eat from a street vendor, and then headed off to the beach. It was quieter there, with only the gentle sound of water lapping on the shore to break the silence.

They walked and talked; learning with almost a sense of urgency everything about each other's lives; that is, every detail they wanted to divulge to each other. For his part, Batim refrained from telling Urla his parents were angels, and Urla omitted the part in her story that would reveal her profession. Neither seemed to matter now, anyway. They were about to fall in love. ...Helplessly and hopelessly in love.

Yet their date ended more abruptly than either could have envisaged, taking both the terran spirits and their ghoulish onlookers by surprise.

Without any warning Batim suddenly fled, leaving Urla shocked and completely mystified.

It happened this way:

Their enjoyment of each other's company was such that the evening passed quickly, and neither had realised it.

Sitting on an old tree trunk, thrown up by the surf in bygone times, they had become engrossed in the mood of the evening, and by a darkening sky mirrored off the calm water. It was perfect.

"Could Eternity be any more beautiful than this?" Batim reflected.

But then, as darkness enveloped them and Urla was in the process of leading him to a secluded spot in the dunes where, as she put it, they could 'spend the night together', the reality of Batim's situation sunk in: he was past his curfew. The door to his hostel would probably be locked by the time he got back; shutting him out. So, all he said in response was that he should leave straight away.

Then, in a rush he was gone; leaving Urla by herself and in complete darkness.

Immediately, Urla felt nervous for, although she had been to the spot many times before, she had never done so alone or at night. With heart in mouth for fear of the dark, and out of concern that she may have lost Batim completely, she hurried back to her modest home.

Batim, too, was sure he had spoiled the relationship.

As he suspected, he could not gain access to his hostel. Curfew was always strictly observed; there would be no exceptions. In a panic he checked to see if anyone may have witnessed his late return. Mercifully, all appeared to be quiet.

He then had to decide what to do next.

There was really nowhere he could go at this unsociable hour. Forlornly, he made his way to the rear of the hostel and found a sheltered alcove near the service entrance to the cookhouse. It smelt unclean, but at least it was dry and warm, for the night had now turned chilly. His head in a spin, he leant against the wall, hardly believing his plight.

None of this was supposed to happen! Batim wailed silently. What started off as a pleasant evening had turned into a fiasco; a situation that was bound to get him into serious trouble.

He had a room to himself at the hostel so nobody was going to worry that he had not returned home. But all the residents were expected to adhere to their strict house rules, and curfew was one of them. His absence, he knew, would not go undetected.

"What would my father think if he could see me now!" he howled inwardly.

There would be no rest for him that night, either: his third in a row without proper sleep. While he struggled to find a comfortable position where he could actually drift off, he thought back to the previous night and the excitement of anticipation, and to the night before that when all thought had been centred on the carnival.

So what had gone so horribly wrong?

Hour after hour he wrestled with the problem. Was he doing something he shouldn't be doing in making friends with Urla? He tried to work out how his parents would react if they knew about her. Would they approve, or be angry with him for not giving full attention to the courses? It was hard for him to understand. Of one thing he was sure, though. If he managed to get back into the Academie without recrimination, he was not going to allow himself to be swayed so easily again.

His association with Urla, he had convinced himself by daybreak, was a thing of the past.

But Lucifer had other ideas.

When Batim shamefacedly emerged from his class the following afternoon: red eyed, light-headed from lack of sleep, and embarrassed by the telling off he received from the registrar, Urla was waiting for him again — not by the main entrance as before, but near the door of his hostel.

She rushed up to him straight away.

Batim stopped in his tracks, a feeling of despondency filling his soul.

How am I to handle this? he pleaded in despair. Hadn't he just got her out his system? The last thing he wanted to deal with right now was an emotional outburst from an abandoned female.

Yet Urla's sudden appearance, rather than threatening rebuke, in fact heralded a more plaintive approach: that of heartfelt entreaty.

"I'm sorry to turn up like this," she said meekly. "I don't want to get you into trouble or anything, but I really need to know why you ran away last night. Was it because of something I did?"

Open-mouthed, Batim stared at Urla; his mind numb from fatigue and lack of inspiration.

A moment later his emotions took over. Why would she think such a thing? he asked himself. It was nothing to do with her! His running off so abruptly was purely because of the curfew. Didn't she realise that?

"Of course you haven't done anything," he conceded.

Given a choice, he would have preferred to avoid any conversation with Urla which might lead to another missed curfew or get him into further trouble. But the sorrowful look in her soft eyes melted his heart.

Helplessly, he found himself apologising — not only for taking off and leaving her alone in the dark, but also for giving her a false impression of the reason for it. Here was someone, he guessed, who through no fault of her own had been subjected to the same kind of nocturnal torment that he endured. How could he ignore her sorry plight in favour of his own?

It would go against all laws of spirituality!

But then he remembered where they were — outside a male-only dormitory. If anyone saw them it would result in another black mark against his name, and so he motioned her to follow him away from the buildings; to anywhere they could talk in private.

Batim desperately needed to speak with Urla now. He felt he owed her an honest explanation for last night's sudden departure.

He wanted to convince her she should feel no sense of guilt; that she was completely blameless: that it was his fault alone.

But these confessions he could not make with people around, forcing them to whisper covertly. His thoughts should be expressed to her openly and without restriction. And there was only one place where he could do that: the wide, sandy beach.

By the time they reached the headland beyond which lay the familiar sand dunes, Batim and Urla had resolved their differences. Although mindful of curfew now, Batim found himself inching ever closer to Urla in spirit. As they started to talk more informally, he slipped his arm across the back of her shoulder, a gesture which she reciprocated by wrapping an arm round his waist. Then, by the time darkness fell, all considerations except their togetherness had filtered out of Batim's head.

Urla took Batim straight to her special grassy hideaway. She knew they would be unobserved there. She never had been, and saw no reason why this occasion might be any different.

...Except, there was a difference this time; she was sure of it now. Batim wasn't like any of the other young men from the Academie she had enticed to this place. They were after just one thing; she always willing to comply. But Batim appeared to be genuinely fond of her. In fact, he seemed to be a genuine sort of person altogether; not like some of the conceited types she was used to dealing with.

A feeling of serenity crept over her; something she had never before experienced in her seedy past. As they kissed for the first time, she drifted off into unfamiliar rapture.

Surely this is love, Urla thought.

But then something gripped her soul as though a clamp had been placed on her emotions.

All at once she felt a change take place and she became more like her old self. Assisted by Slave, Lucifer's nature in her surged to the fore again, and passion overtook love as she fanned the flame within Batim.

"That's better," growled Lucifer at Slave. "For a moment there I thought you were getting all namby-pamby on me. Please don't let her get sentimental again!"

Batim and Urla lay together that night.

It seemed natural to them now: to consummate their relationship. Urla's favourite grassy spot took on a new significance for her as she made love to her new beau. ...Made love as opposed to seduced; for never before had she received love as well as given it. Never before had she known anything but revulsion when it was all over. Batim, she felt in her heart, was her soul mate.

But this was not real love. It was really only seduction: a clever piece of orchestration on the part of Slave to make her totally enamoured of Batim, knowing as it did that the boy could not help but respond.

That was what its master required: for the terran male to fall in love with the terran female.

Slave did not know why Lucifer wanted the seduction, just that it had been requested, and it was Slave's pleasure to comply. It couldn't wait to take the matter further.

Yet Lucifer had nothing further planned for the pair; not at the moment anyway. He had not thought beyond the knowledge, and therefore his own gratification, that when terran nature takes control in their lives, everything good or spiritual recedes into the background. And this he had accomplished in the son of angels.

Batim was now officially a bad boy.

Unfortunately though, Lucifer omitted to inform Slave its task had been completed.

As the hours of night-time wore on, nothing more entered Batim's mind, either.

The fact that he had again missed his curfew, and was involved in an entanglement with a girl his parents would disapprove of, never once occurred to him. All he wanted to think of, with the euphoria of one whose emotions had soared for the first time in his life, was Urla.

'Urla' he sounded in his heart over and over again. 'How I love the name Urla!'

Late the next morning the infatuated pair, dishevelled and hungry but also exhilarated, walked out of the dunes; their arms still wrapped around each other.

However, as the town came into view, the dome of the Academie's library towering above everything except the sun temple, Batim finally woke up to the certainty of his situation, and he felt his euphoric state drop like a stone.

Gradually a feeling of anxiety filled his gut. By the time they had reached the Academie's boundary, his throat was constricted with fear.

Batim froze to the spot; common sense hitting him in the face.

"What have I done?" he cried in panic.

"What do you mean?" asked Urla in all innocence. "You haven't done anything."

"Yes I have," he murmured, his troubled mind now in a daze. "Not only have I broken curfew twice, but I've also failed to show up for an important class."

He looked at her, an expression of misery in his eyes.

"I can't possibly go back; the registrar will tan my hide!"

"Yes!" exclaimed Lucifer. "I've got him! That's one in the eye for you, Salutat! Good work, Slave. You've done very well for a novice!"

Slave puffed up with self-pride and excitement. Straight away it goaded Urla further.

"It doesn't matter," Urla assured Batim. "You didn't really belong at the Academie anyway. Come back to my place – you'll be comfortable there."

Batim stared at her in disbelief.

How could she be so complacent about it? His entire future depended on qualifications gained at the Academie. Couldn't she understand that?

While Urla tugged at his tunic, beseeching him to go with her, he tried to think up a justifiable reason for not complying. But he could think of none.

Batim was completely devoid of inspiration.

And besides, he considered forlornly as he submitted to her resolve; where else can I go now?

Batim was appalled by the amount of squalor in Urla's part of town. It appeared his loyal and captivating friend lived in nothing better than a dingy apartment beneath the fish market. As he approached the steps leading down to it, he felt nauseated by the putrid smell.

But when they went inside and closed the door behind them, he stepped into another world. It was the soothing aroma that first struck Batim: a hint of Jasmine in sharp contrast with the foul smell outside.

Batim breathed in deeply. The scent calmed his senses, relieving the weight of oppression he was feeling.

Urla skipped down her short staircase and walked over to a shelf on the far wall. The casual manner in which she lit an array of coloured candles indicated to Batim that this was something she usually did on entering her home.

And then he understood why. The cheerless cavern was instantly transformed into a welcoming sanctuary, where anyone would feel contentedly at home.

...In fact, the place looked so inviting that Batim almost said to her 'Were you expecting me to come back here?' Yet he refrained from doing so, because his attention had been drawn to a huge four-poster bed in the middle of her room. Instead, he remarked, "Wow, that's a big bed for a little lady like you!"

Urla laughed. Actually, it was more of a snigger, which she quickly suppressed. There's no need to go into that just now, she thought.

Batim strode over and sat on the mattress to test it for comfort. The bed was unexpectedly soft so he lay down, at the same time stroking its embroidered counterpane with his hand.

"Wake me in the morning!" he said jokingly and closed his eyes, pretending to sleep.

"You are such a tease," said Urla playfully. She slapped his bare leg, making him yelp.

He sat up abruptly. "That's no way to treat a guest!" he retorted in fun.

Just then, something caught Batim's eye.

It was on the same shelf as the candles, and glinted pale in their flickering light.

"What's that?" he asked, pointing to it.

He jumped up from the bed to investigate.

It was small and long, with what looked to his untrained eye like a bowl at one end; and it appeared to be delicately made of clay.

"It's a pipe, of course," replied Urla.

"A pipe?" echoed Batim, picking it up. "What's a pipe?"

Urla laughed again. "Don't tell me you've never seen a pipe before? What sort of world have you been living in?"

Batim fingered it inquisitively.

Then he glanced at her and said, "I didn't socialise with many terrans when I travelled with my parents, and have little knowledge of ordinary things like this. So what do you do with a pipe, then?"

Urla couldn't believe his naïvety. "You smoke it, what else!" she exclaimed.

"What? Set fire to it? What's the point in that?"

"No, not the pipe, silly! You put something in here," she said, taking it from him and pointing to the bowl end of the pipe. "You light it and draw the smoke into your mouth through the other end. Honestly...you're unbelievable!"

Batim put the thin end of the pipe to his mouth and sucked. It brought forth nothing except a whistling sound that caused him embarrassment.

"Well what goes in it, then?" he asked in frustration, while searching for something himself.

Next to the pipe he noticed a small urn and removed the lid. It contained what appeared to be dried up leaves. Batim tipped some into the palm of his hand; then he carefully transferred it to the pipe.

"Here, this will do." he said.

Urla lunged at him.

"Hey, what are you doing?" she cried. "That stuff costs a fortune! Give it to me – I'll fill it."

She took the pipe off him, returned its contents to the urn and placed just a pinch of the substance in the bowl.

"There; that will be plenty," she said

"For what?" asked Batim innocently.

"Don't you know what this stuff is?"

182

"No. It just looks like bits of dead leaves to me."

"Oh, it's far more than that!" said Urla cagily. "Here, let me show you."

She took a taper from the shelf and lit it from one of the candles.

"Well, are you going to enlighten me?" asked Batim, beginning to feel that Urla was teasing him.

"Have you never heard of opiates?" she said, watching the taper's flame brighten.

"No, what are they?"

"My love...you are about to find out."

Urla lit the dried concoction in the bowl and gradually inhaled its smoke. For a moment she stood, her eyes closed; holding onto the inhalation before blowing it out in short puffs.

"Ah, that's better," she said with a sparkle in her eyes. She gestured Batim to take the pipe, warning him not to touch the heated bowl.

He held the pipe the way she showed him, put it to his lips and sucked.

Immediately the smoke caught the back of his throat, making him cough violently. When he started to go red in the face, Urla realised he really hadn't tried it before.

Suddenly she was worried, for her clients didn't usually react that way. They generally reached for it even before she did! Was she mistaken in offering the opiate to such an obvious novice?

Urla quickly opened a cupboard door to reveal several earthenware casks; each containing wine.

She removed one and poured some of its contents into a chalice; then she held it out to Batim.

"Here, have a drink to soothe your throat."

By now Batim felt dizzy. He found it hard even to focus on what she was saying.

Noticing this, Urla steadied his hand while he took hold of the chalice.

"What is it?" asked Batim in between coughing fits.

"It's just wine. Drink it."

Batim put the chalice to his lips and hesitantly touched the fermented brew with his tongue. It tasted bittersweet; not exactly what he was expecting. But it was quite nice and, as Urla had suggested, it might soothe his throat.

He took a sip, then a mouthful, swallowing it a bit at a time. Soon his throat felt better, and a warming sensation began to creep through him.

All of a sudden Batim had an overwhelming desire to sleep. His eyes lay heavily in their sockets, and he needed to sit down. He looked around quickly for a chair before his balance deserted him. Seeing none, he sat on the side of the bed and straightaway lay down.

Within seconds he was asleep.

When he awoke hours later, it was dark.

For a second or two Batim could not remember where he was. Then he saw Urla lying next to him, sound asleep.

"Ah yes," he sighed contentedly. "This is nice – so much better than the hostel."

Lying back, he looked around the spacious room. The flickering candlelight; dimmer now that Urla's candles had burnt down, cast dancing shadows on the wall.

Dreamily, he pretended they were sprites. Then, as he watched them, without warning one of them hurled itself at him…

In a panic, he deflected it and sat bolt upright; fully alert and wondering if it was real or just his imagination.

He looked up into the ceiling. The creatures had gone, leaving only dancing shadows again.

Cheekily, Slave reported back to its master.

"What a laugh!" Lucifer chuckled, and then noiselessly called out, "Son of angels, that'll teach you to stay in your own realm!"

Batim's introduction to opiates and alcohol overwhelmed both his senses and his system.

He had never encountered anything so potently mind-altering before, and the realisation that he had touched on the boundaries of Hellion frightened him considerably.

"Don't give me any more of that stuff," he said when Urla awoke with the disturbance.

I'm so sorry," she said. "I didn't mean for it to cause you any harm. It doesn't usually with my....my friends. Maybe you were just too tired to benefit from it properly."

"What is it supposed to do then?" he asked; not at all convinced that anything beneficial could come out of the wretched substance.

Without giving away her usual experience with opiates, Urla searched her mind for an explanation. It's funny, she thought. I've never talked about it before; just smoked it. ...My clients don't usually talk much at these times. This Batim is one strange character!

"Well," she began to explain, "I suppose it gives you the impression of elation. ...A sense of detachment; like your spirit is lifting out of you. Everything seems wonderful, and you feel wonderful. At least, that's what usually happens. Try it again when you're feeling a bit better."

"I don't think so," came his response. "I thought I was going to pass out for a while back there."

All at once Slave, who had been congratulating itself on Batim's flight of fancy, realised it may have been too hasty in playing such a trick on him; for the terran appeared to be rejecting the opiate.

Slave had assumed that Lucifer's ongoing plan would be to make Batim addicted to the opiate; to entice him away from all that he learnt in his cloistered youth? His master must have known that this could not be achieved without Urla's intriguing lifestyle; for alone, Batim was spiritually too strong to be corrupted.

Had it then failed in its responsibilities to Lucifer?

"What do I do now?" Slave asked itself; the remnants of its mind now in turmoil. "If the male doesn't get hooked on opiates he'll never reject his prudish morals. ...And I'll be in big trouble."

Quickly, Slave crept back to its gullible charge.

By now, Urla had got up and was preparing something to eat. She produced smoked fish, bread, a bunch of grapes, and the remainder of the cask of wine. Soon Batim was replete, and warmed through by the rich beverage.

Slave decided to try again. Covertly, it whispered into Urla's ear to encourage Batim with more of the opiate.

Without recognising what she was doing, Urla picked up the pipe, added some more of the dried leaves and lit it. Then she took a draft.

Batim looked on in quiet dismay.

Handing it to him she said, "Try again; only take it more slowly this time."

There seemed no other option for him now, but to do so. With Urla's dark eyes boring into him, Batim could not resist taking the pipe from her. He felt so relaxed after his sleep, the food and the wine, that he would have done anything Urla asked of him.

Gently he drew in a small amount of the smoke and held it in his mouth before blowing it out again. He could not bring himself to inhale properly yet; nevertheless, he instantly received the effect Urla had promised. It was as though his consciousness was being elevated, and he had done nothing to achieve it except draw on the pipe.

"This is incredible!" he murmured with a grin. "It feels like I'm not quite here."

Batim looked at Urla. She seemed different somehow; or maybe it was just his perception that was different. He saw, not a girl but an angel: an angel in terran form – a bit like his mother... Yet he knew Urla was not really an angel. Last night bore testimony to that, he smirked.

"Ah, last night," he whispered, more to himself than to Urla, remembering the heightened senses of passion they both experienced. Then, when he thought about it once more, the senses returned.

He drew in another mouthful of the opiate's powerful smoke; this time slowly inhaling it. His lungs were almost used to it by now, and he suppressed the urge to cough. He would allow nothing to break the spell of the moment, especially when he realised that Urla had picked up his mood and felt the same.

She slipped off her scant clothes and slid between the silk sheets again.

Batim followed suit.

There ensued a honeymoon of passion such as Urla had only ever fantasised over.

It lasted well into the following day.

Batim was now spellbound by Urla and her way of life.

The apartment, with its fascinating trinkets and bright furnishings, was far more welcoming than his room in the hostel: bare, except for his possessions, some utilitarian items and the simple bedstead he had slept on. Urla was looking after his needs very well; lavishing on him all the attention and love a lonely youth could ever wish for. And as for the extras! He could not get over just how easily he had tapped into the ethereal realms after only a few puffs on the pipe. Surely this gave him an edge over his parents, with their so-called natural spirituality!

'I must tell my parents about this some time," he said to Urla one day, when he had been in residence with her for a few weeks.

"I wouldn't do that if I were you," she replied. "Parents don't generally approve...and besides," she added hastily, "I'm almost out of the opiates, so we won't be able to use it for much longer."

It had not occurred to Batim that the supply of opiates might run out, or that Urla might ever need to replenish it. He had just accepted it when offered, and made the most of that and all the other benefits he gained from Urla's hospitality. Neither did it occur to him that during his time with her Urla had received no income, either from him or from anywhere else.

The practicalities of life had never been part of Batim's thinking, for his father left ample funds at the Academie from which he could draw each month; and neither had he thought in terms of paying his way with Urla. So when she said there would be no more of the opiate, he could not understand why.

But then she confessed sorrowfully, "I just don't have the money to buy any more."

From Urla's perspective, this was yet another problem she faced; one she could not divulge to her live-in suitor.

Ever since she fell in love with Batim and brought him into her home, she had not been able to accommodate regular clients: her only source of income. In order to have the money to spend on necessities, she would need to tell Batim about her profession.

Yet this she still could not do; knowing how innocent of such matters he was likely to be.

"Oh, don't worry about that!" he exclaimed in response to her admission. Then, to Urla's surprise he said, "Anyway, you don't need any money of your own."

Urla stared at him dumbfounded. Was he naïve as well as innocent?

"What do you mean?" she asked.

"I mean...I have plenty."

"You do?"

"Yes," he said with confidence; at last feeling important in Urla's life.

Bewildered, Urla frowned. How could he possibly say that? When he arrived he had nothing. Even the clothes on his back were items left by forgetful clients.

Batim saw her puzzled look, and laughed.

"I don't have any here," he said as if reading her mind. "It's the allowance my father left at the Academie – for my use. We can withdraw the remainder if you like. I won't be going back to study, so we can use it to live off!"

All the while Batim was speaking, Urla's eyes began to light up. At length she said, "But that's wonderful. I had no idea... Can we go now? I'm almost out of provisions, too."

Entering the Academie for the first time since abandoning his course, Batim at once felt out of place.

He strode up to the desk, while Urla timidly held back.

She gasped at its impressive interior. Everything was on such a grand scale. The reception area alone would easily be ten times the size of her own room, she guessed. ...And this, but a small part of the whole complex!

The registrar expressed surprise to see Batim again.

"You came back then?" he said with a hint of sarcasm, and made a mark to the effect on an attendance chart in front of him.

"Yes," replied Batim, wondering why he should be so surprised. "Didn't you think I would?"

Then, before the registrar could react, he added, "I have some unfinished business to attend to."

The registrar looked up from his desk, and scrutinised Batim with an astonished expression.

"And what further business could you possibly have with this Academie?" he said in a gruff voice. "Don't you realise you forfeited all rights to your studies when you left…" He checked the dates in his diary. "….Six weeks ago exactly, by my reckoning?"

Batim laughed.

"Oh, I'm not back to study," he said flippantly. "I only came to retrieve the funds my father left for me."

Again the registrar looked at him blankly, as if he was having trouble understanding what Batim meant. At last he ventured, "You are in jest, aren't you?"

"No I am not!" replied Batim indignantly. "That money belongs to me. I want to withdraw it – now!"

The registrar slowly rose from his seat, a scowl creasing his brow that sent a shiver of alarm down Batim's spine.

"Now look here, young man," he said, glaring first at Batim and then at Urla who, sensing something was amiss, had joined Batim up at the desk. "I'm going to explain the rules of the Academie to you. Money left here by parents is for exclusive purposes: to finance scholars' courses and provide an allowance for their needs. If a student leaves; as you did," he said emphatically; "then he relinquishes his right to the funds as well as the right to return to study. Do you understand?"

Batim was horror-struck. He clearly remembered how, with pride, Salutat told him of the generous allowance he was providing for his son. That money was lawfully his, not the Academie's.

"Give me my money!" he screamed at the registrar, and thumped his fist on the desk, causing everything on it to rattle noisily.

"This is great...and I love it!" cried Lucifer, cracking up with laughter. "Go on, boy! Get angry. ...Get really angry!"

Still standing over him, the registrar responded to Batim's outburst with well-practiced composure.

"You can rant and rave all you like, but it won't do you any good. You shall not get any money out of me."

Suddenly Batim saw red. He leapt over the desk, almost knocking the man down, and shook him by the shoulders.

"Now listen to me!" he bellowed into the man's face. "You're a nobody round here – in fact, less than a nobody: you're just a clerk! You are paid to do a job, that's all. How dare you laud it over me! How dare you deny me what is rightfully mine..?"

"...It is not rightfully yours," replied the registrar with remarkable restraint. He deftly removed both of Batim's hands from his person, and added, "The money belongs to your father; not to you."

"And who are you to enforce that judgement?" Batim continued to argue.

He was not finished with the insolent man yet – not until he had received his dues.

"It is the policy of the Academie to hold funds on behalf of parents, and to release a prearranged amount to the student. If the student leaves the Academie, the balance is held in trust until the parents are notified and retrieve it themselves. This has been our policy since the beginning. There is no reason to change it now...not even for you," he added sarcastically.

Defeated, Batim stamped out of the building; his intense anger threatening to overcome him.

Courtesy of Slave, he could not bring himself to accept what the registrar told him: it was too preposterous. That money was his!

And yet, there was nothing he could do about it.

Urla followed on; helplessly watching as her lover's good humour dissipated more with each departing step. All she could do, as he stormed down the driveway, was attempt to keep up with his brisk pace and feebly try to reassure him.

"Don't worry," she gently urged. "We'll work something out; you'll see."

Back in Urla's room again, Batim's anger had diminished only slightly.

He had never felt like this before; had always been able to maintain an even temperament. The offspring of angels, he was placid by nature and benevolent in all his dealings with other people. But this was more than he could cope with. Not only was he denied his rights in being refused the money, but he had also lost face with Urla, having bragged about his finances beforehand. How marvellous it would be, he had thought, if he could support Urla like a husband from now on. But that little dream had vanished; the bubble burst, with no way of restoring it.

Furthermore, he realised with dismay and a feeling of dread: the urn in which Urla kept their opiate was almost empty. It was something he now enjoyed using every day.

In fact, he thought despairingly, he had come to depend on it. No more funds meant no more opiates.

"How will we manage without it?" he moaned.

In response, Urla calmly said, "I told you! We'll work something out! I've still got one or two ideas up my sleeve. ...Well, one, anyway."

"Like what?"

"I'm still owed some money from a..."

Suddenly Urla went quiet. She was going to say 'from a client', but that would have opened up a fresh line of questioning in Batim's mind. She wasn't ready for that yet; not under the present circumstances.

But Urla did not allow for Batim's state of agitation, or for his swift reaction to anything that might irritate him even more.

He was quick to respond.

"...Money from what?" he said curtly; his eyes still wild. "Where could you possibly get more money from?"

Urla hesitated, trying to think of an answer that might appease him and free her from further questioning.

"Well?" he snapped.

"It's... It's someone I..."

Urla faltered, alarmed by the sinister change in Batim's tone. But then a flash of inspiration gave her the answer.

"I sold something a while back and haven't been paid for it," she lied convincingly. "...Some candles, I think."

Do you know where this person lives?"

"Yes."

"Well come on then," he said, motioning her to follow. "Take me to the woman's house."

"It isn't...a woman,"

"Well, the man's house then!" Batim was shouting now. "Let's go, shall we?"

As soon as they reached the client's house, Urla regretted having suggested it.

She had lied to Batim about the reason she was owed money, which she hated doing. But he was in no mood to hear the real reason why a man might be indebted to her. So, assuming she was telling the truth, Batim waited for her out of sight.

He could tell straight away that the dialogue with her client was not going well. When the man roughly shoved her out and slammed the door in her face, Batim felt duty bound to intervene.

He promptly rushed to her side.

Checking first that Urla had not been hurt by the rough treatment, Batim hammered on the door. Then, getting no response, he banged again; this time shouting through the door for the cowardly man to be forthright and pay what was owed.

Suddenly Urla panicked. She needed to decide quickly which was more important to her – payment for services rendered or the esteem in which Batim presently held her; for the latter would most certainly be lost if he discovered her true profession.

Furthermore, Batim might be injured in the process of obtaining payment. Several of her clients had turned out to be aggressive sorts. This person appeared to be one of them. She feared Batim would not endure the beating he was likely to receive at his hands.

As Batim was about to kick the door in, Urla pulled him away. Using all her strength, she dragged him, protesting, further and further from her client's porch; while Batim at the same time hurled abuse in the direction of the house.

A safe distance away, Batim shook himself free of Urla's insistent grasp.

"Why did you try and stop me?" he shouted as though she were the man himself.

Don't yell at me!" she barked back. "It wasn't worth the danger you were in. He might have killed you!"

"I can take care of myself you know! ...And this creature owed you money – money we need!"

"Batim... It's not worth it! We'll be alright."

Yet Urla wasn't so sure; despite her insistence. He was very angry just now. She had reassured him only to lighten his mood, not because she believed it herself.

To make matters worse, when they arrived back at her home, the landlord was waiting for her.

"You are behind on your rent," he reminded her. "Make up the loss by dusk tomorrow, or I will send the bailiff."

"What are we going to do?" she wailed forlornly later that night, when the reality of their situation had sunk in.

Batim, his mind numb, sullenly lay on the bed. He had said nothing since their return. All that crossed his mind was whether he should blame himself or Urla for the mess they seemed to be in. But by the next morning, after little or no sleep, he knew precisely what they must do.

"I think we should leave this city," he announced. "You and I can make a fresh start! Let's get out of this damnable hole and find somewhere better."

Urla, knowing now that her time in the basement room was nearing an end, had no choice but to agree.

"Alright, we'll leave today before the landlord comes back," she said tearfully.

CHAPTER 3

Carrying with them only as much as they could manage, Batim and Urla left for a new life.

It was with considerable sadness that Urla stood on the stairs and looked back into her room for the last time.

Ah, the memories! she reflected; before realising that not all the memories from her time there had been good ones. Maybe this move really would be for the better.

By this time, it was late in the afternoon. With no-one they could approach for accommodation, Urla suggested a good alternative would be her beach hideaway.

Batim had not been to the dunes since their first night together. It was a strange feeling, returning to a place of such significance, yet under different circumstances.

They lay down on the soft grass to sleep.

There was no question of making love on this night. Weariness and uncertainty had robbed them of all passion. Tomorrow would be hectic; and even more exhausting if they were to put some distance between themselves and this soul-less city, as Batim now considered it to be.

The following morning, while Urla snatched a few more precious moments of rest, Batim strolled to the beach and listened to the pounding surf. It was a sound for which he held mixed feelings now. He would miss the coast, the sea and the bustle of port, but not the callousness of the many people he encountered there. Few he actually considered his friends. Resuval was about the only student with whom he struck up any sort of friendship during his short time at the Academie. There had been nobody else, except Urla.

Returning to their grassy retreat, Batim found Urla still asleep. He gazed down at her, wondering what this day and all the days to follow would hold for her. It was hard to imagine life without Urla now. As she slowly stirred and then awoke, he felt sure they would be together forever.

"I'm hungry," Urla said, soon after they set off again. "We need to find somewhere we can get a bite to eat."

"Using what for money, pray?"

"Have you none at all?" she asked in surprise. "I didn't think we were that low."

"Well, I certainly haven't got any; or even anything we can barter for food."

Urla continued walking, deep in thought. Dreamily, she fingered a ring on her little finger. It was a gold cygnet ring, given to her long ago by an infatuated client. But she did not return his affections, and neither did she give back the ring when she sent him packing. She wondered, now, whether they could exchange it for some food.

"Why not?" said Batim when she mentioned it to him. "It looks like the sort of ring any man would like to give to his wife. Who did you say gave it to you?"

It was..."

Urla sighed with the stress of still having to guard her secret. She tried to arrange her thoughts.

"It was given me by...by my father," she lied yet again. At least, he was old enough to be my father, she added privately.

Well into the afternoon, Batim and Urla, drooping from tiredness and the heat, came across a roadside stall.

An orchard owner had erected it to attract the custom of local people on their way out of town. He stood behind the counter now, encouraging them to buy. But instead of responding to his enticement, the two desperate travellers approached him with the valuable ring.

Batim assumed they would be given a fair amount of fruit in exchange for the jewellery; enough perhaps to see them through to the next day. However, the unscrupulous stallholder recognised that the young couple were down to their last saleable item and were in no position to make demands.

In return for their barter he handed them only a small quantity of fruit, stating that the ring was merely worth its melted-down value; that the return on gold bullion was pitiful for a tradesman, and they should think themselves lucky he was considerate enough to take it off their hands.

Urla objected strongly.

Voicing language that would have made even Lucifer blush, she accused him of underhand dealing; a sentiment with which Batim agreed completely.

In a rage, he took hold of the vendor's stall and pushed it over, sending fruit baskets crashing onto the road.

With only slight gratification for the way in which they had been treated, the pair hurried away as the stallholder frantically gathered together his remaining produce before it became spoiled.

"The man deserved it," said Urla when they were well out of sight.

It was quiet out in the countryside. Very little traffic used the road through these wooded hills.

Although Urla had lived in the area all her life she had never ventured this way before. And Batim, more recently settled in the region, had had no occasion to head off into the hills either. So, as far as the runaways were concerned, they were entering unfamiliar territory.

Neither of them even knew where the road led, except that in the distance there appeared to be a mountainous peninsula.

But somebody else apparently knew where it led, for not long afterwards, the rumbling of heavy wheels behind them caused both to stop and see what was coming.

Batim shot Urla a look.

"We might be able to get a ride on it," he said quickly. He remembered how his parents told him about the lift a man called Halished gave them; a lift that turned out to be a catalyst for their mission.

Maybe he and Urla would have the same kind of luck.

With the approach of the lumbering wagon, laden with logs for the mill, it was obvious that there would not be room for even one extra passenger, let alone both of the weary walkers, and so Batim let it go by. The next one to pass, sometime later, did not even respond to his attempts to stop it, inflaming his anger once more.

But for the fact that he was exhausted, Batim would most certainly have hurled venomous insults at the driver.

He and Urla were now both weary and hungry again; the fruit having sustained them only briefly. Neither knew where they were heading, or where they might spend the night; for dusk was not far off, and Urla was showing signs of distress.

"I'm sorry, but I've had enough," she complained. "Can we look for a nice sheltered spot and get some sleep? I don't think we're not going to die from starvation; not today, anyway."

Batim grunted disdainfully. Why was everything so hard for them? His parents didn't have this trouble — their plans all fell into place. Was it because they were on a mission from Yavros, and he merely exercising his own will?

Batim could not determine if his guess was correct. He was too tired to try and work it out.

While Urla rested on the grassy verge, the couple heard the now familiar sound of wheels again, and looked back along the road.

Urla pulled herself up, greatly encouraged when she realised that it was a pair of horses pulling a cart. Maybe they could persuade the driver to stop this time. And then an idea came to her: if she pretended to be ill, he might take pity.

Without telling Batim of her plan, she feigned a swoon; collapsing at his feet shortly before the vehicle arrived. Batim, thinking that she really had fainted, dropped to his knees, but with half an eye still on his potential transport. He did not want to risk missing out again.

As the driver drew level with them, Batim hailed him and begged assistance for his companion.

"Not likely," replied the driver without even slowing down. "I've heard about you two, and what you did earlier to that stallholder – robbing him of his livelihood indeed! You're not to be trusted!"

"What!" cried Batim in surprise.

"What?" queried Urla at the same time; her pretence forgotten, now that an allegation was being made against them. "Surely he can't mean the incident with the fruit stall," she said.

Suddenly Batim's demeanour changed.

All at once his frustration intensified. He ran alongside the cart, swearing violently and demanding that the driver stop immediately.

Stumbling, Urla tried to keep up; hoping to explain in a quieter manner that there must be a misunderstanding, and that they didn't do anything terrible. But her pleading only infuriated the driver more.

Moments later, as Batim reached the end of his tether, something snapped in him. With a burst of failing energy, he leapt up onto the cart.

Batim had only intended to put a hard word on the driver; no more than to force him to stop the cart so that Urla could climb up. For despite her unexpected and very sudden recovery, he was still unsure of her well-being.

However, in the ensuing struggle between Batim and the driver, a disaster occurred.

In retrospect, Batim was never quite sure exactly what took place just then; it all happened so quickly. The driver, startled by the sudden assault, lost his balance as he stood to fight off his adversary. Then, by accident, he fell under the cart; which dragged him under its wheels for quite some distance, before the horses finally came to a halt.

Urla screamed. Frantic, she hurried to the motionless body on the ground.

By now, Batim had leapt down from the wagon and was inspecting the victim.

It was a grizzly sight that greeted them. The driver had been pulled, face down, along the road's rough surface. Urla could see, from the pool of blood quickly forming underneath him, that he was severely lacerated about the head and upper body.

"You've killed him!" shrieked Urla, looking up at Batim; her eyes wide with fear.

"No I haven't; it was just an accident," Batim protested. "We struggled and he lost his balance...that's all. Besides," he added hopefully. "He may not be dead."

Urla squatted beside the driver. She felt for a pulse, but found nothing.

"I think he is!" she cried in alarm.

"No, he's not. He can't be!" responded Batim defiantly. "Here, let me try!"

Yet he, too, found no sign of life.

Suddenly, terror overcame Batim. It looked for all the world that he had killed a man. A twinge of remorse began to filter into his heart, but then it vanished abruptly at the realisation that he was now in serious trouble.

Thinking quickly, Batim said, "Come on, we'll get him off the road."

He grabbed hold of the man's arms, motioning Urla to take the feet, and together they dragged the heavy corpse off the stones and into a shallow ditch, leaving a trail of blood and skin on the road's surface as they did so.

"Right, let's get out of here. We'll take the cart."

Urla was appalled by everything that had transpired, and suddenly felt very sick. While Batim quickly returned to the cart and its waiting horses, she vomited.

"Hurry up!" Batim screamed after her. "We need to get away from here!"

But he could see she was unwell. Reluctantly he ran back to her; then helped her to the cart and lifted her up. Taking hold of the reins, he snapped them over the backs of the horses.

Instantly they sprang forward in an enforced canter.

With the horses maintaining a steady pace Urla, perched beside Batim, turned round frequently to check if anyone was following. She only relaxed her vigil when the scene of the accident was well behind them, and when Batim told her to stop fidgeting.

"For goodness sake, Urla," he said harshly. "Nobody's coming after us because nobody witnessed it! Just relax; you're driving me mad!"

But then, while Urla obediently sat still, Batim said in capitulation, 'If you want something to do, see what's in the wagon. We might be able to sell it for cash. I'm hungry and I want a pipe."

Urla turned round in the seat again. A heavy tarpaulin, secured at all four corners with knotted ropes, covered the contents of the cart. To see what was underneath it she would need to stop the cart and undo the ties. Yet Batim's mood was such that she knew he would not be willing to stop, and so she had no choice but to make the best of the existing situation.

Hanging on for dear life to the side of the pitching cart, she loosened the fiddly knot in the corner closest to her. At length she succeeded, but feeling she had strained every muscle in her body.

Stopping for a moment to straighten her sore back and to draw breath, she pulled back the corner to reveal the contents. And what she saw made her squeal with delight.

Batim, however, misinterpreted her squeal as a shriek of alarm. He cringed and halted the beasts in order to take a look, expecting to see something that would fill him with revulsion.

Instead, he roared with unrestrained laughter.

The back of the cart contained several baskets, each full of freshly baked bread of all shapes and sizes. It looked to the two observers that this was no ordinary delivery of bread, but was bound for an occasion of sorts: perhaps a wedding. But the prospect of a gathering eagerly awaiting food for their table did not matter to Batim and Urla. All that interested them was the fact that here was food to stave off their own hunger.

They hauled out one basket after another. Together they gnawed at the aromatic loaves; then tossed the scraps out for birds, who soon began to flock behind the cart.

Batim revelled in their unexpected good fortune. "This lot will keep us going for a couple of days," he stated as they journeyed on; all thought of how they came by the cart and its welcome cargo conveniently fading.

He prided himself that, just like his parents before him, he could also attract what he needed – and without having to call on Yavros.

In a state of high elation, he shouted within his mind, "Who needs Yavros anyway – I don't!"

Yet, Batim's elation was to be short-lived. His actions may have gone unnoticed by the general population, but one being certainly saw and heard everything; the same being who had made sure that the wagon they stole would make Batim hungry – not just for bread, but for the prospect of further mischief...

Lucifer snorted contemptuously when Batim made his rash pronouncement.

"You ungrateful whippersnapper!" he snarled under his breath. "Don't you know it was I, Lucifer, who saved you from pursuit; not you. It was I who gave you sustenance when you needed it – not you! And you, my friend, must learn the hard way that of yourself you are nothing!"

Batim and Urla feasted bountifully on their find.

Soon afterwards Urla, perched precariously up on the front of the wagon, found herself nodding off to sleep.

"Why don't you lie down in the cart and get some rest," Batim suggested, after several anxious moments when he feared she might fall. "There's plenty of room in the back, now that we've tossed out some of the baskets."

Urla chose not to argue: she could hardly keep her eyes open. She clambered over her seat, and was about to lift the tarpaulin ready to slide beneath it, when something caught her eye.

It was still way in the distance behind them; too far to see clearly. But of one thing she was certain. Whatever had attracted her attention was moving up fast. In fact, it appeared to be coming after them.

"Batim!" she shrieked. "Look!"

Twisting around, Batim followed both her gaze and the direction in which she was pointing. Even as he adjusted his vision to take in the fast-moving spec, he sensed in an instant that somebody meant business. ...But who with? Not them, surely? They were way out in the countryside when Batim took over the wagon from its unfortunate driver. Nobody had been around to see the incident when it happened. What's more, the non-arrival of the cart at its destination could not yet have been detected. ...So the rider of the fast approaching horse could not possibly be chasing them!

...Yet it was.

Batim was unaware that the cartload of bread had been the responsibility of not one man, but two. The first driver had instructed his colleague to go on ahead while he saw to another matter, with the intention of joining him later on horseback. While the latter was catching up, he noticed the bloody mess on the road.

At first he knew nothing of the dead victim's identity, but stopped to investigate because he could not ignore the fact that something terrible had occurred. It was therefore with horror that he discovered the body in the ditch to be his friend.

Assuming the slaughter had happened only recently, he left in pursuit of the offenders who would not, he guessed, be very far ahead.

Within moments came the man's first shout – a distinctive bellow ordering them to halt, which echoed around Batim and Urla in the forest they had now entered.

Straight away, Batim whipped the reins over the backs of the horses, forcing them to pick up their pace. Soon he had them moving as fast as they could, but they were no match for the swiftly moving filly.

Just then, they came to a fork in the road.

One of the roads carried on through a ravine to some significant destination; the other was a rough track leading uphill into the trees.

From Batim's perspective, the obvious route would be the road, so he chose the uphill track.

In an attempt to outwit their pursuer, Batim urged the tired horses up the hill. He quickly discovered they were surrounded by vegetation and well hidden from the road.

Abruptly, he reined in the snorting steeds and listened. Only the sound of their laboured breathing and the distant clatter of hooves coming closer broke the silence.

Batim held his breath, willing the horse and its rider to gallop by. When the sound of the hooves began to fade away, Batim breathed more freely. His ploy had worked.

But then, as he lifted the reins to set the cart in motion again, Urla stopped him.

"Wait a minute," she whispered, listening intently.

"What is it? I don't hear anything."

"That's just it," she said, trying to make out the muted clatter from hooves she hoped were disappearing into the distance. "I can't hear him anymore."

"He's gone, that's why," replied Batim, urging their own horses forward. Don't worry. We're safe now. The prize is still ours."

Then Urla let out a stifled scream.

"No! Stop!" she uttered in an urgent whisper, and held up her hand in warning.

Again the pair listened.

This time, breaking through the stillness of the forest, a different sound was heard: a rustle, then a cracking twig, as though some large predator was careering through the undergrowth in their direction.

"Damn it; he's coming after us!" cried Batim as quietly as his panic would allow. "Come on! Quickly!"

Together the two fugitives leapt down from their treasure and scrambled up into the forest. The noise made by the tracker was soon drowned out by their own commotion as they sought to escape.

Every so often Batim would stop, listen, and motion Urla to do the same, in the hope of hearing nothing but their own breathlessness. But each time they halted, they heard the same stomping sound; increasing in volume as it ascended far more speedily than they. Then, when Batim stopped for the umpteenth time, he realised that but for their panting, all had gone quiet.

It seemed to Batim that either they had given him the slip, or the gradient of the mountainside was too much for him to climb in a hurry.

"Maybe he was more interested in the cart and horses," suggested Urla; not suspecting that he knew of the other driver's demise – and that they were responsible for it.

"Even so, we need to keep going now. The further we are from the road, the safer we will be."

Batim actually had no idea where they were heading, or why. To continue climbing the mountainside just seemed like the best option.

When there had been no sign of the pursuer for some time, Batim started to believe, or at least to hope, that he had given up chasing them altogether. ...And that Urla was right in saying he only wanted the cart and its somewhat depleted load.

Before long the vegetation thinned to little more than barren rock, offering nowhere to hide if they needed to.

Furthermore, it was getting cold.

Not only were they now at a high altitude and on the cooler side of the mountain, but also a fine mist had begun to descend; chilling them both to the bone as it seeped into their clothing.

"I'm getting...really cold now," complained Urla.

She had begun to shiver despite the warming exertion of the climb.

"...Same here," Batim. "I wish I knew...where we are."

He stopped momentarily to catch his breath. Then, with nothing better to do, he forged ahead again.

"We'll stay warmer if we keep moving," he said.

The rocky landscape offered no clues as to which was the best way to go. However, when they came across a stream flowing away from them, Batim decided they must have crossed the apex of the peninsula, and should soon start to descend.

Encouraged, they followed the stream through rocky terrain to the tree line, where they hoped to find shelter.

On their way down, heavy rain set in.

There was little shelter from the downpour now; even under thick forest canopy.

Then, by chance and despite the onset of nightfall, Urla spotted something through the trees.

It was a cabin; or more precisely, a rough shack where logs had been set one upon another to form the walls, and a sloping straw roof erected to channel the rain.

The ends of the straw now ran with rainwater, creating a curtain of water beads which the pair would need to cut through in order to get to the door. Yet, the rainfall was now so heavy that neither cared about the additional soaking they would receive from it, nor whether the cabin was in fact occupied. Their only concern was finding some shelter before they caught their death of cold.

Batim arrived at the cabin first. He rattled the crudely made door to announce his arrival, in case somebody was inside. A lack of response indicated the place was empty.

Assuming this to be so, Batim straightaway pushed the door open; almost falling over himself as it readily gave way to the force of his hand.

The two hurried in.

Urla shivered uncontrollably; for it was bitterly cold up in the mountains, and their mad scramble to find shelter had not warmed her.

Batim looked around the abandoned cabin; obviously unused for some time as the wind had blown bits of brush through numerous gaps in its walls. Yet it was dry, and for now it was their refuge.

The cabin was built decades earlier by a hunter; for deer were plentiful in the region at the time and fetched a high price. To the new occupants, it appeared that the hunter would have utilised the cabin frequently, as the tools of his trade still lay on a shelf. Batim determined this from an old rusty knife and a set of traps; also rusted with age.

In a dingy, dusty corner of the cabin he caught sight of something hanging from the wall. It was a full-sized deer pelt: old and worn, but nevertheless whole. He carefully took down the pelt, shook off the dust and then wrapped it around Urla's trembling body.

For the moment his own need of warmth took second place to hers.

Batim and Urla sat the night out, sleeping but little for the cold. By morning the sun shone again, giving Batim the opportunity to look out over the view they missed during the rainstorm; and a little more closely at the hovel they had just made their home.

"It really is a shamble of a cabin," he remarked to Urla when she came out to warm herself in the sunshine.

But it had been available in a time of crisis, and for that Batim was grateful.

However, without the bread from the wagon, they had nothing to eat and were now both hungry again. Batim wondered how far from civilisation they had strayed, and mounted a hillock to survey his surroundings.

Away in the distance, the coast was clearly visible down a valley. The stream, which had been their guide the night before, continued on its journey to the sea. No great port could be seen at the mouth of this one; only a small fishing village. Squinting in the sunlight Batim made out a dotted line of buildings flanking the tiny harbour. It would take a day to get there, he deduced.

Then he remembered that he and Urla were actually fugitives and should think twice about joining the outside world again just yet.

Their next meal would have to wait.

It seemed to Batim, as he gazed into the distance, that they had no alternative but to remain in the cabin. He was a wanted man without private means, and his plans for the future must be considered with care.

How did I get into this situation? he pondered.

If his parents found out what had become of him over the last few weeks they would be appalled.

He wondered if the Academie had informed them of his dismissal. Surely word must have reached them by now. Batim knew of no other student who had fallen upon such misfortune in so short a space of time. In fact, he knew of no other student who had even been expelled from the Academie at all...

"Why me?" he asked silently, searching his mind for a possible explanation. "What have I done wrong?"

"You've done nothing wrong, my friend," an inconspicuous voice whispered within his mind. "You are exactly where I want you."

Stumbling across the cabin at an opportune time was no coincidence; either. Batim's decision to cross the peninsula instead of taking the coast road – this, too, was all part of a plan...Lucifer's plan.

However, it was fortunate for Lucifer that the rainstorm compelled the outlaw pair to seek shelter within the cabin, instead of merely inspecting it out of curiosity, as he had originally intended.

Neither was it part of his scheme that Batim, while he stood feeling sorry for himself and their plight, should spot the white bobtail of a young rabbit as it bounded into the shelter of some bushes, and thus realise what he could do to alleviate their need.

"Food!" said Batim out loud, his mind snapping back to the reality of their situation; in particular, that they were both hungry. "I wonder if I could catch something."

He returned to the cabin and took another look at the traps and knife the previous occupant left behind.

"What are you doing?" asked Urla; still warming herself in the sun.

"I'm going to try and catch a rabbit," he replied, testing the sharpness of the blade across the back of his thumb. It barely left a dent in his skin.

"What for?" asked Urla. The idea of killing something in order to eat had not crossed her mind.

Batim turned to face her, holding up one of the traps.

"We're both starving. We can hardly go to a market to buy provisions, and there's nothing around here; so we've got no option but this..." he exclaimed, waving the trap at her. "...If I can get the knife sharpened, that is!"

Urla was horrified; she hated the sight of blood. Killing to eat had never before been part of her life experience. She usually bought meat from a stall at the market; ready cured for cooking. To eat meat from a freshly killed animal was barbaric, to her way of thinking. ...And who did Batim assume would prepare it? Not her!

"Batim, do we have to?" she implored, suspecting he would insist on her help. "I don't think I could handle a dead animal – skin it and everything."

"Don't worry – I'll do that," he said, gallantly.

Yet, Batim really had no idea what would be involved when and if he caught anything; he, too, was used to meat cooked and ready to serve. But he had promised do it, and they were both hungry; so there was no time to lose.

With difficulty, he freed the traps up enough to release their mechanism, but the knife, he knew, would be no use unless it was sharpened.

"The hunter must have had an implement on which to sharpen it," Batim told Urla, who regarded him uneasily.

He rummaged among some discarded pots under the shelf, looking for anything that might be of use; but found nothing. Then he noticed a pile of old parchments in the corner from where he had taken down the deerskin.

Picking up the pile to look underneath, some pieces of parchment fell to the floor, revealing incomprehensible markings; but Batim was too intent on his purpose to take any notice of them.

Meanwhile Urla, trying to be of help to him, joined in with the search.

"What exactly are you looking for?" she asked.

"I don't really know. Just anything that might sharpen a blunt knife."

"...Like this?" she said, holding up a flat stone that she had found covered in dust.

"What is it?" asked Batim. He took it from her, blew off the dust, and looked at it closely. "I think it might be flint. The hunter probably used it himself. ...Well done, Urla."

In fact, several more pieces of the flint emerged from the debris inside the cabin. They represented not only the means of preparing meat to eat, but also making the fire on which to cook it. Batim had seen it used before and was anxious to try it for himself.

Urla looked on, forcing herself to learn; then while he went off to set the traps, she made up a fire. After a few attempts with the flint she had coaxed it into life. Then she searched the cabin for utensils with which she could cook whatever the nervous trapper managed to catch.

Yet her efforts proved to be futile, for Batim caught nothing that day.

Twice before sundown he inspected the traps, but no creature had ventured into them. Demoralised and now ravenous, Urla began to feel weak from lack of food. She complained bitterly when he returned empty-handed.

"I can't believe we must go another night with nothing to eat," she wailed as they waited it out in the cabin. "I've never been so hungry in all my life."

Batim went off again early the next morning, when the first traces of dawn had dispelled the darkness just enough for him to see.

Anxious to check his traps again, but also desperate for food, he felt he couldn't wait until the sun came up. In the dim morning light he stumbled round rocks and scraped past prickly bushes to get to the now familiar trap sites. By the time he arrived at the second of them, his legs and hands were scratched and bruised. But his sacrifice was worth it; for the trap held the still-warm body of a large, dead rabbit.

With a shriek of delight and relief Batim pounced on the trap and opened its jaws, freeing the corpse. He examined it closely, with no feeling of remorse for having killed one of Yavros' creatures, but rather ecstatic that at last he had succeeded in catching something.

He was so excited by the success that in his haste to show it to Urla he almost forgot there was one more trap to inspect. As he made his way carefully across the bank that led to it, he looked up and saw her sliding down the hill towards him.

"Look what I've caught!" he exclaimed triumphantly, holding up the rabbit by its legs.

"I heard you shout, but couldn't tell if it was because you'd trapped something or because you've hurt yourself," Urla said breathlessly when she caught up with him. She looked at the rabbit, and was saddened by its wretched appearance.

214

"Well it was the former, glad to say," Batim responded; oblivious of Urla's reaction to his catch. "I've got one more trap to inspect and then I'll be home to skin it." He was looking forward to utilising the newly sharpened knife.

"Home!" laughed Urla. "Did you say 'home'?" But then she retracted her comment. "Never mind," she added. "I'll go back 'home' and get everything ready. I can't wait – I'm starving!"

Urla hurried back to the cabin. She gathered together the knife and the only pot she had found which wasn't broken. The stream was just a short scramble down the slope, and she filled the pot to the brim, predicting there would be some spillage during her struggle back up again. Then she set to work on re-lighting the fire.

By the time Batim returned with only the one rabbit, and then enthusiastically skinned and dismembered it – an operation she refused to watch – Urla was almost ready to cook the meat. With nothing to add to the stew to give it flavour, the resulting meal would no doubt be tasteless, but tasteless food, they decided, was better than no food at all. Then, their spirits brighter, the couple enjoyed their first meal in well over a day. Afterwards, with more energy than before, they contemplated their future.

"I don't think it would be wise to move on from here yet," Batim told her; receiving a stunned look in return.

"But how can we stay?" questioned Urla. "Look at this place...it's a hovel! There are holes in the walls, there's dirt everywhere and it's still got the rubbish from its previous occupant. Can't we find somewhere else? Just the thought of it makes me feel sick."

"There is nowhere else!" insisted Batim helplessly. "We were really very lucky to find this place!"

215

He looked around the neglected cabin, identifying with Urla's revulsion of their surroundings but at the same time looking for a positive element on which to capitalise.

"We could tidy it up," he added, plaintively. "With a bit of effort we can make it fairly habitable."

Urla fell silent.

Defeated, she went outside and sat on the rickety step, while the reality of his implication sunk in. Batim followed and sat beside her.

He slid his arm around her shoulder.

"We'll be alright," he said with encouragement. "We've just proved we can fend for ourselves."

"You make it sound like we'll be here for a long time. ...And I don't want to live off rabbit stew. It was horrible, even if we were hungry!"

Batim laughed. "Yes, I suppose it was tasteless. It was good though, don't you think?" He was trying desperately to brighten Urla's outlook. "We can always try something else. The hunter must have lived independently. If he did it, why can't we?"

Urla sighed. She knew he was right.

Batim sensed her capitulation, and stood up again. "I'm going to get started on the tidy up," he said. "You don't have to help if you don't want to."

Urla reluctantly followed him back into the cabin. After all, she had to admit, they were in this together and so must work together. It wasn't fair that he should be left to do all the clearing up by himself.

It took most of the day to clean out the cabin.

Batim made a couple of brooms from bushy branches, and when each broom began causing more mess than it was sweeping up, he renewed it.

By late afternoon the pair were covered in dirt; with eyes smarting and lungs bursting from inhaled dust. Yet, they also felt a welcome sense of achievement from their day's work, and Batim was relieved to see Urla in a more positive frame of mind.

Amongst the rubbish they found enough good sacking to make up two comfortable beds, and other equipment the hunter once used; including some candles he had roughly made out of bees wax. The sheets of parchment, discarded untidily on the floor the previous day, now lay in a neat pile.

"What do you want to do with that stuff?" asked Urla, pointing to them. "We could use them to light the fire."

"What are they?" asked Batim.

"I don't know. I just tidied them with everything else."

Batim bent over the parchments and delicately picked up the top one. There were about a dozen in all. The piece he held contained strange symbols in columns; now faded with age but each neatly drawn; giving him the impression it was writing rather than artwork.

Urla looked over them, too. She picked up some more of the fragile pieces. They all seemed to contain the same indiscernible markings.

"I've seen this sort of thing before," she told him. "It's a foreign language. They should burn very well, though."

"I wonder what they're doing in a trapper's hut."

"Maybe the cabin was his retreat," Urla suggested.

Batim looked through the remainder and was about to dismiss them as being of no interest, when he came to the last piece, which was different. This was a drawing; circular in shape with symmetrical markings within the circle. And furthermore, he recognised it.

...At least, it seemed familiar.

Then he remembered.

"I know what this is, too," he said. "It's a mantra."

"Excellent!" cried Lucifer. "He's found it. Carry on, my boy. You're doing nicely."

"A mantra?" asked Urla, coming up to take a closer look. "What's a mantra?"

Batim laughed. "That's what I said when I first saw one. By chance I caught sight of a mantra belonging to a fellow student, and asked what it was. At the time he told me it was helpful in focusing on higher things."

"You mean, like praying to the sun?"

"I suppose so."

"Perhaps the trapper liked to 'focus on higher things', too," she said, and added frivolously, "We should give it a try as well!"

Lucifer sniggered. "Well done, Slave – and I didn't need to prompt you with that one! It's heartening to see initiative in a lesser being!"

"Yes, we could do with a little higher assistance," retorted Batim, unaware of the supernatural chit-chat going on around them. "When we've finished work for the day we might set it up and see where it leads."

However, before he could even consider an evening of enlightenment, there was still the problem of finding some more food.

Lucifer had heard their conversation about not wanting to live off rabbit stew, and although he had no idea what that meant, he was astute enough to realise that terran spirits need a variety of food in order to survive. So, before dusk descended again on the mountain habitat, he quickly set the wheels in motion for Batim to find another source of food.

This came in the form of fruit; yet not fruit picked from a tree, but an offering dropped at his feet.

When it landed, Batim jumped back in alarm; until he realised what it was.

"It's a fig," he said, and bent to pick it up.

He looked around to see where it had come from. A large bird sat in a nearby tree, squawking as if to let Batim know he was holding its property.

"The bird must have dropped it as it flew over," he told Urla, who also witnessed the incident. "I wonder where it came from."

"There'll be a tree close by; let's look for it," she said. "We'll go in opposite directions."

As was Lucifer's intention, they found their source of fruit before darkness set in.

While searching, Urla came across a small grove of fig trees on the other side of the stream. She called out to announce the find. Then, filling the folds of her skirt with ripe figs, she made her way back to the cabin.

That night they feasted with welcome merriment. Their humble cabin was beginning to feel more like home now. They had light, heat, food and comfort, and a newfound sense of wellbeing; something that had been missing from their lives ever since they fled Urla's apartment only a few days previously.

And now, Batim decided; or rather, Lucifer decided, they also had an interest: the mantra. Batim was looking forward to trying out the mysterious charm.

As soon as their meal was over he set up the stiff piece of parchment on the shelf, with a candle on either side both for light and dramatic effect. He maintained the colours of the mantra's design showed up better in light from the candles than normal daylight.

Then he looked over it intently.

"There must be some meaning to these markings," he said, tracing over them with his finger. "We should have kept the others. Maybe they would have explained what this one is all about."

He took a step back to get a clearer perspective on the mantra, and found that by merely gazing at the circle, he felt like he was being drawn into it.

"Boy, this is powerful stuff!" he exclaimed.

"Let me try", asked Urla. She leant towards the mantra and peered into it.

Batim held out his arm to stop her. "I don't think you should get too close!"

He collected up the sacking from their beds, placed it on the floor in front of the shelf, and settled down onto it. But in order to look straight at the mantra, he needed to stretch upwards and peer over the edge of the shelf. So instead he moved around until he was kneeling up on his haunches.

"That's much better," he proclaimed and invited Urla to do the same.

"Aren't you supposed to chant something in front of a mantra?" she asked.

"I wouldn't know. This is the first time I've had anything to do with one. But you're right. It does seem that some sort of chant might be needed to help things along. What do you suggest?"

"Alright, Slave," growled Lucifer. "Don't overdo it – there's plenty of time for them to play into my hands. I'll tell you when I want the girl to be involved again."

Unexpectedly, Urla found she could make no suggestions in response to Batim's question.

"I don't know any chants," she snapped. "I just thought it might be a good idea to do it, that's all!"

Urla was surprised by her abrupt absence of inspiration, when the idea had been hers in the first place. Yet she thought no more about it and, sitting back on her heels, knelt before the mantra with Batim.

"Perhaps we should just remain quiet and look into the centre of it," he suggested after a few moments of silence. "It might help get us in the right frame of mind."

"...For what?" Urla asked. "What's supposed to happen when you 'focus on higher things'?"

"Not higher things, you silly girl," chided Lucifer, enjoying her naïvety. "...On my things!"

It was going to be easy taking control of this pair, he chuckled inwardly. Thanks to Slave, he already held sway over the girl's soul. Batim would soon belong to him, too.

As the terran couple quietly meditated on the mantra, Lucifer entered the spiritual conduit they were creating and approached them disguised as white light.

While they focused, their eyes slowly closing with what they thought to be ascending spirituality, Lucifer met his opponent face to face.

Batim was now experiencing a high not unlike his feelings of elation derived from the opiates. He felt as though he was gazing into the centre of Eternity; while all the time seeing only the mind-play initiated by Lucifer to trap them into believing this.

His gullible consciousness became so elevated in false wonderment, and so closed off from true spiritual wisdom, that he truly believed his perception to be reality.

Urla, too, had become transfixed by the experience, but her ability to focus was limited. As a full-blooded terran spirit she could maintain the elevated consciousness for only so long, whereas Batim, with his angel heritage, could have remained in that state forever, had he been given the opportunity.

But he was not given the opportunity.

When Urla had had enough euphoria, she sighed deeply and opened her eyes.

Looking across at Batim, she tried to speak to him; then realised he was not ready to come back down yet. After a few more minutes of quietness, she became bored and lightly touched him on the arm to attract his attention.

The shock of sudden intrusion brought Batim back to reality with a jolt. He cried out, his heart pounding wildly as his spirit abruptly descended back into his body.

Urla gasped in fright.

"Don't ever do that again!" he shouted at her, deeply disturbed by the effect her light touch had on his nervous system. "Don't ever touch me or do anything to bring me back, do you understand? If you do, I will kill you!"

Urla sprang to her feet in alarm, and rushed headlong out of the cabin.

She was frightened of him now. He had never spoken to her like that before. And even though it was completely dark, she felt safer outside than in the cabin with Batim; for she could not understand the sudden change in him. All she did was touch his arm.

Little did Urla know, that in the same moment Lucifer had also touched Batim.

As a result, his reaction to converging forces had caused a momentary arrest in him. Had it not been for Batim's youth and vitality, it would certainly have killed him.

From Batim's point of view, Urla had interrupted him as he was about to enter the realm of Eternity – or at least, what he perceived to be Eternity. He was sure something beautiful had happened just before Urla touched him, and he resented the intrusion. He would have given anything to remain in that state of euphoria; to own something of the same spirit that was within his angel parents. But it was too late. He was back in the cabin, his heart still pounding from the shock of what just happened.

Batim roared with frustration.

Outside, Urla heard his yell and slipped round the side of the cabin, shivering now from shock and the cold of the mountain night.

It was some time before Batim calmed down enough to realise what he had said, and that Urla was no longer there.

He got up and opened the door.

"Urla!" he called plaintively into the night. "I'm sorry! Please come back in; I really didn't mean it!"

Yet the hurtful words still rang in Urla's ears, and she retreated into the shadows – he had threatened to kill her! How could she trust him again? But then she heard his entreaty. It seemed the voice calling out to her was gentle; more like the Batim she had known all this time; not the monster he turned into a few minutes ago. Perhaps he had got over his rage...and it was so very cold outside. Maybe it would be alright to go in...

Cautiously, she stepped out into the dim light so that he could see her.

"There you are!" he said, relieved she had not strayed too far. It would have been impossible to find her in the dark of a moonless night. "Are you alright?" he asked.

"Yes," she said shakily.

With her head down to avoid eye contact she walked straight past him and into the warmth of the cabin.

He followed her in, feeling sheepish and intensely guilty for his behaviour.

"I do apologise for threatening you like that; something came over me and I lost control," he confessed.

"I was frightened – you've never spoken to me like that before. All I did was touch you."

"It may not have seemed very much to you, but when you touched me I was experiencing something amazing in meditation. The shock of being roused from it was more than I could bear. ...I've got over it now, though."

He approached Urla to put his arms around her, but she was not ready for normality, and side-stepped him on the pretext of seeking warmth from the fire.

"If you don't mind," she said; "I'm really cold. I think I'll bring my bed over by the fire for the night."

Throughout the long hours of darkness, Batim felt deeply remorseful for his behaviour, and sorry that this would be their first night sleeping apart.

In actual fact, this was also to be their last night as a couple; for the following day, unknown to either of them just then, they would part company forever.

CHAPTER 4

Urla slept little. By daybreak her nerves were frazzled and her head pounded. During the night she heard Batim, though sound asleep, making strange noises as if haunted by something sinister.

That was how it sounded to her.

In the dimly lit cabin, his noises were unsettling for the uneasy girl, especially after what had transpired earlier.

At dawn she got up and went outside before Batim stirred. The cool air was refreshing, and she breathed in deeply; trying to clear her head and her heart of unwanted pressures.

While Slave's attention briefly wavered, Urla ran down to the stream, removed her garments and bathed in the clear water. She had heard that water cleanses the soul as well as the body, and the real Urla felt in need of thorough cleansing now.

However, the effect of cleansing also alerted Lucifer to Slave's inattention. He screamed at it to get back to work.

Immediately, Urla's sense of well-being was replaced by one of dread, and she returned to the cabin with a feeling of reluctance. She was almost there when a distant sound halted her. At first she thought it was a bird calling to its mate in the early morning, but this sounded terran. Automatically she turned around, and saw a man making his way up the path of the stream. He called again.

Urla quickly realised he was hailing her.

Taken by surprise at this worrying turn of events, she panicked and rushed inside the cabin, closing the flimsy door behind her.

The disturbance woke Batim, who gruffly demanded to know what all the noise was about.

"There's a man coming up the hill!" cried Urla in alarm.

Batim struggled to his feet and hurried to the window. Pulling back a corner of the makeshift curtain, he peered out. The man was almost upon them.

Batim swore under his breath.

"What does he want?" he hissed.

Frantically, he searched his mind for a possible reason for the visit, and came up with only one. ...But surely, he thought, if this man was coming to arrest him for theft or murder, he would not have come alone.

Batim flung open the door. Purposefully, he filled the doorway with his frame to show the unwelcome visitor he was not to be messed with.

The visitor, a tall, middle aged man, breathlessly halted in his tracks just below the cabin.

"Greetings," he said with reserved geniality.

Already intimidated by the unfriendly reception, the visitor recognised a need for caution. There on a mission yet to be accomplished, he elected to tread carefully with the two strangers.

"I wonder if I could speak with you?" he went on.

"What do you want?" said Batim curtly.

Not to be deterred, he ventured closer, looking directly at Batim.

"May I come in?" he asked.

Batim stood his ground. His mind raced as he continued to speculate on why the man had come.

Defensively, he insisted, "No you may not. Stay where you are and state your business."

The visitor sighed, realising his unannounced arrival had caused concern for the occupants of the cabin.

"I think I should explain," he said. "My name is Carva, but that's not important. I'm here because my father built this cabin and used it frequently up until his accident some years ago. He died recently, but not before asking me to retrieve something from the cabin that was very precious to him."

"Like what?" asked Batim, relieved that his interest was in the cabin and not its present inhabitants.

"May I please come in and take a look? It's probably not here, anyway."

Batim was becoming irritated with the man's ambiguity now. He said, "What could we possibly have that would be of interest to you?"

...Surely not the traps and other equipment, he thought to himself – it was all rusted with age. The only other thing the trapper left behind was the pile of old parchments. Perhaps that was it. There was only one way to find out.

Reluctantly, he stood to one side. "Come in then, and be quick about it."

The visitor glanced at him furtively as he did so.

Once inside, he looked around and complimented Urla on how homely she had made the little cabin.

She smiled in response, touched by a sincerity she had not experienced in a long time.

Here's a nice man who cared about his father's wishes, she thought. In his younger days I bet he spent time with him up here.

"I'm looking for a set of ancient manuscripts. They are writings from the east, and were of sentimental value to my father. He said they contained sacred wisdom from an earlier age, although I don't know what he meant by that."

The trapper cast his eyes over the contents of the cabin, expecting to see something that might resemble what he was looking for.

Had he arrived a couple of days earlier, he could well have noticed the parchments scattered on the dusty floor, but now that the cabin was clean and tidy he saw nothing except the mantra still propped up on the shelf.

The parchments containing valuable writings had been burnt along with all the other rubbish. However, this piece of information Batim was not about to divulge.

"As I'm sure you can see, there's nothing like that in here," he responded quickly; anxious to be rid of him.

Urla opened her mouth to comment, but Batim glared at her while Carva was distracted by the mantra.

He moved closer to inspect it. "This might be part of it," he said, carefully removing it from the shelf.

"No it's not!" insisted Batim. He extracted the fragile parchment from the visitor's fingers and put it back. "It belongs to us – to Urla. Doesn't it, Urla?"

Batim refrained from looking at her while he said this: he knew she would not approve of his lying.

However, Urla was alarmed by the tone of his voice and still wary of Batim's present frame of mind. She chose to back him up.

"Yes, it's mine," she also lied. "It helps you to focus on higher things. That's why we are here - the mountain's the perfect spot for it."

"So you see, your father's manuscripts are not here; he must have removed them when he left," Batim continued emphatically, hoping his would be the final word on the subject. "I'm afraid you've had a wasted journey."

"What was so special about the writings?" asked Urla, feeling guilty not just about lying, but more especially that they failed to recognise any significance in the parchments and discarded them.

"I never knew what they said," replied Carva. "It was my father who aspired to the teachings, not me. He was very interested in spiritual matters, especially the ancient philosophies which predated sun worship."

"And he came here for solitude?"

"Yes. Like you, he enjoyed the clean environment of the mountains. He said he felt closer to his creator up here."

Urla liked this man. He was a different type from Batim; older certainly, but much gentler by nature. She felt drawn to him, and wished she could leave this isolated place with him. Yet, she felt sure Batim would not let her go.

By now Batim was becoming impatient with the intruder's chitchat. "If there's nothing more, we'll bid you good-day," he said, holding the door open for Carva to leave.

Upset by Batim's continued hostility, Carva suddenly became annoyed. How dare the arrogant young man treat him like an outsider and try to get rid of him. It was his father who built and therefore owned the cabin, not this young upstart. The fact that he had brought his girl to it and turned it into a home made no difference to the ownership of the cabin. ...Not that he particularly wanted it, himself. He probably would never have set foot in it again, but for his father's request that the documents be retrieved. There was a matter of principle involved here...

"Just remember, my friend," he told Batim who was still waiting by the door. "This cabin belongs to me now. It may be old, but I have a far greater claim to it than you have, so

I'll thank you not to be in such a hurry to get rid of me. What are you really doing here, anyway?"

Urla cringed at the way the situation was deteriorating, and feared Batim would react badly. She knew enough of him now, or at least the Batim he had become, to assume he would not take kindly to such remarks from a stranger, even if the man was right. Abruptly she saw the need to step in before things got out of hand.

"We came in here to shelter from a storm a few days ago, and stayed," she said truthfully. "Your father's tools were very useful in making it habitable."

However, Carva was not convinced of the innocence of Urla's explanation. His curiosity aroused, he looked them both over.

"You're not on the run, are you?" he said, as a thought crossed his mind.

While in the locality, Carva had heard of an unfortunate merchant who was robbed and killed on a nearby trade route – supposedly by a young couple – and that nothing had been seen of them since. Could this be the pair?

Suddenly he realised he may have spoken his mind too soon. If his perceptions were right, then the young man might still be dangerous. He had certainly demonstrated he was very impatient. And if these were the criminals who had killed once already, then maybe they wouldn't think twice about killing again. He decided to backtrack, and withdraw his comment.

Before either could respond he said to Urla. "...But I must be mistaken. You are much too nice to be a fugitive."

Carva deliberately avoided making eye contact with Batim now. He knew without doubt what the girl's partner must be thinking, and hoped fervently that he'd covered his suspicions enough to fool him. Somehow he sensed Urla would not have been involved in the killing itself but was merely caught up in it; for she looked incapable of murder. He sensed, too, that she was unhappy about her present situation because she was so edgy – not just with him, but also with her partner.

For both of their sakes he needed to be careful.

"Alright then, as you're unable to help me, I'll be on my way," he continued jovially.

Carva made to leave, but found he could not.

Just as Batim had at first been anxious to show him the door, he now barred his way; suspecting their identity was no longer a secret. Despite Carva's affable farewell, he was not convinced of the visitor's sincerity.

"Make sure you tell nobody we're up here," he insisted; his hand on the man's chest in restraint.

Carva glared at him and tried to force his hand away.

Batim defiantly grabbed his wrist.

"Then you two do have something to hide?" exclaimed Carva, unable to contain his suspicions any longer. "I was right, wasn't I? You are on the run."

With a snap he twisted out of Batim's grasp.

Batim snarled back at him, "You're just guessing, and you've got no proof. If you know what's good for you, this will go no further. Please leave."

He beckoned to Urla and roughly took hold of her hand as a show of solidarity. However, the strength of his grasp caused her to wince in pain.

"You're hurting me!" she cried and tried to break free.

Urla panicked, for Batim still had her firmly in his grasp. She could say nothing to appease either man; caught now between the two of them.

Then fear got the better of her and she burst into tears.

Angered, Batim smacked her across the cheek with the back of his free hand.

Carva sprung to her defence.

"Hey, stop that! Now I know it was you who killed that poor man," he said, reaching for her. "Urla, do you really want to stay here?"

"Answer him, girl!" Batim shrieked, and hit her again. "Tell him you belong here with me!"

Urla dropped to her knees in a faint.

Fuelled by Lucifer, Batim's anger took over.

He was faced with antagonism on one side and betrayal on the other. His feeling of hostility towards both suddenly prevailed over everything else, and he had just one thing in mind.

"Get out!" he yelled, and flung Urla off like a piece of trash. "Get out both of you – before I kill you!"

Carva helped Urla onto her feet. The two scrambled out of the cabin and its hysterical occupant before he could do them further harm.

They ran down the hill towards the stream, with Batim shouting abuse after them from the cabin.

But then Batim had a change of heart about allowing them to go free, and his anger welled up again...after all two people could now identify him.

His first thought had been to take off in the opposite direction and get as far away from the wretched place as he could. Anybody else would probably have taken that option. But Batim was not his own person any more. He was under the influence of Lucifer, and just then Lucifer alone was pulling his strings.

Batim rushed back into the cabin and grabbed hold of the knife he used to skin the rabbit. Then he ran helter-skelter down the slope, uttering blood-curdling screams after the fleeing pair.

Hearing his screeches, Urla's courage failed her.

She parted from Carva and disappeared amongst the brush edging the stream.

Carva called after her, to no avail. Then he carried on his way down the slope.

Being fleet of foot, Batim soon caught up with the older man. He lunged at Carva; grabbing him around the waist.

Together they tumbled into the shallow stream, flailing and splashing as each struggled to control the other.

Moments later they fell silent; the one slumped dead in the trickling water, now running red with blood; the other waiting motionless in anticipation.

Batim got up and looked down at Carva's pitiful form. The father's knife was now embedded in the son's chest. Batim smirked at the thought.

He bent over his lifeless body and pulled the knife out; a feeling of achievement flooding through him. At last he was free. This man was no longer a menace.

But where was Urla?

Wracking his brain, he couldn't remember whether she separated from Carva at the stream or when the fugitives fled the cabin. In the heat of the moment he had failed to notice her whereabouts; and now he regretted it.

Surely she could not have gone all that far.

But Urla, stimulated by fear, had found her second wind and was well out of sight.

After leaving the stream she followed the line of bushes until it disappeared round the bend. Then, when she felt it was safe to do so, she hurried down into the valley below; never to be seen by Batim again.

By now, Batim was at a loss to know where to start looking for Urla.

Bewildered by all that had taken place, he decided to let Urla go, and reluctantly returned to the cabin.

Everything had happened so quickly that it did not even register with him that he was now responsible for another death. All he knew was that for the time being he was free from pressure.

Back inside, he knelt before the mantra again, for here lay his help and inspiration. Effortlessly he slipped into meditation; his mentor waiting anxiously to meet up with him again.

This time, Batim became aware of an actual presence. Then, assuming it to be the creator, he opened up his soul and let Lucifer in.

Lucifer was ecstatic; at last he had complete control of Batim. His objective reached, he decided to extricate Slave from its duties with Urla as she had become superfluous to his cause.

But what should he do with his minion now?

And then a wonderful idea came to him. He would give Slave even greater responsibility.

Instead of manipulating a mere girl, this time it would dominate none other than Batim himself. Accordingly, with Slave's already proven initiative, Lucifer felt confident that control over the lovechild of his arch-rival would be maintained. What's more, Lucifer realised excitedly; if Slave controlled Batim by actually possessing him, it meant that he would be at liberty to concentrate on a further aspect of his current quest for revenge.

He would seek retribution from the brat's philandering father, Salutat.

Batim remained at the cabin for the greater part of that fateful day.

In his transcendent state the hours slipped by quickly, and he was surprised to discover, when he finally emerged from it, that the daylight was fading.

Concerned now that Urla may have gone for help, he vacated the cabin. Without even closing the door behind him, he left in search of a new life. ...But not before rolling up the mantra and tucking it down the front of his tunic for safe-keeping.

With a flourish, Lucifer passed on responsibility of Batim's soul to Slave.

The cynical sprite from Hellion flew into raptures when Lucifer delivered the news, and would not stop grovelling before him in gratitude.

"None of that!" snarled Lucifer, who still regarded Slave only as a tool, not an identity. Roughly, he pushed it away. "I'm merely giving you greater responsibility – a more important job than the last one – so make sure you don't let me down."

"My master, I could never let you down," replied Slave, still ingratiating itself. "I will always serve you well."

On the other hand, no ritual accompanied Batim's change of guard.

When the time came, Lucifer merely shoved Slave into his soul as the weary terran, having fled through the night, stopped to rest on a bed of soft ferns; sheltered from the weather and possible eyewitnesses.

Batim was so tired that he fell into a deep slumber; unaware that his soul was being possessed. When he awoke the next morning, all he felt was a stiff back and a blinding headache; for Slave had not yet completed its alignment with his spirit. Then, when the aching lifted, he continued his bid to put as much distance between himself and the cabin as possible.

However, there was one small yet significant difference between the old Batim and his new, enslaved persona.

The young athlete had always been agile of mind and body, but once Slave took over, the languid sprite slowed him in his bid to escape. After a while, and considering all that he and Urla had endured of late, he began to think he was unwell.

Batim had never really been ill before; nor even knew what it felt like. Yet, he was sure the dragging feeling he now experienced could not be attributed to anything else. Certainly, it did not occur to him that his soul had been usurped; and by the same sprite that swooped on him in Urla's bedroom.

Now that Batim's loyal allegiance could be assured, Lucifer was free to address what he regarded as the next phase of his work.

Ever since Batim's disagreement with the authorities at the Academie, Lucifer was beginning to suspect that the registrar had not bothered to locate his former student's nomadic parents. This, he determined, must be remedied straight away; for their learning about Batim's expulsion was vital to his ongoing plans.

It was now crucial that he first locate and then inform the terran angels that he had secured the devotion of their wayward son.

Lucifer chortled with delight. He could not wait to see Angelina's reaction when she heard the news; for he had little sympathy for her these days. It was because she took up with Salutat in the first place that he felt the need for revenge. As a dispossessed angel he could never have her for himself, but he certainly wouldn't allow anyone else to have her either – especially not that pompous, interfering angel Salutat.

In order to effectively upset the angelic relationship, he came up with a plan.

As part of their self-appointed mission was to utilise Miekaale, Lucifer decided the best way to locate the pair was to find out where the Golden Angel had been working of late. It should then be a matter of determining which way Salutat was likely to go next. After all, he sniggered in recollection, it would not be the first time he had located Salutat in the mission field.

Congratulating himself for his ceaseless ingenuity, he put his plan to work.

Yet, Lucifer had overlooked a relevant factor when making his plans: his mind rarely functioned on a spiritual level these days.

He was now spending so much time in Eddren that his consciousness had become more like the terran nature he originated. As such, he did most of his thinking on a terran level, and could not get into any kind of meditative state. Thus, when he tried to concentrate on a task, his thinking prevented him from achieving anything.

Then, after frustrating himself with continual failure, he decided it might be better if he changed his location and returned to Hellion; there to focus on his objective without endless terran distraction.

...But could he trust Slave to continue with its duties in his absence?

Slave enjoyed the new experience of having a terran spirit all to itself. Without Lucifer's continual scrutiny it felt a sense of freedom, such as it had not experienced since its own terran life.

During random moments of inactivity, it recalled what that was like.

Ah, those were the days!

There was much to be said for a life of impropriety, even if it did land him in Hellion. However, those days were long gone, and Slave dared not reminisce on a life that could never be again. It was too conscious of Lucifer's authority – and of Lucifer's reprisal if it strayed from the straight-and-narrow path of its new role.

So straight-and-narrow it was from now on. Slave was determined to earn recognition from the great fallen angel once and for all.

And it had a pretty good idea how to go about it.

Despite his new lumbering gait, Batim travelled a long way in only a short space of time. It troubled him that he could not figure out what was causing his sluggishness. ...Maybe he was just plain hungry.

As he passed through settlements and isolated homes in his quest for a safe haven, he became adept at stealing, unobserved, a loaf of bread or a pitcher of the local wine.

Then, after several weeks of travelling around, slowly working his way further into the interior of the country, he noticed that the landscape was becoming desert like.

Batim had heard about deserts from his father – how in another life he had lived in an arid land, and how difficult living conditions were in such a place. So he chose to head away from the desert, especially as he was dependant on vegetation for cover and water for basic survival.

Yet, he still had his knife, and a talent for hunting that was now well honed. He would never go hungry again.

"I am a true survivor," he declared with pride. "I don't need anybody or anything in order to succeed!"

Batim frequently chuckled when he reflected on the many ways in which his cunning had helped him of late; and Slave always saw to it that he went undetected.

One area of the country particularly appealed to Batim. It was warm, fertile, and far enough away from the coastal town that none of the local people would be aware of his previous activities.

After a while he began to feel safer out in the open, and confident enough in his abilities that he would never get caught while stealing. Then one day, when Slave felt sure that Lucifer would approve its choice of location, the sprite gave Batim an incentive to regard the place as home.

It happened this way:

Batim was an accidental witness to a dispute between two brothers. By the time he arrived on the scene, the quarrel had progressed from a verbal argument to physical abuse. He noticed that one of the brothers appeared to be the underdog, even though the unwitting observer felt he was in fact in the right.

During a brief hiatus in the struggle, Batim asked him if he could be of help. This was a gesture that surprised all three men. The underdog brother was agreeably surprised that somebody was willing to help him, the aggressive one was acutely surprised because he considered his brother to be in the wrong, and Batim was probably the most surprised of all when he realised it was the first time he had spoken to another terran for a very long time.

The strange sound of his own voice in conversation made him suddenly tongue-tied, and he wished he had kept out of it. But it was too late. Slave wanted him involved in this dispute, and made sure he would be.

"What has any of this got to do with you?" challenged the aggressive brother.

He advanced purposefully on Batim, at the same time gesticulating with both arms for him to go away. But Batim was unmoved.

"Take no notice of him," said the underdog brother as he stepped between the two. "He's just a bully who won't take no for an answer." Then he warned his sibling, "Don't you think you've said enough for one day?"

"Alright; I'm going," retorted the other and, shaking his fist at Batim, he walked off swearing under his breath.

The passive brother winked at Batim.

"Good; that got rid of him," he said. "...And thank you for your help."

"Maybe I shouldn't have stepped in," said Batim, feeling guilty about interfering in something that was really none of his concern.

"Don't worry about it. I get it from him all the time. You see, we're step-brothers; we have the same father. And just as our respective mothers were very different, so are we. I guess that's where we get our competitive spirit."

"I think I understand," said Batim, still surprised to be socialising with another person after weeks of solitude.

"Do you live around here?" the brother went on.

"No. Well, not yet, although I'm thinking about it."

"Then you'll be looking for work? I'm always recruiting good workers."

"Actually, I haven't thought about that yet."

"Well, when you've made up your mind, come and see me. I live in the big house at the top of the hill."

He pointed to an impressive villa that looked out over the entire region.

"I own the local vineyard, and we'll be picking the crop soon, so don't take too long. I'll pay you well."

Batim could not believe his luck. In only a matter of minutes he had gone from thinking himself a fugitive to being offered employment. What good fortune could have sparked that off?

He would never know it was Slave who initiated his good fortune; for no advancement in Batim's life, but solely to impress Lucifer.

Batim accepted the offer with enthusiasm.

The job at last gave him stability, and something to get his teeth into. For a while, he began to feel he was living a normal life again.

But when Lucifer's minion is in control, nothing good lasts forever.

CHAPTER 5

In the meantime, Salutat and Angelina were oblivious of the happenings in their son's life.

At night, Angelina regularly prayed to Yavros for Batim's academic success, and for his happiness in general. She was unaware, though, that Yavros had long since ceased bestowing graces upon Batim.

As far as Yavros was concerned, Angelina's son had chosen terran nature over his intrinsic spirituality, and was now accountable for his own actions.

Batim, as a full terran spirit, was exercising free will and there was nothing Yavros could do to alleviate or cushion the consequences he would have to face.

Even though millennia had passed since the downfall of Hominus and Womah, free will was still a factor in terran existence and therefore remained important to Yavros. He could have easily withdrawn it from the consciousness of future generations, but chose not to. Without free will he could never hope to recover the voluntary devotion for which he initiated it in the first place.

In times of exasperation he had thought to intervene in a dramatic way and give the terran spirits something of a shake-up; to make them consider what they were doing, and remember just who they were. Yet he knew it was not really the answer. A terran soul's return to him had to be a conscious choice. And so it was with reluctance that he sat back and forlornly watched as Batim faltered.

Yavros actually considered Lucifer's practices in Eddren to be quite insidious. The manner in which he had taken hold of an innocent young man and twisted his values until everything taught him by his angel parents was lost, upset him terribly.

But still he did nothing.

Neither could he forewarn Salutat of his son's disgrace; not even in a dream. It was as though a drama had to be played out, with Yavros merely a spectator; watching and waiting to see the final act.

Yet the final act was still a long way off.

The evangelists enjoyed their work. They were so tuned-in to each other's thoughts and needs that they worked as one in spreading the message about Yavros and Miekaale.

While they toured the country, they enlightened a great many terrans.

However, they also realised that Lucifer's influence, so dominant in daily life, would never allow the terrans to be completely free of it. As a result, few of those who heard the message remained spiritually strong enough utilise the angels' advice in everyday life.

This fact did not cause the angels distress, though. They were well aware how addictive terran nature had become in their lives, and expected a struggle to redeem any souls. But for every one who turned back, first to Miekaale to remove Lucifer's influence and then to Yavros in readiness for the Return, there was rejoicing in Eternity.

Even one redeemed terran spirit, the angels thought, was better than none.

Little more than a year after they left their son at his Academie, the angels reached a stage where most of the viable areas for conversion had been covered, and in order to spread their message further it seemed logical to take it overseas. It was only when they realised they would be absent indefinitely that they considered the need to get in touch with Batim.

At the time, the only means of communication between regions was by messenger; and as a mother, Angelina had reservations about using such an impersonal means when it came to informing their son.

"I really think we should go and see him," she declared to Salutat in the modest tent that served as their mobile residence.

"I suppose you're right," he said. "He'll be wondering what has become of us. We've been so wrapped up in our mission I fear we've neglected Batim of late. The problem is," he went on thoughtfully; "I don't think we've got time to pay him a visit."

"Why's that?" asked Angelina.

Salutat held out a hand-written itinerary, and pointed to an item in their schedule.

"To see Batim and get back for our voyage would take a whole week, and we only have a couple of days before our vessel sets sail. We may have to send a message after all."

Meanwhile, Lucifer had been putting his time in respite to good use. He had painstakingly traced the movement of Miekaale's aura, located the angels' current whereabouts, and subconsciously implanted in them the desire to take their mission overseas.

After all, he guessed, how else could he persuade them to connect with Batim one more time?

As he hurtled through the ethers and into the angels' locale, he caught the tail end of their conversation.

"...Oh, no you don't!" Lucifer exclaimed in a blind panic. "There's no way you'll just send the brat a message before you leave!"

Straightaway, the noise of rushing wind was heard through the flimsy canvas of the angels' tent.

The sound seemed to be coming closer, and became so worrying that it interrupted the angels' deliberations.

"What, in all of Eddren, is that racket?" asked Salutat, mystified why the stillness of their evening had suddenly been overtaken by such an uproar.

He quickly got up and went outside to investigate.

In the distance he could see a spiral of dust picked up by the whirlwind as it passed by. It did not occur to him that might again herald Lucifer's arrival in Eddren, as had similar events in the past. Not even when, after only a few seconds the whirlwind seemed to run out of energy and dissipate, did Salutat consider it to be anything more than a marvel of nature.

"How strange," he mused, returning to the tent.

"What was it?" asked Angelina.

"Just a whirlwind," explained Salutat. "Not to worry; it's disappeared now."

However, while Salutat was briefly out of the tent, Lucifer rushed in to see Angelina.

He sighed, as the affection he once held for her flooded through him again.

Sitting close beside her, he enjoyed the moment in her presence, knowing it could not last. Yet those few seconds were enough, and he appealed to her telepathically not to change her mind about visiting Batim.

Not suspecting where the thought could have come from, Angelina interpreted it as her own.

By the time Salutat returned, Lucifer had gone.

"I've made a decision," said Angelina when Salutat was settled again. "We must not go overseas without visiting Batim; even if it means changing all of our plans."

"Thank goodness," panted Lucifer as he recovered from his exertions.

He was starting to feel old now. Translocating between dimensions was not as easy as it used to be. Furthermore, the shock from a sudden rush of feeling for Angelina was a nuisance he had not anticipated.

He sighed; the frosty cavity that once held his heart thumping painfully.

"Watching my friend find out about her son will not be the joyous experience I'd hoped for," he muttered with a hint of remorse. "I'm sorry, Angelina, I don't want to hurt you; but this is something I must do."

Lucifer's remorse took him completely by surprise. He had spent so much of his time plotting against one soul or another, and weakening terran spirituality in general, that he forgot he once owned feelings.

"Am I getting soft?" he wondered.

Then he remembered a behaviour trait he once instilled in the terrans: that when trapped in an emotional vacuum, to have one's feelings stirred up creates distress. This was something Lucifer felt now as he worked out how to bring mother and son together again.

He only had himself to blame for the feelings, though. It was due to his interference in the beginning that feelings became part of terran nature. If he had kept out of it, the terrans would not have evolved with these emotions, and he himself would not now be suffering.

"I didn't think that one through, did I?" he smirked.

Yet, by the same token, he reflected, if it wasn't for his escapades he would have just wasted away in Hellion, with nothing better to do than contemplate his sins. Had not the last few thousand years in Eddren been both great fun and extremely productive? The occasional bout of remorse was a small price to pay for his achievements, especially when his current target was within reach.

With that calming realisation, Lucifer breathed deeply; refreshing his infernal soul. Angelina's imminent suffering was something he would just have to put up with.

"Let's go back and see him," Angelina insisted. "I really think we should."

"But what about this schedule?" cried Salutat, waving it at her. "I've put a lot of thought into it. There won't be another vessel heading our way for a month or more!"

Salutat looked downcast, but Angelina, still Influenced by Lucifer, stood her ground.

"That doesn't matter. It's more important that we see our son again."

Frustrated, Salutat leant over the table for a moment; his forehead resting in his hands. Then he rubbed his eyes and looked up at Angelina.

She gazed intently at him, silently urging him to agree.

"Why are you so insistent?" he asked at length. "Batim is a grown man now. He doesn't need his parents around. The separation from him hasn't bothered you before now, so why the sudden change of heart?"

"I don't know," she replied passively. "I just realised it was the right thing to do. Besides..."

Angelina's voice tailed off as a lump began to form in her throat.

"Besides what?" asked Salutat with a sense of defeat.

"I miss him," she added, swallowing back a tear. "He's my son. I'd like to see him again."

"Alright! You win – we'll go and see Batim."

Angelina hugged her husband fervently, almost pulling him off the seat. This was an argument she needed to win, and was grateful Salutat did not oppose her.

"You won't regret it. ...And I know Batim will be thrilled to see us again."

Lucifer rubbed his hands together with delight.

"That's my girl! This is going better than I thought," he chuckled. "Thank you, Angelina. ...But I wonder how you'd feel if you knew it was I who put you up to it!"

Salutat found it difficult to revise his completed schedule. It meant he needed to send messages to several distant communities to inform them they would not now arrive until at least the following month.

Angelina felt a sense of guilt for the inconvenience she was causing, and almost backed down when she saw his extra workload. But after the messages had been sent off, she relaxed; knowing they were obligated to the decision.

She must wrestle with her conscience in private.

The day came shortly afterwards, when their packing was complete and the goodbyes said, that the mission angels were at last free to return to the Academie and their son.

As the pair set off on the horse-drawn wagon, Angelina felt a level of excitement she seldom experienced working on the various stages of their mission. That had been work, albeit rewarding work; but this was personal. It was their son they were visiting.

A surge of joy went through her when, during the long journey back, she remembered they were making this trip to see Batim, not a community of strangers; even if the strangers had quickly become friends.

They were used to travelling now; for an itinerant adapts to a nomadic existence, as most people adapt to living in a permanent dwelling.

During their mission they had often been faced with the uncertainty of an unknown reception. This journey would be no different; except, to Angelina's way of thinking, they will have the joy of a family reunion at its conclusion.

When they rounded the final bend in the road and saw again the harbour town, the place where they had married and enrolled their son at its Academie, the year away from it seemed to disappear as though it had never been.

...They were coming home.

A shock to the system is always difficult to bear, and the shock to the angels when they learnt that Batim had been expelled, was devastating.

In effect, they refused to believe it.

Salutat demanded to see the registrar who was absent at the time, and was told he would be not be back for a number of hours.

They waited impatiently; confused and angry.

Why was Batim expelled? When did it happen? Why had nobody contacted them? ...And where is he now?

The unanswered queries between one another came in a steady stream; providing them with no solutions until the registrar had answered them.

When eventually he returned, he found himself faced with set of parents whose alarm over the disappearance of their son was now explosive.

Red-faced, he tried to answer the barrage of questions and insinuations that Salutat hurled at him.

Yet, the irate parents had no choice but to acknowledge the registrar's explanation: that the Academie was forced to expel Batim for breach of policy by ignoring curfew, and for continual absenteeism.

He informed them it happened many months ago, and that the Academie tried unsuccessfully to send a message to Salutat.

However, the registrar did assure them that the funds left for Batim's use had not been touched...

"...Then what's he been living off?" Salutat shrieked, the complexity of their situation becoming more severe with each revelation.

Angelina began to weep.

She had remained silent in disbelief, but the shock of discovery, together with Salutat's reaction, was more than she could bear.

Although worried for Batim's situation, she also feared for her normally gentle husband. Terran spirits, she knew, may be struck by a shock to the heart when extreme anger attacks. Salutat was close to that now.

Tearfully, she tried to console him.

"There would have been a good reason for him to go off like that," she ventured to suggest. "Something awful must have happened to make him relinquish his studies. It could be that he was injured, or became ill and was unable to continue. There are any number of possibilities."

"Then he should have contacted us. I informed him of the places we were planning to visit."

Much to Angelina's relief Salutat, though still angry, was more responsive to her soothing voice now.

She continued in earnest.

"Maybe he couldn't get in touch with us. Maybe..."

Angelina went quiet, disturbed by the thought that had just occurred to her.

"...Maybe he's dead."

"Oh, for goodness sake, Angelina. Don't get maudlin on me," chided Salutat, irritated by yet another consideration to deal with.

"I'm sorry. I didn't mean to upset you."

"Well, let's have no more talk about possibilities. We've got to decide what to do about it, and soon."

Salutat was in control again.

"It's a long time since he disappeared, so if we're going to look for him, we should get on to it straight away."

In a vineyard, a few weeks' journey away, Slave was in top form, directing the life of its new charge.

It had now established Batim in the vineyard with a position that well suited him: tending the grapevines prior to harvest. In addition, the owner had put him in charge of seasonal labourers brought in for the purpose.

This side of the work Slave enjoyed the most, especially as it manipulated the vineyard's owner into giving Batim license to exert authority in any way he saw fit.

Slave was sure Lucifer would not want Batim to become soft in his new lifestyle. As the son of angels, he was at risk of slipping back into his inbred personality: the kind, gentle temperament he once exhibited, and a potential problem which needed constant surveillance. Slave's reputation with Lucifer depended on it. Thus, when it noticed a slight softening in his manner or behaviour, it created a situation which ensured Batim would exercise, and so strengthen, the harsher side of his nature.

Shortly after he was put in charge of the labourers, Batim procured a whip from a travelling salesman.

Encouraged by Slave, he quickly discovered the thrill of using it, and adopted the approach that lazy or deceitful labourers deserved no better than to feel the painful lash of its cord.

Batim quickly honed his skills with the whip, perfecting the art of lashing. Everything from branches to individual blades of grass came within his range. On one occasion he snagged a small rodent as it was sunning itself on a rock. This gave him a special thrill.

All the while, Slave looked on through his eyes; enjoying the same sensations.

In Slave's opinion, taking control of Batim was far more interesting than keeping guard over the silly slip of a girl, whatever her name was. Lucifer had been most gracious in favouring his unworthy servant with a responsibility like this. It knew what Lucifer's goal had been all along – to get back at Batim's father – but it did not know the reason for it. As long as Batim was prevented from regressing, Lucifer would surely be pleased with its work and in due course heap upon it a worthy reward.

Slave could only imagine what that might be. Dreamily, it began to focus on its own initiative rather than the task at hand.

However, the day of the accident brought Slave to its senses; never to stray again.

Batim had been working alone at the vineyard's furthest boundary for most of the morning. Nothing untoward had occurred for several days, and he was contentedly at ease; not feeling in the least inclined towards violence.

Suddenly he heard a yell followed by a crashing sound coming from another part of the vineyard. Fearing damage to equipment that was his responsibility.

Batim hurried over to the site. There, he found one of the labourers lying beneath a collapsed wooden structure

252

from which he had fallen; and the man was indicating he could not breathe.

During Slave's momentary inattention, Batim's angelic sensitivity came to the fore again, and he felt concern for the injured labourer's plight as well as for the structure. With a mighty heave, he lifted it off and shoved it to one side; thus freeing the grateful labourer.

By this time more labourers had arrived, having also heard the commotion.

Once it was established that the injuries were not severe, those present expressed appreciation to Batim for helping a fellow-worker.

Batim had earned a reputation for being inflexible with the labourers, yet had now revealed to them a softer side of his nature. The group's spokesman alluded to this, and praised him for the benevolence of his spirit; a gesture that touched Batim deeply.

But then Slave, who had been daydreaming about the rewards Lucifer would heap on it, abruptly awoke to what was going on.

In an instant, it jolted to attention and took over.

Feeling both the jolt and the surge of impatience that accompanied it, Batim rebuked himself for losing face with the subordinates clamouring around him. He pulled the whip from his belt and angrily cracked it over their heads.

"Alright, it's over now. Get back to work," he ordered. "You're not paid to stand around and gawk!"

Phew, that was a close call, thought Slave, and vowed to curb his daydreaming.

From then on, Slave tightened its grip on Batim's soul; earning the son of angels a reputation approaching that of a despot, as he ruthlessly dealt with even the most trivial of transgressions.

Meanwhile, Batim's parents began their difficult search.

Enquiries made to tutors and students at the Academie; then later on with artisans around the city, all yielded no valid response.

Angelina began to fear the worst again. However, just as desperation started to creep in, they met up with an elderly couple they knew before their mission began, and finally made a discovery.

"I heard he took up with a young prostitute," said the old woman with an air of criticism.

"What!" cried Salutat. "You must be mistaken! Our son would never do that!"

"I'm not mistaken," she retorted. "I saw Batim out with the girl on more than one occasion."

"When was this?" asked Angelina, distressed with the revelation, but anxious to find out more.

"Oh – a long time ago now."

"And have you seen him since?"

"No. Although..." the woman began, but then stopped; reluctant to say any more.

"Go on – please!" said Salutat pointedly.

"I'm not sure if I should tell you this..."

She looked to her husband for support, yet he was as mystified as Salutat.

"What are you talking about, woman?" he barked at his wife. "What more do you know?"

The woman looked forlornly at Angelina, knowing that if she divulged anything further it would likely upset her diminutive friend.

"Alright," she said at length. "You won't like it, though. ...And please don't accept what I tell you as the truth, for it may just be hearsay. Nobody knows for sure..."

Angelina took her by the hand, and beseechingly looked into her eyes. On the verge of tears, she urged, "Please tell us everything, I'm so worried about my son."

The woman relayed how a man had been killed on the road and his wagon stolen; supposedly by a student from the Academie. The girl with him was reported as being a prostitute. A rumour circulated that the young man went by the name of Batim...

Angelina listened in stark disbelief, while Salutat stared at the woman; wide-eyed. Then he astounded Angelina by starting to laugh.

"There's nothing funny about this!" she cried, horrified both by what she had heard and by Salutat's reaction to it.

"Don't you see," he said; still chuckling. "This is insane. How could it have been Batim? He's not capable of killing! We know Batim. We know his heart, and the way that he thinks. Whoever spread this vicious rumour has mistakenly identified the culprit as our son."

"I'm sure you are right," said Angelina in support. "But it doesn't tell us where Batim is now, or what made him give up his studies!"

"Have they caught the pair who killed that man?" asked Salutat; more serious now.

With Angelina's comment sinking in, he was beginning to have second thoughts about Batim's virtue, especially in light of the fact that he did not resign from the Academie, but was expelled.

"I don't think those two were ever found," replied the woman. "At least, I haven't heard if they were caught. I can ask around, if you like."

"Yes, please," Angelina replied, quickly. "Do you think I could come with you?"

"Of course. We could go now, if you've nothing better to do for the moment."

"That would be wonderful. I don't think I shall rest until we've found him."

Angelina breathed a sigh of relief that at last they had a chance of locating Batim.

Over the next few days, Salutat and Angelina moved from one source of information to the next, gleaning facts that might be relevant to their search, and ignoring worthless gossip which, they discovered, was rife throughout the city streets. They heard, too, how another man had been killed up in the mountains; the theory in town being that the same couple might be involved in his murder.

By now, Salutat was less sure of his son's innocence. Yet, the angel in him still found it hard to accept that their supposition could be true.

Only when further information started to filter through did the reality of the situation begin to sink in; for even from outlying regions rumour can spread quickly.

It was not long before the deeds of the vineyard's overlord also became local gossip, as Batim had by now dismissed so many labourers that some turned up at the coastal city.

From his investigations, Salutat discovered that a good source of information was the local tavern; though not all of the gossip could be considered relevant. Nevertheless, spending time there each day, getting to know the local people and hearing their stories, proved to be worthwhile.

It was from one dismissed labourer that he learned the awful truth.

"I know where Batim is," he reported back to Angelina later that night.

Angelina groaned in gloomy anticipation when she saw the severe look on her husband's face.

"Oh, dear," she muttered through clenched fingers. "Do I really need to hear this?"

"I'm afraid so."

Salutat gave detail on everything the labourer told him. He omitted nothing of relevance. The information gleaned had been upsetting when he heard it, and he knew that Angelina would be similarly upset. As such, he could spare his wife no pain, but only comfort her in her distress.

It was several days before Batim's parents felt sufficiently composed to consider what they should do next.

"I'm afraid to go near him now," Angelina confessed when Salutat gingerly broached the subject again. "Our lovely son seems to have turned into a dangerous man."

"But even if he's never caught for the two killings – for which we must now assume he was responsible – we can't allow him to continue in this manner. It violates the ethics we bred in him."

"I know, but what can we do? Batim is a terran – and an adult terran at that. He has free will and is responsible for his own destiny. As angels we don't have the luxury of free will because we're under obedience to Yavros. But Batim is an independent. We have no right to interfere."

"You make it sound like you don't want to redeem him; that his soul doesn't matter now. What sort of mother are you turning into?"

"Salutat, of course I want to redeem him! His soul is just as important as it ever was! But he's a fully-fledged terran spirit. The fact that he's also our son doesn't alter that."

Salutat sighed, a perplexed look crossing his features.

"What do you suggest then?" he asked woodenly.

In his heart, he knew Angelina was right. Yet, they still needed to decide which was more important: giving way to Batim's free, will even if it ultimately caused his spiritual downfall; or find their son and appeal to his better nature. ...To persuade him to give up his chosen way of life for the sake of his soul.

As the latter option came to mind, Salutat determined what they should do.

"We must go to him; there is no doubt in my mind," he stated. "If we don't, I'll not be able to live with myself."

And when Angelina agreed with him, Salutat took her in his arms – both to comfort his wife and to receive from her the support he badly needed.

The next few weeks would be distressing for them all.

Their expedition to Batim's vineyard took two weeks and four days.

In their state of anxiety, the angels felt every jolt during the hastily planned trip. Never before had a simple journey seemed so onerous, and they had been on many.

This was not a trip either of them had wanted to take; unlike the others where the end of the journey promised interesting experiences with new people. Even returning home had been something to look forward to; but this... This was like journeying to the outer limits of endurance and not being sure whether they could get back from it. What's more, the helpful informer from the tavern gave Salutat only a vague description of where Batim's vineyard was situated.

After many enquiries to local vineyards they finally, and with great relief, received a definite clue as to the location of the one they sought.

"It's just over the next hill," they were told.

The young man they described, their informant advised them, was without doubt the overlord of that particular vineyard. He knew of no other overlord like him, for this one was a tyrant.

...And, he added; they would be well advised to exercise caution in their dealings with him.

"Could it really be our son the man was talking about?" sighed Angelina as they set off on the final stage of their exhausting journey. "I wonder if we'll recognise him – and whether or not he'll want to know us."

Tired from their travels, the worried parents chose to rest for the night and tackle their chilling problem refreshed in the morning.

But Salutat could not sleep. His edginess woke Angelina all too frequently, and eventually he left their tent for fear of distressing her.

Salutat stood quietly beside the tent in the darkness.

He stretched his back and tired limbs; then rotated his head to loosen tight neck muscles.

As he did so, he noticed how brightly the stars stood out against the blackness of the sky. 'The firmament of all Eternity,' he once heard Masian call it, and could now understand why.

He wondered if Yavros was looking down on him, but then remembered that the stars were merely part of the physical realm. Yavros himself was within his own soul.

All of a sudden, Salutat had an overwhelming desire to pray. He dropped onto one knee and closed his eyes.

"Yavros, my master," he shouted in a whisper. "Come to me, I beseech you."

This he repeated several times; the sound diminishing with each utterance. A mere hush escaped his lips as he mouthed the words for the last time.

Just then, something came upon him. At first he wasn't quite sure what it was, only that he needed to breathe in deeply, as though something had stirred wthin his soul. It warmed him, delighted him; comforted him. And then he knew it was Yavros. He had not been abandoned.

"Thank you, Master," mouthed Salutat, his hands over his face; the wonder of the moment overwhelming him. "Thank you for coming to the aid of your helpless subject. We need you so desperately at the moment. Angelina and I are in crisis over our son."

"I know," came the response.

Yavros in pure consciousness made no physical sound, but to Salutat, kneeling in the silence, it seemed as though someone had spoken to him.

He leapt to his feet, looking around in alarm.

"Who's there?" he said.

Was somebody close by? Had Angelina woken up and assumed he was talking to her?

He peeped inside the tent, expecting to see her sitting up, but she was curled up on her cot.

Then he realised the voice he heard was just thoughts within in his own head.

Yavros had responded to him.

"I'm sorry, Yavros," he said soulfully, embarrassed that he'd failed to recognise the voice of his own master.

He knelt again in prayer, his focus now deep within his own consciousness.

"Do you know what is happening in our lives, Master?" he whispered inwardly.

"I do."

"Yavros, I don't understand why our son has become so corrupt. What have we done wrong?"

"You have neglected to protect your own."

Salutat straightened up, puzzled.

He opened his eyes, while his own mind tried to grasp the meaning of the strange statement. When he failed to do so, he focused inwardly again.

"I'm sorry, but I don't understand what you mean," he moaned, almost in tears.

"You have not, as my terran spirits say, 'practiced what you preach."

Once more Salutat paused while he tried to grasp the significance of the remark.

Yavros sensed his confusion and continued.

"You must work out for yourself just what I mean. It is not for me to advise you. When you understand, you will know what to do."

Abruptly, the feeling of companionship left Salutat, and in an instant he knew that Yavros had withdrawn. He was on his own again.

For a moment panic seized him. He felt his conversation with Yavros was unfinished; at least, it seemed that way.

But then he remembered something significant: Yavros did everything for a reason. Was he telling him he must work things out for himself, because he was not only the parent of a miscreant son but also an angel in the service of his master? Were he and Angelina not just on a teaching mission, but expected to further their own spiritual growth as well? If this was indeed the case, then Yavros was trying to teach him a valuable lesson. If only he could fathom out what it was.

Salutat's first thought was to awaken Angelina and tell her what had happened, but as she was still asleep he decided against it, and instead went for a walk.

They had camped on the near side of the hill. With nowhere else he would rather go, he laboriously climbed the hill, and arrived at the top breathlessly wondering why he had bothered. But when he looked out at the view, he could only marvel at the beauty of what lay beneath him. Away in the distance, a band of orange light lined the horizon, announcing it would soon be dawn.

Salutat gazed over gently undulating land, upon which morning mist was beginning to settle.

"I wish Angelina could see this," he said to himself.

Just then, down below he saw a flickering light through the encroaching mist:

Somebody was moving about with a torch.

In the twilight he could make out rows of plants, which from the height of the hill looked small, but he realised they must be grapevines – perhaps at the vineyard they had been directed to.

Salutat felt tears welling up. Could the person moving about be their son?

He felt like shouting out; desperately wanting to attract the person's attention. To run down the hill and, assuming it was Batim, to embrace him and tell him everything was going to be alright now that his parents were there.

Yet he knew he should not. That was only what he, the parent, wanted to do. It was not necessarily what their errant son would accept. So with a sigh he turned around and made his way back down the hill to the familiarity of his tent.

A lot had happened in the final hours of that night, and he was still very confused. Maybe Angelina would be able to throw some light on it all.

She was already up when he arrived back at the tent.

Angelina stood outside, a worried look on her face.

"Wherever have you been?" she asked, disturbed by Salutat's absence. "You didn't go to the vineyard, without me, did you?

Without answering, Salutat pulled her into the tent and motioned her to sit down.

"I need to talk to you about something," he said before lowering himself cross-legged onto a mat.

He looked deep in thought.

"What's wrong, my sweet?" she asked tenderly, placing her hand in his.

Salutat meekly told her what happened. He explained how he could not sleep and prayed to Yavros; then how his prayer was answered with a mystifying conundrum.

"What did Yavros say?" asked Angelina; interested that Yavros had responded, and wishing now that he'd woken her up to share the moment.

"He said we have failed to protect our own and accused us of not practicing what we preach."

"What does that mean?"

"I don't know; that's the problem. He insists we work it out for ourselves. Then when we understand, the solution will become clear."

Angelina screwed up her face, trying to grasp what it was all about.

"Yavros was talking about the situation with Batim, wasn't he?"

"Oh, yes. He knows what's been going on. But it seems he's unwilling to help – unless we can figure out where the trouble lies. If we can do that, he reckons we'll know how to remedy it."

Salutat went quiet for a moment while he reflected on possible meanings.

"What do you think he meant by, 'failed to protect our own'?" he asked; thankful to be sharing the problem with his wife now.

"I wish I knew," Angelina murmured.

She fiddled with her garment while seeking inspiration. But then she stopped what she was doing and looked at Salutat as a look of horror crept into her features.

"Oh no!" she cried, struggling to her feet. "Not Batim!"

A tear formed in her eye, alarming Salutat.

Distraught, Angelina forced her way out of the modest tent, suddenly stifled by its claustrophobic smallness. She stood motionless in the chill of early morning; her mind numbed by a sudden realisation.

"For goodness sake, Angelina — what's going on now?" exclaimed Salutat, following her outside.

He noticed she was shivering, and fetched a blanket for her shoulders.

Angelina placed her arms around his waist and sobbed into his comforting chest.

"I'm so sorry," she said at last, struggling to regain her composure. "I've realised something terrible. ...And I don't think I can forgive myself for not seeing it before."

"Whatever are you talking about?"

Salutat now added frustration to his growing despair.

Angelina pulled back, holding him at arm's length. She peered into his eyes, trying to find the right words to drop a bombshell on a loved-one. At last she said, "I think Batim has been taken over by Lucifer. ...And we let it happen."

"What!" Salutat shook her arms off roughly, irritated by what to him was yet another outrageous idea. "You're not serious, are you?"

"Yes, unfortunately I am," she said weakly. "Salutat, just think about it. Lucifer must know we're together in terran form. ...In which case, he would like nothing more than to gain control of Batim and upset us at the same time. How better could he achieve it? In this light, Yavros' comments make perfect sense."

Salutat was not convinced.

It seemed insane to him that their son, the son of angels, could be so gullible as to allow an evil entity into his consciousness and corrupt his soul. What with the upbringing he received and all the love his parents gave him throughout his early years; the driving ambition that encouraged him to study at the Academie in the first place...how could this be; especially after so short a period of time?

Was Batim himself so spineless as to let it happen?

Is the son of angels not in control of his own actions?

Salutat could not bear the thought of it. He wanted to scream at Angelina that she was wrong – horribly wrong. Yet the truth in her words was so overpowering, despite their quiet presentation, that he could not ignore it. And if indeed it was true, then they had let their son down.

...But how?

Salutat struggled with the thoughts racing round his head. The torment he suffered formed sweat on his brow, and he began panting in deep distress.

Once again, Angelina feared for his health.

She tried to comfort him, but this time he would have none of it.

He needed someone to strike out at, and Angelina was the closest. He wanted to shun her for the irrational words she had spoken, as though it was all fabrication.

"Leave me alone!" he screamed at her. "How could you criticise my son like that?"

Angelina was stunned.

"Don't forget he's my son, too!" she wailed. "I don't like to think Lucifer has got his hands on Batim any more than you do; but it must be true! Why else would our gentle son have become a murderer and a tyrant?"

She ran back into the tent, reeling from the shock of her husband's attitude.

In a daze, she sobbed unrestrainedly, and began tidying up the scant belongings in the tent as though getting ready to move on. Yet that was not her intention, for she was merely going through the motions; needing to keep her hands busy while her mind tried to cope with Salutat's rejection of her. But at the same time, she knew him well enough to realise that it was only an abhorrence of reality which caused him to behave that way.

Gradually she came to her senses. Thinking freely again, she knew it would be wrong to let this trial destroy their relationship. As she slowly folded up the last blanket, she resolved to mend the temporary rift that had developed between them.

Angelina went outside again.

Salutat was not there.

At first she failed to see him; but then she spotted the familiar colour of his overshirt through the foliage of a bush, and went up to him.

He was sitting on a rock, absently poking the earth with a twig. Salutat glanced up when he saw her shadow; then, assuming it was Angelina, he looked down again.

Beseechingly, she said to him, "Please don't shut me out, Salutat. We're in this together, aren't we?"

Instinctively, she knelt down at his feet and, receiving no response followed his gaze to the ground.

Faltering, she uttered, "You are treating me...as though it's my fault."

Salutat's mouth quivered.

Angelina sensed he was trying hold back tears. She had never seen her husband weep before. The anguish of all that had happened must have been too much for him.

She leant forward and kissed him on the forehead.

"Forgive me," he said through constricted tears. "I don't know what came over me."

Angelina felt a weight lifting from her shoulders as his anger subsided. She breathed a sigh of relief: perhaps they could talk now.

"It's like something got into me," he went on. "Perhaps Lucifer has sunk his claws into me, too!"

Angelina smiled, as a terran smiles when faced with overwhelming odds: helplessly; not quite knowing what to do next. She raised Salutat to his feet and held him closely, as if so doing he would feel like his old self again.

Meanwhile, Lucifer was in festive mood.

Having monitored the angels' conversation from afar; his attention irresistibly drawn by Salutat's supplication to Yavros, he had indeed goaded the couple when Angelina identified his involvement.

"Naturally, you have me to thank for all of this, Salutat, my friend!" he mocked. "Now let me see you untangle the mess you've created by your negligence. Don't you know I'm always watching you, and will forever trip up both you and your terran family?"

Lucifer jeered in triumph, witnessing first hand to what extent vulnerability renders Yavros' terran spirits useless. He had long since ensured that basic terran kindness, as instilled in them during the early days, cannot easily put on the armour of battle when confronted with evil. Instead it cringes in fear and cowers away from what it regards as an immovable force.

He sat back with his phantom arms folded, a look of pride and pleasure on his face; waiting for his victims' next futile attempt to solve their problem.

267

"Don't forget, you pious angels," he said. "Yavros gave free will to these stupid creatures. Your precious terran son, competently assisted by Slave, is now exercising his 'free will' to the full! You're going to have a battle on your hands if you want to save both him and yourselves!"

The tent had been stripped of all comforts when Salutat and Angelina went back into it. Normally, by now it would have been anyway; for packing everything up was part of their regular routine before contentedly moving on to the next location, and so nothing seemed out of the ordinary. Only this time, they were not so anxious to move on.

They had already known many incidences of Lucifer's interference, but none where he took possession of a soul.

Angelina was aware, perhaps more so than Salutat, that free will played an important part in terran evolution and readiness for the Return. Where a sinister occurrence was evident it was a simple matter of invoking Miekaale. ...But a terran soul who has voluntarily succumbed to infiltration by Lucifer would surely need to be treated differently.

Just as many terran parents have to decide the fate of their offspring, so must they, as angels, choose whether to intervene with Batim's soul, or allow him his free will.

Should they leave him to the wiles of Lucifer for the rest of his eternal life, or summon up all the spiritual help they could find to free him from those clutches?

Salutat and Angelina had some serious thinking to do.

Angelina gathered twigs from the surrounding brush, and rekindled the embers of their dying fire.

"It would be good to have a hot drink to warm us up," she told Salutat.

While he placed a pot of water on the fire and waited for it to come to the boil, Salutat tried to piece together in his mind a suitable plan of action.

Angelina stood back, watching him.

"We won't know just what we're dealing with unless we speak to him." she insisted. "Everything we've heard about Batim is still hearsay. You know how terran spirits can exaggerate. Maybe he's not as bad as they make out."

"...And maybe he is!" cried Salutat. "Remember, we are not just dealing with Batim; there are a lot of unknowns as well. Lucifer may have influenced other souls in our son's life, too. We must tread very carefully."

"Perhaps I should go on my own," suggested Angelina. "I'm sure Batim, even the Batim under Lucifer's control, would be pleased to see his own mother!"

"Of course not!" exclaimed Salutat; then quickly added, "...I don't mean, he wouldn't be pleased to see you, but that you must not go there by yourself."

"I doubt if he'll take kindly to both of us turning up. He might be caught off-guard and shut us out."

"That's right – we can't have him become suspicious. If Batim really is being controlled by Lucifer the rascal will be on the lookout for trickery on our part; in which case we must fall in with him – at least to begin with."

"Oh Salutat, I don't think so. We would be playing into Lucifer's hands; he's always been a quick thinking angel. By now he must know that we'll try to draw Batim away, and will do everything in his power to prevent it."

"That shouldn't stop us from trying, though!" protested Salutat with fervour.

"Amen to that!" Angelina punched the air to reinforce their solidarity. "It certainly won't be an easy task..."

"...Or straightforward. After all, it's our own son we are dealing with. How can know what to expect if we've never come across a situation like this before?"

Angelina paused for a moment as a thought came to her.

"That's just it! We have never come across anything like this before! We've got no idea how Batim will react, or how to handle it. Maybe it's time to seek advice."

Salutat shot her a quizzical look. "Who do you suggest we consult, then? We can't go back to the Academie; they wouldn't be interested. He was expelled..."

"...I know! Obviously I don't intend to seek advice from there! I mean... Well, there's only one place we could go for help, and that's Eternity! We must consult Yavros! If he can't offer advice, nobody can! We're probably overdue for a visit anyway, so could include a mission report with our quest for answers."

"Actually, that's not such a bad idea," said Salutat light-heartedly; he had always admired Angelina's insight.

He nodded in acceptance of her suggestion.

"As you say, Yavros already knows what is happening. Now that we've recognised Batim's situation, Yavros might offer us counsel. When shall we go?"

With eyes brighter than they had been for a long time, Angelina responded to her husband's joviality.

"There's no time like the present!" she said. "We won't get anywhere with Batim as things are just now, so what's to stop us going straight away?"

Armed with renewed hope, the angels prepared to leave for their home realm. Their brief stay in Eternity would be in spirit only, so all the trappings of terranity would need to be secured before they left.

Settling comfortably into the bare tent, with blankets wrapped around them for warmth, the spirits of the two angels slipped out of their bodies and passed once again through the veil of consciousness back into Eternity.

Yavros was expecting them.

He had made a few observations regarding their son's demeanour, and was anxious to talk to the angels about it.

Batim, he had noticed, now carried a different air from the one with which he was born and bred.

There was a disquieting and unusual aura about him. Yavros suspected that his mind was in some way detached from his spirit. ...Or rather, he reflected, Batim's spirit had become closed off from the rest of him. Instead of utilising his intuition, the young man now lived out of his own nature, and had become self-centred.

"Yes, that's what I'll say," Yavros declared in readiness for the angels' arrival. "A terran spirit whose mind is shut off from his soul becomes unapproachable except on its own terms."

Yavros had seen Batim change from the caring, humble spirit to an arrogant, self-serving egomaniac, all because of Lucifer's involvement. This was indeed a perilous state of affairs. Not only had he adopted Lucifer's characteristics, but he also retained his right to choose; a right which was now dominated by Lucifer.

It appeared to Yavros that Lucifer had complete control over Angelina's son now. Unless Batim became aware of the change within him, regretted his choices, and decided to open up his spirit again, he would be lost to both his parents and his creator. And Yavros was sure Batim would not want to be stuck with Lucifer till the end of time!

The situation was really quite harmful...

But then Yavros had second thoughts. This state of affairs was probably sad rather than harmful – sad for his parents and tragic for Batim, as his beautiful soul had no control over the situation at present. However, of greater importance was Batim's current presence of mind, for it could become threatening for his parents if they weren't extremely careful.

The sooner he was able to discuss all of this with Salutat and Angelina, the better.

"I'm glad you've come to see me," he remarked much to their surprise, for they knew nothing of his contemplations on the matter.

Although there was a lot Yavros wanted to say, first he needed to listen to their report on the mission.

"You are to be congratulated on your level of success," he responded at length. "The terrans should be reminded how strength of spirit helps them, and you've done well to accomplish this. Well done, too, for realising you need my help on your little problem. I hoped you'd come to me."

"Is that what you meant?" asked Salutat, "You implied that I would know how to proceed once we had discerned the problem"

"Why yes, of course! You need my guidance, but if I had merely instructed you to come, you would have been none the wiser. As ministering angels in Eddren, I wanted you to use your terran intellect to arrive at the same conclusion. And that you did. I only wish all the terran spirits would do the same!"

Angelina felt more at ease now, and was relieved that he had expected them to seek counsel.

Together the angels told Yavros of the dilemma presently facing them: that they were unsure what kind of approach to use with Batim, and that they were afraid of angering him or scaring him off with the wrong approach.

"It's a difficult one for you to deal with," said Yavros in sympathy. "When you encounter a situation which is the first of its kind, it is difficult to know what to do. You can always learn from things in retrospect; when history has repeated itself often enough to learn from mistakes made by predecessors. But the first time something arises, you cannot know how to act.

"I feel like saying, 'Curse that meddling Lucifer'," Yavros went on; "yet I know it would be a waste of vital energy, and achieve nothing. Actually, if the truth were but known, I am to blame for providing the terran spirits with free will in the first place. What was I thinking of! All I accomplished was their choosing Lucifer over me!"

Yavros shook his head, dejectedly.

Angelina felt sorry for him.

"You weren't to know Lucifer would become a nuisance when you created terran spirits," she reassured him. "If he hadn't been stubborn in refusing your instructions, none of this would have happened."

Yavros looked at her sideways, a sly grin appearing on his face.

"He's a cunning character, alright," he said with a smirk. "You've got to admire his tenacity. His hatred of me is so absolute he keeps thinking up new ways to get back at me. ...But, even though sometimes it seems hopeless, bear in mind that everything happens for a reason. All experiences are lessons to learn from, and this drama is not yet played out; not for any of us. So, in the dark moments that may lie ahead, rest assured that I will be with you."

Salutat was deeply moved by the words of wisdom Yavros shared with them. His master had shown a softer, more compassionate face, as if to demonstrate that real power comes not from might but from comprehension.

Now that he knew what Yavros was thinking – that he was equally unsure of the immediate future – they need not feel inadequate. Yavros would guide them, of this he was certain, and he took comfort from knowing it. But still, the initiative had to come from them.

Salutat thanked Yavros and made to leave, but Yavros stopped him.

"Before you go I would have a word of advice," he said as the need to share his observation of Batim surfaced in his mind. "Your son has changed; he's not the same person you knew of old. He has put on an air of arrogance – the most insidious of Lucifer's traits I've seen in my progeny, and abhorrent to me. Any attempt to confront him may inflame his arrogance and incite him to turn against you. At best he will try to convince you that he is in the right and you are just interfering..."

"...Then how can we possibly get through to our son?" asked Angelina, the apprehension rising again.

"Just be yourselves. Forget, for the moment, that he is anything but the son you love. Embrace him as parents who have missed him. ...And remember that he is also the son of angels and therefore my progeny, too. Appeal to his eternal spirit while you speak with him. It may help draw him away from the evil disposition that possesses him. And now you must go. I will be with you, but I cannot interfere. Summon Miekaale if you sense evil around him; and unfortunately I think there is some kind of presence actually within Batim. I will instruct Miekaale to make your invocation his first priority if the need should arise. So, goodbye my friends, and may your son's spirit be restored to spiritual perfection.

CHAPTER 6

When the angels returned to their terran state, the details of the meeting with Yavros were as difficult to remember as are the content of a dream. It was only in retrospect that they managed to fit it all together.

"We must agree on how we approach Batim," Angelina said as they prepared to move on.

Salutat agreed.

Then, when everything had been secured on the wagon and the horse hitched up, they set off for the vineyard.

Salutat guided the horse in silence during their relatively short journey. There was a lot to think about.

At length, he said, "It would be better if you let me take the lead when we're talking to Batim."

Angelina nodded; she felt at ease about the upcoming meeting with their son now. Having taken Yavros' advice to heart, she was looking forward to seeing Batim again; her love for his spirit having surpassed any misgivings she had about him.

Soon the gateway to the vineyard loomed large before them.

The entrance was a solid structure; its gates shut and barred as if to announce to all who approached them that strangers were not welcome.

Undeterred, Salutat pressed on.

He drove the horse and wagon directly up to it. Then, jumping down from the wagon he strode to a smaller door on one side of the main gates. As he reached out to it, the door suddenly opened.

A stocky man with a mop of black hair came through to meet him. "What do you want?" he barked.

"This is the moment of truth," Salutat muttered under his breath.

Instantly, he recognised the need to convince the man of his integrity or they would never be able to get in.

"We are the parents of Batim, your overlord," he said with confidence. "We heard he was at this vineyard, and would like to see him."

The man looked taken aback. It had not occurred to him that the cruel master of the vineyard actually had parents. But he had been brought up to respect his elders, and was fearful of repercussions if he was otherwise to the parents of his employer.

Immediately he changed his demeanour.

"Welcome then," he said courteously, nodding towards Angelina in acknowledgement of her status. "I will see if the master is available to speak with you. Please remain here until I return."

Salutat glanced up at Angelina as the man slipped back through the side door; shutting it behind him.

"That wasn't too bad," he said cheerfully, and lifted her down from the wagon.

"It's an imposing place – and well guarded, by the look of it," remarked Angelina as a bout of nervousness crept through her. "I wonder if this is Batim's doing."

A few minutes later, a heavy bolt was rammed back on the inside of the main gate.

Creaking from lack of use, one half of the gate slowly opened; the man pushing against it with all his might. Breathless, he suggested to Salutat that they should be able to get the wagon through the gap without his having to open up the other half. Then he told them, "You'll want the building on the right. Your son has been informed of your arrival and is anxious to see you."

Once again Salutat looked at Angelina, and grinned.

Excitedly she climbed back up.

Then Salutat guided their horse through the restricted opening of the immense gate.

Angelina could not help but wonder if Yavros had arranged the easy access to their son.

Experience had taught her that when a venture went smoothly, Yavros was usually involved. However, she also knew that from now on they would be on their own. There could be no help from him where their handling of Batim was concerned. Terran relationships were just that: terran.

Batim stood on the steps, waiting for them.

At first they failed to realise it was him. He seemed to be much bigger than before; older and more mature, even. But mostly they did not recognise him because he sported a beard – a dense, intimidating beard – which looked to his mother like it had not been trimmed for some time.

Angelina gasped. Surely this was not her beautiful son. Perhaps he was waiting inside, and this person was just an assistant who had been sent to escort them in...

"Well, well, what a surprise!" Batim said as they came closer. "I never expected to see you two. How did you find me – and why?"

Angelina could barely believe her eyes; this really was Batim. Whatever had happened to him? He seemed more like somebody else than her own beloved offspring.

"Hello, son," began Salutat; somewhat irritated by the curt greeting, yet also mindful of Yavros' cautioning. "It's good to see you again. You...you're looking..."

Salutat was suddenly lost for words.

"You look very healthy," he settled on. Perhaps it would be safer to speak little to begin with, and just see what his son had to say.

Batim dropped down the steps to greet his mother. He had always loved her, and some of the love surfaced again at the unexpected sight of her.

In one deft movement, he scooped her off the wagon and lightly set her on the ground in front of him.

Angelina looked through the black hair, trying to see his spirit, but all she could see was two black eyes. Weren't your eyes blue before? she thought secretly. Has Lucifer even changed your appearance?

"Son, I've missed you so much," she said, on the verge of tears. "It has been a long time since we last saw you; I'm so sorry."

"Don't worry yourself about it," Batim said casually, and wrapped his arms around her; holding on too tightly.

Angelina winced with the pain.

He released her, apologising.

"You are very strong, now," she uttered warily, rubbing a painful arm. "Your toil in the vineyard has strengthened you physically."

Batim began to sense her uneasiness, but assumed it was due to his coarse handling of her.

In truth, he felt uncomfortable in the unfamiliar role of host, yet he knew they must have come a long way, and that he should offer them some refreshment.

"Come inside," he said, and bounded back up the steps. "You must be weary from your journey."

Salutat started up after Batim but realised Angelina was not following. He turned around to look for her.

Still at the bottom of the steps, she stood motionless and in a daze, trying to absorb the changes in her son.

Salutat snapped his fingers to get her attention; then indicated for her to go with him.

"It'll be alright," he whispered as she caught up with him. "Just take things slowly – there will be time to discuss our feelings about it later."

Meanwhile Slave, still absorbed with its own importance, had once again forgotten to focus. With a start, it realised that a burst of affection had surged out of Batim towards his female visitor.

"What's happening?" it asked itself; now paying closer attention. "Who are these two people, and what was my charge thinking of – hugging that terran?"

Angrily, it stirred within Batim as a reminder of just who was in control.

Batim reacted abruptly with a feeling of agitation. Had his parents come unannounced just to check up on him? Did they know about the expulsion; the killings? Suddenly he was suspicious.

As he led them into the lounging room, he motioned them to sit down, told them he wouldn't be a minute, and slipped out through a side door.

"Something in him just changed," observed Angelina as he went out. "He seems different."

Salutat had noticed the sumptuous fittings and didn't sense it. Then, while he got up for a closer inspection of a tapestry, he asked, "What do you mean?"

"Batim has lost the friendliness he had a moment ago."

"He's probably woken up to the fact that his long-lost parents have come back into his life!"

Salutat laughed at his own whimsical remark, forgetting for a minute that he needed to exercise caution. At the same time, he pointed at a mural of the vineyard, which filled the wall opposite.

"Just look at that! Our boy has done well for himself..."

"...Salutat! Will you pay attention?" Angelina growled; had he lost control of his senses! "Don't get pulled in by all of this, or you are no better than Lucifer himself!"

"I'm sorry. It's just that... Well, I've never seen anything like this before. And it belongs to our son."

"It doesn't belong to Batim; he manages the vineyard, that's all..."

"...It's as good as mine, though!" exclaimed Batim.

The angels swung round to see their son leaning against a doorpost, watching them.

Alarmed, Angelina glanced at her husband. How much had he heard? she wondered, but then was relieved when the old Batim seemed to come to the fore again.

"I bet you never thought I could do as well as this!" he smirked. "Sit down father, and take it easy. I have ordered some refreshments."

In fact, he had requested more than just refreshments.

Slave had aroused suspicions in Batim to the extent that he felt compelled to check-up on his visitors. While he was out of the room, Batim had a servant inspect their wagon for anything that might indicate the real reason for their visit, for they never did explain how they found him.

Batim handed round the drinks.

"So, how did you know I was here?" he asked again as he sat down next to his mother.

Salutat quickly raised his cup in a toast.

"Here's wishing you good health," he said cheerfully; to which the others responded similarly.

Yet the toast was merely a hedge. Salutat was in fact thinking quickly how to answer Batim. This was something he and Angelina had not covered in their strategy, and he felt edgy about the need to say the right thing.

Mindful of Salutat's delaying tactics, Batim looked him squarely in the eye.

"Well, are you going to tell me?" he asked, with an air of impatience.

"What does it matter how we found out?" said Angelina gently, sensing her husband's panic. "The important thing is that we are all together again after such a long time."

Angelina had tried hard to be sincere, in the hope that his instincts were dulled with worldly living.

But she underestimated Batim.

Slave recognised her deception straight away, changing the expression on his face to one of annoyance.

Seeing this, Salutat felt he had no choice but to tell the truth; for if they were to hedge around it much longer they could make the situation worse. The Batim of old might be taken in by an excuse, but not this new persona. Whatever was controlling him seemed to be perceptive and would no doubt be quick to react.

"Son, I have a confession to make," Salutat announced to him at length.

Angelina stared at him. Whatever was he going to say! It was far too soon to divulge what they knew of Batim's recent past. She had agreed that he act as spokesman, but assumed he would use some common sense...

Salutat did not return her look of concern. He was deep in thought, formulating the right words for his admission.

"Your mother and I discovered by chance that you had left the Academie," he said without flinching.

"You did?" responded Batim guardedly; ready for even a hint of criticism.

Salutat sighed privately; then reached into his angelic state of consciousness. Speaking more confidently he said, "Yes, we were to embark on an overseas trip... I presume you still remember our mission?"

He looked up at Batim, who nodded; vaguely recalling the project his parents had been engaged in while he was at the Academie.

Salutat continued.

"We decided, as we have not seen you for so long, that before we departed we should come back for a visit. The people at the Academie told us you had...that you had left, and it was only after extensive enquiries that we found out you were here."

Angelina breathed a sigh of relief. Please don't question us further, she silently pleaded.

But Batim was on the defensive now...and so was Slave. It saw an opening to make trouble and went for it.

"What else did they tell you?" asked Batim; his black eyes flashing menacingly.

"...What else was there to learn?" countered Angelina; uneasy about the direction in which the exposé may head if she left it just to Salutat. "Please tell us why you left your studies? Were you unhappy at the Academie?"

A mother's instincts are wonderful, thought Salutat. He had noticed Batim's defensive stance and was secretly pleased she saw fit to join in the conversation. Angelina might help to maintain a balance.

Batim, the son of angels, fidgeted awkwardly in his seat. As their son, he owed his parents a proper explanation; yet Slave, still firmly in control, decided its charge's activities were none of their business.

The fabricated response came easily.

"The Academie was alright – I just wasn't accomplishing anything by staying there."

In reality, Batim had been getting excellent grades and many commendations; the fact of which his parents were informed when they visited the Academie.

In light of this, Angelina knew her son was deliberately lying. Although she badly wanted him to tell her the truth, caution prevented her from commenting further.

"I'm sorry you felt that way," she responded, trying to maintain a moderate approach – it really was the only way to proceed.

Angelina had also observed that Batim would not tolerate contradiction. Arrogance, she was learning, wields its own authority. If they were to succeed with him they would need to virtually agree with everything he said. From now on it would be difficult to get him to open up while at the same time maintaining good relations.

Suddenly she felt weary of the struggle they were having. Had they bitten off more than they could chew in coming to see him? He was so different now from the young man he used to be. But then she remembered what Yavros had promised – that he was always with them even if he could not interfere.

"I need you, Yavros," she said within her mind. "Please help me find the right words with my son."

Yavros looked on. He was close to tears now, seeing how Batim had changed in his attitude towards his parents. He saw also the disturbing aura around the once innocent young man, and assumed that Lucifer's influence must be deeply embedded in his consciousness by now.

Had he looked closer, Yavros would have seen that the aura was actually a presence: the worthless sprite Lucifer had implanted within Batim to ensure total control.

If he had noticed this he would have also recognised that with its removal Batim stood a chance of reverting to his normal self.

Yet it did not occur to Yavros at the time that Lucifer could be so depraved as to implant another entity within the consciousness of a terran spirit. So the situation went unheeded, and Slave's hold on Batim remained absolute. Yavros could only hope that in time the young man would see the error of his ways.

In response to Angelina's plea, Yavros merely advised her to draw from her intuition, not her emotions.

She closed her eyes, hoping to receive some inspiration, but Batim abruptly broke in on her musings.

"Actually, it was too boring at the Academie," he told her with a haughty expression.

"Boring!" exclaimed his father. "How could the wisdom and knowledge in your courses be considered boring?"

Immediately, Salutat regretted his verbal explosion, and received Angelina's dismayed look with full accountability. Why hadn't he kept his mouth shut?

"I'm sorry, Batim," he chipped in to appease the critical eyebrow raised in his direction. "I was wrong to say that. The suggestion to attend the Academie came from us, and we honestly thought you were happy there...but we must have been mistaken."

Salutat felt sick. His true feelings were eating at him. How he wished he could just come out with the string of questions he desperately needed answers for, or take his son by the shoulders and shake some sense into him. But he could not. Instead, he pulled back from the anger once again, and forced out the words, "Won't you tell us what really happened?" from a throat constricted with bottled-up frustration.

Unexpectedly, Batim went quiet.

Angelina watched him for a sign of renewed irritation. Yet, surprisingly, she could see nothing; for the reason that Slave had become suspicious. There seemed to be more to the parents' questions than they were presently divulging. And while it assessed the situation, Batim was rendered incapacitated.

At length, though unconvinced of their sincerity, Slave restored his senses and allowed him to speak again.

"I'm sorry, what did you just say?" asked Batim, suddenly aware he had not been listening.

This is so strange, thought Angelina. It appeared to her, as she studied the face of her son, that for a moment he'd been absent from his conscious mind, yet she could not fathom out in what way. Was he remembering something? ...Perhaps something from his recent activities, which had temporarily distracted him? And if that was the case, how was he going to react to his parents, knowing as he did that they were looking for answers.

"Your father asked what happened to make you give up your studies," said Angelina, continuing her quiet façade of parental interest, while trying to understand the workings of a disturbed mind.

"I decided not to continue with them; that's all," was his curt and only response.

Then Angelina sensed something else she had not seen before; but the idea of it seemed too preposterous to be real. It seemed to her that Batim was not of one mind, but two; that she detected more than one source of thought within her son. The concept of it troubled her.

By now Batim was starting to get tired of the questions. He had no intention of telling his parents of his relationship with Urla or anything else that went on back then. As far as he was concerned, it was time to end their chat.

"If you don't mind," he said; "I'm very busy and should get back to my work. It has been good to see you both again. I wish you well in your overseas mission."

Dismayed by the abrupt end to their visit, Salutat leapt to his feet.

"But we haven't finished yet," he cried despondently. "There's a great deal more we need to know!"

Batim turned on him.

"What more could I possibly tell you?" he retorted, his anger rising. "I've made a life for myself here – a good life, as you can see," he added, gesturing around him. "I am an adult who is independent of his parents now. The detail of my life is really none of your concern."

"We would still like to be part of it though," Angelina added weakly; hoping to solicit further conversation.

But it was too late. Slave was certain now that the two parents were up to something, and it needed to safeguard its investment.

Batim must get rid of them.

Just then, a loud hammering on the door caused Batim to swing round; annoyed by the interruption.

"What do you want?" he yelled.

The door opened slightly, and a servant timidly peeped through the gap.

"I'm sorry, Master; I didn't know you had company," he whimpered. "I have an urgent message – would you mind coming with me for a minute?"

Batim sighed petulantly.

Without answering the servant, he said to his parents. "You see...I really am busy!"

"Alright," said Salutat, defeated. "We'll leave now and let you get on with your work. Thank you for seeing us."

He gave his son a hug, which Batim returned without emotion. Then, crestfallen, Salutat brushed past him to get to the door.

The servant pushed the door open for him; and held it for Angelina to leave, too. Yet she was reluctant to forsake her son just yet.

She clung to him, her tears flowing freely.

Batim exchanged glances with the servant as if to say, 'This is annoying but it can't be helped'.

"Please don't forget the family who love you," Angelina sobbed. "...And don't relinquish your spiritual roots, either. They are what really sustain you. I will pray to Yavros that you may not be lost to him forever."

It was only after separating from him that she realised she had spoken without thinking.

All of a sudden Angelina was afraid. Had Batim heard her, understood the implication; guessed, even, that she knew more than she was revealing?

She looked at him for the final time: directly into the dark, impenetrable eyes that should have been blue.

Only the cold, hard stare of someone whose patience had run out looked back at her. It was the look of someone who just wanted to be rid of a nuisance.

Angelia's heart sank – and with it, her spirit. She turned away and walked outside with Salutat.

Together they left the vineyard, feeling more desolate than any terran spirit had ever felt before them.

At that moment, Angelina was sure her son, the son of angels, was lost to Yavros forever.

Batim found it hard to concentrate on his work during the days that followed his parents' visit. Something disturbed him terribly, although he could not work out what it was.

In fact, Slave was keeping him restless. The determined phantom had now delved more deeply into the thoughts of Angelina and Salutat. ...And in doing so, it learnt more about the motives behind their visit than they had indeed divulged to their son. Theirs had been no casual visit; but rather, Slave deduced, the parents were after juicy titbits of gossip about their son and his antics.

Slave flew into a rage when it identified their pretence, and vowed Batim would not rest until he was made fully aware of it. Having inveigled its way into his soul, it now no longer regarded itself as the the interloper, but as the host personality himself; its own thoughts and wishes replacing Batim's; the real host little more than a shell.

Consequentially, Slave took the deceitfulness of the two parents very personally. And when Batim began taking his restlessness out on his workers, Slave saw an outlet for its own anger.

One night, Slave communicated directly with the mind of Batim for the first time.

The phantom could not talk, for Lucifer had not given it that ability. Instead, it forced impulses into Batim's head, which transposed into thoughts and then manifested as a terrifying nightmare.

Thus, in the early hours of the morning, Batim cried out as if in pain, and awoke in a cold sweat.

Straightaway, a servant ran into his quarters to see if he was all right and found Batim sitting on the side of his bed; trying to recover from a panic attack.

"Yes...I'm fine," Batim snapped at the servant. "Go back to your station.

The servant shuffled off, leaving Batim more distraught and restless than ever. ...Only this time, he knew why.

"Damn my interfering parents," he hissed loudly. "Why did they have to come snooping around. They must have found out I was expelled. All those bogus questions about why I left the Academie – what rot!"

Batim leapt up from the bed and, still shivering, threw a cloak round his shoulders. He stamped over to the window and looked out at the inky night; his mind racing.

"What else could they know?" he growled; his minding racing. "...A damn sight more than they let on, I bet!"

He was angry now; the painful awakening having rattled his nerves. Together with the notion Slave imparted, his mood had become explosive.

By morning Batim had settled down very little.

During the sleepless hours his pent-up anger needed to find release. Yet, rather than take his frustrations out on his servant, he decided to channel them into something more constructive.

He began to plan the strategy for a new project; one that would deal with the matter once and for all.

Later, when the morning's chores had been completed, he gathered a small band of trustworthy employees – men who were obedient to his every command whilst at the same time ruthless in disposition. Then, after whittling the group down to only two, he took them into his confidence.

"This is what I want you to do," he said.

During the course of the morning, Batim directed them regarding the substance of his plan. When he had finished, he discreetly took out the whip he always kept in his belt. Without warning, he lashed the ankle of one of the men; who fell to the ground, shocked by what Batim had done to him but otherwise unhurt.

Both men looked at Batim in fear.

"That was just an example of what I'll do if you fail me," he told them. "...Now go."

In the meantime, Batim's parents hastily left the district.

Confused and demoralised by what took place at the vineyard, they had no sense of purpose any more, except the need to get away from their son as quickly as possible.

Only an overwhelming impression of failure occupied the hearts of the terran angels. The look of contempt in Batim's black eyes had troubled Angelina. Her sensitivity had great difficulty in coming to grips with the outright rejection she suffered at his hands.

It was unheard of for a son to deal to his mother so...

"I don't think I will ever get over it," she confessed to Salutat during one of their many periods of silence.

There was nothing Angelina wanted to talk about now. They had no enthusiasm for continuing their mission, and their attempts to redeem Batim had met with failure. He was a stranger to them, and best forgotten.

...But how could a mother forget her son?

"You'll get over him in time," Salutat assured her. "As he implied, he is his own master now. Nothing we do or say will influence him. Lucifer has too firm a grip on him."

"All the same, I will always worry and, of course, we must pray for his redemption."

Angelina's self-esteem plummeted; she felt only misery.

With a spirit that constantly seemed to be down in her boots, she could think only of the negatives that haunted her. The positive aspects of their missionary life, which had so lightened her heart beforehand, were now a thing of the past and should indeed be consigned memory.

Salutat did his best to encourage her, but as a terran male he was less emotional than his wife and could not share her feelings to the same extent. And because he could not share her pain, neither could he understand it; to such an extent that, when many days had passed and Angelina still remained in the doldrums, he finally ran out of patience.

"I wish you would snap out of it!" he ordered when he could take her sullenness no longer.

"I wish I could snap out of it, too!" Angelina wailed indignantly. "Do you really think I like being so upset? It's a situation we never experienced as angels, and I've had little occasion to feel downhearted before now. But this is something I can't seem to handle by myself. Please don't be cross with me. I promise I'll try to cheer up, but I really do need you to be patient and give me time."

Salutat relented. He could see the struggle his terran wife was having, and his angel compassion came to her aid.

For her part, Angelina tried to lift her spirits, if only for her husband's sake. She deliberately took note of the little things around her that had always brought her joy: a lovely sunset, a beautifully formed blossom, or the cheeky bird that one day alighted on her knee to steal a piece of fruit from her fingers...

Slowly she began to feel like laughing again. The more she laughed, the better she felt. It wasn't long before her efforts started to pay off, and Angelina found herself joining in renewed plans for their mission.

She had almost forgotten the Return and Miekaale, so distracted had she become with her own worries.

"When we last spoke with Yavros he said he would send Miekaale if ever evil overcame us," she reminded Salutat one day. "D'you know, we never did summon him. I guess we were too absorbed in our domestic problems to give him thought. I've wondered since then if he would have made a difference to our visit with Batim."

"Who knows," Salutat replied. "It makes little difference now. Anyway, Yavros won't interfere with terran free will, so Miekaale couldn't have done anything to alter Batim's acceptance of Lucifer's influence."

"I'm not sure only Lucifer is involved, though."

Salutat abruptly stopped what he was working on; his curiosity aroused.

"Angelina, you're not making any sense."

Ignoring his comment, Angelina went on.

"I don't suppose you noticed it at the time, but there was something odd about Batim when he was speaking."

Salutat smiled; impressed that Angelina was once more talking about their son objectively. But her train of thought was worrying.

"What are you referring to?" he asked uneasily.

"It was an observation I made about him at the time."

Salutat sat down on the grass, with Angelina following suit – it was good to be conversing naturally again.

Trying unsuccessfully to recall their conversation with Batim, he said, "Tell me what you saw."

"This was not so much what I saw, but what I sensed. It was as though Batim had a twofold consciousness."

"Twofold?"

"Yes; I know... It does sound strange, and I'm sorry for being so vague. But there was a sort of duality to him while he was speaking."

"But that would have been Lucifer's influence..."

"...I'm aware of that! But this was different. Some of the time it wasn't Batim talking – it was this other..."

Angelina searched for the right word.

"There was another 'being' inside of him."

"Another soul?"

"I suppose so."

"How can you have two souls in the one person?" asked Salutat with scepticism.

"I...I don't know," Angelina replied self-consciously.

She suddenly realised how foolish her statement must have sounded.

"But I swear it wasn't Batim speaking. At the end, when he wanted us to leave, his reaction seemed like somebody else was goading him."

"It must have been when that man came to the door."

"No, there was more to it than that. I noticed it first in his eyes. They weren't Batim's, but those of an alien being. Somebody else was looking out at me through our son's eyes. Does that make sense?"

"I understand what you are saying, but I don't think it can be done. Surely, it's one terran spirit, one soul. When we inherited these bodies all those years ago, we did so after the souls of their original inhabitants had departed. I'm sure what you saw, or rather, what you think you saw, was just the result of Lucifer's influence."

"Salutat, aren't you forgetting something? In your last mission, you took over the body of a living person."

"That was different..."

"...How? The principle was the same."

"I know. But it was a spirit sent by Yavros to utilise one of his creations. What you are suggesting is impossible. No entity in Eddren is capable of possessing another soul; not even Lucifer. ...Only Yavros can do that sort of thing! Surely you understand that."

Angelina gave up. She would receive little support for the theory from Salutat. Her rationale could not be proved, and nothing less than proof would make him believe her.

Yet, although she had no choice but to drop the subject with her husband, she could not let it go. The thought of Batim being taken over by another soul may have worried her, but it also gave her just a faint glimmer of hope; for if this possession had been forced on Batim, and if it could be exorcised, she might get her son back.

"I want to talk to Yavros about it," she told Salutat not long afterwards.

"You're quite serious, aren't you?"

Angelina nodded. "I can't get it off my mind. But it's just a theory at the moment, and on my own I've no way of finding out whether or not it's right."

"Alright then; a chat with Yavros might help you resolve it once and for all. Do you want me to come with you?"

Angelina thought for a moment.

"Would you mind if I went by myself this time?"

"Not at all. I've got some repairs to do on the wagon, and it will give me the chance to do them while your spirit is away. I'll try not to disturb you."

So, with hope in her heart, Angelina settled comfortably in the tent again and slipped back into Eternity.

When she arrived in the realm, Angelina found disorder in her community. Something had occurred which caused a ripple of trepidation among the normally docile angels.

At first she paid little attention to it; her mind focused on the need to speak to Yavros. But when she discovered that he was in conference over the same troubling matter, she made enquiries as to what had happened.

It transpired that one of the souls banished to Hellion was missing.

Every so often a census was conducted within the realm to make sure that none had left without arrangement. The most recent census revealed that one soul could not be accounted for.

"...But surely, that would be Lucifer." Angelina said to her informant, a returned angel guardian she had never seen before. Then, as an afterthought, she said, "Did you know Lucifer is in Eddren at present? He's still ruining terran spirits, my son included!"

Her informer looked baffled by the odd remark from an angel, and a stranger at that; for he had no knowledge of either Angelina or the life she had been living in Eddren.

With a superior expression unbefitting one of Yavros' angels, he responded, "Obviously I know where Lucifer is! ...You're new around here, aren't you? At least, you're not one of the regulars."

Angelina suddenly regretted having said anything. Even in her home realm she was feeling out of place. She had gone back there solely with the intention of speaking to Yavros; not to become embroiled in local affairs. ...And whatever had become of the angels? They certainly didn't behave like this in her day! Had Lucifer's influence filtered through to Eternity itself; that even angel guardians were now tainted? She hoped not.

...Or maybe she had just struck the one bad apple in the whole barrel.

The thought of it made her chuckle.

"I wonder what the angel would think if he knew I'd referred to him as a bad apple. He would consider me to be crazy – a poor example to other angels – and no doubt have me shipped off to Hellion!"

Angelina decided to have no more contact with her angel peers.

While Angelina sat waiting for Yavros to finish his meeting, she saw a familiar face. It was Masian.

She leapt up in delight; and with relief that not all of the angels were now strangers.

"How lovely to see you again; I've missed you!" Masian cried with joy. "Have you been in Eddren all this time?"

Angelina felt a little more at ease. He had been a good friend to her in the past, and she was in need of one now.

"Yes. Salutat and I have been on a mission to promote Miekaale and the Return," she said politely; although her heart urged her to speak on a different matter.

Angelina wanted to rush headlong into the whole story of Batim, so great was her need of sharing it with Masian. But she held back. Masian would not be able to absorb it all in one go. Maybe, after she had consulted Yavros he might be willing to see her. Masian's opinion and advice would be invaluable.

Drawing breath, she went on, "I'm waiting to talk with Yavros, but afterwards I would very much like to see you."

"Yes, of course. You know where I live. Just come round any time. Are you and Salutat back home for good now?"

"Oh no; I'm by myself – just visiting because I need to consult Yavros," she said with sadness in her voice. "I shall return directly to Eddren when I've spoken with you."

Masian noticed a hint of melancholy in her voice, and wondered what the trouble could be. As an angel who had never been to Eddren, it was difficult to comprehend what conditions were like for those who had worked there.

Waiting patiently for Yavros, Angelina's thoughts remained centred on Masian. She knew it would be hard to explain her dilemma to him; yet even having someone to whom she could pour out her heart gave her comfort.

She was working out her explanation for Masian, when angels of various ranks emerged from Yavros' chambers. After the last of them had left she rose to her feet and peeped through the still open door. Yavros sat at his desk, a perplexed expression on his face.

Angelina knocked gently.

"May I come in?" she asked.

"My goodness! What a surprise!"

Yavros' face suddenly lit up, and it gave Angelina joy to realise he was pleased to see her.

"I was wondering how things are going with your son. Is that what brings you back to Eternity so soon?"

Angelina entered the room; glancing around to make sure they were alone.

"Something is troubling me, Sire, and I would like to get your opinion on it."

"Right then; come and sit down. I just have one matter to attend to, and I'll be with you."

Yavros indicated where he wanted Angelina to sit, and then left the room. In his brief absence Angelina elevated her consciousness, remembering how Yavros taught her to communicate from her intuition rather than her emotions. She was contemplating this when he returned.

"How can I help you?" he asked, sitting down beside her. "There aren't still problems with your son, are there?"

"Well, actually that's why I've come to see you."

With some hesitation, Angelina recounted to Yavros all that took place during their visit with Batim.

Yavros was astonished that they had been unsuccessful in talking with Batim.

"Did you not call on Miekaale?" he asked.

Angelina looked at him with embarrassment.

"No," she said apologetically. "It didn't actually occur to us at the time..."

"...Why not? I offered him to you! It's no wonder you got nowhere with your problem. This would have been an ideal opportunity to avail yourself of Miekaale's services. After all, it is what you preach to others, isn't it?"

Angelina fidgeted awkwardly. How could she get him to understand how different everything seemed when they were confronted with their own son? How even their composure was so upset they could not think clearly? How she as a mother became so drained by Batim's dominance that all thought of Miekaale's help dissipated..? But Yavros was correct. What right had they to consider themselves competent ambassadors if they couldn't even put into practice the spiritual principles they preached to others?

Suddenly she felt ashamed.

For a moment, Yavros' chiding blurred her thinking. She sat in silence, momentarily lost for words; dumbfounded by the recognition of error Yavros had awakened in her. She hoped he did not regard her as a failure.

"I apologise for the oversight," she said with remorse.

Would no-one try to understand the difficulties of being both angel and terran...not even Yavros?

"No, I'm the one who must apologise," he said, seeing how unhappy his words had made her feel. "I don't fully understand the problems you must have faced with Batim. To me it's all so simple − call on Miekaale when evil is present. It always works! But I assume, not being a terran,

I underestimated the intensity of terran feeling, and how it can disturb your spiritual sensitivity."

Angelina relaxed a little. Yavros had not condemned her for the error; albeit an understandable error. But there still remained the reason for her visit. She still needed to seek verification from him that she was on the right track in her way of thinking.

All at once a sense of weariness came over her. Devoid of inspiration, with no idea how to describe the duality she had seen in Batim, she wondered how she could continue. Yavros would surely think she was insane.

But Angelina did not take into account Yavros' powers of intuition and recollection.

"So tell me, what else brings you here?" he said. "I can see there is more to this visit than an update on Batim."

Angelina looked up at him, pleased he was encouraging further conversation. She blinked to clear her head, and to gain some focus on the theory that haunted her.

She responded immediately.

"I think my son may be possessed by another soul," she said outright.

Yavros looked at her enquiringly.

Instantly, Angelina regretted being quite so direct. He does think I'm mad, she guessed.

"What do you mean by 'possessed'?" Yavros asked.

Angelina fidgeted with embarrassment. How could she describe what nobody has ever witnessed before?

"It's hard to explain," she began. "I noticed something about Batim when we were at the vineyard, which might explain why he has become so violent recently."

"Go on. This is fascinating."

Yavros leant forward to pay closer attention.

He trusted Angelina. After all, she was still an angel, despite her mission in Eddren. Her spiritual qualities were intact, even though the pressure of her terran nature could be overwhelming – as she had just demonstrated by her unusual imaginings.

"What did you see in your son?" he asked.

"I saw another being in his eyes."

"Did you, now?" exclaimed Yavros.

This was unheard of. Not even Lucifer was capable of inhabiting a living terran.

"How do you know it was another entity and not just the result of Lucifer's influence?"

Angelina sighed, desperately trying to find the words to describe her observations. At least Yavros was listening to her, and did not regard her as a deluded angel, confused by too long in terran form.

"For one thing, when I looked into his eyes, I saw a kind of empty blackness, whereas Batim's eyes are usually blue. Whatever has influenced him has also possessed him, and it was looking out at me through his eyes."

"Did you question Batim about it?"

"Oh no! He was on the defensive – or at least, the thing inside of him was. Whenever we tried talking to him, he would instantly contradict us. It was as though this other being had such a hold on him that it did not recognise us as anything but intruders. Our son Batim would have been happy to share his experiences, but not this creature. I've never come across anything like it before. Do you think I could be right?"

"You may be; I can't know for sure. Lucifer is certainly getting more cunning as the ages slip by. It's possible he may have discovered a means of actually possessing terran spirits rather than just influencing them."

"It wasn't Lucifer himself; it was some other entity. I'd have recognised Lucifer; I know I would."

"But where would Lucifer find another soul who could be manipulated like that? My realms are only Eternity and Eddren, and..."

"...And Hellion!" cried Angelina, feeling more confident about her idea. "Isn't there a soul missing from Hellion?"

"My goodness, you're right!" said Yavros, alarmed by the implications. "There has indeed been a soul reported as missing – and it disappeared at about the time Lucifer last gave us the slip. I wonder how many more he's got lined up for terran invasion!"

Yavros lapsed into deep thought, leaving Angelina both speechless and no closer to solving her problem.

"Yavros, how can I help our son?" she asked at length. "That is my primary concern just now."

"Yes...I know it is," he answered kindly, placing his hand over hers. "It's my concern, too. But of greater concern to me just now are the implications this has on terranity as a whole. I must have a conference with Miekaale."

Yavros got up from his seat, and rang for assistance.

"Angelina, would you mind very much if we terminated our conversation?"

Angelina looked at him in surprise. "...But what about Batim's situation?"

"If I can solve this problem with Miekaale's assistance, it will help Batim, too."

Yavros escorted Angelina from the room.

"I'll get back to you and Salutat when I've decided what to do," he told her. "There's some urgency here – in terran terms, anyway. So please forgive me if I get right onto it."

"Yes, of course – and thank you for seeing me,"

Angelina had responded to him politely, but really she was numbed from the shock of being ushered from Yavros' presence.

301

What do I do now? she asked herself.

...And then she remembered Masian.

Angelina's friend and mentor welcomed her warmly.

"I can't describe how good it is to see you again," he confided. "Life around here isn't the same without you and Salutat. How is he, by the way?"

"He is well, thank you. Did you know we got married?"

Straightaway Angelina realised Masian might not know what she meant by that.

"What is 'got married'?" he asked; unthinkingly reading her mind.

As Angelina suspected, Masian had no knowledge of life as a terran spirit.

"Marriage is the love bond between male and female terrans. They get married in order to procreate and keep the species going."

"Oh, I see," he said with only moderate understanding. "...And did you?" he added.

"Did I what?"

"Procreate? Did you keep the species going during your life as a terran spirit?"

Angelina laughed.

"Yes we did," she said brightly; enjoying the moment. "We have a son called Batim. In terran terms he is a grown up young man now..." Angelina hesitated briefly; then she added, "...That is why I wanted to talk to you. We are very worried about him."

Masian's brow creased; the kindly mentor empathising with his favourite angel. He had heard of the difficulties experienced by terran spirits as a result of Lucifer's grip on them, and hoped the two angels – and their progeny – had not been affected by it.

"In what way are you worried?" he asked.

Angelina again recounted the recent events; especially her suspicion that Batim was possessed, and that Yavros thought there might be some basis to her theory.

"Has Yavros made any suggestions to help you?"

"Not yet. However, he wants to discuss with Miekaale how best to deal with this and any similar occurrences."

Masian paused in thought for a moment.

"I wonder if Lucifer has singled you out because of your liaison with Salutat. He always had a soft spot for you, if I recall. He may even be jealous, and this is a way of getting back at you."

Angelina groaned. "I'd like to think he wouldn't be that cruel, but now I just don't know. There's one thing I'm sure of, though."

"What's that?"

"Lucifer is not going to give up his influence over Batim without a struggle, and this is worrying me. How can you evict an alien entity from another person's soul? I do hope Miekaale and Yavros manage to come up with a strategy? It's hard for an angel living in Eddren at the best of times, but having to deal with…"

Angelina suddenly stopped; unable to finish what she was saying. Her face ashen, she clutched at her chest as a tugging sensation caused her heart to miss a beat.

Masian saw a frightened look on her face.

"Are you alright?" he asked, confused how something could be ailing an angel.

On the verge of blacking out, she replied, "I don't really know… I feel as though I'm…"

Angelina passed out – and also out of sight; leaving Masian alone and wondering what just happened.

Without warning, she found herself being yanked back into the physical dimension.

She awoke in her body with a start.

Salutat was shaking her.

Trying to adjust, she blinked and looked up at him; then blinked again. For the face looking down at her was bruised and bloodied.

"Angelina; thank goodness!" gushed Salutat. "I've been trying to bring you back for ages. We are in great danger here and must leave. Somebody is trying to attack us!"

Though shaken by the abrupt re-entry into her body, Angelina sensed the urgency in Salutat's voice, and rallied quickly. But her first concern was her husband. Whatever had happened to him?

"Look at your face!" she gasped, gently touching a fresh bruise on his cheekbone. "Are you badly injured?"

Salutat flinched.

"No! No, I'm fine," he retorted impatiently. "I'll tell you what happened on the way. Now, please help me pack up the tent. There's no time to lose."

Angelina could scarcely believe any of this: One minute she was enjoying a productive conversation with Masian, yet in the very next moment, she was being goaded into action by her husband who, for some reason, had been beaten up.

Soon, Salutat cracked the reins over the horse's head and set it in motion. As the wagon slowly moved off, he nervously looked around.

"There's a bandit in the bush over there," he stated. "I knocked him unconscious, but don't know how long we've got before he rallies. The other bandit disappeared after I chased him."

Salutat's agitation reflected in his voice. He cracked the reins again, forcing the struggling horse to pick up its pace.

Angelina sat beside her husband, anxiously speculating on what had taken place.

At last Salutat's apprehension began to lessen, and he eased the horse back to a canter. The crisis, it seemed, was over for the time being.

"Will you please tell me what happened?" she asked; her anxiousness only slightly diminished. "You said there were two bandits."

"Yes. They appeared out of nowhere and ambushed me while I was loading the wagon."

"Ambushed you? Did they steal anything?"

"No. I got the feeling they weren't thieves so much as thugs. They seemed to want me, not our belongings."

"Oh, Salutat – surely not! How could they have known who you were, or where you'd be?"

"A comment from one of the bandits made me realise what they were after. The man I eventually knocked out said, 'This is him.' Then the other one said something like, 'We'd better be sure or the master will flog us.' I believe I got the better of them in the end, because one bandit was unconscious, and the other had gone. Mercifully, neither went into the tent where you were still sleeping. But I felt we needed to get away quickly and tried to wake you. I hope it didn't cause you any harm?"

"No, I'm alright now. I'm more concerned about you."

Angelina noticed his swollen knuckles and the way he winced when he tried to move.

'Poor Salutat,' she thought tearfully. 'If only I had been here to help him. Who could have done such a thing?'

Unknown to anyone, including Lucifer, it was Slave who ordered the attempt on Salutat's life.

Convinced that Batim's parents knew of his activities, Slave now regarded them as a threat; not just to Batim but also to its own survival. With Batim's free will long since usurped, it was Slave who now made the decisions; for even if Batim had known about the attack on his father, he could have done nothing to prevent it.

The escaped bandit hurried back to the vineyard with both of the horses.

Too cowardly to admit to Batim that the object of the attack had turned on them, he lied that although Salutat left his partner for dead, their quarry was overcome.

Throughout the assailant's report, Batim stood before him; his lips pursed in concentration, giving nothing away.

But Slave took in every word.

To bolster his position in Batim's eyes, the man grasped at a chance to also add sentiment to his tale.

"I regret to advise that my colleague did not recover from his injuries," he again lied; in the full knowledge that his co-conspirator had merely been knocked unconscious. Furthermore, he deliberately omitted to confess that, in bringing back both of their horses, he left the other bandit with no means of returning to make his own report on the botched job.

His own report delivered, he waited for his master's congratulations on a job well done.

However, whilst the Batim of old might have believed the story without question, Slave knew better.

A cunning character always recognises its own kind, and Slave was well aware how readily people of low character will lie to save their own skin. It instantly saw through the man's deceptions, and took control.

"Liar!" roared Batim with absolute authority. "How dare you try to deceive me?"

Shocked by his master's response, the unfortunate man cowered as Slave raised up within its host, ready to attack once more.

"Tell me what really happened, degenerate, or you will surely die!"

The man had no option but to tell the truth; yet only part of the truth.

He was still reluctant to disclose that Salutat had not been killed as instructed on pain of death, as he feared the outcome if he did so.

But Slave was too wily for him and outwitted him with every comment.

Before long, the hapless bandit found himself admitting to his master the very truth he had been trying to hide.

"What!" roared Batim. "You disobeyed my orders!"

"He was too strong for us!" the man wailed. "He came at us with supernatural strength. I've never seen anything like it. We both had him pinned to the ground and he still managed to get free!"

"You have failed me!" roared Batim again. "For this you must die!"

"Sir... Please! Have pity on me – I did my best!"

"No, you did not. You could have followed him and seen where he was going; so that someone far more competent than you might succeed where you failed!"

"I'm sorry. Please forgive me!"

The man grovelled before Batim; his hands clasped in petition. But Slave's anger knew no bounds.

Batim called out for his servants, two of whom reacted swiftly and rushed to his side. Unwavering, he told them to bind the man, take him outside and execute him.

The man screamed in terror as he was led away. Then he fell silent.

Batim walked over to the window. Without feeling, he gazed on the grizzly sight. The man's body lay lifeless on the dirt, his decapitated head lying beside it. Already the ground was stained red with his flowing blood.

"Good riddance, you scum," rasped Slave.

Batim turned back into the room.

With a look of pure evil, he mumbled, "As I can't trust anyone else to this job properly, it appears I'll have to do it by myself!"

Then he strode outside, slamming the door behind him.

CHAPTER 7

Salutat headed for the coast. Traumatised by his near miss at their camp, he wanted only to put the past behind. And the best way to forget what had happened, he decided, was to keep busy. He and Angelina would pick up the unravelled threads of their overseas mission, and book another voyage.

It was raining when they arrived at port.

As luck would have it, a local market was in full swing, which gave Salutat the opportunity to sell their belongings in order to pay for the voyage.

Yet, this meant they would now be restricted in their activities in the meantime.

Salutat was happy to put up with a bit of hardship while they waited the few days for their boat to arrive. Angelina, on the other hand, saw things differently. She insisted they move into some form of accommodation rather than put up with any hardship.

"There's no value in catching a cold," she said wisely. "It will be hard enough living in another land. We don't want to start off with one of us taking to our sickbed as well!"

Salutat reluctantly agreed. Before nightfall he booked them into a small lodging house close to the docks.

On the day their vessel was due to arrive in port, Salutat went down to the dockside to take a look around.

He had little experience of docks or shipping, and the sights, sounds and smells with which he was confronted fascinated him. Noisy gulls swooped without fear, picking up tasty titbits discarded from the boats, and the garbled sound of voices could be heard from a docked vessel as its cargo was prepared for offloading.

Salutat wondered if this was the boat that would take them overseas, and scoured its length in a vain attempt to discover the name. Disappointed, he realised this could not be the one; for theirs definitely had a name. If only he could remember it...

By now, Salutat's curiosity had been aroused. Excited by the prospects ahead, he returned to their lodgings to find out from Angelina what the boat was called, and when it was due in.

Yet Salutat did not go back there unseen. Unknown to him, somebody was watching his every move.

It was Batim.

Slave wasted no time in initiating the pursuit of Salutat, methodically searching Batim's mind for clues as to where his parents might be heading. When the recollection of an overseas mission surfaced, it quickly deduced that they would no doubt head to the nearest port; a calculated guess in which Slave had utmost faith. So it was with little surprise that Batim sighted his father at the dockside a couple of days later.

Keeping well out of sight, Batim watched the older man make his way back to his lodgings, and again when he later returned to the dock; armed with the name of the boat.

With the name of the vessel implanted in his mind, Salutat selected an embankment from where he could observe the comings and goings in the busy dock. As each vessel arrived, he dropped down to take a closer look.

At last his patience was rewarded.

Here it was…the 'Persimon'.

He watched while its bulky cargo was unloaded, and the vessel's few passengers disembarked. He wondered where they came from, and if any of them knew about Yavros and Miekaale.

…Probably not, he reflected; for the message had not yet spread that far. An idea of such significance would take time to catch on with terrans of other cultures.

"Hopefully it won't be too long before our message will have spread throughout the whole of Eddren," he thought when a twinge of excitement for the months ahead caught his breath.

For a moment the trauma of recent days slipped to the back of his mind.

Later on, he went into the shipping office and checked Persimon's departure time. An old mariner confirmed that the ship would leave at noon the next day as scheduled. Salutat hurried back to give Angelina the happy news.

Also with keen anticipation, Batim gathered from Salutat's interest in the boat that his parents were indeed planning to leave on Persimon. Once Salutat left for home, Batim also slipped into the shipping office, and made the same enquiry of the old mariner.

The mariner was bemused that two men, who looked so alike they could be related, should come in one after the other in relation to the same vessel.

That night Batim lay low; hiding in a disused wooden crate close to the water's edge. With Slave in charge, he no longer questioned the activities he was engaged in, and mindlessly responded to its every whim. In the morning he strolled along the wharf, helping himself to food from the countless crates and barrels which had been opened for inspection by the port authorities.

Slave made sure his actions went undetected. It could not allow its host – the one who would soon elevate it in Lucifer's estimation – to be caught pilfering.

The morning seemed to drag on for Batim. There was very little he could do except hang around; waiting until his parents turned up at the dock.

The shipping office attendant recognised the muscular youth from the day before, and saw from his demeanour that he was getting bored. He decided, as there was still time to spare before Persimon's departure, that he would put him to good use.

"Come here, lad," he said curtly when he caught Batim watching him at work.

Batim looked around to see who in particular the man was calling.

"Surely it can't be me?" he grumbled. "Nobody would have the gall to address me as 'lad'!"

"Yes, I'm talking to you," the mariner stressed, pointing directly at him. "Come over here. I've got a job for you."

All at once, Slave's indignation was aroused. Someone was making demands of its host...and that would not do at all. Batim was at the dock for a purpose, and nobody must interfere with the plan.

"What do you want, scum?" Slave growled, surprising even Batim with its ferocity. "Go away and leave us alone."

The mariner was shocked. Never in all his years had he been spoken to so rudely by a mere adolescent. And what did he mean by 'us'? There was nobody else around...

"Are you waiting to board Persimon?" he ventured, still hoping he might be able to get some work out of Batim.

"What has that got to do with you?" screamed Slave with outrage at the mariner's audacity.

The old man gave up. He retreated back into his office, fearing Batim might hit him. He could not get over the evil look in eyes blacker than anything he had seen before.

That youth is crazy, he thought, shutting the door and bolting it.

Shortly before noon, Salutat and Angelina arrived at the dock, along with other passengers.

Batim observed his parents' arrival, and unseen made his way to the gate through which they would pass before embarking. At the last minute, he jumped out in front of them, preventing them from going through.

Angelina let out a shriek in surprise at seeing him again so unexpectedly.

Quickly, Salutat stood in front of his wife to protect her. He feared this would not be a sociable meeting.

"Son, you gave your mother a fright!" he cried. "What are you doing here?"

"I couldn't let my parents go overseas without saying goodbye now, could I?" sneered Slave; its sickly smirk painted on Batim's face.

Straight away, Angelina recognised the voice of Batim's intruder: so different from his own.

"I don't know who you are, or why you are doing this," she said fearfully. "Please leave my son alone. You are not welcome in him!"

Salutat looked at her agog. Whatever was she saying? Had Angelina lost control of her senses?

But then he remembered her claim that their son was possessed by another spirit.

He turned back to Batim and tried to see what gave her that impression. As soon as he looked into the menacing eyes he knew exactly what she meant. This was definitely not Batim.

Suddenly he sensed danger.

Salutat looked around, hoping there might be people close by to give them a feeling of security, but the other passengers had already embarked. The estranged family group appeared to be alone.

"Kindly step out of the way," he ordered Slave.

By now he had ceased to regard the entity before him as his own son.

"And where do you think you're going?" shouted Slave, only briefly fazed by the realisation that both parents now knew of its presence.

Salutat extended his arm to push Batim aside. As he did so, a flash of bright metal caught his eye.

He tried to dodge the slashing blade of Batim's knife, but it caught him on the wrist, and he cried out in pain.

"Are you mad!" screeched Salutat, clutching at his now bleeding arm.

Angelina screamed.

"Batim!" she cried. "Don't let the fiend do this to you. Take control again, my son."

She rushed forward, hoping to push Batim away from Salutat before he slashed again with his knife. But she was too late. Slave had already plunged the knife deep into Salutat's gut, and cruelly wrenched it out again.

Salutat slumped to the ground, writhing in pain.

Batim stood over him; his face expressionless.

"It's done!" Slave shrieked wildly within him. "I have avenged Lucifer's honour! How he will glorify me!"

Angelina gaped in stunned disbelief.

"Salutat!" she cried in terror, and dropped to her knees before him.

He lay curled up, clutching the wound in his abdomen; now bleeding profusely.

"No, my love!" she pleaded. "Surely not...I can't believe this is happening!"

She looked beseechingly up at Batim, as if in some way he might be able to undo the damage now done.

Indifferent to her appeal, Batim stood motionless while Slave gloated over its prize.

Bending over, Angelina gently cradled her husband in her arms.

Salutat reached for her wrist. Then, weakened from loss of blood, he uttered something she could barely hear.

Angelina positioned her ear close to his mouth to catch his words.

With a final effort he murmured, "Miekaale..." Then he fell back, dead.

"Oh no," she moaned, her face buried in his bloodied hair. "Salutat, please don't leave me..."

Angelina wept hysterically, clutching the inert body of her husband; gently rocking him like a babe in arms, as if to somehow comfort him.

But then unexpectedly his voice seemed to speak inside her head. "Miekaale..." it said again.

She looked at Salutat's face, thinking he had spoken to her; hoping with a passion that perhaps he was not dead after all. Yet the life had gone from his empty features.

I must have imagined it, she thought.

"Get up you stupid woman!" commanded Slave, as the boot of her son prodded her ankle.

Angelina rose to her feet, covered with blood. All of a sudden, her grief exploded into anger and she turned on Batim. Beating him on the chest with clenched fists, she yelled abuse such as she had never done before.

Just then, two dock workers appeared, disturbed by the commotion. They paused for a moment to weigh up the situation. It was obvious what had happened.

Batim faced them, the knife still bared; Salutat's blood staining the deadly blade.

"Come on, you fools! You can't touch me now," rasped Slave, its crazed and victorious look bursting out of Batim's eyes. He waved the knife at the two men.

They stood a way back, afraid; then exchanged glances for courage.

The senior of the two muttered to the young dockhand, "I saw this creep over by the office earlier on. He looked like he was up to something."

Angelina said meekly, "Please don't harm my son."

"Are you alright, lady?"

"Yes, I'm unhurt, but my husband is dead."

Angelina felt faint with shock. She was on the point of swooning, when Salutat's voice again sounded in her head; much louder than before.

"Miekaale!" it said. "Call...on...Miekaale!"

This time, Angelina knew where it came from.

It was indeed Salutat; and the realisation of it restored some of her strength. Her angel husband, in dying to his physical form, had reverted to spirit. Angelina could not see him, but she knew without doubt that he was present. And she knew also what she should do.

Raising her arms to the heavens, she shouted for all she was worth: "Miekaale! Save us!"

Immediately, a gust of wind blew through the gateway and surrounding buildings. Angelina could see nothing, but in an instant she recognised the mark of the great Golden Angel. In her mind's eye she saw the sword-wielding being alight on Batim, catching him off guard and hurling him to the ground.

Miekaale stood over him, one foot on his head, his right arm raised high ready to plunge his fearsome sword deep into the antagonist.

Slave cowered in fright; unable to comprehend exactly what was taking place. One minute it had been riding high, and the next...

It really had no idea what would happen next; only that its newfound status appeared to be in jeopardy.

What did happen astonished everyone present.

The two rescuers heard only the rushing sound and witnessed the young man's fall. Slave felt a gripping terror as the point of a sword was aimed at it, and unwittingly let go of its host. Batim, freed at last from Slave's hold, passed out from exhaustion. And Angelina heard something she never thought she would hear.

In a consciousness elevated out of sheer desperation, she heard Miekaale the Golden Angel speak.

"Go from here, you insidious creature!" he demanded, addressing the now insignificant wisp of a sprite cowering in a dark corner. "I am Miekaale, Golden Angel of Yavros. You shall go back to Hellion where you belong. ...Now!"

Rebellious to the last, Slave turned on him with one last show of resistance.

"You can't tell me what to do! I am the representative here in Eddren of the mighty lord Lucifer. It is you who shall be banished, not me!"

Yet Miekaale was unmoved by the shallow threat; such was his authority.

In a flash, he plunged his sword into Slave's quivering shadow and lifted it high. Then he flung the still screeching spectre through the veil of consciousness, and deep into

317

the furthest recesses of Hellion. And finally, to reinforce his actions, Miekaale followed in its wake.

Slave would never again return to Eddren.

Meanwhile, Angelina stood panting beside the dead body of her husband and prostrate form of her son.

She knelt beside Batim and stroked his hair. It seemed to be a lighter shade than before.

...How strange, she thought.

The supervising rescuer asked if he was alive.

"Yes," she said thankfully. "He should be alright now."

"Do you realise he must be arrested and taken to the guardhouse?" he asked.

"What?" she said; mystified. Had not the real murderer been evicted?

"But of course he must," said the other, joining in. "He has just killed a man."

"Let me explain something to you," said Angelina, rising to her feet to confront the rescuers, who suddenly seemed more like enemies. "This is my son," she said, pointing to Batim. The incident was a family affair. It was my husband he killed, not some stranger! You have no reason to take him away. ...And besides...he's all I have left now."

"Even so," the young one persisted. "He has committed a heinous crime and must be arrested before he can harm anyone else."

"But he won't...I know he won't!" she insisted. "He's no longer a threat to you or anybody. When this happened it was because an evil spirit possessed him; but my son has come free of it now. So you don't need to worry about his actions anymore."

The two men looked at each other, suspecting grief had caused Angelina to lose her mind.

"Come with me now," insisted the supervisor.

He took hold of her by the elbow to lead her away, but Angelina resisted and shook herself free.

"Leave me alone!" she shrieked, at once fearful both for her son's safety and her own.

She looked down at Batim as the young dockhand tried unsuccessfully to rouse him.

He lowered a bucket into the harbour and emptied its contents over Batim, splashing Angelina in the process.

She gasped with the sudden coldness of the water.

Batim also gasped, and then stirred. As he came to, his eyes rested on the sorry sight of his father lying dead on the ground. For a moment he remained still, while trying to remember where he was and what had just taken place. But his memory was sketchy; so completely had he been dominated by Slave. Then he noticed the men. Their stern features told him all was not well.

With difficulty he lifted himself up; only to slump back down as a dizzy spell came over him.

Defiantly, Angelina placed herself between Batim and the two men.

"Can't either of you see that my son isn't a threat to anyone now?" she asserted; vainly entreating the seamen to leave them both alone.

Ignoring her, the supervisor was adamant.

"Please move out of the way and let us take him to the guardhouse," he demanded.

In desperation, Angelina flung her arms around Batim's stooped shoulders. They really were going to arrest him! She must not allow them to; it wasn't right!

...But she was powerless.

The two men hauled Batim to his feet.

He looked over his shoulder at Angelina, and she saw again the blue of his natural eyes.

"Oh, my son," she sighed tearfully.

Batim tried to maintain his balance but, weak from the ordeal, his knees crumpled beneath him.

Supported by the captors, Batim was dragged away from his dead father and protesting mother.

Angelina could only stand and stare; not yet knowing if she should remain with her husband's body or follow after them to see where they were going.

She decided on the latter.

The seamen escorted Batim to a cell at the rear of the shipping office.

The old mariner was shocked to realise that the stroppy youth had been arrested.

"What has he done?" he asked the two men when they re-emerged with a large key, which its bearer placed on the desk.

"See he doesn't escape," the supervisor barked without answering his question. Then he strode past him to make his exit.

Once he had left, the mariner looked quizzically at the younger one.

With unsanctioned authority, he responded with, "He stabbed his old man to death."

The mariner's jaw dropped in disbelief.

"They were in here not all that long ago – separately. This one must have been lying in wait for his father! No wonder they looked so alike."

Just then, Angelina entered the office.

"Could I please see my son?" she asked pointedly.

"He's out the back," the young man replied, pointing to the door. "You'll have to be quick, though. The bailiff will be taking him away soon."

"The bailiff?" she repeated. "You mean..."

"...He'll be sent to jail until he goes before the tribunal."

"But he's my son! You can't do that to him!"

"I don't care, lady. Your husband's killer must be judged according to the law – even if he is your son."

"You don't understand..." she insisted. "There's more to all of this than any of you realise."

Angelina's slender frame stood dwarfed between the two inflexible men. Suddenly she felt any further attempts to plead her case would be futile. From her perspective, the reasons for securing Batim's release were justified. But neither of these two would listen, and they certainly were not going to let him go. It looked like Batim was destined to spend the night in jail.

"Do you want to see him or not?" the young one asked impatiently.

"Yes! Oh yes – please!"

Angelina slipped in behind him as he opened the door. Batim was sitting on a stone bench against the far wall; his head bowed.

She slowly walked up to him as the door slammed shut behind her.

"Son," she said, a lump forming in her throat. "However did all of this happen?"

Batim rubbed his eyes.

She could see moisture glistening on his cheek. He had been crying.

You poor child, thought Angelina. How bewildered you must feel. That horrible creature left you in an appalling predicament.

She took hold of his wrists to encourage him to stand. When he did so, she wrapped her arms around his waist; her head buried in his chest.

After a moment Batim responded.

"Is my father really dead?" he asked.

"Yes," she answered sorrowfully, but then she changed her mind. "Well...actually...no..."

"...What do you mean?"

Confused, Batim pulled back and looked at her.

"Do you mean to say he didn't die, after all?"

"Well, yes, he did – in a physical sense..."

This is going to be difficult, she thought.

"...But since then, he has spoken to me spiritually. Your father has reverted to his original angel form. I hope to see him again soon."

"Are you going to die, too?"

"No, son. I'm not going to die. I'm just going to visit him in Eternity. It's where we come from, if you recall."

"Oh, yes. I remember now."

Batim slumped down on the bench; exhausted. He fell silent, withdrawing into his private thoughts.

It seemed to Angelina that the struggle to understand his situation was more than he could cope with, and she suddenly felt helpless.

There was nothing she could do for him now; for in the terran world he had committed murder. And even though she knew there were extenuating circumstances involved, they would not be justification for his release.

"Can I come to Eternity with you?" asked Batim, still in a daze.

"I wish you could, but I don't think it would be possible; not until..." Angelina groaned with the thought of what she was trying to say. "...Not until you leave this realm and can meet up with your father again."

"...And until then?"

Angelina shook her head sorrowfully. "I'm afraid that's out of my hands."

The noise of a key rammed into the door startled them. Angelina turned around, and saw that the supervisor had returned; accompanied by a bailiff.

"You'll have to leave now," the supervisor told her.

Panic overcame her, and she rushed to Batim's side in a vain attempt to protect him.

Immediately she was pulled away and escorted out.

"What are you going to do with him?" she asked.

"That's for the tribunal to decide."

"May I please go with you?"

Angelina was afraid now that she might lose track of his whereabouts.

"Of course not," replied the supervisor. "Jail is no place for a pretty lady like you."

He looked Angelina up and down with a lustful smirk on his grimy face.

She could guess what he was thinking, and shuddered.

"Then will you at least tell me when I might be able to visit him?" she asked.

All at once the supervisor lost his patience.

"Look, I can't tell you any more tonight! Go home and get some rest. ...You've got things to do, anyway."

"What do you mean?"

"Have you forgotten already? There's a dead body out there. You need to make arrangements for his corpse..."

Angelina felt faint. This was getting too much for her.

"...He's been taken to the town morgue," interrupted the bailiff.

Angelina gasped.

"To the morgue...when? Nobody told me my husband had been moved!"

Despair was creeping into Angelina's demeanour now. She felt surrounded by the enemy with nowhere to turn.

But again was heard the voice within her head.

"Pray, Angelina, pray."

Yes, of course, she thought.

"Yavros, I need you," she said under her breath.

"What did you say?" asked the old mariner.

"I didn't say anything," she muttered; conscious of the fact that she was lying.

"Go home and get some rest," emphasised the mariner. "You're going to have a long day tomorrow."

"Home? I have no home! We are... We were transients. We've been staying in lodgings and were about to board the Persimon, ready to further our activities overseas. There is nowhere for me to go now."

The mariner felt sorry for her. "You can come back with me if you like. My wife would be happy to put you up for the night."

Angelina looked at him with gratitude and thanked him; then added silently, 'Thank you Yavros, too.'

There was no time left to say goodnight to Batim. The supervisor and his sidekick hauled him to his feet, and with little resistance lead him out of his cell.

Angelina weakly called to him; urging him to also pray for Yavros' help. ...But he could not hear for the clanking of leg irons as they were being attached to his ankles.

"Is that necessary?" she appealed to the mariner.

"It's standard practice for criminals," he replied.

"My son is not a criminal!" she insisted.

The mariner looked at her curiously.

"Of course he is. How can you doubt that?"

Angelina sighed. "Never mind," she said. "You wouldn't understand."

The mariner's wife, a caring woman slightly older than her husband, expressed surprise when he came home with a female in tow. But a brief explanation set her mind at rest.

On seeing Angelina's drawn features and blood-stained clothing, her heart went out to the unexpected guest.

Later, after being cared for by the kindly soul, Angelina lay on a makeshift bed; her aching head and heart relieved only slightly.

Despite her exhausted state, she found it hard to sleep; so much was going through her mind. She gazed up at the bevelled roof, unable to believe she was there at all. She should have been on the Persimon with Salutat; on their way to a new adventure. Instead, his corpse lay on a cold impersonal slab somewhere in the city. Her son, no doubt, was shivering the night away in jail, and she... She was in a stranger's house; albeit resting in simple comfort; thanks to Yavros and to the benevolent mariner.

While she tried to make sense of all that had happened, something occurred to her. There was but one good thing to come out of it all: she had her son back.

Batim, though in dire straits right now and facing an uncertain future, was his normal self again.

If only she could persuade the tribunal of this – that Batim himself was not to blame for the murder; that he was, at the time, possessed by an evil spirit... She would have a difficult time trying to convince him of such a thing, but she must at least try. ...Or would he just think she was a crazy woman, and lock her up in an asylum? She sighed; too exhausted to think about it anymore.

Angelina closed her eyes, expecting to drift off into some form of sleep again.

Instead, she found herself translocating to Eternity.

Salutat, lingering within the veil of consciousness, drew her spirit towards him.

"At last; I've been waiting for you to fall asleep," he said in a tone which seemed to be chiding.

Angelina had not anticipated a return so soon; especially when she saw her dead husband very much alive.

Caught up with terran affairs so much over the past few hours, she had almost forgotten that Salutat was still living; that terran death is only final to the physical body, not to the spirit.

It took her a moment to remember this fact. And when she did, the relief was overwhelming.

"Salutat! My goodness, I can't believe you look so well!" she said, embracing him. "Your passing wasn't too much of a shock for you, was it?"

Salutat grinned. "I'm alright now; although it was a bit shocking to be killed off like that."

"My poor darling," said Angelina with compassion. She winced at the thought of what he had been through.

"After I'd been stabbed, it was quite strange. I felt like I was popping out of my body. My spirit seemed to separate from it and hover above everything. I could see you and Batim. I could even see that nasty little sprite manipulating him. And then I called out to you, if you remember. I saw Miekaale in all his brilliance. He looked at me and smiled. And then, when the demon ran off to hide, he picked it up on the end of his sword and tossed it away to who-knows-where. ...Did you see that?"

"In a way I did. ...At least, I knew Miekaale was there. But I must have been very emotional, because I could really only sense what Miekaale was doing in my mind's eye. It was wonderful to witness Batim at last coming free of it, though."

"What a blessing for you to have him back – in spite of all the drama."

"Oh, yes. ...Although things aren't all that blessed at the moment."

"Why is that?"

"He's been arrested for murder."

"What do you mean? ...For my murder!"

Angelina nodded; then realised how strange that must have sounded.

"...Even though Batim wasn't really to blame?" Salutat went on.

"Yes. How can I convince the authorities that a demon made him act that way?"

Salutat suddenly looked anxious. "We must stop them – get him out...anything that will help him!" He paused as a worrying thought came to him. Then purposefully he said, "They might have him put to death!"

"Oh, Salutat...surely not? You don't really think they'd go to that extreme, do you?"

"They might! I know they execute terrans for far lesser crimes than murder."

Angelina cried out in terror at the thought...

...A second later, Salutat was no longer there and she had awoken in a cold sweat on her bed.

"Oh, bother!" she wailed breathlessly. "I wasn't ready to come back yet!"

Angelina spent the remainder of the night worrying about Batim's fate.

In vain she tried to re-enter Eternity so that she and Salutat could find a way to resolve it. Yet all she succeeded in doing was agitating her already frayed nerves.

In despair, she arose and went out into the early dawn light; the moon still brightening the landscape. Anxious for solace, she walked down a jetty close to the mariner's home and onto the foreshore.

Looking out to sea, her attention was drawn to the thin silver line of the moon's reflection upon it. A part of her longed to follow the line, towards the life she and Salutat were supposed to have embarked upon the previous day. Her heart heaved with the pain of its memory – of what should have been, and of what was now occurring.

How unreal it all seemed.

As she stood in silence by the edge of the ocean, the incoming tide began to gently lap her toes; its chilly water bracing. Soon she needed to step away from it, and walked along the water's edge instead.

She tried to communicate with Salutat once again. It was important she secure his aid now. She did not know how best to help her son, and was terrified of doing the wrong thing.

During his missions in Eddren, Salutat had developed a certain worldly wisdom that she knew she lacked. If she could discuss her dilemma with him again, it would make all the difference... But the foreshore was not the place for translocating. The only place she could hope to achieve it was in the privacy of her bed.

She looked up at the sky. It was lightening steadily now. Maybe if she hurried home she could spend some more time with Salutat before the household's morning routine began...

Angelina was almost back at her temporary abode when she suddenly came to a halt.

She had heard a voice, and was not sure where it came from. Was it someone calling her – or could it be Salutat's voice within her head again? She held her breath while she listened; hoping...

...There it was again: little more than a whisper.

"Angelina, do nothing," it said.

"Salutat!" she exclaimed under her breath, and listened more closely...but there was no more.

What can it mean? she wondered.

As Angelina quietly re-entered the mariner's home, she felt sure Salutat had, in his simple missive, relieved her of responsibility towards Batim. For this she was grateful. But at the same time, she was flooded with a sense of isolation from both her husband and the strength she needed from him at the moment.

Loneliness is very much a terran emotion, she reflected with increasing despondency in her heart.

Throughout all of this time, Salutat had been busy.

He had determined that there was only one person he could ask for help in this matter, and that was Yavros.

After Angelina's abrupt departure from his side, Salutat attempted to re-connect with her, but without success. He understood very well how the terran consciousness must be at peace in order to commune with the ethereal, and Angelina's state of mind was far from peaceable just now. Furthermore, as an experienced inhabitant of both realms, Salutat knew how difficult it is to send more than a short message from one dimension into the other.

The mind of a terran spirit can absorb only a sliver of spiritual insight before it tries to take over, and shuts off the channel of communication.

...But then had come the period of tranquillity during Angelina's early morning walk. In that snatched moment, Salutat had acted quickly. The sliver of insight reached its mark. All he did was convey Yavros' simple instruction to take no action.

Yet that was enough. Angelina understood.

By the time the instruction was successfully delivered, Yavros and Salutat had come up with a viable solution to the family's dilemma.

In actual fact, Yavros had been astounded that Salutat saw the need to consult with him so soon after Angelina's visit. After all, had he not already imparted his wisdom to her?

However, assuming the visit also concerned Batim, he politely enquired after the boy's current status, expecting from Salutat the report of a satisfactory conclusion to the unfortunate incident.

"It's a bit more serious than all we've told you so far," Salutat informed him categorically.

Yavros reacted indignantly.

"Excuse me! What could possibly be more serious than one of my terran spirits being usurped by a mere sprite implanted by Lucifer?"

Salutat grimaced. Reluctantly he replied.

"How about, when Lucifer's sprite deliberately kills off your ambassador in Eddren – as a direct affront to you?"

Yavros looked anxiously into Salutat's eyes. "You don't mean... Lucifer hasn't harmed my Angelina, has he?"

"Oh, no!" exclaimed Salutat, shocked that Yavros might consider the possibility. "No, not Angelina... Me!"

"You? But how can that be? You're hale and hearty..."

"...Lucifer had me killed!"

Yavros stood back and scrutinised him, expecting to see a difference in his bearing.

"I don't understand," he said at last. "You look the same as ever."

"He didn't kill off my spirit – nobody could do that! He killed my body." And then Salutat went quiet. "You're not going to like this," he went on. "It was by the hand of our own, very terran son that Lucifer had me murdered."

"You're joking! Not even Lucifer would be so stupid as to kill my most important mission angel in Eddren! He's gone too far this time!"

"It's alright, Sire. There's been no harm done; except to Batim, of course."

"I'm almost afraid to ask," said Yavros, forlornly. "What has happened to Batim?"

"Are you not already aware of this, Sire?"

Salutat was confused now. He had assumed Miekaale responded to Angelina's invocation at his behest, and that Yavros had since kept up with developments. ...But he was giving the impression he knew nothing about it.

"Should I be aware of something else?" Yavros asked by way of reply.

"Angelina called for help, and Miekaale immediately appeared. Was it not you who sent him?"

"There was no order from me. My Golden Angel has instructions to respond to you and Angelina directly. He must have taken the initiative alone. I'm afraid I've been involved with other problems concerning Lucifer."

A look of despair crept over Salutat's face. "Oh dear... What problems, Sire? What has Lucifer been up to now?"

"I'll bring you up to date in a minute. Just finish what you were saying about Batim."

Salutat drew breath and gave his report: that after his body had been killed, Miekaale drove out the sprite, thus freeing Batim.

"...But that's wonderful!" exclaimed Yavros. "You and Angelina must be very relieved."

"Indeed we are. But that was the beginning of Batim's problems, not the end."

"I don't like the sound of this," Yavros moaned.

"Batim has been jailed for my murder, and I suspect he may be put to death on account of it."

Yavros suddenly writhed as if in agony. This news was the last straw for him in his battles with Lucifer.

For a moment, Salutat feared that Yavros was about to fragment under the strain, but at length he rallied.

"Is there no end to this tyranny?" Yavros cried; wringing his hands in fury.

"Do you mean with Lucifer?"

"Of course! He has caused so many problems in Eddren; you wouldn't believe it! Everywhere there is disharmony. My beloved offspring are actually fighting each other now. Whole nations are warring against other nations; most of the time in the name of Lucifer's trumped up sun religion! Fathers have been turned against their sons, and husbands are deserting their families. Honestly, Salutat, I sometimes think it will never end. A little hardship challenges the soul, but what he's doing is so destructive! Even your son is now in mortal strife because of him!"

Yavros sat deep in thought for a while; then looked up at Salutat.

"Is this why you came to see me?" he asked.

"What do you mean?"

"Did you come because of Batim's imprisonment?"

"Yes – and to seek your advice."

"Then we must do something about it."

Salutat's heart leapt with relief.

"Thank you, Sire. Angelina is very anxious to help him…"

"…No, not Angelina. Please don't involve her. This is too big a problem; I'll handle it. I know exactly what to do…"

A resolute look came over Yavros' features.

"…It's about time this benevolent creator started to fight back!"

CHAPTER 8

Batim was brought before the tribunal the following day.

It was a clear-cut case, his accusers insisted; backed-up by testimony from the workers who witnessed the crime. The accused had committed a murder, and the procurator wasted little time in passing sentence.

He informed the terrified youth: "The law states, 'A life for a life'; therefore you give me no choice but to impose the death sentence upon you. I will decide by which means later today."

After a brief hiatus while he penned his pronouncement onto parchment, he went on, "I cannot comprehend how a personable young man like you saw fit to commit murder. In my opinion you don't look capable of it! ...And your own father, too! It's unheard of in these parts. Don't you have anything to say in your defence?"

Batim, standing with his hands bound, looked directly at the procurator.

There was so much he could have said; but where to start, and what was the point? How could he tell them he had no recollection of killing Salutat, and that it grieved him just thinking about it. ...Or even that his memory of the last few months was sketchy, as though someone else was living his life rather than him. But he could say none of these things. They refused to come out, because he knew the people he must convince – the stern, accusing men of the tribunal – would not believe a word he dared to state. ...And whatever he even uttered would be misconstrued and held against him. So he stayed silent, dropping his gaze to the floor, away from their reproachful eyes.

"Well, boy; have you nothing to say?" the procurator asked impatiently.

Batim looked up at him again.

Meekly he said, "No, Sir," and then added before it was too late, "...I didn't mean to kill my father."

"But you intentionally stabbed him in the stomach. How can you stand there and deny you intended to harm him?"

Suddenly Batim's fighting spirit began to rise up in him. If he was going to be punished for a murder he didn't really commit, then he would go down fighting!

"...Something evil made me do it," he blurted out; but then regretted it when a murmur went round his accusers.

He glanced at the faces of the men who held authority over him. Some of them shook their heads disapprovingly and others, it appeared, found his statement amusing.

"You don't understand!" he shouted, addressing all the men. "You think I'm a murderer, but I'm not!"

"Alright, I've heard enough," exclaimed the procurator. "Take him away!"

"No!" cried Batim.

He struggled as two sentries grasped his shackled arms and led him out.

"This is an injustice. I am innocent!"

Batim's voice tailed away while the heavy door clanked shut behind him.

"That's one we're best rid of," said one of the tribunal. "Who knows what other crimes he may have committed in the past?"

The means of execution was announced just before dusk.

There were various forms of execution in regular use at the time. They ranged from a quick death by beheading for lesser transgressions, to a fearsome punishment for more serious offences. The law decreed that murder and crimes of treason against the state warranted an extreme form of punishment; one deliberately chosen to deter others from similarly offending.

At the request of the procurator, the latter form was to be Batim's fate. Angelina's gentle son was destined to die in the suffocating coils of a giant reptile trained especially for the purpose.

Yet, this was no ordinary snake, but one renowned for its apparent enjoyment of the task.

Not only was it a horrendous way for anyone to die, but it was also performed publicly, as an added attraction to the regular contests held in the city's arena.

"Announce it from the plaza," the procurator instructed his aides. "The execution will be held tomorrow at noon."

While all of this was taking place Lucifer, oblivious of the mess he had caused, made an unscheduled visit to Hellion.

More and more of late he felt the need to re-establish his presence there; to avoid losing all status in the realm, as nearly happened on a previous occasion.

While on this visit, he happened to run into Slave.

Lucifer almost overlooked the nondescript nuisance. Its aura had become so reduced as a result of shock, and its demeanour so weakened by the humiliating eviction from Eddren, that it was barely present; causing little more than an irritation in the general maelstrom of Hellion. So the fact that Lucifer noticed it at all could only have been put down to chance.

However, there was no twist of fate at play in uniting the two, but rather telepathy: a psychic connection born of like-minds working in Eddren, although neither would have acknowledged it as such.

"Slave!" bellowed Lucifer, causing the emaciated critter to shed its phantom skin. "What in all of Hellion are you doing here? Why aren't you still in Eddren doing your job? You're supposed to be controlling that boy!"

Slave was flabbergasted. The unexpected appearance of its master caught it completely by surprise. Lucifer was the last individual Slave thought it would run into there, and certainly the last it wanted to run into; unsure as it was if Lucifer knew of recent events.

So, still smarting from the sudden demotion, it stood quivering before its master, reluctant to raise its head in anything but shame.

"Well, numbskull, what d'you have to say for yourself?"

Slave fidgeted, wishing the bitter, swirling ethers would conveniently swallow it up…or at least provide it with a means of escape. Backed into a corner, it had little option but to face its examiner and try to think of a very good reason why it was no longer at its post.

But then Slave had an idea… Had it not accomplished its self-appointed mission to dispose of Salutat, and therefore was entitled to take a sabbatical? Maybe all was not lost with Lucifer, but merely about to change direction…

"My lord, there is something I must tell you," it said in a manner to arouse Lucifer's sense of intrigue. "I have some tidings which will gladden the heart of the mighty Lucifer."

Lucifer was unimpressed with Slave's boasting; in fact, it rather sickened him.

"Pray, what tidings could you impart that would be of any interest to me?"

"I have…" announced Slave, puffing itself up to dazzle the recipient of its smooth talk. "I have succeeded in my allotted mission. Your unworthy servant has effected that which your heart desires the most."

Lucifer curled his lip in scornful disbelief.

"What are you babbling about?" he said.

Slave missed the sarcasm.

"Tell me," it continued. "What is your greatest desire?"

"…Just at the moment? To be rid of you; you snivelling little fiend. Now stop this nonsense and get back to work. Have you forgotten I gave you a job to do?"

Slave grinned at Lucifer.

"My work is already accomplished," it pronounced with great satisfaction.

"Accomplished? Says who? Not me! I will tell you when it is accomplished!"

"But there is nothing more to be done!"

Lucifer snorted petulantly; he would get nowhere with his irritating minion without hearing what it had to say.

"Go on, then. What's the wonderful news?" he uttered with less than a hint of enthusiasm.

Slave grinned again; at last it had Lucifer's full attention. How he will love me for my deeds, it thought glibly.

"Well…" it began. "If you remember… Some time ago you embedded me in Salutat's son…"

"Yes, yes. Hurry up…I haven't got all day to listen to you twittering."

"You wanted me, through the boy, to make life difficult for Salutat…"

"Idiot!" growled Lucifer. "Obviously I remember why you possessed him. Get to the point. …Don't waste my time on something I already know."

Slave paused briefly to gather its thoughts. This was not going well. If it wasn't careful, its moment of glory might slip into insignificance. Maybe it should forgo the build-up to avoid further ire from Lucifer…

"Okay… In short, I disposed of Salutat for you," he said without further delay.

"You did…what?"

"I made the stupid son dispose of his irritating father!" Slave exclaimed with pride. "There…aren't you pleased?"

Lucifer suddenly lost all pallor. Dumbfounded, he stared blankly into the dense ethers; unable to speak as though shocked into silence by what he had heard. Then he slowly mouthed, "What did you just say?"

"I said…"

"I heard what you said!"

Slave's words had begun to sink in now.

"How can you stand there and make an outrageous statement, which can only be a lie?"

"It is no lie, Master. I carried out your wishes. You hated Salutat, and I got rid of him for you."

"My wishes? You carried out my wishes..!"

Lucifer angrily stamped the ground, causing the acidic ethers to swirl around them.

"…You don't know what my wishes are, because I have never told you my wishes, you inconsequential upstart!"

By this time, Lucifer was so enraged that the disturbance, much to his dismay, began to attract attention.

Soon had gathered a crowd of unsavoury characters who, like Slave, had been banished to the stinking halls of Hellion. Disgusted by the sight Lucifer, without warning, grabbed Slave and hauled the squawking sycophant off to a more private place.

There, he sat Slave down again and said a little more quietly, "I think you had better explain."

Slave had no choice but to tell of the goings-on which preceded its abrupt return to Hellion. However, in its own interests, quick-thinking Slave prudently omitted the part about Miekaale's intervention. Rather, it attempted to give the impression that it voluntarily let go of Batim after the killing, leaving the boy's soul available for Lucifer's further amusement.

Lucifer listened intently to the prattle. Not believing a word, he drew the conclusion that out of self-interest Slave had manipulated Batim into killing his father. Then, when this factor hit him where it hurt the most, he howled with anguish.

"I didn't want him killed, you ridiculous creature," he wailed. "I just wanted to lure his son away from Yavros; to get back at Salutat for marrying Angelina! You knew that! You were merged with Batim to manage the pubescent's allegiance to me; not to do any real harm!"

"But surely this was your dream – to be rid of Salutat altogether?"

Slave could see its glorification waning as the moments slid by and needed to think fast. Maybe it could persuade Lucifer that killing off Salutat was the right thing to do...

"...And you're trying to read my mind as well, are you?" retorted Lucifer.

"No! I just..."

"...Aaagh! I can't stand this anymore! How could I have ever trusted you?

Lucifer was beside himself with grief now.

Everything he'd done in Eddren was to annoy Yavros. The warring, the arrogance of terran nature; even the fracture he had successfully created between the precious terrans and their maker...that was all a prank. There was no real damage done – except to Yavros' pride. All down

339

the ages he had always known where to draw the line. ...But killing a missionary angel!

I've surely overstepped the mark this time, he thought. Yavros must be so angry with me!

For only the second time ever, Lucifer knew what it was to feel afraid.

"Don't you realise Yavros will bring all of Eternity down on my head now?" he screamed at Slave.

"I don't understand why you are so upset," said Slave, still trying to validate its actions. "Salutat is an angel. He's immortal! I only killed off his body to get him away from your lady friend!"

Lucifer's eyes flashed with rage.

"And what do you suppose Salutat is doing right now?" he asked, sarcastically. "Is he sitting back thinking, 'never mind, Lucifer. I'm not really dead so it doesn't matter'? No. He will regard it as a slight against Yavros himself, and I will be even more hated in Eternity than I am already!"

Lucifer slumped in a fragmented heap.

Slave had never before seen him look so disconsolate: so pitiful, so worthless...so vulnerable.

All at once, every bit of loyalty it had ever felt towards him — admittedly for its own gain — dissipated into thin air, and it looked on the slimy ghoul with contempt.

"In which case, I hope you get what's coming to you," it said in rejection of all accountability. "If you weren't such an evil bastard, none of this would have happened!"

"Get out of my sight!" shouted Lucifer, and snatched at the insignificant wisp standing before him.

But Slave was alert and on the defensive. Too quick for the old master, it shot out of reach in a flash; then took off into the distance.

Lucifer yelled after it.

"That's right! Avoid me, you puny little individual! From this time forth, you will be no more than a speck of dust blown along on the caustic winds of Hellion. You deserve nothing better!"

Back in Eternity, Yavros knew nothing of the uproar in the underbelly of his universe; he had more pressing matters to attend to.

Thanks to an angel guardian home on respite, he had learnt of Batim's whereabouts and what was to become of him. There is no time to lose, he realised in near panic.

"This is a matter of the gravest urgency," he advised a group of practiced angel guardians; hastily summoned to form a strategy.

However, one angel in particular was excluded from the gathering. Now considered to be too emotionally involved in the unfolding drama, Salutat was not invited to have a role in the exercise. Yavros needed strong and impartial individuals who would not become distressed by it. With a degree of reluctance, Salutat honoured his angel's vow of obedience to Yavros and backed away; to leave his son's predicament in the hands of others. Instead, he acted on a suggestion from the group to bring Angelina home for the duration of the exercise. Both he and Yavros agreed that Eddren was no place for her just now. Her angel sensitivity would not be able to stand the negative blows she would have had to endure.

Grudgingly, Angelina agreed.

Once provision was made for her body and her spirit fortified against stimulus which might yank her back into Eddren, she joined her husband in Eternity.

By the end of discussion the group of angels had agreed on the part they were each to play in the ensuing mission.

"This exercise will be faultless," Yavros told them; each participant acknowledging that the plan was infallible.

However, the angels did not take into account one very important factor: Lucifer's fickle character.

It was not long before they learnt that even for an angel of Yavros, pride sometimes goes before a fall.

Unaware that he was the focus of angelic attention, Batim lay on a bare stone ledge in the prison cell, pondering his inevitable fate.

He knew he was to be killed at noon the next day, but not the manner of his execution. According to the prison governor, withholding this information heightened the sense of fear in a prisoner, and made him more aware of his sins against society. But all it achieved with Batim was to make him withdraw even further into his shell.

"What have I done to deserve this?" he said quietly to himself, while his new cellmate slept.

He placed his hands behind his head and surveyed the dirty roof of the cell; gazing almost beyond it as if to some great deity on high.

Batim turned over to face the wall. It was so close that even in the darkness he could see tiny holes. There were so many, in fact, they almost appeared to be some kind of writing; not unlike the oriental print in the cabin he shared with Urla. He sighed with remorse as he remembered her; for he had not given his lover so much as a thought since that time, and now wondered what had become of her.

How easily things can change, he realised. One day he was a confident student in the Academie; the next, he had been expelled. ...And after that, his life just seemed to unravel. Whatever happened to bring it about?

In his ignorance, Batim had no knowledge of Lucifer's infiltration of his character– unlike his parents. They were well aware that when Lucifer gets his claws into a terran spirit, the poor soul has no conscious knowledge of such.

Even when he was finally free of it, Batim little sensed that something of the like had taken place. The concept of being physically taken over by an evil spirit would be too bizarre to consider; and so he was left wondering.

...Or maybe, he reflected, he was just a bad person after all, as his captors had tried to make out? There was always that possibility.

He thought about the crime for which he was being punished. He had killed Salutat. He, Batim – dutiful son of angel parents – had killed his own father! It just couldn't be! Even after his farce of a trial, when the reality of his actions had been rammed down his throat, he still could not grasp that he'd actually done it.

How could he have done it! He loved his father! He bore him no malice, and yet apparently he stalked him and then plunged a knife into his belly – and right in front of his mother, too! The thought of it appalled him.

"Oh, my dear mother, what have I done to you?" he cried silently; tears beginning to form.

He sniffed them back, and then remembered the burly man on the bed opposite him. He could not risk being seen weeping. Dealing with a criminal's taunts would be as bad as the punishment he was about to face.

Early the next morning, after a night where Batim slept little and woke in a panic on several occasions, he finally decided to get up. He could not bear the thoughts which kept going round his head. The only way he could avoid them was to remain awake and concentrate on what was going on inside the prison.

Very soon he heard the now familiar clattering of food bowls being shoved through the bars of each cell, and although he felt quite sick to the stomach, he realised he was actually very hungry. Yet, when the jailer arrived at his cell, the cellmate snatched Batim's bowl from his hand and laughed when its hapless recipient protested.

Feeling even more tearful after so little sleep, Batim retreated to his bed.

Now completely demoralised, he huddled in the corner, his face to the wall. "Let's get this over with," he pleaded inaudibly. "I can't take any more."

As the sun climbed higher, Batim drifted off to sleep. He was now so resigned to his fate that he felt surprisingly peaceful. But his sleep was short-lived. He awoke with the sound of a key opening up the gate of his cell. They had come for him at last.

A pang of horror shot through him when he realised his time to die had come, and he faced up to his captor with a look of terror.

Roughly, the jailer turned him round and secured his hands behind his back. Then he whispered something in his ear; a sickly grin on his face.

"You're for the snake, my friend."

At once, the cellmate glanced up at the jailer, and Batim noticed the expression on his face. It was almost one of compassion, as though he was thinking, 'you poor thing'. But Batim had no knowledge of the boa constrictor, and was left in ignorance of what would happen.

In the split second he had to think about it, he assumed he was to receive a fatal snake bite.

That wouldn't be so bad, he assumed.

His reassurance did not last long.

It was a long walk to their destination.

Batim, bound and dragged along by his cruel jailer, also suffered the added disadvantage of being blindfolded; so that when he arrived at the arena he was exhausted, and sported a large bruise on his forehead from a painful fall on the way.

Yet, still he had no idea where he was.

Assuming it to be a place of execution, he was mystified by the noise of a crowd roaring, laughing, jeering; sounds such as the cheers he heard during the Academie's athletic event in which he once participated.

Suddenly, for a brief moment, he wondered if this had all been a nightmare; that the last few months were but a terrible dream from which he was about to awaken; that he would find himself in his own bed at the Academie, and that everything was alright after all.

But then the jailer yanked at the rope securing him, and he realised it was not a nightmare. This was the real thing. Only, why had they come to an arena? And then it dawned on him: The arena was not used for athletic games, but combative sport.

He had heard of places like this. Prisoners were fed to the lions, offered to ferocious bears or forced to submit to blood-thirsty warriors. But where did the snake come into all of it?

Batim sighed dejectedly, too exhausted to think about his fate any more.

Dispirited now, he calmly waited for his turn to be brought into the arena. Batim had no idea what might take place and could not be bothered even contemplating it.

He remained blindfolded right up until the last minute. Hour after hour he was subjected to cries of anguish when each new victim was shoved out into the arena; to face the waiting foe and an exhilarated crowd hungry for a kill. He suffered with them through their death screams, as if each torment and annihilation was not just theirs, but also his to endure.

Batim died many times over that morning.

When his turn came, it was almost an anti-climax. As he was led out, still blindfolded, it seemed that the arena had gone quiet. For a moment he thought he had already died; so bewildered was his mind. He imagined he was passing through a peaceful open space, with fresh, cool air; to a tranquil place beyond the pain of death, and he was being gently led up an ethereal staircase to meet the creator.

But then the blindfold was removed, and he opened his eyes to the reality of his situation.

The crowd had fallen silent in anticipation, not because they had left the arena.

They were all still there – thousands of them, not daring to breathe; waiting for the arrival of the snake.

Numbed by the realisation he was not in some idyllic place, Batim barely understood the scene which lay before his dazzled vision. The glare of sunlight in eyes long covered helped to mask the sights which surrounded him.

He pretended it was just an illusion which, if he closed his eyes again, would go away. But it was not an illusion.

When he was prodded from behind, making him quickly take stock; he discovered he was standing on the edge of a three metre drop. No longer could he hide in his own little world; now he needed all his wits about him. This was it. This was reality.

This was the moment he had been dreading.

Batim was standing on a ledge overlapping the rim of an open-topped cage; which was circular in shape, wider than it was high, and made of bamboo latticework.

The cage was constructed in such a way that from the outside everything taking place could be seen, but nothing from within it could escape.

At last Batim came to his senses enough to look around.

The steps he imagined would take him to a peaceful place, were now being pulled away from the cage. Instead, a rope ladder dropped for him to descend into the cage.

Again he was shoved to get a move on, and obediently took hold of the ladder.

Once down on the ground Batim stood motionless; like a caged animal waiting for something to happen.

With eyes now accustomed to the light, he noticed an aperture to one side of the cage at ground level, and he wondered what it was for.

It was a good-sized opening, something a child could fit through but not a full-grown man. Then he saw through the latticework that a tunnel, similarly constructed, led out from the aperture to the side of the arena.

With renewed horror, he remembered about the snake.

A large tunnel must be for a large snake.

Suddenly any preconceived theories on how he was to die dissipated.

This was not to be the poisoned nip of an unassuming serpent, but something else: something he could not as yet envisage. It looked like this creature was going to be a monster. A terrified shudder went through his weakened frame, and his legs seemed not to support him anymore.

He leant against the side of the cage for support.

Just then a gasp went around the arena, followed by a stunned silence. Somewhere a woman screamed; another shrieked, "Look at the size of that thing." Pampered ladies up at the front fainted at the thought of what they were about to witness.

Batim picked up on their anxiousness, but because of the angle of the tunnel and the fact that the aperture was covered, he could not see the snake. Yet, triggered by their fear, panic began to set in.

Without thought, Batim attempted to climb the side of his cage and again was prodded; this time with the point of a sword.

He cried out in pain, and clasped his hand to his neck. Blood seeped through his fingers.

There was no escape from this, it seemed.

Then the cover was drawn back, and at last Batim saw his adversary: It was huge.

The creature quickly slithered into the cage; the speed at which it moved taking Batim by surprise.

As it had done many times before, the snake followed the circumference of the cage until its head touched the tip of its tail; in effect, forming a perfect circle. For just such a demonstration was the cage designed.

Terrified, Batim realised he had been encircled by a single gigantic snake.

With eyes tightly shut, he stood frozen to the spot; not daring to move a muscle, to breathe or even to think of what might happen next.

But what did happen next confounded both victim and spectators alike.

Invisibly from above, a small band of angels descended just as the snake slithered into the cage. Unknowingly, Batim was encircled by both the physical presence of a dangerous reptile, and also the absolute power of Yavros in the form of his angels.

Yet, even if the ethereal beings had been visible, Batim would not have seen them. He had already withdrawn into the private sanctuary of his afflicted mind. So he did not witness the subliminal counsel the angels offered to the snake, nor the gentle shield of protection they laid upon the petrified youth. He just stood there and waited.

He waited for the end...waited for the jaws of the beast to consume his flesh, or for its coils to crush his body. He waited expectantly; resigned now to his fate.

But then, after a while, he realised he was still waiting; still alive...still in one piece. As he came to again, out of the refuge of his own imaginings, he noticed that the crowd seemed confused. They were talking amongst themselves; pointing at him; even jeering. And as Batim shifted his gaze from the faces of the people in the crowd to the ground on which he stood, he noticed to his surprise that the snake was no longer there.

He swung round to face the aperture again; just in time to see its tail disappear back into the tunnel.

The snake had gone...and he was still alive.

Batim could not believe it.

This has to be a dream, he thought; not knowing what to do next, and not daring to accept his good luck.

He considered scaling the side of his cage again, but saw the fixed look on the face of the sword-carrying jailer and realised it would not be a good idea.

What's more, his audience seemed angry; disappointed even. They were looking forward to a spectacle. They had paid good money to watch the snake perform and to see justice served on a murderer...

But there had always been a longstanding law in the city that if a contestant in the arena managed to survive, he was granted his freedom. This was a well accepted fact, if not well received. The spectators, too, had no choice but to recognise it. So the rope ladder was again thrown over the cage wall, and Batim invited to climb over it.

Ignoring the taunts of the crowd, he timorously set one foot ahead of the other towards freedom.

In Eternity, the group of angels congratulated themselves on their success.

Salutat and Angelina joined them in their merriment.

"How readily the snake bowed to the higher will," said one of the angels.

"Yes, far more willingly than any terran spirits I worked with," laughed another.

Then a third ventured, "How fortunate we learnt that the lad would be given freedom if he survived the cage!"

Salutat stood up and responded with humility.

"Angelina and I are deeply grateful to you all for coming to our son's rescue. As you know, I can't return to Eddren because I no longer have a terran body, but Angelina must go back. And now, thanks to you all and to Yavros, she has somebody to go back to."

"Amen to that!" came the response.

The sense of relief that the frightful episode was finally at an end overwhelmed Angelina. When visiting Eternity in angel form she retained something of her terranity, and although she could not weep physical tears, she felt all the emotion associated with it. Such was the case now. As she privately shed tears, she hoped none of the angels noticed. Only Salutat would understand the concept of tears. The others would probably think she was unwell in spirit; which she certainly was not. And so she remained slightly apart from them.

After making another gesture of thanks to Yavros, the group were about to disperse when another angel burst into the room. His worried features and the disturbed atmosphere he brought in with him, indicated to everyone present that something was wrong.

"I don't know how to tell you this..." he confessed to the astonished group.

Salutat came forward to greet him.

The messenger looked into his eyes, perceiving in the great angel an anguish yet to be felt.

"What is wrong, my brother," Salutat asked.

Angelina looked on, fearing that something was amiss with Yavros.

"Is it the Master?" she asked.

"No," he replied, giving her the same heartrending look he gave to her husband. "It's your son, Batim."

"Batim! Oh no..." she said uneasily, cupping her hands over her mouth.

"...What's happened to Batim?" asked Salutat.

"I'm sorry to be the bearer of bad news, but he's dead."

Angelina let out a long, piercing scream.

The other angels gasped in surprise at Angelina's rather unconventional behaviour. Then, not knowing how to deal with emotion from one of their own kind, they each slowly shied away from her. Yet their discomfiture also contained a degree of guilt that their celebrations appeared to have been premature.

Unable to believe the news she had just heard, Angelina sought out her husband, who put his arms around her.

While she sobbed into his breast, Salutat gallantly hid the shock that he, too, was feeling.

"How did it happen?" he asked the messenger.

"Somebody with a sword decided your son should be executed after all."

"Do you mean, it wasn't the snake?"

"No. It happened after Batim left the cage. Apparently, the guard in charge of him was to receive a bonus for a successful execution. He couldn't handle seeing Batim go free, so he killed him."

"How do you know all this?" asked Angelina; well aware how easily terrans misinterpret facts. It was imperative that they be given an accurate report of what happened.

"An angel guardian who had been present in the arena told me."

Salutat released Angelina and took the messenger aside. He spoke to him out of earshot of his wife.

"Thank you for the information; we will deal with the matter from here."

The angel left, along with the other group members. It seemed appropriate to leave the angel parents to discuss their son's situation privately.

When they had gone, Angelina rushed her husband.

"It's all lies!" she wailed. "It has to be! The angels saved him – Yavros saved him. How could he now be dead?"

"I don't know," said Salutat. "Something obviously went wrong after the escape..."

"...Then there's only one course of action to take," said Angelina, shaking her head in disbelief.

"What's that?"

"I must get back to Eddren and find out what really happened. This has to be a terrible mistake and I'm going to prove it for myself!"

With that, and before Salutat could warn her against becoming embroiled in the situation, Angelina was gone. She awoke in her body; fully in control and fired up ready to begin her investigations. She would establish once and for all that the messenger was mistaken.

But Angelina's investigation proved fruitless; Batim was indeed dead. Everything the messenger told them was the truth; except for a factor yet to be revealed to the angels of Eternity.

Although it was the point of a sword that killed the jubilant survivor, the deed was actually initiated by Lucifer.

As far as he was concerned, if he was to be wrongfully punished for the killing of Salutat, he may as well get some compensation for it by disposing of Batim, too.

After Slave's confession, Lucifer had engaged in some honest soul-searching. At first he felt a deep sense of guilt about Slave's treatment of Salutat, and embarrassed that he naïvely allowed the sprite to follow a personal agenda as though doing his bidding. He balked at the knowledge that something so useless could even think of identifying with his greatness, and felt nauseous that it grovelled before him in such an impertinent way.

But then a realisation started to enter Lucifer's troubled mind: Even though it wasn't his own fault Salutat died but rather Slave's doing, he would still be blamed!

This made Lucifer angry – angry and frustrated; because there was absolutely nothing he could do to avoid Yavros' condemnation.

Of course, he could not know this for certain because nobody from Eternity had challenged him over it. Yet, the more he speculated on it, the more niggled he felt towards Yavros for something that was still only supposition. Thus, the greater his resentment of Yavros' assumed judgement on him, the firmer became his resolve to retaliate.

So it was a last minute decision on Lucifer's part to act in the way that he did, and have Batim finished off.

Anyway, he reflected, why should he care what Yavros thought? He was already in just about as much trouble as he could be, so he might as well get some gratification out of it.

In retrospect, he determined, it served the boy right for allowing an alien force to infiltrate something as precious as his immortal soul – and then to leave himself wide open to further infiltration, even when he was free again. That was just asking for trouble! Why didn't the asinine creep protect himself from another attack?

Batim, Lucifer declared, deserved to die!

In reality though, Lucifer was indeed to blame, despite his protestations to the contrary; for it was he who degraded Yavros' terran spirits in the very beginning. And it was the angst in Lucifer's nature that penetrated the jailer's mind, giving him the motivation to plunge his deadly weapon into Batim's heart.

It did not occur to him that in having Batim killed he would be hurting his beloved Angelina, and that by taking her son away from her forever, he was denying the object of his affection some much-needed comfort in her old age.

Lucifer still thought of Angelina as an angel: a creature of immortality for whom an incident of this nature would be no more than a passing phase. He could not imagine the life of a terran spirit, for he was not one. Neither did he think in terms of weeks and years; only in the eternal present of Hellion. So he could not know the despondency with which his reckless act would plague her throughout the remainder of her life, or suffer guilt for inflicting such pain on the one person he would never deliberately hurt!

Of intentional neglect Lucifer was innocent. Of all else he was unspeakably guilty.

For the moment, Angelina knew none of this. In fact, she knew nothing of Lucifer's involvement in her son's death at all; only that her fervent wish was one minute granted to her and the next minute snatched away.

As an angel she could have accepted the tragedy to be the will of Yavros and moved on to his next assignment for her. Yet as an angel in terran form she saw the whole affair from a different perspective.

Within one and the same consciousness, she embraced the understanding of an angel and the bitter passion of a bereaved wife and mother.

It was all too much.

In the space of only a few days she had lost both her angel husband and her terran son. Salutat, she knew, was alright. He was strong in character and had recovered from the shock of physical death quickly. What's more, he still supported her, if only in spirit.

But Batim was another matter.

He had only ever been terran. He had not maintained the spirituality taught him by his parents; certainly not in the latter part of his life. And when Lucifer came along and lured him further away from his roots, he had nothing to fall back on.

Angelina had assumed that once they released him into the world he would be spiritually grounded for the rest of his life. But she had been mistaken, because in the long-run it gave him no support at all. He was now dead, and she had let him down.

But then, even in her anguish, Angelina began to realise that she and Salutat were not entirely at fault. They did everything for their child to the best of their ability. Had they not given him the opportunity for a good education, even though their purpose as terrans was their mission in Eddren, not to be parents? Did they not communicate with Yavros as soon as they realised something was amiss in Batim's life? And when he was in jail for a crime that

Lucifer initiated, were they not inspired to do everything in their power to save him?

Then what went wrong?

Angelina wracked her brain to find an answer. After a lengthy period of denial as to its probability, she came to only one conclusion: it must have been Yavros' will that Batim should die. Yes, that was it: he allowed it to happen.

Yavros was to blame for her son's death!

The awareness of this shattered Angelina.

For the first time in angel history, she lost her faith in Yavros. She even thought she hated him. Something deep inside her was so disillusioned, so hurt and so angry that she disconnected from the spiritual, and functioned only in the physical.

Angelina's devastation was remorseless and seemingly without end. Not since Lucifer's exile from Eternity had an angel harboured such deep feelings of resentment against their master.

If Yavros was testing her dependability with this, she was failing miserably.

CHAPTER 9

Salutat helplessly witnessed his wife's decline; attempting in vain to communicate with her. But she became so bitter and depressed that he could not connect with her spirit.

Meanwhile, Angelina's terran health was suffering too. It was only when her despair reached its lowest ebb; when she was so weak that the anger faded into numbness and her mind momentarily stilled, that Salutat managed to get through.

He came to her in a dream.

In her deranged state of mind she barely allowed it into her consciousness. By the time she awoke the recollection of dreaming had gone. Yet each night Salutat persisted; saturating her spirit with the love of both himself and of Yavros. ...Until one morning she found that the numbness had left her, and she woke up with the warmth of spiritual awareness in her heart.

"At last!" he cried when they finally united. "I thought I'd lost you forever."

"I'm sorry," she replied. "Batim's death was more than I could take."

"I know, and I wish I could have supported you, but you wouldn't let me in... Angelina, promise me something."

"What's that?"

"While you are still in physical form, if you feel yourself slipping again, come straight back here. And when that's not practical, at least connect with me. I can't help you if you fail to do that."

"I don't want to go back to Eternity," she admitted.

"What do you mean? Of course you do; it's your home! You have me here; and Yavros of course."

"It's Yavros I can't face at the moment."

Salutat was shocked. He had never heard her speak this way before. She loved Yavros; was devoted to him. Why would she not want to go to him?

He asked her to explain.

Angelina hesitated to express her feelings. It would come across that she had lost her devotion and was therefore unworthy of her angel status. But if she could not confide in Salutat, then who else could she talk to?

Taking a deep breath, she made her confession.

"But that's how all terrans feel when their spirits are low," he said after she had finished. "I know from my own time there, that when you're down in the dumps you tend to think negatively; then when your spirits lift you're more positive. How do you feel about everything now?"

Angelina thought for a moment. It was true: now that she was feeling a little better in herself she did not resent Yavros quite so much. The angel sense of loyalty in her had been partially restored. However, she still did not want to see him. She still blamed him for Batim's death, and it hurt her to think Yavros allowed it to happen; especially in light of the effort he made in sending the angels. But more than anything, she did not understand. More than anything, she wanted to know...why?

"You won't know the answer to that if you don't talk to him," maintained Salutat. "He's exactly the same Yavros as he ever was. I spoke with him quite recently, and I can tell you, he is distressed by what happened to Batim. He's also concerned about your present infirmity. Our son's demise was definitely not his doing."

"You're just saying that out of loyalty to him!"

"No, I'm not!" cried Salutat; anguishing over her abiding doubt. "Angelina, it's obvious you are still dispirited and therefore negative. Please don't dwell on this or your spirit will degenerate again."

"I can't help it! The thoughts won't go away!"

"Well, talk to Yavros! It's the only solution. And if you won't, then I will!"

"...No! No, I wouldn't want you to speak for me; I'll go. Yavros will think poorly of me if he knows I'm reluctant to see him. Just give me a few minutes to put my body on hold, and I'll come over."

Yavros was indeed expecting a visit from her.

He anticipated Angelina might be confused and look for an explanation as to why, after all their elaborate plans, Batim still died. However, he did not anticipate that she had set her heart against him, and was taken aback when she responded less than cordially to his greeting.

"I think you'd better sit down so we can discuss this," he told her seriously; sensing now that their conversation would not be easy. Having assumed the role of comforter to the grieving mother, of mentor to a troubled angel, he certainly had not expected a rebuff.

Whatever was going through her mind!

Angelina wasted no time in getting to the point.

"Why did my son have to die?" she demanded to know. "Why did you instruct the angels to save him; only to let that horrible soldier pierce his heart? I don't understand you at all!"

Angelina's frustration gave way to sorrow as her terran emotions came to the fore again.

While she sat quietly sobbing, an act which in itself was disquieting to the Grand Master of Eternity, he composed himself to give her the answer. There was a well-defined element of cause and effect involved with Batim's death, but explaining this to a distraught mother and convincing her that he was right, would take some doing.

"First of all, Angelina," he said. "I must tell you how sorry I am about your son…"

"…Sorry!" she shrieked, and then curbed her outburst; remembering where she was. "How can you state that you are sorry, when it was you who let him die?"

"Why do you say that?"

"…Because you had control of the situation. You sent the angels, for which I was very grateful, but once Batim had escaped you allowed him to be killed right after you'd saved him… I cannot understand why you would do it!"

"I didn't do it! I did not 'allow' Batim to be killed! That's ridiculous! Why are you insisting I am to blame?"

"…Because you are!"

"Be careful, Angelina; don't overstep the mark, please."

Yavros was beginning to feel annoyed with his normally rational subject. Angels were passive and obedient. They were not supposed to be free thinking individuals at liberty to turn against their master.

"I'm sorry, Yavros, I didn't mean to. It's just that…"

Angelina suddenly found herself at a loss. She paused for a moment to gather her thoughts, and then continued.

"…Alright then, if you insist you're not the one to blame for Batim's death, just who is?"

"He is, of course."

"What? Are you suggesting he killed himself?"

"No, Angelina…! Think about it… I saved Batim from the punishment laid down for him. Is that correct?"

"Well...yes," said Angelina in reluctant capitulation.

"It was a punishment which Batim unjustly deserved. Is that also correct?"

"Yes, but...."

"....And why did he not deserve to be punished?"

"Because it was not really Batim who killed Salutat, but Lucifer's minion."

"So what have I done wrong?"

"Nothing...I suppose. You just... I think you..."

Angelina was struggling now. She was beginning to see how terran emotion could have clouded her judgement. Either that, she decided crossly, or Yavros knew he had the upper hand and was taunting her...

Quickly, she changed her rationale. If she wanted to get anywhere with him, she would need to be objective; and calmer in her questioning.

"Alright then...you may not have allowed his murder, but you did abandon him," she said at last.

"Oh, I see... Now I understand why you might feel bitter towards me."

Yavros broke off in thought. He moved away from her to give himself some space. Then, having drawn wisdom from his surroundings, he turned back.

"It seems I need to jog your memory about something," he went on with a stern tone of voice. "It is not my duty to make everything perfect for the terran spirits, even if they are my offspring. Lucifer's interference has left them with different priorities; yet the purpose behind their creation is still to seek me within their souls. This has always been my objective in helping them out; not to give them an easy time as they dance to Lucifer's tune. If they don't seek me out when they're in trouble...then I cannot help them."

He reminded Angelina that even before Batim entered the cage, he was no longer possessed. Therefore, after he was helped to escape, as a terran with free will he became accountable for his own choices.

"...And choose, he did," Yavros went on. "However, in exercising his free will, Batim made a critical error. Even though he was delighted to be free, he failed to consider a factor which, for him, was the difference between life and death; one that most terran spirits fail to consider when they find themselves in a predicament. Batim did not turn to me for ongoing spiritual support...or even acknowledge me in any way."

Angelina stared at him, dumbfounded. Had Yavros just told her Batim was responsible for his own death?

"You could have saved him for me!" she asserted. Did Yavros not realise how important her son was to her, now that Salutat had reverted to his angel status?

"Sadly, I could not. You obviously don't understand the empowerment I bestowed on terrans with the gift of free will. It is a force in itself – not unlike the force of the wind. Harnessed, it can be put to good use, as in the sail on one of your mighty vessels, but left unchecked it creates havoc. Free will is the same. It must be controlled by its owner. Batim was born an independent spirit, and even though he was the son of angels he failed to control free will for the benefit of his soul. Furthermore, he did not seek spiritual protection even when he was at his most vulnerable; and suffered the consequences for it..."

"...Then he was as good as free, and still you sat back and allowed Lucifer to take him!"

Angelina's tirade was relentless. The terran spirit in her refused to leave Yavros' presence without some sense of justification for being angry with him.

"Dear Angelina...this is becoming tedious. Why can you not accept what I'm telling you?"

"Because I still think you're at fault."

"Alright then, let's try again: Lucifer's influence gave the terrans another option they could choose over me; which we call terran nature. In the case of Batim, his own terran nature prevented his eventual escape. The first thing he should have done, when the snake disappeared, was to acknowledge me; to thank me, even. ...But he didn't."

"...And how would he have known it was you who saved him if he couldn't see the angels?" retorted Angelina.

"That doesn't matter. These days, only the most astute terrans seem to recognise my presence in their lives. Most don't attribute little miracles that happen for them to my intervention; they just put it down to luck. When Batim did not acknowledge me in the cage, I assumed he would do so soon afterwards – as he was taught in his childhood by you and Salutat. But again, he didn't because he regarded the escape merely as good fortune! Do you understand what I'm getting at?"

Angelina could see her argument slipping away. Even though she began to think Yavros was probably right, her anguish remained, and until she had released all of it she couldn't help but attack him.

"If Salutat and I did such a good job of bringing him up, then is it not obvious that during his torment he was too distressed to remember you?"

Yavros sighed and pondered her words for a moment. Her logic was correct, but not her understanding of reality. For the sake of her ongoing status as an angel, he needed to somehow change her argumentative stance. Perhaps he could accomplish it by way of a comparison...

"Okay Angelina; I'm going to use an analogy to explain my point. Imagine the following: On your return to Eddren from seeing me now, you absent-mindedly walk out into the street and are knocked down by a wagon. Who is to blame for the accident? You...? Me...? Or is it Lucifer?"

"What has this got to do with Batim?" asked Angelina, too weary now to try and discern Yavros' riddle.

"Everything! It concerns consequences: the outcome of actions. Everything a terran does in life is governed by them. Not rewards, not punishments; just consequences. If you eat poisoned food – even if you're not aware it is poisoned – you will die. If you forget to connect with me – even if you are usually well-connected with me – you will suffer the consequences. It's not my negligence; it's yours. It may be unintentional negligence, but nevertheless the onus is still on you. For me to operate fully in your life you must retain your link with me. Do you understand?"

"I think so," conceded Angelina. "I don't like your logic, but you are right. If Batim had stopped and thought about you, the outcome would have been different?"

"...Possibly. He had reclaimed his free will; which meant he was accountable for his actions again. Batim had plenty of time to harness his freedom of choice and seek me when he was in his prison cell. At one time he did seem to look up – but not enough to invoke me. When I saved him from his punishment, I did it because it was the correct consequence for the injustice done him by Lucifer. After that, he was responsible for his own actions. ...And in this instance he attributed his escape purely to good luck"

Angelina suddenly thought of something. "After the angels left," she ventured; "Lucifer must have urged the guard to kill Batim. In light of what you've said, they each suffered the consequences of terran nature...in which case you could have saved them both from Lucifer!"

"Being possessed by an evil spirit is not the same as inheriting Lucifer's characteristics. One is an invasion; the other is an inherited trait. Possession I can help with when invoked. However, terran spirits must work through the traits they inherited from Lucifer if they are to recognise

364

where real strength comes from. If Batim had invoked me, I would have sent Miekaale. ...But he didn't."

Yavros sat back, his lesson concluded.

On the other hand, Angelina had by no means finished with Yavros.

"Batim might have turned to you once he'd recovered, but now he won't have the chance to because he is dead." Then, as a thought came to her, she asked, "Where is he, anyway? Is it possible for me to see him?"

Yavros looked at her curiously.

"I don't understand why you're asking this. Batim's soul was empty when he died. He is not in Eternity or I would know about it – and he's certainly not in Hellion, because I didn't send him there. I'm afraid he doesn't exist now; like countless others before him."

"That can't be right, Yavros! I won't believe he doesn't possess an immortal soul. I know where his body must be right now – in the common grave. But surely his spirit will have gone somewhere, too!"

"What makes you think that? Eternity is for the souls of terrans who connected with me during their lives. Hellion is for spirits who lived evil lives and need to learn a lesson. Batim was neither. There's nowhere he could go..."

"...Are you trying to tell me that there is nothing after death for the dispossessed; for terran spirits who omitted to connect with you, but who otherwise lived reasonable lives? Where are they all now?"

"Do I have to repeat myself, Angelina? They don't exist anymore. How can they? I've created nothing for them, and I have no interest in their fate..."

"...Even after all this time? That seems a bit callous!"

"Don't get judgemental with me again, please. I formed only three realms. You must learn to accept that."

Suddenly Angelina's anger was replaced by concern. This new revelation gave her something more to worry about. Surely Batim's soul did not die along with his body!

With a growing sense of guilt and fear, Angelina began to realise that, while her focus had been on self-pity and her continuous resentment against Yavros, she had not given Batim's immortal soul a second thought.

In a daze, she returned to Eddren.

Disillusioned with spiritual logic, she felt she should live a purely terran life while she tried to adjust to the concept that Batim might not exist anymore.

It did not make sense to her that a soul could cease to exist just because its body had died. Had she not already witnessed terran spirits detach from their bodies at the moment of death? Her own terran form once belonged to Cefire. Where were Dymas and Cefire now? They must be somewhere! It was all too confusing...

Meanwhile Salutat, concerned about Angelina's wellbeing, arranged for her to meet up with an old family friend who lived on the outskirts of town.

Although no longer Angelina's spouse in a terran sense, Salutat wanted his widow to feel secure while she lived out the remainder of her years in Eddren, and sensed the two women would be good company for each other.

Maella, also recently widowed, was an easy-going sort of woman. The arrival of Angelina back into her life, at a time when company was what she needed the most, came as a welcome surprise. And from that time on, Angelina benefited from a different kind of companionship from that experienced as a missionary with her husband.

If nothing else, it took her mind off recent problems.

However, domestic peace and idle chatter could never be Angelina's chosen way of living, for underneath it all she was still an angel.

Now that she had neither a family nor her mission on which to focus, she could not adjust to the role of lively companion for someone else, but rather sought one of quiet, reflective living. What she needed most of all was seclusion so that she could think about her lost husband and son, and get back to her angel roots: a feeling that began to resurface in her with the passing of time and the healing of her heart.

Maella knew nothing of her companion's birthright, and would have found the idea of angelhood unfathomable. So Angelina kept it from her and maintained their friendship on a social level.

But her façade of the good companion could never be maintained.

There came a time in later years when Maella's endless banter became more than she could tolerate. As a result, Angelina found herself avoiding contact with her ...And the more she sought refuge from her, the more she thought about her son.

Though many years had now passed since his death, she still missed him terribly.

As well as missing his company, the question of Batim's soul also returned to her everyday thinking; haunting her waking hours and invading her dreams. She desired only to be by herself in order to contemplate the mystery of his whereabouts. Before long, she recognised that she really should do something about it.

At length she decided to explain to Maella what was on her mind, and why.

Surprisingly, Maella understood.

"I've often wondered what happened to my own dear husband," she admitted. "As you suggest, it doesn't seem logical that the person dies completely – like snuffing out a candle. Certainly, I would like to think there is something of him that still lives."

Buoyed up by Maella's interest, Angelina determined to find out as much as possible about a terran's soul, and if indeed it was immortal; a fact of which she was not yet certain. And there was only one place she could hope to get some answers...

Angelina translocated back to Eternity during a rare and welcome break from routine, when Maella was off visiting relatives. Salutat had not been communicative with her of late, and she was looking forward to seeing him again. But mainly, she hoped to consult someone else. ...Not Yavros, the thought of whom still made her feel uncomfortable, but her old and trusted friend Masian.

The esteemed sage was overcome with compassion for Angelina when she turned up all of a sudden.

He embraced her warmly.

"My dear, I was so sorry to hear of your loss," he said; quite emotionally for an angel.

Masian had learnt of the angels' rescue mission, and the tragic event which followed. He had attempted to find Angelina to console her, but by then she was something of a terran recluse, having taken up residence with Maella. So Masian's emotional embrace was as much relief to see her again as it was to offer her consolation.

Angelina responded tenderly to his gesture. This was the first spiritual warmth she had felt since Batim's death. It came to her that she must actually be recovering, if her heart could open up enough to receive affection.

"Thank you for your caring words, Masian," she said. "Although Batim's death came as a shock, I have learnt to move on with my life."

"How are you filling your time now?" he asked, leading her through to his sitting room; a room so familiar to her.

How Angelina loved that room. It represented wisdom, and an angelic soul with whom to share her burdens. For a moment she became lost in pleasant memories and the delight she felt to be there again...

"Did you hear what I said?" Masian asked, noticing her brief absentmindedness.

She came to with a start. "I'm sorry Masian, my mind was on something else. Would you mind repeating it?"

"I wanted to know what you're doing these days, but I can see I should have asked how you are in yourself. There must still be a lot of sorrow in your heart."

"I'm not as bad as I was," she replied in all honesty. "To begin with, Salutat showered me with his love – spiritually, as he no longer has a body. But nowadays I'm not unwell in spirit so much as perplexed about something...which is why I came to see you. I wondered if you might be able to help me."

"Does it concern Batim's death?"

"Yes – and no," she said, making Masian regard her curiously. "It concerns Batim, but not his death as such. I had a long chat with Yavros a while ago, and he explained why Batim died even though he'd been rescued by the band of angels..."

"...And I can imagine what he said!" quipped Masian. "I bet he wasn't too sympathetic."

Angelina grinned. "No, he wasn't. Even now I still have a few reservations about his logic. But that's not the query which brought me here. It has to do with my son's present existence and possible whereabouts."

"Do you mean, where his immortal soul might be right now?" ventured Masian.

"Yes!" she exclaimed, surprised at his response, and encouraged that he understood her point of view. Masian had often demonstrated that he was of one mind with her. Heartened, she continued. "Do you think Batim has an immortal soul, then?"

"Of course! Terran spirits have souls just like angels..."

"...And that after the death of the body, the soul lives on in another form?"

"Naturally!"

"Yavros didn't seem to think so. He maintained that once an ordinary terran spirit has died, it doesn't exist any more; except for the spiritualised souls who go to Eternity and the wicked ones who finish up in Hellion. And that doesn't make sense to me!"

"I think the problem there is that he is too emotionally involved with his terran spirits. It causes him pain to think of the millions who die never having taken the trouble to know him. He won't consider the possibility of their souls living on. But they do; of that I am sure."

"...So you reckon all those souls are still in existence? Yavros says not, because he hasn't established a realm for them to go to."

"That doesn't mean they don't exist!"

"Well, if Yavros hasn't created a place for them, where can they be?"

"That's obvious! They've created one for themselves!"

Angelina stared at him in wonderment and disbelief; trying to grasp the idea he had just presented to her.

The concept of another realm was so amazing, it might just be true. Masian was not one for idle comment. He must have some justification for thinking along those lines.

...And if it was true, then perhaps there was yet some hope for Batim.

"How do you know all of this?" she asked him. "I mean, what makes you so sure there's another world out there?"

Again Masian smiled at her. It never ceased to give him pleasure when Angelina looked to him for advice, and he knew for a fact that this visit would prove to be beneficial in her quest.

With joy in his heart, he answered the question.

"I know it's there, because I've seen it."

"Really!"

Masian watched as Angelina's wonderment turn into excited fascination. But before she could ask for more, he slipped in a further comment.

"...Actually, I've sensed it rather than seen it. And I've had my impression of its existence confirmed by reports from other angels, although this is not widely spoken of. But it's a definite reality."

"Then Batim is still alive!" she stated excitedly.

Masian was elated. In the space of only a few moments he was witnessing a transformation in her. The depressed angel who came to his door had become a revitalised spirit right before his eyes: the spirit of the Angelina he had always known.

For her part, Angelina's depression finally lifted, leaving her with the promise of an avenue which she could now pursue in the quest to find her son.

"I think I should point something out though," Masian went on. "I don't know what kind of reality it is; only that it exists. From what I understand, there is something of a no-mans-land suspended between the physical and what we know as the spiritual; where there is no substance, form or order, but merely the existence of millions of souls. I'm told it even has a name. They call it 'Astralus'."

371

"Astralus...well, I never! You said angels have spoken to you about it. Could you tell me what they may have said?"

"Certainly. For millennia, angel guardians of lost terran souls reported a phenomenon: something they witnessed as their charges died. What's more, each reported seeing the same thing. It appears that when terran dies, the spirit hovers above the body for a while and then disappears. Apparently it can't be seen by terrans, but angel guardians with their heightened senses can see it quite clearly."

"I know what you're talking about!" cried Angelina as her own recollections sprang to mind. "I've had a couple of similar experiences. Salutat and I were actually involved in one of those occasions."

"That's interesting," responded Masian. "Would you be willing to tell me about it?"

Masian listened with interest as she repeated the story of Cefire and Dymas. This was a subject which interested him keenly. Unknown to Angelina, he had kept a journal of similar incidents, which he hoped to present to Yavros as proof of the fourth realm's existence. He thanked Angelina for sharing her experience with him, and asked if he could document the information.

"Please do!" she exclaimed, thrilled to have someone so interested in what she had to say on the subject. But then she went quiet as a thought crossed her mind.

"What is it?" he asked, noticing her pensive expression.

"I wonder..." she said. "Do you think the angel guardian who witnessed Batim's death may also have seen his spirit leave his body?"

"He may have. Would you like me to enquire?"

"Oh, could you? That would be so helpful," responded Angelina with enthusiasm.

"It would be my pleasure. I'll ask Salutat to work on it, and contact you when he has the information."

"Thank you, Masian. You are very kind."

Angelina sighed as the weight of grief finally lifted from her heart. She glanced with affection at Masian.

He returned the glance; happy to have been of help.

Masian was looking forward to his investigation into Batim's death, both for his own journal and for Angelina's sake. How marvellous it would be, he thought, if she could contact her son again.

"I suppose I should get back to Eddren now," Angelina conceded, and then grinned. "I would much rather sit here and talk some more about this new place... What was it called – Astralus?"

"Yes; Astralus; and it isn't a new realm. It's been around for a long time, but not many angels seem to know of it, either in Eternity or Eddren. I have a feeling we're going to hear a lot more about Astralus from now on, though!"

PART FOUR: RETURN FROM ASTRALUS

CHAPTER 1

After her exciting discovery, Angelina found it difficult to settle back into the routine of daily life; for her main focus had shifted from the activities of an ordinary terran to a brand new mission: that of searching for her son.

This proved to be a struggle as she tried to maintain the appearance of normalcy before her companion, as Maella still had no idea of her true identity.

Angelina's thinking was now more angelic than terran. Her greatest desire was to hear from the angel guardian who witnessed Batim's death. Only with him could she hope to freely discuss it.

Unwittingly, Maella eased the burden for her; knowing that Angelina loved to talk about the afterlife and their deceased loved-ones. Yet, although Angelina longed for a chance to talk about Astralus, it meant she would have to reveal her true identity, and this was not something she wanted to do while waiting for some news from Salutat. ...Maybe one day, she promised herself, but not just yet.

If in the process of finding Batim she could also help Maella with her quest, then so much the better. But right now her burning desire was to find her own kin; not someone else's.

During this time, Salutat had been briefed about his role in the search for the angel guardian.

Recognising that the task might take a while, he tried to contact Angelina to advise patience. However, once again her terran eagerness to hear from him was so strong that she again shut him out. Then, when the information at last came to hand, Salutat had to use drastic measures in order to attract her attention.

One night she awoke in a panic; her ears ringing.

"I'm sorry, Angelina. I didn't mean to bellow at you like that..." said the usually polite Salutat. "...but you were too eager to receive my report, and I couldn't break through your anxiousness to give it to you!"

Angelina laughed with relief when she realised who had shouted at her, and that there was no cause for alarm.

"Salutat! It's wonderful to hear from you again," she mouthed for fear of waking Maella in the next room. "Can I come over? I lose something of the conversation when we try to talk across the dimensions. Besides," she added, "I'm looking forward to seeing you."

Salutat felt a sense of relief to link up with Angelina, for his investigations had been all-consuming of late, and he knew he was neglecting her.

It had also distressed him that he was elsewhere during Angelina's visit with Masian, but being asked to find the angel guardian on her behalf had somewhat made up for it. At least he would have the chance to talk with her in person now. Salutat, too, had missed his spouse.

He greeted her with renewed affection. His life as an angel was very different from his terran experiences, and he missed their physical contact. Memories of the precious moments they had shared as man and wife still surfaced occasionally; for the role of the terran male wasn't all hard work – there had been many good times as well.

Yet Angelina's translocation just now was for a specific purpose; not to revisit the past. As such he must waste no time in getting to the point. In his investigations, Salutat had not only discovered the name of the angel who saw Batim die, but had already conversed with him.

"Oh Salutat!" exclaimed Angelina; this was more than she had hoped for. "What did the angel have to say?"

"He described to me what he saw that awful day; and I can tell you, it upset me hearing about our son's death in graphic detail."

Angelina shuddered at the thought. "I'm not surprised. Please go on, if you can."

Salutat continued.

"He told me his terran charge had gone to the arena as a spectator to see the boa-constrictor at work. Apparently the shameful character liked to indulge his primal instincts, and that was why the angel guardian had been given this particular assignment..."

Angelina screwed up her nose, imagining how low the terran spirit must have sunk to want gratification in such a debase way.

"...Anyway," Salutat went on. "Once Batim had escaped from the cage, the terran was taking his leave of the arena when there came a loud yell, followed by stunned silence. The angel said he looked back and saw that the guard had plunged his sword into our son...

Salutat paused; briefly overcome with emotion.

Angelina gave him a moment; then she continued with renewed purpose.

"What else did the angel guardian witness?" she asked on tenterhooks, while Salutat collected his thoughts.

"You were right," he said at length. "As you and Masian suggested, Batim's spirit did leave his body at the moment of death. Even from a distance, the angel distinctly saw a wispy form separate from the body; then hover above it before vanishing into thin air. Batim's soul, it would seem, does live on."

Angelina could stand the tension no longer. Pure terran feelings took over, and she wept for joy and relief.

Salutat also found himself overwhelmed.

"This means the door is finally open for us to find him again," Angelina sobbed.

She looked deeply into Salutat's now reflective eyes.

He returned the look, expecting still to see heartache in her, but instead he saw the joy of hope – a hope they had both been longing for.

"Now I can begin my search," she said eagerly. "Now I have a chance of finding out what happened to our son."

When Angelina returned to Eddren this time, she did not go back there alone.

Salutat, though now in angel form, wanted to support Angelina in her pursuit of Batim's soul, and asked Yavros for permission to act as her companion.

"Well, yes, you can go, but I still think you'll be wasting your time," insisted Yavros.

Yet, Yavros owed this angel a debt of gratitude for all of his mission work in Eddren, and despite his reservations about a possible fourth dimension, he decided to relieve Salutat of his duties.

Angelina's heart leapt for joy when he told her; raising her hopes that their new joint mission might actually meet with success.

Salutat chuckled at her childlike enthusiasm.

"Your positive outlook will do this mission the world of good," he joked. "...In fact, if you were any more positive about it, all the souls in Astralus would rush joyfully into Yavros' arms and we might have no mission at all!"

"That wouldn't be such a bad thing!" retorted Angelina. "There's nothing Yavros would like more than to have the dispossessed souls return to him. And naturally we would love to see Batim come home to Eternity... There is still one thing that bothers me, though."

"Oh, what's that?"

"How are we going to operate, with me in physical form and you in spirit? I can't keep putting my body to sleep to come on the same level as you."

Salutat thought for a moment; then said, "However we work, we'll need to function in an entirely different way. We've been angels together, and we've been terran spirits together. But we haven't worked in both guises at the same time. I think we must forget how we have worked before. The only way we can do that successfully is if I assume the role of angel guardian with you."

"Does that mean I won't be able to see you?"

"Not while you are awake. You can't see my spirit while you're in your terran consciousness; only when you leave it during sleep. But I can still guide you, just as the angel guardians do with their charges. Am I making sense?"

"Yes, I think so. I often wondered how angel guardians function, and if their charges ever take any notice?"

Salutat laughed. "I'd say, not too many, by the number of souls who must be going to Astralus rather than coming home to Eternity! What do you think, though? Do you agree it's a good way to function?"

"It certainly sounds logical. We'll try it after I wake up in the morning."

Angelina vividly recalled her night-time conversation with Salutat. Adopting a listening attitude, she waited to hear his voice again.

Salutat groaned when he noticed this. He knew only too well that as soon as she brought her mind into play, his spirit would not be able to contact her.

By mid-morning Angelina was becoming frustrated by Salutat's apparent tardiness. Then, during the evening her frustration turned to contempt; for it seemed he was toying with her.

Only when she fell asleep exhausted was he finally able to get through.

"At last!" he cried. "I've been trying to reach you all day! You really must learn to relax. Please don't strive to hear me, because it doesn't work that way."

"Sorry," she said sheepishly. "I forgot how hard it is to tune into spiritual things while in the terran consciousness. I won't make the same mistake again."

The next day, honouring her promise, Angelina allowed her thoughts to drift just enough for Salutat to connect with her.

Stilling her mind for any length of time proved to be more difficult than she envisaged, and frequently she lost him in a sea of terran thought. Only after much practice did she manage to keep her thinking mind detached while they conducted their conversations.

The only obstacle she needed to overcome now was her interaction with Maella.

Angelina's sociable friend knew nothing of the exchange taking place under her roof. Throughout the next day she frequently tried to draw Angelina away from her musings for some purpose of her own.

Distracted by the continual interruptions, Angelina left the house and hurried to the beach in order to focus. Once there, to all appearances it looked as though she was out for a stroll. Keeping her head down, she did not want to give the impression to any onlookers that she was just a crazy woman talking to herself.

Telepathically, Angelina asked Salutat, "So where do we go from here?"

"The next step will be to locate this Astralus," Salutat replied. "I'd never even heard of it till recently."

"Nor me – not before Masian told me about it, that is."

"Then we must do some researching. I'll ask round the angel community."

"It might help if you speak with Masian. He's forming a journal on Astralus from information given to him by angel guardians on their return from duty."

"That's a good idea. I'll get on to it straight away, if you don't mind."

"Oh...does that mean you are going to disconnect from me now?"

"Yes. Are you alright with that?"

"Of course. I just want to know when you are likely to contact me again so that I can be prepared. We don't want a repeat of the last fiasco!"

"We certainly don't! The best time to connect with you is just before you arise for the day."

"Alright, I'll be watching for it."

"No, don't watch out for me!" he cried, exasperated.

"...You know what I mean!"

Angelina was now concerned that remaining in physical form could be a hindrance to working on a higher level; for the more she tried to relax, the more tense she became.

"I wish I didn't have to be a terran spirit anymore," she cried forlornly when, for the umpteenth time during the night, her forced attempts to relax prevented her from sleeping. As dawn approached she began to think herself inadequate for the task ahead; so tired and disgruntled did she feel after her restless night.

In her opinion, the body she inherited from Cefire had now served its purpose.

"Surely I don't need to be in physical form any longer," she moaned inwardly, hoping someone in Eternity might hear her.

"Don't be so maudlin," Salutat responded.

He actually felt sorry for Angelina and empathised with her situation. It must be difficult, he assumed, to live a life of duplicity. But terran she still was, and so must make the best of it until such time as Yavros decided to free her from the obligation.

Angelina stirred, dragging herself out of the dark state of consciousness which was neither sleeping nor waking. Was that a voice she just heard, or only her imagination?

"Angelina, wake up!"

"Salutat! Thank goodness you're there."

She sighed with relief that she hadn't shut him out with her unwanted anxiousness. Then she remembered his self-appointed task.

"Did you speak with Masian?" she asked.

"I did indeed."

Angelina leapt out of her bed and flung a wrap around her shoulders. "Just give me a minute to attend to some necessities," she said; "And then you can tell me all about your discoveries."

Salutat chuckled to himself. He knew exactly what she was referring to. He had heard it called 'ablutions' and was something all living creatures needed to engage in during the day. This was part of terran life he happily dispensed with once he left his physical body.

He waited patiently for Angelina to return to her room. She did so carrying a mug of steaming herbal tea.

384

"Maella was up. She made me a drink." Angelina settled herself into the bedside chair in order to focus on Salutat. "What did Masian tell you?" she asked at length.

"In addition to the information he gave you, he's done some investigating, and held a meeting of returned angel guardians to ascertain just where Astralus is."

Angelina listened with interest, her eyes closed to aid concentration. Though keen to hear everything Salutat had to say, she found herself nodding off to sleep; a fact which Salutat noted.

He prodded her inwardly to hold her attention.

"Sorry, Salutat," she muttered as she came to. "I'm still very sleepy."

Realising that sitting comfortably did not aid alertness, Angelina got up and walked over to the open window for some fresh air.

"That's better. I'm less likely to fall asleep on you now! What were you saying?"

Salutat continued.

"There appears to be a point in consciousness where Astralus can be accessed – not unlike when we translocate from Eternity to Eddren. In other words, you don't change your actual location; only your state of consciousness. But, according to Masian, angel guardians don't follow their charges into the afterlife; they just watch them go. So the actual point of entry remains a mystery."

"That doesn't help us very much," remarked Angelina; a little disappointed. "Perhaps we need to be in attendance when a terran spirit dies so that we can follow him!"

"Yes, that was the impression I got when I discussed it with Masian."

"Or..," said Angelina, and tailed off when an improbable solution came to mind.

"Or what?" asked Salutat.

Angelina cupped a hand over her mouth, not daring to mention it. After all, carrying out the idea would be like an echo of a previous incident.

Salutat was wise to her, and said, "I know what you're thinking, there."

"You do?"

"Yes. ...And it probably would be the only way to find out for sure."

Angelina was stunned. The idea of arranging her own death, when it came to mind, had seemed so contrary to Yavros' rules for his terran spirits, that she dared not even voice it. And yet here was Salutat, not only understanding what she had in mind, but also agreeing with her. After all, their terran predecessors had done it. If Dymas and Cefire could survive their suicide, then why couldn't she?

Yet, it was too bizarre an idea to even contemplate.

"I'm beginning to wish I hadn't thought about it at all, though" she admitted.

Angelina suddenly felt giddy at the prospect of her own death, and sat back down. However, she could not dispute the fact that physically dying in order to discover what happened to the spirit afterwards was an entirely logical way of locating Astralus.

She asked Salutat, "When you died to your terran form, did you not see anything of this other place?"

"No," he replied. "If you recall that incident, Miekaale came to my rescue. Before he freed Batim, he whisked me back to Eternity as I was in shock. Though, with the benefit of hindsight, it would have suited our purpose if I had gone to Astralus first. ...But then, it's not a foregone conclusion that I could have escaped from it."

"Oh dear...is Astralus a dangerous place?"

"No; not from what Masian told me, anyway. He thinks it's more like a no-man's land."

"I remember now," said Angelina. "...A place suspended between two dimensions."

"Yes; something like that."

Angelina slipped into deep thought. "If I were to die and pass over to Astralus," she said at length. "Do you suppose I might get stuck there? I wouldn't be much use to Batim if we couldn't get out."

"I'd be with you," Salutat replied. "And we will summon all manner of spiritual help. What do you think then?"

Angelina sighed intensely.

"It's certainly worth considering," she said. "I'm getting really tired of being terran. I need my angel status; I need your company...but this is more important than any of my own feelings just now."

"I tell you what," said Salutat after some reflection. "If you're concerned about it I could consult Yavros..."

Angelina grunted. "He's very sceptical about the whole issue of Astralus."

"I know, but he might be sympathetic about your desire to return to angel status. We don't have to tell him the gist of our discussion."

"Oh, I'm not sure..." said Angelina guardedly. "It would be deceiving him, and that wouldn't be right."

"Well, what do you suggest, then?"

"Let me give it some..."

A knock at the door suddenly broke her concentration. Angelina gasped with the shock of such an abrupt return to full consciousness.

She cried out in alarm.

Maella flung the door open noisily.

"Angelina, I want you to come to the market today; it would do you good," she gushed. "I've heard there'll be a band of minstrels playing, and while we're there we could look for the blue fabric I have in mind for my new drapes… Are you alright, Angelina? You seem a bit flustered."

"Yes…thank you," Angelina replied impatiently, and then quickly added, "Well actually, I'm not feeling very well at the moment; I have a bit of a headache. Would you mind if I don't come with you?"

Disappointed, Maella backed down. "No, that's alright, my dear. I just thought you'd enjoy the outing."

"Thank you, Maella, but I'm very happy as I am."

Angelina smiled at her friend; not wishing to hurt her feelings; but inside she felt like she was dying.

How much longer must I live this dual life? she thought.

After Maella left, she called for Salutat again.

Aware of the break in communication, he had remained with her in case the interruption may have aggravated her nervous system. He was right: Angelina was faltering.

"I'm still here," he said to reassure her. "This need for a life of duplicity is wearing you down, and it's worrying me. Give our idea some thought, and get back to me as soon as you possibly can."

"I will," she responded, and burst into tears.

Since Salutat's departure from physical life, and especially now Batim was no longer with her, Angelina's dislike for a terran existence had compounded. By now, the only way she could cope was by frequently shutting herself away. She craved solitude and silence; for the focus in her life now was regular contact with Salutat.

Even Maella's chatty, friendly disposition was too much for her fragile nerves.

More than anything, she longed for Eternity. And yet, the prospect of going through the painful process of dying filled her with terror.

What would it be like, she wondered; to actually have your physical body rendered lifeless?

All she could think of was the terrible ways in which her husband and son died. She had witnessed terran death a number of times, and each incident happened in dramatic fashion; she knew nothing of dying gracefully. Yet, in order to locate Astralus and then go home to Eternity, she had no choice but to undergo the process of dying.

Maella's husband died, she recalled. Was he killed, too? She decided to find out.

"Gracious me, no!" Maella exclaimed almost laughingly when Angelina broached the subject. "Who would want to kill my darling husband? He was well loved by everyone. No, he died of the sickness."

"...The sickness? What is that?" asked Angelina who had had little exposure to terran ailments in her time.

Assuming Angelina wanted to know which sickness was responsible for his death, Maella replied, "He was unwell for quite a while. In the end the tumours in his body ate away the good flesh, and he succumbed..."

Angelina waited considerately while Maella relived the distressing experience. Then she asked, "Were you present when your husband died?"

"Yes. I remained at his bedside till he slipped away from me forever. It was very upsetting...I loved him dearly."

Maella was becoming emotional now.

All at once, Angelina realised she had been insensitive in bringing up the subject, and saw the need to regress.

"I'm sorry, Maella; I didn't mean to cause you suffering. Please forgive me."

"There's no need. It would probably do me good to talk about it now and then. Why did you want to know?"

"Oh, no reason," said Angelina, quickly trying to justify her need to ask such personal questions. She could hardly inform Maella that she had contemplated her own death. Even so, it was shameful that she should resort to telling a lie; for she did have a reason for asking – a good reason. But it was something she could share with no-one on the physical plane.

The next time Salutat conversed with Angelina, he gave her surprising news.

"I've been to see Yavros and arranged for both of us to speak with him. Can you leave your body and come over?"

"...Right now?" she asked, stunned by his request. She had assumed they would discuss a move like this before acting on it.

"Yes, if you can."

"But it's already morning. You'll have to wait till tonight. It's impractical for me to come over during the daytime now. Have you forgotten we live in a world of time and space in Eddren?"

"You are right; it did slip my mind. Come through this evening then. I'm sure Yavros won't mind a slight delay. He always loves to see you."

"...I'm not so sure about that," Angelina said to herself as she began her chores.

Throughout the day Angelina's mind was racing.

This interview with Yavros could be the cornerstone for her future; but after her disastrous last meeting with him, she feared for the outcome.

Initially, she had hoped that Yavros would allow her to just walk away from her physical form forever; to stay in Eternity, leaving her body to die off back in Eddren. But that wouldn't be fair on Maella, she conceded. The still-grieving soul would have yet another death to deal with...

As the day wore on, Angelina thoughts swung between desire to leave Eddren and a sense of loyalty to someone who was still a good friend. Maybe she should just leave it up to Yavros. He usually knew what was for the best; at least, she hoped that was still the case.

By nightfall, Angelina was so apprehensive about the upcoming interview that she could not calm down enough to translocate, and in desperation called out to Salutat.

"I can't do this!" she cried subconsciously, when sleep continued to elude her. "Salutat, please help me!"

Salutat understood how she might be worried about discussing suicide. Anyone would be. It had been different in his case, for death was forced upon him. But making a voluntary decision about dying to the body must never be easy. ...And what of Yavros? What would he think of the suggestion? It was not surprising Angelina's anxiousness had become ingrained. Yet Salutat was also eager for her to arrive, for he did not want to keep Yavros waiting.

A swift response to her cry for help was needed.

Frantically, he thought how he could do this.

Then, as if prompted from within, Salutat remembered Yavros' special team of angel counsellors. It was formed to support returning guardians who experienced emotional trauma during their missions. Healing was brought about by bathing the angel guardian with soothing balm. Almost without thought, Salutat found himself invoking them.

Moments later, Angelina drifted into a peaceful sleep. She was by Salutat's side in no time at all.

"Quickly," he said as she awoke to the fact. "Let's get to Yavros before he gives up on us!"

"I won't hear of it!" came Yavros' thunderous response to her request for release. "Angelina, do you know what you are asking of me?"

Angelina shrunk back in fear. She had overstepped the mark with Yavros again, and he was angry with her. Didn't he care that living as a terran spirit was draining her soul these days?

"But Yavros," Salutat said in support. "Angelina is not a natural terran spirit; she's an angel. The only reason she took on physical form was to engage in a mission for you; a mission which is long since over. She doesn't need to be terran anymore. ...And," he added passionately, "Angelina badly wants to come home to begin her search for Batim."

Yavros looked up at the two pairs of eyes regarding him intently. Their determination to win him over was alluring, but there was nothing he could do to accommodate them.

"I'm sorry Angelina, but I cannot bring you home yet," he told her.

"Why not?" they cried simultaneously.

"Because I have no means of separating you from your body – permanently, that is. Even now you are joined to it by the silver cord, and nobody has the right to sever that; not even me. I know there are a number of ways a terran body can die, of which you two would be far more familiar than I am. ...Remind me what they are?"

What's this: a quiz? Salutat asked himself; exasperated.

"There's sickness and accident," responded Angelina in automatic response. "...And old age, of course."

"I was killed," muttered Salutat condescendingly. "And some people kill themselves..."

Where is all this leading? he wondered in despair.

"Well, think about it," Yavros went on. "Angelina is not sick, and is much too careful to have an accident. She is far from old and nobody would want to kill her. In physical terms, Angelina, you are still a healthy middle-aged terran spirit with many years ahead of you. ...And you must live out those years until death finally catches up with you. You cannot resettle here before that time…"

"…Oh no!" groaned Angelina, her features showing the pain of disappointment. She had been sure he would allow her to return.

"Don't you know…how much I hate living this dual life?" she stammered through rising tears.

Yavros fell silent. He sensed her pain, but he had made his pronouncement and there was to be no arguing; for there was another reason behind his decision, one which only time would reveal…

All at once Salutat recalled the other option they had elected to mention. If they were to broach the subject of suicide, it must be now. …And by the sad look on Yavros' face, Salutat surmised, he might yet capitulate.

"Well then, Sire," he said quickly. "Angelina should be granted dispensation to end her own physical life – many terran spirits do, you know. Would it not be acceptable for an angel in physical form to do likewise?"

"I know many of my progeny end their own lives," he replied sadly; "but I abhor it and, regrettably, they are held accountable for it. Suicide is a slight against the purpose of their creation. The circumstances which drive them to it may be defensible, but not the act itself. However, suicide for Angelina would not only be punishable but also way beyond the pale because she is an angel under obedience to me, and I have said, 'No'. Angelina's status as an angel would be severely jeopardised if she chose to go against my wishes on this."

Yavros looked directly at her when he spoke the words. Again, it was his way of telling her to be careful. She was his angel and therefore had no say in the matter.

Yet, there was also a veiled appeal within his look which said, 'Keep going, Angelina. I can't tell you the reason; only trust me and you will see...'

Salutat took note of Yavros' fixed look, and the chastening effect it was having on Angelina. But then a thought came to mind which, he hoped, might just sway Yavros' opinion once and for all.

Quickly he said, "During my first mission, I inhabited a body for my work, and then left it to come home again. Couldn't Angelina do the same?"

"No, Salutat. You're not thinking straight here. When you left that body it was still occupied. It didn't die. Its resident spirit merely took over again. If Angelina vacates her body now, it will die because presently her spirit alone sustains it. In effect, she would be committing murder. ...However," he continued on a cheerful note to assure them he was not an ogre. "Angelina is free to come back to Eternity for a visit whenever she likes."

Angelina felt she was doomed.

Never before in Eternity, or even in Eddren, had she been so down in spirit; so forsaken by the one being who could actually do something to help her.

"If I must stay there," she mumbled, the constriction in her throat making it difficult to talk. "Would you allow me another mission...to keep me occupied? I couldn't...bear living only...as a terran...for the rest of my life."

Yavros laughed knowingly, but then regretted it when he saw the look of confusion on Angelina's face.

"Angelina," he said. "From now on you will have plenty to keep you occupied."

"What do you mean?" she asked.

"You'll find out in the fullness of time."

"What did he mean by all of that?" Angelina asked Salutat on the way out.

"I wouldn't know!" replied Salutat, angered by the lack of success and Yavros' unhelpful remarks. "At times I just don't understand him. He's all-knowing and yet he will not attempt to see things through our eyes. It's like he doesn't care anymore."

"I think Yavros has changed in his attitude towards me," she said miserably. "It's so unfair. Do you honestly think he doesn't care about us?"

"He certainly gives that impression. But maybe it is we who have changed; not Yavros. The other angels wouldn't question him the way we have. Perhaps we are behaving more like terran spirits than angels, and he doesn't like it."

"I wish I'd never taken on terran form," cried Angelina forlornly. "Returning to angel status and finding Batim is more of an illusive dream than ever."

"Don't forget, you are still depressed because of what happened to Batim. Focus your attention on finding him. When you've make some progress you'll cheer up about everything else as well."

Yavros looked on as the two unhappy figures walked away.

He sighed in lamentation for their suffering, and for the cruel way he treated them. But it was necessary. He dealt with them that way for a reason.

Yavros was convinced that only by remaining terran and going through all the tribulations she would have to face, could Angelina hope to find Batim.

"No other angel has such a vested interest in locating the mysterious realm of Astralus than Angelina," he declared when she had disappeared through the veil of consciousness; for he was beginning to accept that there was indeed such a place.

"If anybody can find it, Angelina, surely you can."

But right now he felt wretched.

Yavros was certain he had just lost the loyalty of his two finest angels.

As he went back to work he wailed in frustration, "Will there ever again be happiness in Eternity?"

CHAPTER 2

If it wasn't for Maella's generous nature, Angelina's spirit would have struggled through the next few weeks.

She had taken Yavros' ruling hard; not even attempting to grasp his reasoning, or to understand why he had such little consideration for her plight.

"I'm angel, not terran!" she declared emphatically while alone in her room. "How can he be so mean as to relegate me to a life of terran hardship?"

But then she realised what she was saying. She should feel sorry for them; not for herself. Terran spirits were also Yavros' creations. They were his offspring, not his subjects as were the angels. But for Lucifer's intervention over the millennia, they would be ranked above the angels by now.

Yet, terran spirits nowadays did not match the intended image for them...thanks to Lucifer.

It was all too confusing. ...Oh, to be an angel again!

To take her mind off self pity, Angelina tried to involve herself in Maella's activities. With a bit of effort she found she could even generate some interest in her good works. ...And there were plenty of needy terrans who depended on kindly souls like Maella.

"Come with me to the gardens in the morning," Maella suggested to her one day. "Homeless young men gather there for company. I've started taking them freshly-baked bread and some fruit from our trees. They seem to like it."

Angelina was in the habit, now, of accepting every task Maella offered her. Yavros had said there would be plenty to occupy her during the remainder of her life. Maybe he meant working alongside Maella. If this was the case, then she would be obedient to his will. So she agreed to every request, accompanying her companion to the market, to visit sick friends...and to feed the young men.

There was a considerable gathering in the public gardens for so early in the morning. Angelina watched as hunger brought out both the best and the worst in the youngsters; some of whom were no more than children. While most of them waited patiently to be offered nourishment, others pushed and shoved in order to be served first. Always gracious and understanding, Maella did not chide them but gently said, "You must be the hungriest!"

Angelina marvelled at Maella's generosity of spirit; she sincerely enjoyed doing good works. It caused Angelina to wonder why she herself felt unable to share in the richness of Maella's enthusiasm. But then she realised why. Maella was fulfilling her vocation. She had been a wonderful spouse in her time, and now was sharing that benevolence with those less fortunate; for it was in her nature to do so. Angelina, on the other hand, was not yet able to achieve her heart's desire, but merely remained active until she could go where she felt her spirit belonged: back to Eternity to begin her search for Batim.

The thought of him again, especially in the presence of all the young men, brought tears to her eyes.

"Oh, my son," she inwardly sobbed as she looked into faces so desperate for a bite to eat.

These youngsters were very different from Batim. They seemed innocent and natural; not arrogant as Batim had become in his latter days. But also, she thought, they have clearly not yet been invaded by Lucifer.

Why was that? Watching them, it seemed obvious: they did not pose a threat to him. They were too destitute, and in some cases too sickly to want to struggle against him.

As she witnessed their gratitude to Maella, she realised there were some among them who were, in their humility, already closer to Yavros than many of the terrans she had come across in her time.

Without realising what she was doing, she offered up a prayer for them.

When she left the gardens that day, Angelina felt she had learnt something valuable. Only true humility can bring a soul close to Yavros. She wondered if Lucifer was aware of this and planned to capitalise on it. She hoped not.

"They're good boys, really," Maella commented on the way home. "They just need someone to love them."

"Don't they have homes and families?" asked Angelina.

She thought back to Batim's early years, and how she and Salutat did everything they possibly could, under the circumstances of their mission, to give him a wholesome upbringing. They thought they'd succeeded. ...In fact, they did succeed! It was only when Lucifer took hold of Batim in their absence that their son began to change. Surely these boys also have families to give them stability until they go out into the world...

"A lot of them were orphaned" Maella explained. "And some have been abandoned by their families because of financial hardship. It's quite sad. I do what I can for them, although it isn't much, really."

Nevertheless, even though Angelina's heart went out to the young men, she knew she could never share Maella's passion towards helping them. Something more urgent still tugged at her heartstrings...

After a while, Angelina stopped going to the gardens with Maella. The reason she gave was that she felt ashamed her concern for the boys was pity rather than love: an excuse Maella could not easily accept.

"I don't understand; I thought you liked helping me!" Maella chided; far more critically than Angelina considered was justified – as though her voluntary help should now be regarded as a regular commitment.

All Angelina could do in response was to apologise and retreat; for discounting Yavros' will upset her more than suffering Maella's annoyance.

"I'm sorry, Yavros," she mouthed into the ethers. "I just can't do it anymore. I don't have my heart in it, and that's not fair to you."

She wondered why she heard nothing back from him.

From then on, convinced she could do nothing while she remained alive, Angelina stayed at home to focus on what she regarded as her true vocation: the soul of Batim.

She thought of him often. Where was he now? Was he alright? What was he doing?

How she wished she could get some answers.

One balmy night, when the level of humidity in town was higher than usual, the air in Angelina's room seemed thick, making each breath laboured. Even with the window flung wide open, the pressure in her temples intensified and she started to develop a pounding headache. Then, when she tried to sit up, she felt giddy.

As she lay helpless in the stifling gloom, her mind began to slip into an altered state of consciousness. Suspended somewhere between waking and sleeping, she thought for a moment that she was seeing things.

At some time during most nights Angelina habitually made the transition back to Eternity. She looked forward to it as a means of escape from physical reality. But the state she experienced now belonged to neither realm. This pain was drawing her into a dream world she had not before come across.

All the same, she could not help but notice, even in her discomfiture, that when suspended in this unfamiliar state of consciousness she somehow seemed detached from the pain. And this made her want to stay there. But still, she knew it was not real.

...At least, she assumed it was not real.

The next morning she felt more like herself again, for the cooling air helped alleviate the pain.

Later, she told Maella about it.

"It sounds like you had a migraine," Maella suggested. "I've heard they can affect you in some strange ways."

"Well, this was really strange — as if I was somewhere else, but not in a place I would recognise."

"What do you mean?" asked Maella, who had no idea of Angelina's nightly excursions out of her body. The most Maella had strayed in spirit was within the context of her dreams; and that, unknowingly.

Angelina did not feel like explaining herself further just now; for she would need to choose her words carefully to help Maella understand, and that was a task beyond her capability at present. In response, she told her, "I suppose it was a kind of daydream."

However, the illusions, which had been clear even in her sickly state, haunted her for days to come.

These were different from anything else she had come across before; and as yet, she was unsure if they were real or merely the product of an afflicted mind.

It was now high summer in that region of Eddren, with steamy nights becoming a regular occurrence.

Before long, during a particularly heavy, airless evening, Angelina began to feel another migraine coming on.

"Oh, no...not again," she complained when she realised what was happening.

Maella, unable to resist an opportunity to provide help, gave her a fragrance to help her settle. But it was too late. By midnight the migraine had set in. Angelina knew she would be in for a rough night.

Despite the strange sensations inside her head she tried to ignore the pain and focus on getting some proper sleep. But then she found herself slipping into the unknown state again. Reluctantly, she conceded that she had no choice but to go with it and wait for the migraine to pass.

However, this time she regarded the phenomenon from a different perspective.

Despite her discomfort and a great desire to sleep, she was fascinated by the vista that had, of its own accord, presented itself to her. Slowly her focus shifted from her own suffering to something that was giving the impression of being in another dimension.

Later, when the migraine had passed and her mind was clear enough to recall the experience, she tried to evaluate what she had seen.

...And there was only one way to describe it.

"It was like a swirling mist of thought," she told Salutat the following night; convinced he would be interested in the effect of the migraine. "But that's not all I picked up from it," she added. "I heard something, too."

"The mist made a sound?" asked Salutat, trying to quell the scepticism that was arising in his mind.

"Yes. It was as though the substance was wailing. And I felt a great sorrow: a sort of heaviness. ...Not heavy like a rock is heavy but the kind of heaviness you feel when you are downhearted. It was most disturbing, and even though I was relieved to come out of it, part of me wanted to see more. But I wouldn't voluntarily trigger another migraine just to achieve it!"

"It's funny you should use the word 'heavy'," remarked Salutat, showing some interest now.

"Why do you say that?"

"Because when I was talking to the angels recently, one of them used the same word in connection with Astralus. He said he felt there would be a 'heaviness of heart' in a place like that."

"Do you know why?"

"Not especially. But maybe the souls who go there have no proper home, and are lost. They can't come to Eternity as they didn't connect with Yavros while they were alive, and so they go to the no-mans-land of Astralus. It makes sense to me that they might be unhappy there."

Angelina perked up.

"So the place I touched on could be Astralus?"

"...It might be."

"I don't believe it! After all this time I thought the only way I could access Astralus was after my death; but maybe the opposite is true: that I can only locate it by remaining in my body!"

Angelina was excited now; it seemed she had stumbled upon something relevant to her search for Batim.

Salutat offered her a word of caution.

403

"Although the state you have encountered could well be Astralus, please don't assume anything yet. It might just have been the effect of the migraine. And you don't want to be drawn into something that's merely a flight of fancy. You will need to confirm it is Astralus before proceeding much further."

"You're probably right. It's a pity you can't accompany me on these migraine excursions – I could use the support. If my vision really is Astralus, I'd be nervous about going there alone."

When Angelina awoke the next day, she found that she had a whole new perspective on life; for there appeared to be real purpose in her remaining alive after all.

What if she was right – that she could access Astralus while still in terran form? Had it ever been done before? And if anyone else knew about this place of no substance, how could she contact them? She was certain, now, that it would be unwise to try and enter such a mysterious realm alone or without knowing more about it. But apart from Salutat, she knew of no other terran spirits who had ever shown signs of being sensitive to its existence.

...Except, perhaps, Maella.

How strange, she thought, that the only person she really associated with these days, was also the one person who might be willing to explore an alien territory with her. She had assumed that no living terrans would be familiar with the name Astralus; yet the existence of it may in fact be widely known in Eddren, if little acknowledged. After all, the angel guardians got their information about it from somewhere! Perhaps they learnt of it from their charges.

Maella might know as much as the angels do, but just hasn't mentioned it...

What a startling realisation! The more Angelina dwelt on it, the more she read into it. She began to consider that her connection with someone so keenly interested in life after death might not just be a coincidence.

Was their friendship being orchestrated by Yavros for this express purpose?

Come on now, Angelina, she chided herself. Stop all this speculating; it's too early. You haven't even broached the subject with her! Don't assume anything of Maella until you're sure of your facts!

"Have I heard of...what?" Maella exclaimed when Angelina timidly brought up the subject. "I'm very sorry, but I don't know what you're talking about. Whatever is...Astralus?"

Angelina's spirit dropped. Perhaps I was mistaken about this, she thought.

But then she changed her mind when Maella added, "Is it connected with our favourite topic – the after-life?"

"Yes! Yes, it is!"

Suddenly Angelina panicked. For a couple of days now she had convinced herself that Maella must be the one to approach about Astralus; but now the time had arrived, she unexpectedly hesitated. How could she describe the theory without going into her recent conversations with Salutat? And if she did touch on that, then she would also have to explain just who Salutat was, thereby revealing something of her own identity – an entirely separate topic which would really taking some explaining...

Angelina grimaced inwardly: Oh dear, what have I got myself into now?

"Have you been thinking about your son again?" Maella asked; and when Angelina nodded she added, "Yes, my husband has scarcely been off my mind, too. I can't stop thinking about the wonderful life we had together; it's so disquieting... So, what is this Astralus place? Does it have something to do with your son?"

"...It might!"

"What do you mean by that?"

"Come and sit down, Maella. Something has come to mind which may be relevant in my search for Batim — and your search for your husband. I would really like to discuss it with you."

At last Angelina felt she could talk about her discovery.

She briefly told Maella how she came across the name Astralus and what it was, although she made no reference to the angels. She spoke of the migraines and the strange experiences she had when adversely affected by them that convinced her she had found Astralus.

Maella, however, was dubious.

"It sounds more like wishful thinking to me," she stated. "Believing the after-life and your hallucinations to be one-and-the-same-thing does not make it fact."

Level-headed Maella did not share Angelina's sensitivity of vision. Over the years they had been together, she had come to consider herself the wiser of the two; which meant that her scepticism was unquestionably right and Angelina must be deluded.

"I know it might only be wishful thinking on my part," admitted Angelina passively. "It's a start, though."

"What makes you think these hallucinations are actually a real place?"

"Because of a remark someone said, which happened to correspond with what I experience in a migraine."

"And as a result of this, you've concluded that you're in possession of the truth!"

"Not concluded!" snapped Angelina, growing frustrated with Maella. The older woman seemed intent on belittling her suggestion. "I just wondered about it...and also, I was hoping you might know something about Astralus which would help us both in our quest."

"I'm sorry, Angelina, but if you expect me to believe in the imaginings of someone suffering from a migraine, then you need to think again. The after-life is of far greater significance than that. And..." she added with a sly chuckle. "...My husband is certainly not inside your head!"

Angelina felt humiliated by Maella's rejection of her idea. She had assumed her confidante would listen without bias to her Astralus theory; but she was wrong.

Furthermore, Angelina was angry. Did Maella profess to know more than her, or regard her own pre-conceived ideas about the after-life as fact? How dare she assume her own precepts were right and Angelina's wrong, when neither of them really knew the truth?

As far as Angelina was concerned, there was only one way to find out who was right, and that was to prove it.

"But how can I prove something so illusive if I only go into that state when I have a migraine?" she asked Salutat later on. "Evidence like that would not be considered proof!"

"It might not be good enough proof for someone like Maella, but you and I know differently. And which is more important, what terran spirits think they know, or what we in Eternity really know?

Angelina took comfort from Salutat's comment.

She had forgotten how fickle the terran personality can be, and that the opinion of an individual is not necessarily the truth even if it is deemed acceptable.

"Look what happened over sun worship!" she stated in testimony. "Fact is fact, and if I can verify that Astralus and my visions are the same, then no-one will be able to refute the substance of it, whatever Maella thinks!" The only way I can validate my theory is to explore the midway state of consciousness further – even if it means inducing another horrible migraine.

Angelina groaned at the prospect of yet more agony, but there really was no other way to find out for certain.

The next night she closed the windows, making her room as stuffy as possible, and then settled into position. It was not long before the familiar tightness in her head indicated the onset of a migraine.

With more reluctance than enthusiasm she allowed it to take hold.

"I must be crazy to put myself through this again," she mumbled when her head began to throb. "I hope it's going to be worth it!"

As the migraine progressed, her mind drifted into the dreamlike state. Yet, rather than allow it to drift aimlessly, she remained alert to what was happening; mindful now of possible dangers.

The first sensation she encountered was one of slipping through a tunnel; an occurrence she failed to notice during previous migraines. This was not unexpected, though; for a similar experience usually preceded entering a new state of consciousness.

However, there was a subtle difference this time from other translocations: If she opened her eyes she could still see the trappings of her bedroom even while experiencing the sensation of slipping. This provided her with an added sense of security for taking the process further.

Thus, knowing now that she could return to normality at any time, she began to relax.

Soon the sensation of slipping was replaced with one of floating in a swirling sea of nothingness.

As her senses adjusted from coarse physical thought to fine ethereal impulses, she began to perceive that the sea of nothingness actually contained something. Once again she saw and heard the strange impulses that caught her attention last time.

Surprisingly, the impression of wailing was deafening, and yet there was no sound at all. The 'thunder of silence,' was how she later regarded it.

But how could I possibly describe this to Salutat? she asked herself.

She noticed that except for the perception of heaviness there was no evidence of life in any form. Angelina could see nothing at all, just as she could hear nothing. Yet she could still feel it within her heart: tiny entrails invading her soul and drawing her into the emotional turmoil which seemed to be the only element that made up this place.

"Surely this is Astralus," she said out loud.

In doing so, Angelina woke herself up.

Annoyed, she realised that her head was hurting more than she could tolerate. With great difficulty she sat up for a moment; gasping for fresh air but not wanting to break the spell completely. After drinking some water, she lay back down to pick up the threads of the excursion.

Soon she was in her peculiar place again: still feeling, floating and listening, but not knowing where she was or what to do next.

Hardly daring to think in case it also jolted her awake, she tried to fathom how she could find out more about the place. If in fact it was Astralus and invisible souls were present, she did not want to risk becoming embroiled in emotions. Her sole purpose was to locate her son. As that was the case, she could really only do one thing.

"Batim," she whispered gently, trying not to disturb the ethers. "Batim, are you there, my son?"

Suddenly Angelina felt stupid. Maybe Maella was right, and this was nothing more than a hallucination.

Yet it didn't feel like one. Although she could see and hear nothing, her surroundings seemed real.

"Batim," she said again, projecting her thoughts beyond her own aura and into her surroundings.

Then she became a little more adventurous and started to move about within her consciousness; seeking anything that might be recognisable.

As she moved, she noticed a slightly different feeling: something more exclusive than the one of heaviness she just experienced. This was specific, and it was close by. A sense of sadness infiltrated her soul, as though someone was sharing their life's story with her. Was this real or just her imagination?

"Be careful, Angelina. You don't yet know what you are dealing with," she reminded herself.

Perhaps the chat with Maella, though upsetting, had actually prepared her for this sojourn into the unknown. At least, she now knew to exercise caution.

She ventured further on, listening in her heart for new impulses. For a while there were no more. But then she came upon what appeared to be a cluster of impulses; as though souls — if indeed they were souls — had grouped together and she was picking up their emotions.

The feelings they emitted were so familiar to her; so terran, that she could no longer think of them as anything but terran souls.

Their emotions soon became overwhelming. They even mirrored her own state of mind during the dark moments of recent years. She understood what each meant; what the souls must be going through. And despite the warnings to remain detached, she began to develop a deep sense of compassion for them.

She wanted to cry. There was so much sorrow around her, it was becoming more than she could bear...

Angelina squirmed in her sleep – in torment as well as suffering the pain of her migraine.

This she recognised, and decided perhaps it was time to terminate the experiment.

With a struggle she pulled herself back to full waking consciousness, carefully got off the bed and opened the window wide to let in much needed fresh air. After a few deep breaths she felt better.

"What am I supposed to do now?' she enquired of the ethers as, exhausted, she lay back down again.

In no time at all she had fallen soundly asleep.

Angelina kept out of Maella's way after that.

While she was conducting her experiment she avoided communication with her as much as possible for fear of repercussion, should the topic come up again. She neither wanted to discuss it with Maella, nor give any clues as to her recent activities.

In fact, her discovery became so precious, Angelina did not even want to discuss it with Salutat.

She declared emphatically, "Salutat has not been to the place, and wouldn't understand what I'm seeing, so I will keep it to myself until there is definite proof!"

But proof of her breakthrough seemed ever out of reach. Night after night she encountered nothing but the same heartrending impulses.

After a few weeks she began to feel discouraged and not a little weary, as it was upsetting her sleep pattern. So she decided to conduct the experiment on alternate nights and give herself an opportunity to have a good night's sleep in-between.

But then something happened; something which caught her by surprise – and changed everything.

On arrival in the new dimension one night, Angelina felt a number of impulses were unusually close by, and strained her senses to ascertain what they were.

She was still reserved when it came to identifying the place, or what the impulses actually were. In her heart she wanted to believe this was Astralus, and that the impulses emanated from souls. But without evidence she could not be certain, so refrained from coming to any conclusions.

...Until one of them spoke.

At least, it appeared to speak.

While the impulses continued to press around her, she felt sure she heard something: not with physical hearing, but in her mind. Something was communicating with her telepathically.

...And it said, "Welcome."

When she heard it, Angelina was at first afraid. She had spent so many unproductive nights in the swirling mist that she had got used to the idea of being detached from the environment. This new development came as such a shock that she did not know how to react.

Yet again: was it real or imagined? She could not tell.

In alarm, she woke herself up. Mercifully, the headache did not prevent her from taking stock of the situation, and although nervous now of going back in, she also felt a hint of excitement that she might at last be onto something.

Soon she was back in the mist...but the vocal impulses were no longer evident.

Bother, she thought to herself. Have I scared it off?

"I'm sorry," she called through the ethers. "Please don't leave on account of me."

Again she felt foolish. Surely she must have imagined it. Was she now doing nothing more than talking to herself? But then the cluster of impulses came back; one of them more dominant than the others.

Assuming, this time, that it really was a soul, she quickly called out to it, "Hello...my name is Angelina."

The response was immediate.

"Welcome to Astralus, Angelina." The soul said. "They call me Dymas."

"Dymas!" cried Angelina, and jolted awake.

Then she realised what she had done.

"Oh no! I don't want to lose this!"

As she sank back into sleep once more, she found that the thrill of discovery had broken the connection, and she could not regain it.

For a moment, a sense of anti-climax coursed through her, and tears welled up in her eyes. But then she realised what just happened.

"I've actually found Astralus!" she cried out loud; joy at last replacing disappointment.

And this time she couldn't wait to tell Salutat.

"I was right about the migraines!" she exclaimed when, unarranged, she crossed over and caught Salutat off guard.

He had been in conference with an angel guardian and initially resented the interruption. But then he saw just how elated she was.

"You look like the cat that's got the cream," he laughed, causing the angel with him to regard them both quizzically.

"I feel like it, too!" laughed Angelina, unable to contain her elation.

Oblivious of the fact that Salutat was with an angel, she excitedly described her latest discovery.

"Slow down!" Salutat blurted out when Angelina was in full swing. "I can't understand what you are saying!"

"Sorry, but I'm overjoyed about this!"

"I can see that! ...Only, I don't really have time to chat at the moment!"

Just then Angelina noticed the other angel.

"Oh dear, have I interrupted you?" she said in apology. "I just wanted to tell you who I met in Astralus."

"Met? You mean you've actually spoken to somebody? Not Batim, surely."

"No, not Batim. Do you recall the name of the terran who inhabited your body before you?'

Salutat looked puzzled. He had actually inhabited two bodies during his missions in Eddren.

"You know..." urged Angelina. "...The couple jumped off the cliff and we entered the bodies. Don't you remember their names?"

"Oh yes. I certainly remember the incident, but I don't quite remember the name of..."

"...It was Dymas."

"Of course... Is he the one you met in Astralus?"

"Yes! Isn't that wonderful?"

Salutat felt guilty for neglecting his associate now, but this was too significant to ignore.

"I'm very pleased for you," he said. "Did you discover anything about Batim?"

"Oh no; it's much too soon for that! I didn't even get a chance to speak with Dymas."

"Why was that?"

"I was so delighted to meet him that I accidentally woke myself up. ...And then I couldn't wait to tell you."

"So nothing else has happened since then?"

414

"No. Why do you ask?"

"It's just that I must get back to my colleague here. Do you mind?"

Angelina was taken aback. Salutat seemed very distant. Perhaps she had just caught him at a bad time.

"No, I don't mind. Can I contact you later; when I learn some more?"

"Of course..."

On awaking in the morning, Angelina reviewed her strange conversation with Salutat.

He had seemed almost to resent her visit. Had she done something to upset him? ...Or was he beginning to draw away from her? After all, he was no longer her spouse, no longer the terran father of a terran son; but pure angel again just like before they began the mission. As such, his priority would naturally revert to doing Yavros' will. Maybe from now on she should approach him less casually if she wanted to retain his support.

"Henceforth," she declared, "I will only contact Salutat when I have something to tell him about Batim – if I ever have anything to tell him about Batim!"

Even so, the realisation saddened her. For the first time since Salutat's terrible murder, Angelina felt she no longer had a spouse. She was now completely alone.

"But there's no point in dwelling on it," she told herself sternly. "It gives me even more reason to find Batim!"

Unfortunately, Angelina's attempts to proceed any further were thwarted through no fault of her own.

Later that week saw a change in the weather with the onset of autumn. The nights became cooler and therefore less helpful for someone who wanted to induce a migraine headache. Though grateful for successive nights of good sleep, it upset her that she could not bring on a migraine; her only access to Astralus.

"There must be another way to do this!" she asserted at length. "It's a certain state of mind that enables me to slip into that dimension, not the headache itself. Surely I can create the state of mind independently of a migraine."

Yet, despite a succession of experiments, touching the right spot in her consciousness continued to elude her.

"This is so frustrating," she cried forlornly. "I've already found Astralus, and now it's being taken away from me!"

But then she remembered something from when she first started delving into the new dimension.

After her last talk with Yavros, Angelina had wondered if he knew more than he was willing to admit.

Assuming this to be the case, she now considered that he may have rejected her wish to die because he knew the migraines were the key to entering the illusive realm. If so, then perhaps he could also offer advice on how else she could gain access. Surely Yavros would know what to do.

What she needed was unrestricted access through a permanent point of entry – and soon; because even if the humid weather returned, it would not last forever.

With determination in her heart, she called in on him.

"I hear you've been busy, Angelina," Yavros remarked with a glint in his eye. "I told you there would be plenty to do!"

Angelina laughed, remembering how, in their recent meetings, she felt Yavros was being unkind. But now she was making some progress, she could see that his stance had been necessary.

"Sire, I never thought I'd have occasion to say this," she began, still grinning. "But I must thank you for everything you've put me through just lately."

416

"Really? And why is that?" he asked, feigning ignorance of her implication.

"...Because if it wasn't for your insistence that I remain alive, I would not have discovered Astralus."

Angelina looked up at him to check his reaction. What were his honest feelings towards the concept of Astralus? Maybe now she would find out.

"So you located the mysterious realm then?" he asked, as though expecting nothing less from his trusted servant.

Angelina's spirit leapt – he believes in it after all! The realisation was heart-warming.

Yet, although she felt the excitement in her heart, she showed no sign of it on her face. There was still a long way to go in her conversation with this secretive superior.

"Yes," she said without expression. "I made entry into Astralus. ...And I met one of its inhabitants."

"...Not Batim?" Yavros' face lit up, but when Angelina shook her head, he resumed his passive countenance.

"No, not Batim, unfortunately. It was Dymas, the terran spirit who's body Salutat inhabited when we began our mission together."

"How do you know that?'

"He told me his name; although I didn't make headway with him on that visit," she admitted dejectedly. "I was so excited about meeting him that I broke the connection and woke up in my body. Since then I haven't been able to get back into Astralus."

Yavros looked thoughtful for a moment, as if trying to work out a perplexing problem. "You gained access only when you had the headaches, didn't you?" he said, more as a statement than a question.

"Yes, but how could you have known that?" exclaimed Angelina in surprise.

Yavros smirked. "I suspected something drastic was the only way," he confessed. "That's why I arranged for the climatic conditions to bring it about. It's a pity they could not be maintained. ...My fault for initiating the seasons! Perhaps I can help you enter Astralus another way, then."

"I know access is initially through a certain place in my consciousness," she told him, quietly pleased her hunches had been right. "But I can't work out how to pinpoint the spot, or how to make the transition without having those headaches. I came to see you in the hope that you could suggest something."

"Have you thought of using a mantra?"

Assuming he was speaking in jest, Angelina gave a half laugh. "A mantra? Goodness; I haven't seen one of those since my angel training! They're not still in use, are they?"

"Oh yes. They have always been an excellent means of focusing, and I don't believe in dispensing with a system that works. A mantra might be just what you need to get into Astralus if you don't want the headaches. I'm sorry about that, by the way. I know how you suffered. But your willingness to suffer demonstrated something important to me."

"What was that?"

"...Your determination! The way you tortured yourself just to achieve your goal inspired me to take an interest.

"Thank you...but I was no martyr for the cause. I just knew it was the only way I could hope to find my son. If there was another way, I don't think I would willingly have suffered the pain. And now you say a mantra might help?"

"It's worth a try, don't you think?"

"Certainly. Can you suggest a mantra for me to use?"

Yavros sniggered. "Angelina, I rather think you are the only person who could formulate the mantra, don't you? Astralus is no longer a strange place to you, so finding your way in using a mantra shouldn't be too difficult. Please let me know how you get on."

"I will," replied Angelina with the enthusiasm of one who has not applied herself to the task ahead; a task she was yet to begin, let alone complete.

Only when she awoke the next morning, with Yavros words resonating through her head, did the enormity of his request finally sink in.

When most of her misgivings had faded, Angelina began to seriously ponder Yavros' suggestion.

The thought of using a mantra to access Astralus gave her the shivers; for only she knew the dangers associated with this particular unknown. Whilst she was grateful to Yavros for making the suggestion, she still had no idea how to go about formulating one. Without guidance she could finish up anywhere!

The task seemed so problematic that, even though her heart yearned to access Astralus again, Angelina shunned his idea as a challenge.

She wondered if Maella had ever utilised a mantra, but had not the courage to ask. Yet, apart from Maella there was really no-one else she could approach who might be able to help. Not even Salutat or Masian had attempted to enter Astralus!

The prospect loomed large that if she ever wanted to access Astralus again, she must tackle the problem all by herself. ...And when you're alone and don't know what to do, she lamented, those prospects can seem very gloomy!

Such became Angelina's way of thinking.

Had Yavros outsmarted her this time: by recommending something beyond her capability as yet another test?

The problem was, even though she used many mantras during her angel training, she had never formulated one. If an angel placed a mantra appropriate for the purpose in front of her, complete in every detail, she would have no problem achieving her objective by way of it. Of this, she was sure. Yet, she was also sure she must be dreaming if she thought one might magically appear before her eyes.

"But what if it did?" she thought with a sly grin. "What if I imagined it before my mind's eye rather than sketched one out on parchment?"

The idea seemed unlikely, but it was her only hope. And if it didn't work... Well, there's no harm in trying.

"Yes, that's what I'm going to do," Angelina pronounced with renewed enthusiasm.

Focusing via her third eye, Angelina visualised the outline of a mantra she could use to gain access to Astralus.

Initially, it registered nothing structured but was merely an abstract form in her head. Until some detail had been filled in she could go nowhere, and this she accepted.

It was strange, she noticed, that once the basic outline had been established she had a feeling her responsibility towards it was at an end. ...As though it was now over to the higher powers within her soul to fill in the details and show her the way.

Does that mean, she thought to herself, that the best thing I can do towards completing this mantra is to forget all about it? ...How absurd!

Angelina chuckled at the idea. It seemed a contradiction in terms – that the best way to achieve something was by doing nothing. But this was not the same as wanting to see a clean house and then disregarding it, or sitting back idly when the provisions for the week needed to be procured. This was different. It involved special vibrations out of the higher planes: spiritual impulses more finely tuned than in normal terran thinking. As she had discovered on several occasions before, only a peaceful mind can hope to convey spiritual signals to the waiting senses.

"Alright," she conceded. "I give up. Whoever up there is pulling the strings on this, I will work with you."

She wondered if Salutat was involved, but decided he couldn't be; other matters were his priority now. Perhaps no-one was involved at all except for her; and the spiritual powers which, as an angel, she knew to be at her disposal.

"Is that what I must do now?" she said aloud. "Should I be looking into myself for the inspiration to complete this mantra? But that brings me back to where I was before – doing something instead of nothing. ...Except, the effort on my part shall be from my spirit, and not from my head! Okay, Angelina," she said with renewed purpose. "What is your spirit telling you to do?"

The answer, when it came, was so logical she wondered why she hadn't thought of it in the first place.

The object of the exercise was to find her son, so the focal point in the mantra should be...Batim.

When she fashioned his image in her mind's eye, she conjured up a mental picture of him – not the person of sinister habits he became, but the fresh-faced youngster she had always loved. As the mix of happy and painful memories from his terran life crept into her mind, she realised that thinking about him emotionally would be counter-productive to her objective. So she shook off the maternal feelings, put on a more angelic countenance, and carried on.

The next point to consider was her brief meeting with Dymas: did he somehow recognise her? If so, he probably had no idea why she might want to enter Astralus. Yet the fact that he introduced himself to her must have signified at least a degree of interest in her arrival.

"Yes," she declared. "Dymas is most certainly important in my quest to find Batim."

From then on, vital elements to be included in the mantra revealed themselves to her waiting mind; not all together but one after another: as and when they were needed in order to put the picture together.

Gradually Angelina began to understand why she had struggled with the idea of formulating the mantra. Rather than visualising it as a complete picture, she was in fact piecing it together, layer upon layer. Each portion formed a composite mental picture of its own as well as adding to the whole. And only when finishing touches were needed in order to complete the mantra did she realise what each part should be.

Lastly, she placed upon the outer aspect of the mantra the point in her consciousness into which she would slip when the migraines took hold.

This, when she was ready to begin her journey through the unfamiliar realm, would be her starting place.

But would it work? she wondered.

...There was only one way to find out.

CHAPTER 3

Making sure her body would not be disturbed, Angelina prepared to enter the mantra.

With eyes closed, she placed the picture in the window of her mind, and inwardly stood back to gaze upon it.

As she did so, she noticed something remarkable. The mantra appeared to have been transformed from a static picture into a living vista of many dimensions. Instead of the abstract impulses she had set one upon the other, she now witnessed a world of light and colour, and clarity of form that stretched away to the distant features of her son: the focal point of the mantra.

For a moment the image of Batim seemed so real her heart went out to him, but she broke away to stop herself from racing out of control towards it. How tragic it would be, having come this far, to forfeit reality in favour of mere vain imaginings.

Angelina took a deep breath to steady herself, and to diffuse the spell that might lead her to disaster.

One thing at a time, she insisted and, taking another breath, started again.

"Oh, Salutat," her soul cried out. "I wish you could have been here for this."

But as usual, she was alone.

The mantra's point of entry she recognised immediately, for even the recollection of her past migraines made her feel nauseous. However, in this instance she affirmed that the reaction was nothing more than memory, and laughed it off. Then, fixing the next aspect of the mantra in her mind, she moved on.

"This is too easy," she said, humming quietly.

Again, she restrained herself. She was still operating in an unknown area which could hold many hidden dangers. Angelina wondered, as she patiently waited for each level of the mantra to unfold, if she was the first living terran spirit ever to enter the enigmatic Astralus; then reminded herself that she had only succeeded thus far because of spiritual connections.

As she progressed, carefully establishing a firm foothold in each level of the mantra before attempting the next, she likened it to climbing up a steep hill. She was alone and vulnerable, but as long as she stepped carefully and kept her objective in view, she could feel confident about her progress.

...But then she met up with Dymas.

Angelina saw him out of the corner of her eye long before she reached his level in the mantra.

He appeared to be waiting for her; peering through the layers ahead of his in readiness to catch her attention.

To a small extent it distracted her. However, she had learnt by now to remain calm and allow the mantra to pull her through, stage by stage without deviation. Yet when Dymas' intentions became more obvious than she could ignore, she found herself being irresistibly drawn towards him.

"Angelina! Now I know who you are! You're one of the spirits who took over our bodies, aren't you?" he cried as she veered in his direction.

The unwelcome deviation threw Angelina off balance, and for a moment she feared she had wrecked the experiment.

Breathless and visibly distressed, she chided him.

At once he realised he had acted hastily.

"I'm so sorry," Dymas said. "I've been anxious to meet you ever since I first saw your face. You look so much like my darling Cefire would have looked, had she lived on in terran terms. It is a privilege to meet you."

There was no doubting his identity now. After their first encounter, Angelina had questioned whether the wispy apparition who said he was Dymas could possibly be the same one as Salutat. But now she was certain. In him she recognised the same compassionate features she grew to love in her husband, and was moved almost to tears.

As Angelina and Dymas briefly scrutinised one another, each felt the same sentiments, yet at the same time knew they were talking with a complete stranger.

Before I move on, thought Angelina, I must explain to Dymas just what happened the day he and his lady-friend leapt off the cliff...I owe it to him.

Angelina quickly drew Dymas away from the magnetic pull of the mantra.

Travelling through one, she had found, was enlivening, but also a noisy experience. The rush of energy generated by its unfolding layers created a vortex such as she only witnessed once before during a whirlwind. However, as soon as they were clear of the mantra, the surroundings quietened down.

Angelina caught her breath. Anxious not to release her hold on the mantra, she swung round to bring it under control. To her relief, the vortex had stabilised.

"That's better, we can speak properly now," Dymas said when Angelina turned back to him.

"Yes, that would be wonderful," responded Angelina in all honesty. She had been longing for this moment, if only to enquire about Batim.

Angelina glanced around. The environment here was like the swirling mist she experienced during her migraines.

Although she could not make out any form, she sensed a greater air of permanence than when viewing it distantly in the mantra.

This time, it seemed she had arrived somewhere.

"What is this place?" she asked Dymas.

"Why are you asking me something you already know?" he replied jovially. "It's Astralus, of course."

"So Astralus is real after all," she muttered contentedly, more to herself than to Dymas.

"It's as real as we make it," he stated, picking up on her comment.

"What do you mean by that? And who are 'we'?"

"Astralus is a place of imagination. If you have a glowing imagination it comes alive. If you don't, then you see and experience nothing but the sensation of a swirling mist." Dymas gestured in a circle as he went on, "There are more souls here than currently inhabit Eddren; souls who have nowhere else to go. They just hang around with nothing better to do; it's very sad. Would you like to meet some of our inhabitants?"

"No!" snapped Angelina, not wanting to get involved in the drama of the place.

Then she regretted her explosive response when she saw the shocked look on Dymas' face.

"I'm sorry, I didn't mean it that way, but I'm not here for a visit. I'm actually trying to locate the soul of my son. His name is Batim."

"Is he a recent arrival?"

"Yes...though years ago in physical time. He was only a young man when he died."

"I'm sorry to hear that. I'm afraid you will find it difficult to locate him. They tend to get lost in the mist when they pass on from Eddren – unless there is someone waiting for them. I don't suppose your son had anyone?"

"No, he didn't. But what makes you say he would be lost in the mist?"

"Because he'll be a waif by now..."

"...A waif!? That sounds awful. Surely not!"

"Yes, I'm afraid so...and probably fragmented, too."

"Dymas, what kind of talk is this? You're worrying me."

"Sorry, but these are things you should know. When a soul arrives over here without support – a waif – he literally has nothing to hold him together, and his form dissipates in the mist. That's what the mist is – fragmented souls. You're surrounded by them now."

Angelina cringed at the thought. She felt the ethereal skin at the back of her neck start to crawl, and shuddered.

"You seem to be alright." she said, looking Dymas over. "In fact, I even recognised you. Why was that?"

"...Because I wasn't alone when I passed on. Cefire and I intentionally left Eddren together. We were – and still are – very much in love. And, although at the time we had no idea what was going to happen after our deaths, it was our love for each other that buoyed us up and stopped us from falling apart. Incidentally, as you may have guessed after what I said earlier, we saw you two slip into our bodies. It surprised us, I can tell you. We felt sure they would be smashed to pieces..."

"...I'll tell you what happened later," promised Angelina.

She looked around, suddenly realising she had not seen anything of Cefire.

"Where is Cefire?" she asked with concern. "Is she not with you anymore?"

"Oh, yes. We'll always be together. ...Perhaps I should explain. When we first got here, we saw what conditions were like: that most of the souls had become fragmented, and only a small percentage appeared to be alright. After a while, Cefire discovered the reason for it – which I just mentioned to you. She recognised a common denominator where the unaffected souls were concerned, and that was love: they all had somebody to care about them – like a deceased father welcoming a son, or a husband greeting his wife. ...Or even multiple deaths from disasters, where close family ties maintain their togetherness. That's what keeps souls from fragmenting. But they tend to be in the minority. Unfortunately, most souls who arrive here have nobody to greet them."

"Where are the souls who did not fragment? I haven't seen any apart from you."

"Unaffected souls are usually busy people with plenty to do. They seem to fall into two groups – just as in physical life, where some are helpful and others are self-serving. The self-serving ones take themselves off to form colonies or enclaves which they've made into ethereal versions of the environment they came from, or perhaps which they aspired to when they were alive. Generally, they keep themselves to themselves. And who can blame them, really? But there are also the helpful souls: people who are grateful to have the love which sustains them – Cefire and me included. They do everything they can to bring love into the existence of the waifs and hopefully make them whole again. You haven't seen any of the helpers because they are away working. There's a great need here, you know. And to answer your question about Cefire – she is in the furthest reaches of Astralus at the moment, trying to bring love to a group of orphan souls. Orphans are the souls of children who passed on with nobody this side to look out for them. Fortunately, she's getting on very well with her approach. One of the youngest souls is beginning to take on form again. It is most gratifying for Cefire and her helpers. She works very hard with them..."

Angelina was fascinated. Until recently she had no notion of the realm's existence, let alone all the activity going on in its four corners.

To her, Astralus appeared now to be a complete realm in its own right; one which had developed structure thanks to good souls like Dymas and Cefire. ...And to think Yavros once discounted it as worthless fabrication.

She smirked knowingly; then retracted her cheekiness in case Yavros was eavesdropping on the unfolding events.

Here is another parallel universe, she thought; a fourth dimension and a very real place at that. Hitherto everyone in Eternity assumed there were only three dimensions; yet this place has probably been in existence almost as long as Eddren and Hellion. How could it have gone undetected? Could it be, as she once suspected, that Yavros denounced all terran souls who refused to connect with him because it hurt too much to think about them? In his opinion, once they died that was it – they did not exist anymore! Yavros decreed the same of Batim when questioned regarding his whereabouts. Was it a matter of 'out of sight, out of mind' for ever and ever?

For Yavros maybe – but not for her!

...Although, she conceded, he has changed in his way of thinking now, and acknowledges that Astralus exists.

Just then, another amazing thought crossed her mind; a revelation which would explain a lot:

If Eternity has had no awareness of Astralus, could the opposite also be true? Could it be that this realm is such an unhappy place because, while still in Eddren its inhabitants only worshipped the sun? If this is true, then nobody in Astralus yet knows about the richness of Eternity. What if she were to tell them about it, and perhaps help to bring about their return to..?

Suddenly Dymas' voice broke into her musings.

"...Angelina, you've drifted away from me. Did you hear what I was saying?"

Dymas had interrupted Angelina's train of thought in the middle of what, to her, seemed to be the most incredible revelation of all time. This was a matter she must take up with Yavros. Surely these poor wretches could be helped? But right now, she owed Dymas an apology for appearing to be rude.

"I'm sorry," she said. "I must have been lost in thought. Please forgive me. There is much to take in just now."

"Yes, and so far none of it has helped you in your quest to find your son."

Angelina smiled as another thought crossed her mind.

"I suppose you could say he was your son, too – yours and Cefire's."

Dymas looked aghast. Was Angelina suggesting he had an heir? What an amazing idea! Yet on further reflection, it wasn't so amazing. Cefire was with child when they ended their lives, and Batim, so he understood, was the progeny of his and Cefire's bodies...

"Well, what a thought!" he said. "That makes it doubly important he's found." Then he added sheepishly, "Did he look like either of us?"

"Yes, he favoured his father in looks, so you could say he did resemble you. ...But I need to explain something: Batim wasn't the child Cefire carried when you jumped off the cliff. She; that is, I lost that baby. I guess the adversity of everything that happened was too much for it. Batim came along after we were married. But you can still think of him as your own, if you like!"

It was obvious from the change in Dymas' demeanour that the idea of having a son was new to him.

He had long accepted that he relinquished the right to become a father when he and Cefire decided to end their lives, and that of their unborn child.

All of a sudden he remembered something else. "Didn't you say your son died while still a young man?"

"Yes...probably about the age you were when you gave up your body."

"What happened? Would you be willing to tell me?"

Angelina was prepared for this. As custodians of his and Cefire's bodies, she felt obliged to elaborate on the lives she and Salutat had been living.

But where shall I begin? she asked herself. There is so much to tell.

Certainly Dymas witnessed the entry of the two spirits into their bodies. Would he be able to accept the secret she had been keeping from Maella; namely that she was an angel? But then she would need to explain about Eternity; which might be too much for a simple resident of Astralus in a brief explanation. Her angel background was a different topic...and she was anxious to continue with her journey through the mantra.

So she briefly gave Dymas details which just concerned Batim; information any mother might tell of her son. She told him how Batim grew up accompanying his parents as they travelled the country in their work. How he attended the Academie, and was later killed by a swordsman who bore him a grudge. She decided against explaining about Lucifer's infiltration, or that Batim murdered his own father and was sentenced to death; it seemed irrelevant to their conversation at the moment. That, too, would have to wait for another occasion.

Dymas listened as though hearing about his own kin; his interest becoming personal. The boy seemed more like a brother to him, once he learnt they were roughly the same age when they died.

Before he realised what he was saying, he blurted out, "Can I join you in the search for him? I'll be able to help!"

Angelina was stunned. The unexpected request distorted all her plans. Lost for words, she said, "Oh...I don't know..."

All the same, the idea of having the help of someone she now trusted was appealing. In many ways she was getting tired of working by herself...and Dymas had already helped her; for which she was grateful.

Yet, how could she complete the mantra with a divided consciousness? She needed every second of focus to work through it step by step. There was still the image of Batim, the focal point of the mantra, to pursue. If she allowed Dymas to accompany her she might finish up ruining the one method by which she was confident of locating him. Was it not Yavros who assured her the mantra was the right way to go? Dymas may be an expert where Astralus was concerned, but he was not a mentor in her journey. Yavros was the one she must depend on; not a terran soul.

"I'm very sorry, Dymas," she said. "Although your offer of help is appreciated, I would not be able to complete the mantra properly if somebody else was with me."

"I understand how you feel," said Dymas, disappointed. "...Though it would have been a real adventure to look for our...for your son."

Angelina said goodbye and reluctantly left him standing alone. She slid back into the mantra; taking a moment to re-adjust and focus her attention again. Then, as the image of Batim beckoned, she felt herself moving forward. Yet, Angelina did not begin the final part of her journey in the way she had intended; for on the spur of the moment, Dymas contravened her wishes.

A split second before the veil of consciousness closed on him, he leapt into the mantra.

Thus, when Angelina moved ahead in her quest, Dymas was right behind her.

It was a well-known fact in Eternity that when somebody makes a spontaneous decision, often it is made for them rather than by them. Such was the case with Dymas. In effect, he joined the mantra without realising what he was doing. Thus, when he found himself enveloped by images, he wondered what had happened.

...But Yavros knew.

By now, Yavros' doubt had been well and truly silenced and he believed in the existence of Astralus as well as did Angelina. However, the extent of soul life in this fourth dimension left him completely speechless. As Angelina had stated, here was an entire realm which was unknown in Eternity until recently. Thanks to her endeavours, that had all changed. As far as Yavros was concerned, his intrepid angel was worthy of the best support he could offer her.

It impressed him considerably that she placed so much faith in him with regard to the mantra; for Astralus was unknown territory to everyone but its occupants. Yavros now worried that, being a sensitive soul, Angelina may not know how to handle the difficult situations which could arise during her experiment.

It was for this reason he urged Dymas to accompany her on the rest of her journey.

Unfortunately, Yavros omitted to inform Angelina of his decision – nor did he allow for her reaction when she saw Dymas had gone against her wishes.

"Why did you follow me!" she cried with rage; fearing, as she had already implied, that she might not now be able to complete the mantra.

"I don't know. I just...did," he replied self-consciously. How could he make her understand that he entered the mantra not of his own volition, but in response to an urge?

"I said I can't have you with me," she said, exasperated and thrown out of step. "Now what am I going to do?"

Hastily she glanced ahead of her to make sure Batim's image was still in place. To her relief, she saw that it was. Then she looked back at the receding vista and realised it was too late to insist Dymas leave.

Defeated, she groaned in frustration.

"Sorry, Angelina," he said, embarrassed for what he had done. "I didn't mean to make you angry."

"I'm not angry as such. It's just that finding Batim is so important to me; I can't risk jeopardising my actions in the mantra. Surely you can understand that!"

"Yes, of course. But I don't know why I followed you! ...Impulse, I suppose. As you can see, though; I can't really go back now."

Angelina sighed in reluctant submission. There was no point in chiding him further. They would just have to make the best of the situation.

Angelina returned the focus of her attention to the next stage of the mantra.

It seemed to her that Batim's image was looming in her mind's eye more quickly than before; so much so that it threatened to overwhelm her with its intensity. Abruptly she reminded herself that this was only an image, not the real thing. It was time to move from the mantra image to the soul of Batim himself.

With heart in mouth, Angelina carefully realigned her focus in order to bring this about.

She chose not to inform her uninvited passenger of what she was doing. Working alone in consciousness had so far been productive and, for her, deeply satisfying. She felt like she was working on the venture in partnership with Yavros, and that meant a lot to her. The thought of revealing such a sensitive operation to a virtual stranger seemed like a betrayal of trust. But it quickly came to her that unless she was to evict Dymas somewhere along the way, she really had no choice but to include him.

For his part, Dymas also recognised that the image of Batim was beginning to dominate. It seemed unreal to him that the imposing phantom face could embody the true Astralus, and especially a fragmented soul like Batim; for it gave a false impression of what Angelina should expect. To his mind, the image needed to be brought down to size in case it swamped the persona it represented. Yet, he chose to say nothing for fear of offending Angelina. One thing he had learnt in the last few moments was that his presence, and therefore his opinion, was not wanted.

If it wasn't for their respective stubbornness, Angelina and Dymas would have recognised that they were actually of like mind and travelling in sync: a situation orchestrated by Yavros himself for their mutual benefit. However, at that moment, each was too introspective to notice.

While all of this took place, a rumour was circulating in the angelic realms that the whereabouts of Astralus had been discovered, and that a person from Eddren had already ventured there.

Fortunately for Angelina, Yavros had placed a shield of secrecy over the experiment so that her identity would not be disclosed until she was back safe and sound.

He wanted only Dymas to be involved; not every well-meaning angel who had shown an interest in the illusive realm. For, despite his lack of spirituality, Yavros now felt that Dymas was the only soul who could help Angelina in her quest. So, bypassing his principle of trusting only those from his own realm, Yavros had handed over his beloved angel to the care of a transient terran.

Despite all of the secrecy surrounding her experiment, rumours about it provided their own impetus throughout each of the known realms. Although Angelina's name was never mentioned, her expedition was now a major talking point – not only in Eternity, but also in Hellion.

...And the individual most interested to hear all about it, was Lucifer.

Up until now, Lucifer had no inkling of a place called Astralus. He thought he knew all there was to know about the realms of Yavros and only reluctantly allowed himself to be persuaded of its existence.

Yet, once his interest had been piqued, there was no stopping him; except for the fact that even with his best efforts he failed to glean information, because no-one but the anonymous explorer knew how to access Astralus.

So, it was with growing frustration, that Lucifer found himself unable to do anything except stomach each new, exciting rumour as it came to his ears.

Lucifer's inability to learn about Astralus augured well for Angelina; for it meant she could continue with her search without interference. What's more, Lucifer's absence from the fourth dimension ensured that she would not need to explain to Dymas just who he was; or, just at the moment, what he might get up to.

Had Angelina known of Lucifer's interest in Astralus, she would have worried he might discover she was the one involved. Even more concerned would she have been if he learnt of her desire to find Batim. But she had little need of such fears, for her obliviousness was yet another bequest from Yavros to facilitate her work.

In fact, since Batim died she had not given Lucifer even one thought; and neither would she. Just now there was room in her consciousness for only two things — Yavros, whom she placed before anything else...and Batim.

With the spirit of Yavros firmly embedded in her heart, Angelina proceeded along the mantra; the image of Batim constantly before her.

To the relief of her companion, she reduced the size of the image so that it filled only her third eye and not the entire mantra. Yet, in order to bring Batim into perspective she now needed to visualise his real presence and diminish the mantra image to just a memory. The young terran she loved was no more; neither was the tyrant he turned into, courtesy of Lucifer. But what had become of him since his arrival in Astralus?

When it came to formulating a new image of her son, Angelina really had no idea what he looked like.

She voiced her concern.

"Don't forget he will be a fragmented soul right now," Dymas reminded her.

"Thank you, but I am aware of that!" she hissed; still reluctant to regard Dymas as anything but a spectator. The idea of her son being fragmented was clouding her ability to picture him at all. In near panic she turned on Dymas.

"Dymas, will you please keep out of the way! I can't even visualise him, now."

"Then call him," Dymas retorted.

With encouragement from Yavros, Angelina's tolerant companion was beginning to understand how he could help. Although he knew nothing of the promptings within him, he recognised what they were urging him to say.

At last Angelina saw reason: Dymas was right.

Fragmented soul or not, surely Batim still recognised his own name!

Maybe, she reflected, Dymas could be useful after all.

"Batim," she called softly as she arrived at the focal point of the mantra. By now there was nothing beyond it but the swirling mist.

Fear began to fill her, and she wondered for a moment if she was out of her depth with something she really knew nothing about.

"Call him again," said Dymas, watching intently for any sign of life in the impenetrable haze.

"Batim, my son; are you there? This is your mother. I've been looking for you."

Still there was nothing.

Just then, Dymas sensed something.

In his mind's eye he perceived rather than saw the faint image of a waif crouched in a corner: the wispy form of a soul curled up so tightly it might never open out again.

"I think I see him," he whispered to Angelina. "At least, I have an impression of him."

"Where!" cried Angelina, desperately straining to make something out.

But the image was only visible to Dymas.

"I can't see anything at all!" she wailed in frustration.

Again Dymas peered into the mist.

"Well I'll be... D'you know, Batim might not actually be fragmented!" he said with growing intrigue.

"What do you mean? Could he still be whole?"

His focus sharpening with each glance, he said, "I think he is. There must be something...different...about him. I've never known a waif to remain whole before, but this one seems to be intact. I would say he's just...lonely!"

Angelina's heart leapt as only a mother's heart can.

The longing to leap the gap that separated her from her son became unbearable, and she started to cry.

"Oh, my dearest Batim," she lamented. "I can't bear to be apart from you any longer. Can you hear me?"

Dymas concentrated his attention on the waif in his mind's eye, but it neither moved nor gave any indication it heard her cries. For a moment he suspected he had merely conjured up the image to see something for himself.

"Batim!" Angelina cried again, this time directing her supplication out into the ethers. If he was no longer in her mantra, then perhaps he was somewhere close by. "I love you, my son. Please come back to me...I need you!"

The pain in her heart was unbearable.

Again Dymas looked at his image. If it really was Batim, surely he would have heard his mother by now. Then, as he peered more closely, something remarkable happened.

While Angelina was pouring out her heart, the phantom form began to change. Astonished that something was at last happening, Dymas saw a hint of normality within the dull, wispy form.

Was Angelina finally getting through to Batim, or was it just his imagination?

"Keep speaking to him," he urged her; hardly daring to breathe in case the effect was lost.

"Batim," she called again; sensing now that something positive might be taking place. "I've missed you so much. Can't you feel the love I have for you? Please talk to me!"

Suddenly Dymas saw movement. It wasn't much: Batim just seemed to heave, as if slowly drawing breath. Yet as he did so, the colours in his aura began to intensify.

Dymas grinned, exciting Angelina who knew nothing of his vision.

"I wish you could see this," he said. "I think he's starting to come around."

"And is it Batim?" Angelina asked anxiously.

"I think so. ...And he is responding to you. Try again."

"What else can I say?"

"...Whatever comes into your heart."

Angelina was crying now. "I love you, my son," was all she had left to tell him. "I want to give you everything; you deserve better than a place like this. Let me take you back to Eternity; I love you so much..."

Batim, whose soul had been in limbo for a very long time, was sluggish in accepting that something wonderful could be happening to him.

In the world of Astralus he had become something of a curiosity, for most waifs fragmented soon after arrival. A waif that did not fragment was a rare spectacle indeed.

"What's so special about this one that he's still whole?" the other waifs wondered while jealously toying with him.

Had they and all the other inhabitants of Astralus been better informed, they might have realised that the son of angels could not possibly become fragmented. But they were unaware of such spiritual facts, having no knowledge of angels, or of Yavros and Eternity.

Neither did Batim understand about fragmented souls or waifs...nor what was expected of him in that peculiar and sometimes creepy place.

He just saw himself as the butt of other people's jokes, and it hurt him terribly. Over time he had descended into a deep rut of hopelessness; not wanting to interact with other waifs, and not knowing where he was or even why he was there.

And that was how he had remained – until now.

His mother's first attempt at reconciliation with him went unheard and unnoticed.

Since his arrival, Batim had not even heard his name spoken; so it took a while for the fact that someone was voicing it to sink into a mind stripped of all thought.

But the insistence of the person calling him soon began to infiltrate his heart and, surprisingly, it warmed him.

Recovering but slowly, he could not comprehend what was happening. Everything he had experienced since his arrival in Astralus had been too strange to contemplate. This new development was equally strange. What was he supposed to think?

Even when Angelina first mentioned she was there, he could not grasp it.

But the love she poured out became irresistible to a heart deprived of any form of normality, and without even meaning to, he began to respond to her.

"Mother?" he uttered in little more than a whisper.

Angelina gasped.

"Did I just hear something!" she exclaimed.

"I don't know," Dymas interjected. "But I certainly saw something."

"What!"

"He moved! He actually stirred...and his colour seems to be improving."

Angelina tried to see Batim through her mind's eye, but he was still was not visible to her.

"Tell me where he is!" she cried, bursting at the seams to reach out to him.

"I don't know where he is!' replied Dymas; her agitation making it difficult to concentrate. "Settle down, will you, and I'll try to locate him."

Dymas moved away from her to avoid distraction. He was just as anxious to find Batim as Angelina, but needed quietness in order to pinpoint his location.

"Where are you going?" she shouted after him.

"I'm not going anywhere!" he answered back, trying desperately to hold onto Batim's image. "Just relax; you're interrupting my focus. I'll tell you when I find out."

But there was no need for Dymas to search further; for the lonely soul, warmed by the love his mother propelled towards him and energised at the prospect of meeting up with her again, took the initiative.

While Dymas focused on an image, the soul of Batim, much to Angelina's overwhelming surprise, appeared not in her mind's eye but right in front of her.

Angelina shrieked; first in alarm and then with delight.

"Batim! You're here!" she cried at the top of her voice as she rushed to embrace him.

Dymas swung round to see what the commotion was about. His heart melted when he saw what, for him, was a wonderful sight: the reunion of two souls. Angelina's joy was in finding her son, but the elation Dymas felt was in beholding the restoration of a soul; and he was deliriously happy for them both.

His first impulse was to run forward and embrace them. Yet he could see, even from a distance that this was a very private moment; so respectfully, he kept out of the way.

But as it turned out, Dymas' assistance was needed far sooner than he might have expected; for when he looked again, Batim was alone.

Angelina had inexplicably disappeared.

What had occurred remained unclear.

From Dymas' viewpoint, one minute he was witnessing the ecstatic reunion of a mother and son; in the next, the mother had vanished leaving her distressed son wondering what was going on.

As a new wave of insecurity washed over Batim, the colour began to drain from his fragile form.

This, Dymas noticed straightaway. Fearing the worst, he rushed to his aid – it would be inconceivable that he might fail the rejuvenated soul so soon.

Yet, as he drew closer to him, Batim seemed to rally.

"Father! Why are you here!" he exclaimed in surprise, mistaking Dymas' familiar features for those of Salutat.

Dymas sighed, partly with relief that Batim was alright, and partly because he did not fathom how to explain the mistaken identity.

This was a strange experience even for him.

"Batim, I'm sorry, but I'm not your father; I just look like him," he said. "My name is Dymas. I came with Angelina to look for you."

Dymas winced as he offered his explanation; it sounded so false. But he had no idea if Batim knew of his parents' past. On the spur of the moment he could think of nothing better to tell him...

"So where did my mother go?" Batim asked; confused by Angelina's sudden disappearance.

He looked around; expecting her to reappear.

"To be honest with you," said Dymas. "I don't know."

As had happened many times before, it was terran nature that yanked Angelina away from her son.

While her spirit was embracing Batim's long-lost soul with a release of energy, her reclining body shuddered so violently, it caused a disturbance in Maella's household.

Although in ethereal terms Angelina seemed to have been away from her body for a long time, it was really but a few minutes since she complained to Maella that her head hurt and she needed to lie down. And when, not long afterwards, uncontrolled sobbing was heard coming from her room, Maella became concerned that something was terribly wrong.

Unflinching, she investigated. As she entered the room, the sight which greeted her filled her with alarm. Angelina, apparently asleep on her bed, seemed to be experiencing a dream so traumatic that not only was she sobbing, but also writhing as if in terrible pain.

Maella hurried over to her. Worried that Angelina was having some kind of fit, she shook her by the shoulders to bring her around.

Angelina awoke to find Maella leaning over her.

The shock of being dragged back from such an intense and important event was too much. Recognising now that she had lost Batim, she started to howl at the top of her voice.

Maella panicked. Angelina had never behaved like this before, and she did not know what to do. The only course of action she could think of was to pat Angelina's hand, tell her there was nothing to be concerned about and offer a drink of water.

"I don't want water!" Angelina shrieked, not realising it was her own worrying conduct that had summoned Maella to her room. "Don't you know where I was just now? I was with Batim!"

"I'm sorry," said Maella sheepishly. "I didn't realise you might be dreaming about him. No wonder you're upset."

"I wasn't dreaming about Batim – I was with him! ...You don't understand."

Angelina turned away from Maella and began to weep softly into her pillow.

"Please...leave me...alone," she stammered, doubting she would ever find her way to her son again.

Distraught, Maella left the room. Angelina was right: she didn't understand. ...And what had she done that was so dreadful her friend should react in such a way?

She would have a word with her about this outburst. It was unacceptable behaviour from a house-guest...

Meanwhile, Dymas was faced with the uneasy decision of what to do with Batim.

Thinking quickly, he noticed that although the soul's fragile condition had deteriorated only slightly, receiving a shock so soon rendered him vulnerable. It was imperative, therefore, to prevent him from slipping back. ...And the best way he could do that, Dymas decided, was to engage him in conversation.

He would introduce Angelina's rejuvenated son to his new home realm.

But what Dymas wanted to tell him, and what Batim wished to hear, were two completely different things.

Batim, more like his old self again, immediately demanded to know why his mother had searched for and found him, had subsequently disappeared, and how he was to get out of the accursed place he was stuck in with no idea as to why he was there.

If he had taken some time to think about it, he might have vaguely recalled his imprisonment, the cage with the snake, and his narrow escape from it; yet the detail of what happened afterwards would forever remain a blur. All he did remember was somehow looking down at his body, and the next minute being in this weird place, where everything was nothing-in-particular, and people weren't really people but only fragments of people...

It had all been terribly confusing.

However, his time spent as a recluse had also provided him with a welcome escape from his troubles. Batim's life as a terran had been far from straightforward, and to be in a place where no-one knew his history came almost as light relief to the weary spirit, despite initial taunts from others. Dreary though his stay in Astralus had become, it was a form of freedom in itself... But right now, he wanted Dymas to tell him why he'd relinquished it for little more than a breath of fresh air in his mother's presence, and for a shallow promise to go with her to Eternity.

Now, he faced loneliness and pain in full consciousness, rather than the freedom he felt in his state of nothingness.

"Mother, how could you do this to me!" he wailed.

For his part, Dymas felt great empathy for the now fully-integrated soul.

His work with waifs and fragmented souls was such that concern for Batim was part of his conditioning. Yet, he was also developing a personal interest in Angelina's son who certainly bore a strong resemblance to him. He had begun to look on Batim as his own kin, and recognised a need to help him adjust to living in Astralus – no longer as the lonely waif, but as a fully integrated soul.

In his experience, deceased terrans considered Astralus to be the afterlife and prepared for their eternal existence there. This, he decided, was where his duty towards Batim should lie. He would therefore show his new charge some of the more interesting places in Astralus, and help him prepare for the future.

Dymas knew of an area where Batim might settle well. There, he could meet souls of similar temperament and intellect. In time, he sincerely believed, Batim would find peace and contentment as a resident of Astralus – with or without his mother.

His theory on the subject he quickly imparted.

Unfortunately, Dymas did not take into account the fact that Batim was the son of angels – parents who taught him well in his youth. He already knew of an afterlife that was much better than the one Dymas hoped to offer him. The helpful spirit who was taking him under his wing would get nowhere with this independent soul...

"Are you telling me you don't know why my mother left without a word?" Batim asked his attentive host.

"Yes, I'm afraid so," Dymas confessed. "It possibly has something to do with the fact that she's a living terran. Maybe she needed to go back to Eddren all of a sudden."

"Now I'm really confused. Is she dead...or something?"

"No, your mother is still very much alive. She has spent all this time agonising over your death…"

"…My death? What do you mean by that?"

"Don't you remember? You were pierced with a sword, and died. Your spirit found its way here. Angelina grieved for you terribly. Then she learnt about Astralus and how to locate you. I happened to be here just when she needed help, and together we were able to find you. Don't worry, Batim, I'm sure she will contact you again. Angelina seems to be very resourceful. And, of course, you could always try to reach her! Can you imagine the joy it would bring you both if you did?"

"Just at the moment I don't know what I want to do," Batim retorted forlornly, the shock that he was no longer alive still sinking in. "I don't even know who or what I am anymore."

CHAPTER 4

Angelina was inconsolable. Her sense of loneliness at again being separated from her son intensified with each passing day. She missed him more than ever, especially now that she had actually touched him.

As time went by her encounter with him, though strong and bright in her mind with constant recollection, began to seem more like a lovely dream. It would have been easy to convince herself of that fact, but for the deeper awareness that it had been real.

The further use of her mantra did not enter her head; for she had never thought beyond its initial purpose at all. Her objective in using it had been to locate Batim, and she had done that.

But the time came when the ache in her heart drove her to action again. The need to consider what she should do about Batim became paramount.

Should she go back into the mantra, she wondered, or just wait until she died before connecting with him again?

At least she knew where he was.

It was a difficult dilemma for the weary angel. To wait the many terran years she had left was unthinkable. Yet travelling through the mantra had proved to be a draining and precarious activity while she still occupied a terran body. She envied the animals of colder climes, and their long winter sleep. These days she could not manage even a nap without interruption. How wonderful it would be if she could enter Astralus and not have to return to Eddren. Then she could guide Batim home to Eternity and reunite him with his father.

And best of all, she could introduce him to Yavros.

Yet, these fantasies she shook off. She was dealing with the realities of the situation, not the ideals; realities that must be either resolved, if she was lucky, or just visualised for the rest of her life.

"There has to be a way!" she reasoned. "With Yavros' help I succeeded with the mantra; surely I can get beyond this stage too! It's time I consulted him again!"

As she translocated back to Eternity, Angelina wondered if Yavros had monitored her progress through the mantra. It would suit her well, she decided, if he already knew what transpired, for recounting the detail was beyond her just now. To her delight if not surprise, she discovered he knew of everything, including her indiscretion with Maella.

"You did very well!" he told her proudly.

"Thank you, Sire..." she said with customary politeness.

Yet, whilst she appreciated his words of praise, she had not come to seek acclaim, and without hesitation got on to the purpose of her visit.

"...Then you must also know why I am here," she went on less politely, but quickly checked her stance before, yet again, she said the wrong thing.

"Yes, I can imagine why you would wish to see me at this time," he said, overlooking her manner. "I'd prefer to hear what you have to say, though."

"Isn't that was obvious? I must get back into Astralus."

"What is stopping you?"

"Nothing, and everything!" she exclaimed, exasperated. "I don't know how to get in there, now. Using the mantra was unnerving and I'm not sure I could do it again."

"Why not? Who do you think enabled you to complete the mantra last time?"

"Dymas, of course. Is that what you mean?"

"...And who made sure Dymas accompanied you?"

Angelina said nothing; stunned by his remark. She had not even considered Yavros initiated the move; although, in retrospect Dymas did say he was urged to follow her.

"...And who do you think is making sure Batim's being looked after by him in your absence?"

Suddenly Angelina realised what he meant. As she saw the tender expression on his face, she realised that Yavros had been there for her all along; that despite her reservations he was looking out for her still.

But if that is the case, she also wondered, then why was she faced with her present dilemma?

Struggling to contain her emotions, she asked him.

His response was not what she hoped to hear.

"There have been several occasions during your terran life, when I have left you to work things out for yourself. This present dilemma is yet one more. You have all the tools you need at your disposal; I have placed no obstacles in your way. Alter your terran activities to accommodate visits to Astralus just as you do when you come here. ...But I must also advise you to do one more thing."

"Oh dear...what's that?"

"You must inform Maella of what you've been doing. She seems rather unhappy with you at the moment. If you enlighten her as to your recent investigations, she will no doubt be helpful to you."

But Yavros was mistaken. Maella was no longer the sweet, accommodating soul Angelina had been living with.

Maella's tolerance of her reclusive ways had diminished of late. ...And there was a definite reason for the change of heart, which had nothing to do with Angelina's behaviour, but rather involved another entity altogether.

Lucifer liked nothing better than a disturbed terran spirit. He saw in it an opening to be exploited, and when Maella began to harbour disapproving thoughts towards Angelina, he soon recognised another chance to influence her.

Although Lucifer was not wise in his way of thinking, he was by no means dim-witted. In his own way, he was as astute as any of the angels and twice as cunning as well; which meant he never missed an opportunity. An opening such as this soon attracted his attention, as the slightest touch on a spider's web draws its occupant to the victim. Very quickly, he realised that he could learn a lot about Angelina's aspirations through her friend Maella.

Yet, fondness for Angelina was not his only motive in wanting to infiltrate Maella's consciousness. He was also on a fishing expedition.

Lucifer had heard that the latest topic of gossip – the existence of Astralus – was also of interest to Angelina. He was curious to know why an angel from Eternity should bother herself with something that could be nothing more than a rumour.

Maella, he concluded, may be a source of information there, but her infiltration would need to be subtle.

Lucifer realised early on that if he was to learn anything at all, Maella must not detect his involvement. Angelina, he knew, had enough experience of his past interference to recognise the signals. So he lay low, waiting for another indiscretion on Angelina's part before executing his plan.

Accordingly, when Angelina chose her moment to make confession and reveal her interest in the fourth dimension, Lucifer was all ears.

And what she told Maella astounded him.

To learn that Astralus was real after all, and had been since the beginning, came as a shock to Lucifer's ego. He listened earnestly while Angelina described the conditions there, and how she met up with Batim. And he chuckled to himself as she tried to validate the inexcusable behaviour that had distressed Maella.

When Angelina had finished her story, Lucifer grinned triumphantly. He now had all the facts.

"...And facts," he assured himself, "are very useful tools in the hands of someone as artful as me!"

It was then he set to work on Maella.

No sooner had Angelina completed her revelation than Lucifer's tentacle of hate slipped into Maella's heart, and the woman started to feel extremely annoyed. In fact, she took great exception to the revelation.

Is Angelina going mad? Maella wondered while pausing to evaluate the situation.

Never before had she heard such outrageous claims! They were merely recollections of a dream and contained not one element of reality. How could a lowly house guest expect someone as intelligent as her hostess to accept this rubbish as fact? Perhaps Angelina really was going insane. Or at very least, she had been under such strain lately that it was all getting too much for her and she was mistaking hallucination for reality...

"I'm sorry, Angelina," she said. "But I can't accept your ludicrous notion that there's an afterlife such as you have described. I believe it is but a product of your imagination, borne of prolonged grief over your son, and that in your delusions you believe it to be real."

Astounded by the rejection, Angelina's jaw dropped. What happened to Yavros' pledge that Maella would be helpful? she wondered.

She could not understand how such a critical comment might be the outcome of her honest confession.

In a daze she stared blankly, trying to take it all in.

"Are you listening to me?" continued Maella, as Lucifer capitalised on the moment.

"Yes," responded Angelina passively.

"And what do you have to say about it?"

Maella's tone of voice was relentless in its accusations.

Angelina lost her nerve. "I don't know just what to say," was all she could manage.

"I cannot tolerate this behaviour from you any longer!" Maella exclaimed as though at the end of her tether. Then, drawing breath, she carried on with renewed vigour.

She reminded her of how she was a sociable person who loved company, and that Angelina's reclusive nature was making it difficult to maintain her way of life. Then, at length she rammed her point home by stating that she had put up with it only out of deference to her house-guest...

"Do you understand?" she demanded to know.

Angelina nodded without resistance.

"I've been unhappy about the situation for some time," Maella went on. "And I very much regret that I have come to a decision."

Angelina looked up at her, wary of what was to come.

"I think it would be better for both of us if you found somewhere else to live," Maella announced emphatically.

Somehow Angelina had been expecting it.

454

Angelina knew the two of them had drifted apart of late; that as the outsider it was her duty to move on, and that Maella was entitled to live her own life in her own home according to her own dictates.

Although satisfied that she had always been a friend to Maella, she could see how her current interests rendered her more of a burden than a help. And looking at it from Maella's' perspective, she did tend to behave a little oddly.

She sighed as the resignation of her fate sank in.

Looking deeply into her friend's eyes, Angelina told her that yes, she did understand. But as she did so, she also found herself searching those eyes for Maella's soul, and to her horror, she could not see it. Instead she saw only a steely black stare; a harsh coldness which seemed to have taken over from the usual smiling eyes of her friend. The last time she came encountered something like that was when Batim was possessed...

"Oh no!" she cried to herself. "Not Maella, too!"

Angelina quickly looked away from her, careful not to reveal her recognition of the sinister influence.

Lucifer by himself she could handle; after all they were old friends, and he did have a soft spot for her. But when he lurked behind a terran spirit's mind, he used their free will as impenetrable armour, and she knew she would never be able to get past that.

Angelina pretended she did not notice him. Instead, she chose to submissively go along with Maella's request.

"When would you like me to leave?" she asked, anxious now to end the conversation.

"...When you've made alternate arrangements," Maella replied, softening a little now that the solution to all her worries was in sight.

Although Angelina had nowhere to go, she chose to leave as soon as possible.

With Maella still under Lucifer's control, there was no telling what else he might do if she were to stay. It was possible, she realised, that he knew of her conversation with Maella, and was capable of jeopardising her plans for returning to Astralus. The sooner she left the better.

"Oh, Lucifer," she thought bitterly as she packed up her belongings. "Will we ever be free of your interference?"

Meanwhile, in Astralus, Batim had been thinking.

Whilst he had no interest in Astralus as a home realm, he was enjoying his relationship with Dymas, in that his chaperone's cheerful banter kept his spirits up.

Now an expert in diplomacy, Dymas often used banter as a ploy for just such a purpose; and in Batim's case he was determined to keep his charge's soul intact until he could stand alone.

When that moment arrived, Batim recalled something Dymas suggested just after Angelina disappeared.

At the time, he had glossed over it; not recognising the significance of the counsel. But now that his demeanour was more stable he found himself revisiting the idea that if Angelina was unable to return to him in Astralus, then he should contact her.

It looked, if he was ever to see his mother again, that this course of action was the only option open to him. Dymas had mentioned Angelina's mantra. Batim vaguely recalled from his past life that he had already used one; although, in retrospect, he now realised it could have been responsible for his downfall. But it meant he understood the principles of mantra use, and just as his mother put one together to find him, so he could easily formulate a mantra to find her.

Not only did the notion appeal to him, but success seemed highly likely; so, without informing Dymas of his plans, he initiated its design straight away.

It was a wiser and fully accountable Batim who began the personalised mantra; for he knew the dangers associated with it now.

If adversity breeds strength, then he also believed that adversity gives rise to a great deal of wisdom where once there may have been foolishness. So with greater caution than on past occasions, Batim chose the elements to place within his mantra. Soon he had confidently set them in order of priority, and was ready to try it out.

Finding a place to concentrate on it was not difficult in Astralus. Fragmented souls, he had learnt, only take any notice of you when you are conspicuous. So Batim slid off to an out-of-the-way spot on the periphery of the realm, and receded into his phantom form once more. ...Only this time, it was an act of will that rendered him formless, not the recurrence of his depressed state.

With his mind focused, the mantra soon began to open up before him.

It vexed Lucifer greatly that Angelina chose to vacate her home straight away. Losing her physical presence so soon lessened his chances of finding out how to enter Astralus.

In an attempt to detain his prey, he had Maella implore her to wait until she had found new lodgings.

Yet Angelina could still see Lucifer in Maella's eyes, and was more determined than ever to get away quickly.

But for the atmosphere in the house, she would have preferred to stay; for she wanted to consult with Yavros again from the privacy of her room. However, leaving was of greater urgency than seeing Yavros. So, having said her goodbyes to Maella, she aired a silent plea for Miekaale to protect her from Lucifer's influence, and left.

When she finally closed the door behind her, with no idea where to go, Angelina felt a glow of confidence that Miekaale would indeed honour her request.

It was strange, she discovered as she slowly increased the distance between herself and her past; that the further away she went the happier she started to feel; for she now had no obligations to terran spirits. She could be herself again. And that meant she was free to travel to Eternity or re-enter Astralus without having to consider the opinions of anyone else.

On Angelina's mind now was not where to spend the night, but how to regain contact with Batim. As darkness fell and visibility diminished, she found a convenient spot, unrolled the blanket she had brought with her, and settled in. By this time she was hungry and feeling chilled, but she didn't mind. She was where she wanted to be: at liberty to travel the other realms.

Yet, as Angelina adopted the frame of mind needed to begin her travels, something occurred which she could not have expected.

Unknown to her, Batim was systematically progressing through his mantra.

Just as she once made his image the focal point of her mantra, so Batim placed his mother's face squarely in the centre of his own. And as luck would have it, at the precise moment she began her meditations, unobtrusively nestled under shrubbery somewhere out in the countryside, Batim reached her.

Angelina could not believe her luck. Surely the image of Batim's face in her mind's eye must be fantasy? After all, she had only just begun what she assumed would be another difficult and lengthy search for him.

Just for a moment it occurred to her that Lucifer might be playing tricks again; for the soul that greeted her was more confident than the weakened spirit she abandoned during her own mantra travels.

Only when he spoke did she realise that he was actually in her presence.

"Batim, is that really you?" she cried.

"Yes, mother," was the passionate response.

With a flourish, Angelina let go of her terran connection and allowed herself to sink freely into Batim's embrace. Unencumbered by restraints, they held on to each other.

"You're not going to suddenly leave again, are you?" joked Batim at length.

"No; no never again," responded Angelina with equal cheerfulness. Then, as the trauma of that occasion arose in her memory, she said, "I'm sorry about that, by the way. Something happened which dragged me back to the terran realm, and I've spent a long time trying to extricate myself from it. But I'm free now, and it will never happen again... Where are we, by the way?"

Angelina glanced at their otherworldly surroundings. To her surprise there was colour, and as she looked closer she could see what appeared to be flowers. She and Batim were standing in a garden setting; though not the kind of garden she might recognise in Eddren. The aura around everything was definitely ethereal in substance.

But were they in Astralus or Eternity?

"I think it must be the outer reaches of Astralus," said Batim. "I came here for solitude while I travelled through my mantra. Not many souls come out this far – they're too busy trying to get their own lives together."

"I wonder what lies beyond," said Angelina; and then she realised. "Oh my goodness! Can it be? Are we actually on the edge of Eternity?"

Batim recoiled in alarm.

"Mother, if you're right, then I won't be able to go any further. Only angels are allowed in Eternity, aren't they?"

"Where did you get that idea?" she cried. "According to Yavros there's a place there for all terran spirits who turn to him...and that includes you!"

"I don't think he would let me in, though. I didn't lead an exemplary life," said Batim.

"Then perhaps it's time to introduce the two of you; and sort this out once and for all. Stay here, Batim. I'll be back in just a minute."

For Angelina, translocating from Astralus into Eternity was as effortless as stepping through a portal.

In their garden setting, the two souls had been so close in consciousness to Eternity that they were almost there. Only Batim's sense of unworthiness to make the transition prevented them from passing into the realm together. To Angelina's way of thinking, all it would take for him to be granted entry was Yavros' forgiveness of his indiscretions.

Excitedly, she approached Yavros' chambers. She found him in a state of readiness.

"Don't you think I've been waiting for this moment?" he told her. "There's nothing more precious to me than the redemption of a lost soul. And when that soul is your son... Well, what more could I wish for!"

With great raptures Yavros welcomed the soul of Batim into Eternity. His had been a difficult journey; however, with the help of his mother and his own determination not to remain a waif in Astralus, he had achieved it.

In Eddren, some weeks' later, the decomposing corpse of a middle-aged female was found wrapped in a blanket.

Her body discarded as a terran sheds his cloak, Angelina had no further need of trappings. She had gone home to be with her family.

This was a triumph Lucifer could never claim.

Batim discovered, once the euphoria of his welcome into Eternity had subsided, that this was not the culmination of his journey but merely an intermediary stage.

"Of course, you realise you have not actually earned the right to remain in Eternity," Yavros informed him; a fact of which Batim was not aware.

"I don't understand what you mean," he retorted with a hint of disapproval. "You laid out the welcome mat for me, so what have I done wrong?"

"Nothing; not since your physical death, anyway. ...And once your admirable mother located you in Astralus, you have certainly made every effort to improve yourself..."

"...Then I say again," Batim stated emphatically. "I don't understand why I haven't earned the right to stay here."

Batim could see his eternal future slipping away before he'd even got started.

Yavros paused for a moment; then answered him.

"There is a reason for this, but the explanation should come from your mother. Like all my angels, and all who have preceded you, Angelina understands the difference between a terran soul who has earned the right to an afterlife in Eternity, and one who has not. After some training I believe you will also be a fully-fledged member of Eternity. But in the meantime, I advise you to speak to your mother about it."

Angelina laughed when Batim informed her of Yavros' attempts to pass the responsibility onto her.

"The sly old fox," she said in fun, and then remembered she was an angel again now and must leave her terran expressions behind. Correcting herself, she said, "Yavros had a purpose in asking you to consult me over it. I can see what it is now."

Again she chuckled.

"Mother, are you going to tell me, or must I guess?"

"I'm sorry for being so vague. Yavros wants me to tutor you in readiness for the Return. This was his way of letting me know what I must do."

"What do you mean by 'the Return'?"

"Well, sit yourself down, and I'll tell you all about it..."

So the training of Batim's soul began in earnest.

Angelina taught him that although he was received into Eternity, his soul was far from ready for the Return, thanks to Lucifer's interference; that only terrans who reject his nature and false teachings, and acknowledge Yavros as their creator, can be restored to Eternity after their death.

She told him how, out of the millions of terrans who had passed through Eddren since its creation, only a small proportion readied themselves for the Return during their physical life. The remainder, as Batim had witnessed, were destined to a life of nothingness in Astralus. ...And because none of the souls in Astralus knew about Eternity, none had made the transition from it. ...Except for Batim.

"Does that mean I'm unique?" he quipped.

"I guess so!"

Angelina enjoyed tutoring her son. She was discouraged, though, to see how much negativity still remained in his soul. Even after Slave's eviction, it looked like much of the training received from his parents had been forever lost.

It seemed that Lucifer was now well practiced when it came to aligning the souls of terran spirits with his own.

As his tuition progressed, Batim began to see how such ignorance was shared by all the terrans he encountered, both in Eddren and in Astralus – he never heard even one of them mention Yavros or Eternity.

While he was telling her this, Angelina remembered a thought that once crossed her mind: Were she and Salutat naïve in abandoning Batim to worldly influences during his time at the Academie? Would they have been better to direct their mission energies to the city environment; in order to stay near him and therefore offer him spiritual support? If they had done so, the dramas Batim went through might never have happened! But no use dwelling on the past, Angelina declared. It was all water under the bridge, and time to move on. Nothing of that mattered any more. She and Batim were reunited. Her mission now was to return him to a state of unity with Yavros.

Batim often spoke with his mother about the conditions in Astralus. Angelina regarded his reminiscences as therapy. He had been through a lot since his time at the Academie, and she knew the anguish caused by Lucifer's infiltration of his soul must have stayed with him throughout his lonely sojourn in Astralus.

Yet one topic surfaced more than any other during their talks: the awful feeling of unhappiness. He encountered nothing positive or beautiful while trapped in that part of Astralus. There was nothing to lift the spirit, he informed her; or to give the waifs a sense of self-worth.

"The first time I felt anything positive," he said; "was when you and Dymas spoke to me. After that I started to respond. But it was definitely your love that did it!"

Angelina's soul shone as she listened to his words. She understood perfectly why he might have cause to say it.

She told him, "Dymas explained to me that only souls who have someone to receive them in Astralus are likely to remain whole. Those who have nobody to support them become fragmented."

"I didn't fragment!" exclaimed Batim.

"That's because you were different. Your connection to the angelic world protected you from fragmenting. Dymas was the one to notice it! And it was only your connection with your father and me that convinced Yavros to make an exception, and let you come through to Eternity."

"I feel for the others then, having nobody to care about them," Batim reflected, realising how lucky he had been. "What a difference it would make to their existence if they did have someone!"

Batim's words struck a chord in Angelina's mind.

Would having someone care about the souls in Astralus make a difference to their existence? ...And if that concept was taken one step further: the tutoring of each soul, just as she was now tutoring her own son; would it lead to their enlightenment?

Angelina's mind felt like it would explode with the possibility of it. Yet so far, of all the individuals currently in Eternity, only she and Batim had experienced Astralus. To most others in Eternity, Astralus still retained its mythical and therefore alien qualities.

As for the souls in Astralus... Angelina was certain none had heard of Eternity, either. If indeed they did learn of it during the course of their terran lives, the advice must not have been heeded, or by now they would have linked up with Yavros in Eternity.

This was a tricky problem to resolve; but one that could be full of potential with the right approach.

Under the circumstances, she thought, it would be good to get a second opinion as to the possibilities.

Angelina had frequently mentioned to Batim the name of her mentor, Masian; yet since their return from Astralus she had not paid him a visit – an oversight she sought to speedily redress. She also wanted Masian to meet Batim, in the hope that the three of them might be able to come up with a plan.

Masian was fascinated to hear more about Astralus, for it had generated a great deal of interest around Eternity.

In some circles the new realm was no longer regarded with scepticism, but rather hailed as the greatest discovery of all time. And now that Yavros accepted its existence, Astralus received more credence from the entire angelic community; especially from Masian, who now recognised Angelina as the primary authority on the subject.

As such, he leaned on her every word; eager to hear hers and Batim's ideas.

"It's so sad to think of those poor souls suffering from a lack of love," he said, genuinely moved by the description of the fragmented souls. "How has Eternity allowed this to go unobserved for so long? It's absolutely dreadful. Surely there's something we can do about it?"

"I don't doubt there is," said Angelina, reassured by his supportive attitude. "But of one thing I am concerned. We must tread carefully if we do try to help them."

"You'd think they would welcome some love into their lives, especially the spiritual love Yavros has for them."

"Not necessarily. They are pretty stuck in their ways; in Lucifer's ways. When you don't know what spiritual love is, the concept of receiving it can be intimidating. They might prefer to continue living the unhappy lives they're used to, rather than have unfamiliar feelings stirred up."

"I'm sorry, Angelina, but I cannot accept that you are right in your thinking."

Masian's understanding was based only on the precepts of a gentle sage who had spent his entire existence under Yavros' panoply of care.

Not having experienced suffering or lack of support, he could not grasp the possibility that love might be rejected by a soul in Astralus.

"Not all of the souls would be intimidated," responded Batim in support of both angels' viewpoints. "Plenty would soak up love like a sponge if it was offered to them."

"A sponge...what is a sponge?" asked Masian, anxious to fully comprehend what Batim was telling him.

Batim and Angelina exchanged amused glances.

"A sponge is something terran spirits use to bathe their bodies," explained Angelina. "It soaks up water very easily. Batim used the word to show how readily some of them would receive love into their lives."

"Oh, I see..."

Suddenly Masian felt out of his depth with the two ex-terran spirits. They held something of an advantage over him, in that the pair now had a diversity of experiences to call upon. Each could claim knowledge of three of the four realms – may Yavros forbid that they might ever need to enter Hellion! ...Yet he knew only Eternity.

He decided to bow to their joint better-judgement and honour their opinions.

"Do you have anything in mind which will help them?" he asked Angelina.

"Well, I have been doing some thinking, and Batim and I have discussed it. But we are far from coming up with a constructive suggestion. There is one other person I would like to bring into discussion on the subject, though."

"Who's that? ...Yavros?"

"No – Dymas. He's an experienced resident of Astralus," she said at length.

Batim looked at her as if to question her reasoning, but before he could say anything, she continued.

"Dymas is someone I met up with in Astralus, and from whom I learnt a great deal. He also looked after Batim until he was well enough to follow me. He and his partner Cefire are very experienced in coaching dispossessed souls, and in the ways of Astralus in general. I believe Dymas would be an ideal consultant. There is one problem with the idea, though."

"What's that?" said Masian and Batim together.

"Dymas doesn't know about Eternity."

Angelina paused for a moment while they processed what she had said. Then she continued.

"There would need to be a lot of preparation before we take anything to those poor souls. For one thing, we must enlighten Dymas as to Yavros and Eternity, and educate helpers from here about conditions in Astralus. Somehow, I don't think this project is going to be as straightforward as it sounds."

Her missive delivered, she scrutinised the other two.

She observed that Masian was becoming bewildered by their conversation, and the expression on Batim's face indicated he was starting to wonder whether it was worth the effort.

Angelina chose not to comment; for it had occurred to her that, in any event, she was in for a struggle.

But what else can I do? she mused. Returning those souls to Yavros is imperative! Yet it's not a decision I can make alone... I need to consult Yavros!

He liked the idea immediately. Since Angelina's return with Batim, his interest in Astralus had increased steadily, and he, too, felt a need to help the souls there.

Dismayed to learn about the waifs, he wondered how something as beautiful as his terran spirits could end up in such a sad state of fragmentation. Something terrible must have taken place in Eddren throughout the eons of time since their creation.

...And only one entity was responsible: Lucifer!

But there was no point in feeling angry with him all over again. It would neither achieve anything, nor benefit the souls in Astralus. So Yavros once more swallowed his angst where Lucifer was concerned, and focused on Angelina's proposed task.

"I think you have some significant insights here," he remarked when she had expressed all her thoughts.

"There appears to be two ways of going about this," she said. "We could all translocate to Astralus and gather up as many willing souls as we can at the risk of losing others. Alternatively, we could go there one at time and discreetly isolate souls who are ready for the Return."

"Or..." Yavros interjected; "...we could begin by flooding Astralus with love, and see what happens."

"What do you mean, 'flood Astralus with love'? Would we not be required to actually go there?"

"Not to begin with. You see, I have also been thinking about this," he stated. "I would gather up all the citizens of Eternity, both angels and returned terran souls, and reveal the plan to them. The existence of Astralus is common-knowledge now, so everyone would know what I'm talking about. With a united effort we could simultaneously open up our hearts and pour out our love into Astralus; and, as I said: see what happens!"

"Oh, Yavros!" gasped Angelina in awe of his suggestion. "If only that would work!"

"Are you saying it might not?" retorted Yavros.

"I'm sure it would work in principle. But in practice... Well..."

"Well what, Angelina?"

Angelina hesitated, trying to find the right words.

She needed to explain to Yavros that Astralus had built up its own environment; that its residents were no longer the people of Yavros, but self-willed identities.

She told him how the intact souls exist in similar fashion to their lives in Eddren without thought of enlightenment, and that the waifs were so fragmented they wouldn't care.

"If spiritual love flooded an unsuspecting world," she said, "it might be regarded, not as a saving grace but as an alien force, bearing in mind many inhabitants of Astralus won't know what spiritual love is. The level of resistance you'd encounter might be quite frightening."

Angelina sighed in frustration.

Had Yavros forgotten the reason for the existence of Astralus in the first place? ...That it was Lucifer who lured the terrans away from their creator, thereby preventing them from entering Eternity; that all Lucifer offered was a false concept, leaving them with nothing better to take its place. ...Unless it is introduced to them gradually?

Taking a deep breath, she continued.

"Just as the angels of Eternity slowly came to accept the existence of Astralus, so the idea of Eternity will take hold in the souls of Astralus only if it is similarly introduced...of that I am convinced. ...And bear in mind," she proclaimed finally. "You haven't been to Astralus, so you can't know what the conditions are like!"

Yavros was somewhat offended that Angelina rejected his suggestion – he thought it was a good idea. How dare she claim to know more about his universe than he did! Was he its creator...or Angelina?

For some time afterwards, he refused to speak to her, leaving her in a quandary as to how to proceed.

"I must have said something to displease him," she later told Batim when he asked what Yavros thought. "He's not talking to me just at the moment. Unfortunately I have a nasty habit of being outspoken with him. Maybe this time I've gone too far."

But it was only hurt pride which prevented Yavros from getting back to Angelina; not denunciation; for the next day, Yavros assembled the Golden Angels and several prominent members of the angel community to discuss the matter. Angelina was also asked to attend.

Nervously, she complied.

Yavros drew Angelina up to sit beside him. Alarmed by the move, she assumed he was going to make an example of her: to teach the others how insubordination would not be tolerated.

Remembering only too clearly what became of Lucifer after he contradicted Yavros, she awaited his judgement with apprehension.

But instead, he congratulated her on the initiative she had taken where Astralus was concerned, and her desire to help the souls there. Then he spoke to the assembly about everything the two of them discussed at their last meeting. And finally he admitted that he now realised she was right in her way of thinking: that to flood an unprepared world with spiritual love might be counter-productive. He would go along with her suggestion that the problem should be approached gradually.

With relief and gratitude Angelina thanked him.

"Don't thank me yet," he told her. "There is still a long way to go; and neither do we know if your proposal will work any better than mine. However, in deference to your knowledge of Astralus, I've decided to give you a chance. But, if it doesn't work… Well…we'll just wait and see."

Angelina had an uncomfortable feeling, when she left the meeting, that in a way Yavros was taunting her. Did he expect her to fall short in her efforts, so that he could say 'I told you so'? She hoped not.

Nevertheless, she saw the need to act cautiously in her dealings with Yavros from now on. …And she needed to succeed in her venture; if only as a matter of pride.

"Shame on you, Angelina" she chided herself; horrified at her own admission. "Fancy putting pride ahead of the needs of those souls! Pride is a terran emotion, an age-old product of Lucifer's infiltration. There is no place for it in the mind of an angel!"

With Yavros' blessing, Angelina arranged for a small group of angels to prepare for translocation to Astralus.

But before any of them could make the move, first she and Batim needed to have an in-depth chat with Dymas; for he still had no knowledge of Eternity. It was essential he be brought up to date – which included describing to him where Batim had been of late.

"Yes, I did wonder where the two of you disappeared to," Dymas responded when Batim apologised. "My first thought was that you had fragmented…but apparently not, by the look of you!"

Dymas stood back to scrutinise the strong soul standing before him.

"…And you, too, Angelina. You both look so much more contented than when I last saw you. What have you been doing in your absence?"

"That's why we are here, Dymas," said Angelina. "We need to tell you where Batim and I disappeared to."

This is going to be the hardest conversation I've ever had, thought Angelina when they found somewhere quiet to talk. How do you introduce a new concept to someone who thinks they already have all the answers?

She raised her eyes skywards seeking help.

"Help me, Yavros," she whispered into the ethers. "The success of this whole exercise hinges on convincing Dymas of your existence."

All the energy she and Salutat expended during their missions in Eddren was nothing compared with the effort required for this conversation. The inhabitants of Astralus knew nothing of Eternity and believed theirs was indeed the afterlife. It was not a foregone conclusion they would want to know otherwise. ...And that included Dymas.

"I really need you, Yavros!" she called out silently while Dymas asked what she wanted to talk to him about.

As she opened her mouth to speak, Yavros' reassurance came. His warmth filled her soul and the words began to form in her head.

"Thank you," she uttered as she relaxed into what she hoped would be a very productive chat.

CHAPTER 5

"So you really have no idea where Batim went?" Angelina asked the mystified Dymas.

"I told you; I searched for him everywhere."

"Did you consider that he may have left Astralus?"

"That crossed my mind. But I don't know where else he could have gone to, apart from Eddren; which would not have been possible. And there is nowhere else...is there?"

Angelina paid no attention to his remark and carried on with her questioning.

"If I told you Batim was in neither Astralus nor Eddren, would you believe me?"

Dymas glanced at her; then thought for a moment.

"I would have to say both yes and no. But...what other place is there?"

This is it, thought Angelina. Help me, Yavros! She took a deep breath, drawing in with it all the spiritual strength she could find.

"Batim was with me....in Eternity."

Angelina watched closely for his response.

The blank expression revealed that he could not fathom what he was hearing.

"Eternity? Where and what is that?" he exclaimed, and stared pleadingly at Batim for support.

Yet, in him he saw only a half-grin, as though Batim alone shared his mother's secret.

Dymas laughed. If the only way he would get any sense out of this pair was to go along with the joke, then so be it.

"Okay," he smirked. "Do you intend to explain what this is all about or leave me wondering? ...Where and what is Eternity? It sounds fascinating."

"Eternity..." Angelina continued with confidence; "...is a third realm. It existed long before Eddren was formed."

Dymas listened dumbfounded while Angelina introduced what, for him, was a strange new theory.

He pulled sceptical faces as her story unfolded about Yavros and the angels, Miekaale and Lucifer, Eddren and terran spirits.

At first he thought he was being tricked; that her concocted tales were a joke, drummed up as an excuse to validate Batim's sudden disappearance.

...Except that Batim substantiated Angelina's remarks with discoveries he had made for himself.

"I've met angels – I've even spoken with Yavros," Batim said with enthusiasm. "I never thought I'd believe anything like that, but they're real! You should see the angels when they're all together. It is the most amazing sight you could ever imagine!"

By the time Angelina had completed her description of Eternity and all that had taken place down the millennia, Dymas began to see that they were not making it up, but rather he was learning something of profound significance.

Though he was speechless, Dymas' changing expression spoke volumes to Angelina. Suddenly everything he knew about life in Astralus seemed inconsequential, and even though he no longer had a physical body, he felt the need to sit down.

"Sorry; I've given you a lot to take in," said Angelina, identifying with his bewilderment.

She questioned whether her tutorial was actually too much for him all at once.

Dymas smiled at her reassuringly.

"That's alright; I'm fine, really. It just takes some getting used to: the notion of an ethereal realm which outshines Astralus in every way. But somehow this makes perfect sense. I always felt the afterlife should be better than what we've got here," he said. "The concept of a loving creator even answers all my innermost questions. Do you realise that it represents hope for the fragmented souls? What a fantastic prospect that is!"

He looked up at Angelina in wonderment; then sprang to his feet again.

"I feel like rushing off and telling everybody!" he cried, energised by the exciting revelations. "Where is Cefire? I must tell Cefire!"

"Dymas, slow down," urged Angelina. "I do understand how you feel, but please don't get carried away. Just enjoy the moment and we can take it further later on."

He sighed impatiently.

Never before had his spirits been so high. He felt he would burst at the seams if he couldn't share the news with somebody straight away. Yet Angelina was right. He did need to slow down. ...But how? He was like a horse chafing at the bit.

And then Batim had an idea.

"Mother, do you think we could take Dymas to Eternity with us? I bet he would love to meet Yavros"

Dymas gasped in anticipation.

"Oh, I'm not so sure about that," she replied. "Yavros is very particular about terran spirits earning the right to go into Eternity."

"But look at him, Mother. He's motivated! It's like he has been reborn!"

"Yes, that's exactly how I feel!" exclaimed Dymas. "...Or maybe, I'm going from the darkness of this place into the light of something much better."

"See, Mother! How could Yavros possibly refuse him?"

Outnumbered, Angelina laughed.

"Alright; it does appear as though Dymas has had some kind of reawakening. I'll see if we can take him back...but only for a visit, mind you. It will be up to Yavros whether or not he stays!"

In fact, Yavros was equally excited about the prospect of this particular meeting.

When Angelina told him about Dymas' enthusiasm, he felt sure this was a new type of terran soul: someone who experienced a change of heart. And that gave him a great deal of encouragement. If one soul from Astralus could see the truth, and acknowledge mistaken beliefs, then maybe others could, too.

"He hasn't acknowledged them," corrected Angelina. "I don't suppose he even considers he's been mistaken in the past. Dymas didn't know of any other existence until just now, so how could he have been in error? But telling him about you and Eternity has certainly had a profound effect on him. It was like something within his soul suddenly woke up, and he came to life. ...And now he can't wait to meet you!"

So Dymas was brought before Yavros. He became the first soul ever to leave Astralus in full recognition of Yavros as the creator of Eternity, and of himself.

Over the millennia, many terran spirits had died to their physical lives with Yavros' name on their lips, and were welcomed into Eternity. He loved each of them as much as any of the angels. But Dymas was special; even more so to

Yavros than Batim, whose rescue from Astralus had been achieved through Angelina rather than made voluntarily. Dymas acknowledged Yavros within his heart even before they met. This touched Yavros deeply.

With open arms, he welcomed Dymas like a long lost son into his presence.

"Are there many more like you in Astralus?" Yavros asked him when their exuberance had settled down.

"Oh yes, Sir," said Dymas. "There are as many souls in Astralus as there are..." He paused while searching his mind for a comparison. "...As many souls as the stars in the night sky back in Eddren. There must be millions!"

"And do you think they could all be saved?"

Dymas laughed. "I'd love to think they might respond as I did, but I doubt it really."

"Why is that?"

"...Because the souls there are in many different states of consciousness. Some are whole, some are fragmented. Some seem happy with their existence; some angry or sad. Others, I would say, are just lost. You can't generalise...but anything is possible."

Angelina had listened in rapture to the joyful reception and discussion between Yavros and his new subject. She felt it might not be considered impertinent if she joined in the conversation, especially as an idea had come to her.

She said, "Yavros, do you mind if I suggest something?"

"Of course I don't mind!" he gushed; in the best mood she had seen in him for a long time. "What do you want to say, my dear?"

At that moment, Angelina felt she could have asked Yavros for Eternity itself and he would have granted it; so buoyant were his spirits. She smiled that she was included in his merriment.

However, when it came to voicing her idea, especially as both Yavros and Dymas were waiting for her comment, she found herself struck dumb.

"I wondered, Sire," she said hesitantly; "whether you would like to take a look at Astralus, yourself."

Yavros stared at her, open-mouthed, while the effect of her words sank in.

"Do you mean, to interact with the terran souls there?" he asked at length.

Angelina hesitated again. "Well... Not necessarily visit them as such, but maybe just...take a look."

Angelina suddenly felt ill at ease. Had she spoken out of turn again and was about to be refused?

Yet, Dymas caught her meaning and, still bouncing with enthusiasm, glanced optimistically at Yavros.

"I think that's a wonderful idea!" he said brightly.

Angelina drew breath with relief that Dymas had agreed with her. Together they awaited Yavros' response.

Again Yavros paused in thought before pensively saying, "D'you realise I have never before been outside Eternity?"

"Yes, I know," said Angelina, all at once self-conscious for making such a rash suggestion. "I'm sorry, Sire, I should not have proposed it."

"...But now I come to think of it," he said, continuing his train of thought. "There's no reason why I can't extend my horizons and visit the mysterious realm of Astralus."

Dymas cheered, raising Angelina's spirits again.

What is it about Dymas? she thought. His joyfulness is so infectious! Unknowingly she grinned with delight.

Yavros' expression now was one she had not seen on him before. It was like the look of excitement on Batim's face when, as a child, he received a gift on his birthday. Yavros, it seemed, was experiencing a new lease on life;

for at last he had a chance to do something about the situation with terran spirits.

All down the ages, while Lucifer's negative influence spread throughout Eddren like an enveloping fog, Yavros had suffered the anguish of watching his beloved offspring slip away from him. Eternity's fallen angel had so cleverly inveigled his way into terran consciousness that latterly he need not even be present for his influence to direct their lives. Yavros had assumed that all but the most resilient terrans were lost to him forever. Yet that, it appeared, was about to change. He was at last witnessing the enlivening of a soul once lost to him and the expectation of many more to come. Why would he not pour into his new adventure all the energy he could muster?

Yavros' mind was made up.

"Dymas, will you show me around Astralus, please?" he asked spontaneously.

"Certainly Sir...but I recommend that you go just as an observer for now. You really cannot imagine what it's like until you see it for yourself..."

The coordinates for entering Astralus were still only known by Angelina. Instinctive judgement had taught her to guard their secrecy; at least until a degree of security had been established. So when the time came to introduce Yavros to Astralus, it was Angelina who took the lead.

However, even the most diplomatic counselling the pair could impart did not prepare Yavros for the atmosphere he would encounter in the realm.

To see even one of his beloved creations reduced to a fragmented soul and imprisoned by its own will brought him immeasurable grief. He instantly regretted that he had never before allowed himself to believe in their continued existence.

"How could I have let things deteriorate to this level?" he moaned, the pain in his heart forcing him to turn away from the distressing reality. "This is…terrible! What kind of benefactor am I…that I allowed it to happen?"

"It wasn't your fault, Yavros!" insisted Angelina. "You weren't to know they still existed. Astralus has been secret for so long that nobody knew about it. Don't forget, the terrans who died without knowing you are the ones who formed it; not you. And likewise, they are responsible for the conditions here."

"Rather like…Hellion," murmured Yavros, struggling to speak. "I once…established it for Lucifer alone…but it has developed…a life all of its own. Did the same…also happen in Astralus…without my even knowing…about it?"

"It looks like it," agreed Angelina." But I repeat, it still isn't your fault, Sire." Then she added as an afterthought. "I think we both know whose fault it is!"

By now Yavros was so consumed with grief he could not take in what Angelina was suggesting.

"Fault…?" he mumbled. "Whose…fault…?"

"Why, Lucifer's, of course!" she said, not yet aware of the extent of Yavros' pain. "If it wasn't for him, Astralus would never have existed. All the souls from Eddren would now be with you in Eternity!"

Lucifer…," Yavros mumbled again; his mind numb with the shock of what he was seeing. "Yes… Lucifer…"

Just then, Angelina recognised that something was wrong with Yavros. The atmosphere in Astralus was affecting him so badly, his spirituality seemed to be dissipating.

Angelina panicked.

"I need to get Yavros home," she said to Dymas with a sense of urgency. "I'm afraid he may fragment if he remains here any longer, and that would be disastrous!"

Quickly she pulled both Yavros and Dymas through into the brighter realm. The effect was immediate, and Yavros recovered at once.

"Why did you do that?" he asked with indignation; not realising the danger he had been in. "I haven't finished my inspection of Astralus!"

Much to Angelina's dismay, Yavros seemed to be cross with her again.

"I'm sorry, but I really had no choice," she insisted. "You were being negatively affected by the atmosphere and in danger of fragmenting your spirit. I don't need to remind you, Sire, that if you don't have your spirit, your universe doesn't have you! Naturally, I could not let that happen."

"Then I suppose I should be thanking you instead!"

Angelina looked at him; unsure whether his remark was made sarcastically or out of genuine gratitude. None the wiser, she responded mechanically.

"That's alright, Sire..." Then, to change the subject, she added, "How do you intend to proceed from here?"

"I honestly don't know. It was certainly a shock, seeing the conditions in Astralus. You weren't exaggerating when you described them. I don't think I will ever quite get used to the idea of my terran souls being anything but perfect."

"They're only that way because of their separation from you. Once you awaken their hearts, they will recover."

Dymas, who was also astonished by the abrupt withdrawal from Astralus, listened carefully to Angelina's conversation with Yavros. He now understood just how important the terrans were to their creator.

As a terran soul who had been born again in spirit only recently, Dymas' burning desire to share his good fortune re-surfaced with even greater intensity.

"Sir, I have an idea," he said.

481

"What is that, my friend?" asked Yavros, with interest.

"It seems to me that Astralus is not a fitting place for you as there's so much negative energy present."

Yavros laughed. "You're not wrong about that! What do you suggest?"

"If it's alright with you, I'd really like Batim and Angelina to come back to Astralus and introduce the 'Return,' as you call it. Angelina has already implied that many souls there are only fragmented because they have no feeling of love. They've become separated from their spiritual roots, which is you. We need to find a way to re-connect them..."

"...Without upsetting them!" Angelina insisted, taking Dymas by surprise.

"What do you mean by that!?" he asked.

"Despite our enthusiasm, we must be very careful with the souls in Astralus. Just imagine...if you had been in a dark cave for a long time and then somebody dragged you out into bright daylight, it would be blinding for your eyes, would it not?"

"Yes, I suppose it would," he said. "But what bearing does that have on the task before us now?"

"Don't you remember? When you had your awakening, you said it felt like you'd been brought out of the darkness of Astralus and into the light of Eternity."

"Yes, of course. But I wasn't 'blinded' by it..."

"...Because you were ready for it. Yet, when I first told you about Eternity, I detected a hint of scepticism. I'm sure that if you weren't ready for your awakening, you would have rejected the idea of it...and may have been abusive towards me because it contradicted your own beliefs."

Dymas gave it some thought.

It was true: Angelina's strange theories did meet with his resistance at first.

"I used to think I was well informed about such matters beforehand," he admitted. "What you told me did seem to contradict everything I believed in!"

"Then can you see how souls who are not ready for the Return might react the same way?"

"I guess so. But what's the answer? How can we know if a soul is ready for the Return?"

"The three of you will just have to take your chances," ventured Yavros, fascinated with the perceptions of these two souls, so experienced now in all facets of life. "Just as Angelina could not have known if you would be receptive, so you won't know if your message will be acceptable to the souls in Astralus. They may love you, or they might try to chase you off. I would say you must be prepared for both, and not be too disheartened if you meet with more rejection than success. Even one redeemed soul out of a thousand is better than none at all, don't you think?"

"At least we won't have Lucifer trying to make things more difficult for us," said Angelina.

"Why would you say that?" asked Yavros before Dymas could make the same enquiry.

"He doesn't know how to get into Astralus," she told him laughingly. "He attempted to find out before I passed on from Eddren..."

"...What do you mean, 'passed on'?" asked Yavros. "You make it sound as though you died."

"I did! ...Though not intentionally. I became so involved with my spiritual work that I forgot all about my body. And then, one day, I realised the spiritual cord connecting me with it had gone. And that was that! I can't say I'm sorry – as I'm sure you realise," she added, glancing side-long at Yavros to test his reaction.

...Had she not begged him to let her come home often enough in the past!

"Well I never!" exclaimed Yavros. "I didn't realise you no longer had your body. Though, come to think of it, you have been spending quite a lot of time around here lately. Now I know why!"

For a moment Yavros was bemused by the revelation of Angelina's departure from physical life. How natural she made it sound. What a pity, he thought, that except for souls who were confident of coming straight to Eternity, terran spirits seemed unable to view death so calmly. The ones who passed on to Astralus, it seemed, have generally struggled with it.

Yet another form of self-punishment; he reflected; and one which could have been avoided had they not yielded to Lucifer's influence.

Suddenly Yavros realised his mind had wandered. "Sorry, Angelina, what were you saying about Lucifer?" he asked. "...That he can't access Astralus?"

"That's right. I alone hold the coordinates for Astralus, and I think it's best to keep it that way for now. If nobody else knows how to get in, then Lucifer won't succeed in manipulating them."

"But what if he tries again with you?"

"Don't worry on my account, Yavros – I'm always on my guard where that old friend of mine is concerned; he isn't exactly subtle," Angelina responded with a smirk. "He may be clever, but he always manages to announce his arrival."

In fact, the one thing that annoyed Lucifer ever thereafter was that he could not find out how to enter Astralus.

Angelina really had the edge on him this time.

For the first time since he fell from grace, Lucifer had to be content with contemplating what might have been. He could but ruminate on how Angelina and her associates were identifying eligible souls, incarcerated in Astralus thanks to his own efforts. It grieved him to think that the effectiveness of his work was now being undermined, and that there was nothing he could do about it.

However, as the centuries rolled by and he noticed that only the most destitute of souls were turning to Yavros, he relaxed a little; confident that his life's work had not been in vain after all.

It appeared there was still plenty of mayhem worth pursuing in Eddren!